STRIKING EDGE

KELSEY BROWNING

STEELE RIDGE
www.SteeleRidgeSeries.com

TEAM STEELE RIDGE
Edited by Gina Bernal
Copyedited by Martha Trachtenberg
Cover Design by Killion Group, Inc.
Author Photo by Anne Yarbrough Photography

Print Edition, March 2019, ISBN: 978-1-948075-20-6
For more information contact: kelsey@kelseybrowning.com

NOVELLAS

Sexy contemporary romance

Amazed by You

Love So Sweet

BOOKS AVAILABLE BY TRACEY DEVLYN

NEXUS SERIES

Historical romantic suspense

A Lady's Revenge

Checkmate, My Lord

A Lady's Secret Weapon

Latymer

Shev

BONES & GEMSTONES SERIES

Historical romantic mystery

Night Storm

TEA TIME SHORTS & NOVELLAS

Sweet historical romance

His Secret Desire

BOOKS AVAILABLE BY ADRIENNE GIORDANO

PRIVATE PROTECTORS SERIES

Romantic suspense

Risking Trust

Man Law

A Just Deception

Negotiating Point

Relentless Pursuit

Opposing Forces

HARLEQUIN INTRIGUES

Romantic suspense

The Prosecutor

The Defender

The Marshal

The Detective

The Rebel

JUSTIFIABLE CAUSE SERIES

Romantic suspense novellas

The Chase

The Evasion

The Capture

LUCIE RIZZO SERIES

Mysteries

Dog Collar Crime

Knocked Off

Limbo

Boosted

Whacked

Cooked

Incognito

CASINO FORTUNA SERIES

Romantic suspense

Deadly Odds

JUSTICE SERIES w/MISTY EVANS

Romantic suspense

Stealing Justice

Cheating Justice

Holiday Justice

Exposing Justice

Undercover Justice

Protecting Justice

Missing Justice

Defending Justice

STEELE RIDGE CHARACTERS

The Steeles

Britt Steele - Eldest Steele sibling. Construction worker who has a passion for the environment and head of Steele-Shepherd Wildlife Research Center.

Miranda "Randi" Shepherd - Owner of Blues, Brews and Books aka Triple B and Britt Steele's love interest.

Grif Steele - Steele sibling. Works as a sports agent and Steele Ridge's city manager.

Carlie Beth Parrish - Steele Ridge's only blacksmith and Grif Steele's love interest.

Reid Steele - Steele sibling. Former Green Beret and head of Steele Ridge Training Academy.

Brynne Whitfield - Owner of La Belle Style boutique in Steele Ridge and love interest of Reid Steele.

Mikayla "Micki" Steele - Steele sibling and Jonah's twin. Master hacker.

Gage Barber - Injured Green Beret and Reid Steele's close friend who comes to Steele Ridge to help run the training center. Love interest of Micki Steele.

Jonah Steele - Steele sibling and Micki's twin. Video game mogul and former owner of the billion-dollar company, Steele Trap. Responsible for saving the town of Steele Ridge, formerly known as Canyon Ridge.

Tessa Martin - Former in-house psychologist at Steele Trap and Jonah Steele's love interest.

Evie Steele - Youngest Steele sibling. Travel nurse.

Derek "Deke" Conrad - Commander of SONR (Special Operations for Natural Resources) group and love interest of Evie Steele.

Joan Steele - Mother of the six Steele siblings.

Eddy Steele - Father of the six Steele siblings.

AUTHOR'S NOTE

Dear Reader,

I so hope you not only enjoy Shep and Joss's story, but that you fall a little bit in love with Puck, too. Although Puck is obviously fictional (too bad, right?), he is partially modeled on my dog Pharaoh.

We raised our very own service pup in training—a Labrador/golden retriever cross—for Canine Companions for Independence from 2012–13. As required, in May 2013, we turned him in to the organization for advanced training.

Exactly one month later, we received a call telling us that he wouldn't be able to finish the program due to a minor heart condition. With seesawing emotions, we brought him home. Although we were delighted to have our beloved pup back, we also grieved. Our dream of Pharaoh providing love and support to someone who needed him was over.

He now lives the life of a normal family pet, but he spreads joy wherever he goes. Hotel elevators, Home Depot aisles, and friends' homes. He makes people smile, helps them reminisce about lost pets, and soothes them much as

Puck does Shep. Pharaoh sometimes acts as our very own family therapy dog, snuggling close or overtaking our laps when we're upset or sad.

Several of his siblings from the P litter were ultimately placed through the CCI program. From retrieving the remote control to providing encouragement during challenging physical or emotional times, these dogs allow their owners to live independent lives.

If you know much about service dogs, you know they are incredibly well behaved. So if you read the "temptation" scene in this book and think a service dog wouldn't react that way, I'll just claim author license. :-)

As I'm sure many of you are aware, service dog fraud has become commonplace in the US, with people claiming their pets are service or comfort animals in order to give them access to places where animals are normally not welcome. Sadly, this type of fraudulent and selfish behavior damages the efficacy of legitimate service dog programs like Canine Companions for Independence.

If you or someone you know could benefit from a true service animal, I encourage you to contact a well-established and reputable program.

K-

To all the puppy raisers who selflessly take in and ultimately give up these dogs. Your love and early training are the foundation of a dog's ability to provide support, companionship, and comfort to others. Thank you so much for your sacrifice, selflessness, and generosity.

And to the special people who are on the spectrum. I tried my best to write a book worthy of Shep Kingston. If I missed the mark at times, please blame it on the fact that I'm merely neurotypical.

STRIKING EDGE

KELSEY BROWNING

STEELE RIDGE
www.SteeleRidgeSeries.com

1

WHY IN HOLY HELL COULDN'T PEOPLE BE DOGS? DOGS WERE just better in every way. Loyal. Trainable. Incapable of conversation.

"Puck, sit." Shep gave the gentle command to his golden retriever, careful not to communicate the agitation crawling through him like a kicked-over pile of fire ants. Obediently, Puck plopped down his haunches on the ground, but he whined up at Shep.

He knew. Puck always knew when Shep was starting to lose his cool. When he was edging toward overload.

Shep hunkered down in front of his dog, the prickle of mountain grass under his knees, and Puck settled his chin on his shoulder. The feel of his warm breath, his steady heartbeat, provided much-needed grounding.

Shep stared up at the wooden support tower above them silhouetted against the mountains of western North Carolina. His boss, the owner of Prime Climb Tours, had summoned him out here to the zip line course, yanking him away from his weekly check of the rock-climbing equipment. He often did that, pulled Shep from one task and assigned him another.

How many times had Shep tried to explain to Dan that such requests—okay, demands—degraded the quality of his work?

Shep took several chest-expanding breaths. It was okay. He would get back to the equipment. Back to the order of his day. As his brother Cash would say, this wasn't nothin' for a stepper. Shep didn't always understand idioms, but he'd learned this one meant that he could stomp his way through whatever pile of shit he was facing.

Puck touched his nose to Shep's neck, indicating he could feel the overload receding.

"What would I do without you?" He gave Puck a stroke down his back and stood. His dog would wait here until Shep returned.

He climbed seven staircases up the zip line tower to find the group of middle schoolers had already zipped across, leaving Dan "The Man" Cargill alone on the platform. He was just clipping his harness into the trolley—the metal housing of wheels that slid along the cable—with two carabiners, one that would actually carry his weight and another gimmicky one that he carried everywhere. Shep told him, "Dan, I can't pick up this group. I'm in the middle of—"

"That's not why I asked you out here." Strangely, Dan's voice was full of excitement instead of the frustration it usually held when he was talking to Shep. "You're never gonna believe this. I got a call from some muckety-mucks out in California. They're filming *Do or Die* right here in North Carolina, and they want Prime Climb to supply the local guide."

"Okay." What that had to do with him, he hadn't a single clue.

"Apparently, their other setup got canceled, so we're second choice, but who the hell cares?"

"Congratulations." He was fairly certain that was an appropriate response to Dan's enthusiasm. "Have a great time with that."

"Uh…" Dan cleared his throat. "They had a couple of special requests. After studying the Prime Climb website, they requested you as their guide."

"No thank you," Shep said and turned to climb back down the tower.

Dan caught him by the shirt. Dammit, he knew Shep hated that. Knew Shep didn't like to be randomly touched.

"I wasn't asking, Kingston." A tight smile stretched across Dan's moon-pie face. "You *will* guide the group from *Do or Die.*"

"Why?" Unable to look at Dan's lopsided face a second longer, Shep averted his gaze, hoping the view of the mountains would soothe him as it usually did. Shortleaf and pitch pines spiked toward the sky and hardy oaks hugged the hills. They seemed to guard and protect the Nantahala National Forest and the Great Smoky Mountains. That was where Shep wanted to be right now, not standing here talking to his boss.

"Because they asked for you."

"Why did they ask for me?"

Dan mumbled something.

"What did you say?"

His boss's lip curled, and he released his grip on Shep's shirt. "Apparently, they looked at your picture on the Prime Climb website, and you have the so-called *image* they're looking for in a local guide. I offered to lead the group, but they said something about wanting a guide in his prime. Whatever the hell that means. This is what prime looks like." He raised his arms and flexed his biceps, apparently ignoring the quarter inch of fat that had developed around the muscles.

"Why do they need someone local?" Dread was sweeping over Shep, the way it did when he was being backed into any kind of corner. He shoved his hand into the pocket of his climbing shorts and fingered the length of paracord he was never without. "Don't they have that survivalist guy? Tiger or Bear or something?"

He knew damn well the TV show host's name was Buffalo Moody.

"They contract with a local guide on every trip."

"It's not like they're climbing K2 or something." He tied a quick slip knot with the cord inside the pocket, but that didn't soothe him one damn bit. A bowline didn't make him feel much better.

"You know better than anyone, Kingston, that a bunch of urban softies have no business stumbling around in the mountains by themselves. They'd get themselves killed for sure. Besides it's only four days, and the competitors are celebrities. Who wouldn't want to rub elbows with famous people?"

Shep wouldn't. Four days babysitting a group of snotty celebrities sounded like a level of hell even Dante never imagined. "It's a stupid show." Something like *Survivor* meets *Bear Grylls* meets *Mean Girls*. Three famous people competed with one another for airtime and bragging rights.

"Maybe, but it's the hottest reality show on TV right now, and the producers have promised Prime Climb Tours a mountain of cash. And it's like they say, you can't buy this kind of publicity."

"Then send Celia." Not only was she a more than adequate guide, Celia actually liked people. She was constantly smiling at and chatting with the clients who booked tours through Prime Climb. Unlike Shep, who wished their customers were into silent retreat type adventures.

Dan gave a wait-just-a-damn-minute wave to the guide standing on the opposite platforms with ten kids who were, if the jostling and joking was any indication, getting restless. "They don't want Celia. They want *you.*"

WWMD? What would Maggie—his big sister, law enforcement professional, and all-around badass—do?

She would probably stare down Dan, stating one more time in a cold voice that she would not guide a group of pansy-asses on a stupid trek in front of a TV camera. And Dan would probably shit his pants.

The right side of Shep's mouth lifted.

But then again, Maggie was the sheriff and rarely had to do what someone else told her to do.

"Let me put it this way," Dan said. "You guide this group and I'll give you a bonus from the fee they pay me. You *decline* this opportunity, and you'll be looking for another job."

That brought Shep around. Rarely did he look into other people's eyes, but right now he needed any and every clue to determine if Dan was bluffing. Was bullshitting him. "Say that again."

"You heard it the first time. Do this, and you'll be rewarded. Don't, and you can kiss your paycheck good-bye."

Realistically, the check itself didn't mean that much to Shep. He had a pretty simple life. Little cabin in the woods, a truck, and a dog.

"But you know I'm your final stop around here, Shep. No one else wants to work with you."

Fuck Dan for being right. Shep had either worked for or

been rejected by every other outdoor outfitter and adventure company in this part of the state. Those who'd hired him in the past manufactured reasons to strike him from the payroll within a few weeks. The others hadn't bothered to hire him in the first place. They'd either heard about him through the grapevine or he'd blown the interview.

And why the hell did anyone need to sit down and interview a wilderness guide? If he or she was physically fit, exhibited appropriate skills and certifications, that was what mattered most. But no, everyone wanted their employees to say "I love people," "I'm a people person," or some other kumbaya crap.

Potential employers would rather hear a lie than the truth. When they asked Shep that question, he made it clear that people were something he tolerated because that was the only way he could get paid to do the things he loved. Hiking, climbing, rafting, zip-lining. He did it all.

And he did it damn well.

In huge part due to the way he was raised, a little differently from his four brothers and sisters.

When he was ten, his parents decided to take him out of public school. Other kids didn't like him, many teachers didn't understand him, and a so-called normal education didn't fit him.

So he spent the rest of his childhood being what they now called free-range. Like a chicken.

His dad had called it life.

Shep had once read a book that labeled it unschooling.

It all meant the same thing—that he'd been allowed to explore the things that interested him.

Guiding for an idiotic TV show did *not* interest him.

But maintaining his independent lifestyle did. And if he lost his job, he wouldn't be able to keep the news from his family. They would rally behind him, try to lift him up. Maybe even badger him into moving back in with his mom and dad.

Uh-uh.

Shep liked being able to live his life on his own. He'd discovered it was much easier than sharing a space with others, even people who claimed to love him.

"Fine," he finally said, and even he could hear the grudging tone of his own voice. "But you better tell the TV people that we do things *my* way. If they have a problem with that, then they can go fuc—"

"How 'bout I handle that?" Dan cut him off. "And I'll make it clear that you're the expert in these mountains."

"It will take me at least a week to check and double-check all my equipment." On a tour like this, he would need more than just day hike basics. "So when does this damn thing start?"

Dan stepped off the platform as he said, "Tomorrow morning."

It was drizzling in Southern California, making the trail she was running on a mini-mudslide. And because Joss was staring up at the sky, paying more attention to the rain, a magic weather unicorn, than she was to where she was going, her foot slipped, and she went down on one knee.

The fire road near her home in the Santa Monica Mountains was littered with sharp stones, and one made a painful acquaintance with her kneecap.

Before she could get her feet under her again, it began to rain harder. Maybe she'd somehow caused the skies to spit. After all, the sun had seemed dimmer ever since...

Since she'd abandoned and betrayed the people she loved most in this world.

Maybe the only three people in the world who loved her.

No, that wasn't entirely true. *Everyone* loved Joss Wynter. After all, she'd filled arenas full of screaming rock fans.

But her band—Chris, Winston, and Miguel. They knew and loved the *real* her.

When she and the rest of Scarlet Glitterati had hit the big-time music scene nine years ago, Joss had been dissected by every industry publication, featured on every blog, and interviewed on every major media outlet.

They described her as a fusion of the best of female artists. The vulnerable songwriting of Joni Mitchell. The sexy charisma of Debbie Harry. The velvety power of Stevie Nicks. The playful cheekiness of Katy Perry.

So Joss was either one-of-a-kind or some kind of Franken-musician.

But the fearlessness of Tina Turner? That, she could no longer lay claim to.

She pushed herself up from the ground and resumed her run, trying to ignore the two men following at a respectful distance. They knew better than to offer help.

Joss didn't want help. Didn't deserve help.

And after *Celebrity Scoop* published an article about how she'd gone behind her bandmates' backs to negotiate the terms for a solo career, the public had turned on her. The tabloids and social media had been full of so-called news about how she'd put the band on a helicopter while she'd stayed safely on the ground in a billion-dollar multimedia company's limo.

Headlines like *Superstar Singer Guilty of Band Betrayal, Joss Clinches Solo Career by Killing Off Band,* and *Scarlet Glit-*

terati Blood on Wynter's Hands were accompanied by stories of how Joss had hired the private helicopter that had crashed minutes after takeoff.

Now, people who'd once adored her made death threats.

The applause she'd once reveled in had turned to apathy at best, anger at worst.

As she approached her house, she slowed to a walk, barely registering the incredible Topanga retreat she owned. At over six thousand square feet, it had retractable glass walls that opened to a pool and breath-stealing views of the canyon. When was the last time she'd pushed back those walls?

She couldn't remember, and she avoided them today, entering the house through the garage instead. Her home was no longer a respite. It felt like a prison of her own making.

In the past, when Joss felt alone or sad or just misunderstood, she'd reached for her guitar. Now, Fiona—her favorite old acoustic with a scarred body and abused tuning keys—sat propped in the corner of her living room.

After the accident, she'd shoved the guitar deep into the coat closet, but the next morning, Fiona was back in the great room. As if Fiona had opened the closet door and strolled out by herself just to mock Joss. The incident shook her, but when she mentioned it to Jerry, her manager had gently reminded her that she was prone to sleepwalking when she was under stress.

And she'd been suffocating under ten tons of the stuff for three months now.

She couldn't stand to look at her much-loved guitar for another minute. The jittery feeling that constantly crawled under her skin threatened to burst out. To finally eat her up. She needed…something.

Anything.

So she reached for the phone and punched speed dial to Jerry. He answered before the second ring as he always did with her.

"Hey, Jojo," he said, his voice booming with a bit too much cheer, like he thought he could pour the emotion into her and fill her up. "I was just thinking about you."

"I can't stay in this house anymore. I need...I need something. I can't breathe." Even when she was outside, the air pressed in on her, maliciously compressing her lungs.

"I thought we agreed you would lay low for a few more weeks. Long enough for some other shit to hit the fan and for people to forget all the *caca* in your life."

"I'll wear a disguise. Pretend I'm covering Scarlet Glitterati songs." She could hear the desperation in her voice even though her hands were shaking and her stomach was heaving at the thought of touching that damn guitar. "I will sit on a stool in some shithole bar out in the Valley. I'll do anything to stop the"—Silence. Grief. Guilt. —"boredom."

Jerry sighed. "Maybe you need more appointments with Dr. Whitmore."

"If my therapist comes here any more often, the rags will start the rumor that I'm sleeping with her. And although I have no problem with nonbinary relationships, and she's an attractive woman, that wouldn't do a damn thing to help this situation."

"Neither would you wandering around Los Angeles in the state you're in."

"I am dying." She was. Just as surely as... *Shut it down.*

"I did have a nibble of something, but you would hate it."

"I'll take it." Joss's heart lunged against her ribs. "Whatever it is, I'll do it. Smaller venue is fine." In fact, that would be best. Fewer people to witness any meltdown that might attack her on stage. Because if she wasn't out there, wasn't in front of people singing and making them love her, then she would no longer be anyone special.

"It's TV."

Okay, TV would be forgiving. If she flubbed up, froze on stage, forgot the lyrics, they could just edit out any mistakes.

"Tell them yes." Maybe her lungs were tight as she said it, but she couldn't be in this house, alone with all the ghosts, any longer. "I don't care if it's an award show. Hell, I'll even do something on *American Idol* or *The Voice*." She could be a judge like Katy or Kelly. That was even better. Safer. She would be able to win her way back into the public's hearts without singing a note. "When do they need me?"

"You'll have to catch a flight at—"

Her heart did something inside her chest that should've been anatomically impossible. "No helicopters." She'd sit in twelve hours of LA traffic hell if she had to.

"This show doesn't film in LA, so you'll be on a plane."

A plane. Maybe she could do that. She'd known she would have to fly again at some point. Surely it would be easier to keep her cool inside a big, enclosed metal tube than inside of something the size of a bumblebee. A tiny insect that could fall out of the sky so easily.

"You'll have to hop on a red-eye to the east coast, but if you're serious about doing something, this is our best option. You could take a sleeping pill to get through it."

East coast. New York. "You got me a spot on Jimmy Fallon?" Doing the *Tonight Show* would be tough, but Jimmy was known for being kind, for having a light touch when needed.

"Not exactly, Jojo. But I promise that if you do this show, do a good job and open up a little, people will come around, stop blaming you. Heck, if you work hard enough, you might even win the whole thing."

"Win?" She paced back along the huge glass doors, purposefully avoiding the corner where her guitar sat. "Win what?"

"I'll text you the airline ticket as soon as my assistant can book it."

Foreboding smothered her, and she gripped her cell so hard that her knuckles ached. Why wasn't Jerry telling her the name of the show? "Where am I flying?"

"Direct from LA to Charlotte, North Carolina. From there, we'll have a driver take you out to a place called Steele Ridge."

That... that sounded like a town with a population slightly smaller than New York City's. "And then?"

"And then you'll woo back your fans by winning the reality show *Do or Die.*"

2

SHEP STOOD A GOOD FIFTY FEET FROM THE CHATTERING crowd gathered near Deadman's Creek. Unfortunately, Dan had *accidentally* alerted half the damn state of North Carolina that *Do or Die* would begin filming today. Shep's boss had been strutting around, bragging that he was solely responsible for snagging the attention of the show's producer, and with every minute that passed, the waiting mob became louder and more impatient.

Shep didn't need to absorb any of their restlessness or edgy excitement. This was a job to him. All this rah-rah crap was just that.

Stupid crap.

And it looked as if it was making Maggie's life a bitch today. She had deputies posted all along the creek banks. So far, the worst that had happened was a jostling match gone wrong when Donny Preckwinkle caught an elbow to the eye.

Shep lifted his chin in the direction of the ambulance that was serving as a first aid station. His brother Cash was over there, smiling his Don Juan smile and treating a couple of cases of late season heatstroke. Since both patients were pretty girls in their early twenties, it was more likely they were actually suffering from firefighter fever. Cash had always been a female magnet.

Those two women would be disappointed when they discovered Cash was happily locked down these days. He might smile and flirt on occasion, but he loved Emmy McKay. So much that when they were together, the ferocity of their feelings made the air quiver with something Shep didn't really understand.

Probably because he didn't understand how to love another person. And Shep didn't like to think about things he didn't understand.

Beside him, Puck sensed his unease and leaned against his leg.

Stroking a hand over the golden retriever's silky head, he said, "I know, buddy. I'm tired of waiting, too."

He reached into his pocket for his length of cord and tied a series of knots—a barrel hitch, a double overhand, and a fisherman's knot—to keep his cool. The original agreement was that the *Do or Die* people would arrive in Steele Ridge at noon. It was now 2:08 p.m.

For some reason Shep would never understand, many NTs—neurotypicals—had no concept of time. To him, being punctual was as natural as breathing. If he said noon, he meant noon. Not 11:59 or 12:01.

If this was the way the TV crew planned to operate during filming, Shep would be having a meeting with them. The holy-come-to-Jesus kind.

"What're you frowning about?" Maggie posted up beside him, her eyes still scanning the crowd for any signs of trouble. "You going on overload?"

Shep grunted at her mention of the term his family used

when he was coming close to hitting the wall. When he became so overstimulated or anxious that he had a hard time controlling all the quirks that made him different. Well, at least the ones that tended to really freak people out. Like listing aloud all the flora and fauna native to the state, body rocking, and knocking his head against hard stuff like the sweet gum tree behind him.

"I'm okay." For now. "But I already know the trip with these people is going to be worse than I thought."

"Mr. Optimism strikes again." Maggie laughed and gave him a quick hip bump. "Maybe it'll go better than you think. After all, these are famous folks. Maybe you'll be forced to share your tent with a pretty actress."

"I don't like to share my space. You know that," Shep stated. That had been one of his ex-wife's many gripes about him. Shep liked his space—both physically and mentally. Amber had been forever trying to crawl into places with him. And it had made Shep feel as if he'd been shoehorned into a tiny teepee with a T. Rex.

"I was just kidding. I bet they all bring their own tents. Don't you think, Way?" Maggie asked as their brother strolled up. Way was the middle Kingston sibling. He blew in and out of town for work and on his own whims. Maybe his years in the Marines had given him a taste for freedom.

"Tents? Have you *ever* watched *Do or Die*?" Way cut Maggie a sideways glance that Shep filtered through his file of facial recognition prompts. Most kids used flash cards to learn stuff like letters and multiplication. Shep's dad had adopted them to try to teach him how to read other people's expressions and body language.

But they were still like Swahili to him most of the time.

He *thought* Way's side-eye at Maggie meant some kind of

ridicule. "Mags, I am not a hundred percent sure, but I think Way is patronizing you."

"I think you're right." But rather than take a shot back at Way, Maggie just shook her head and said, "No, I haven't seen the show. I have better things to do on Wednesday nights than watch a bunch of celebrity city slickers whine about the state of their manicures after being forced to climb all the way out of their limos."

"Jay takes a limo sometimes," Shep said, thinking about his sister's pro athlete boyfriend. "Does that affect *his* manicure?"

Maggie dropped her forehead into her palm and laughed. "I'm sorry. I was being sarcastic. Yes, Jay does ride in a limo sometimes. One of those pro football player perks. But so far as I know, he's not into manicures."

"Then I don't understand…" Shep trailed off because sometimes a topic wasn't worth going into. Sometimes he understood that he just wasn't going to understand. So he asked Way, "Do you watch *Do or Die*?"

"I've caught it a time or two." Way stuffed his hands into his pockets and looked away.

"Your neck is getting red, which I think means one of two things. You are uncomfortable with admitting you watch the show. Or you are lying. Or maybe you are aroused"—he glanced down at his brother's crotch—"okay, it's not that."

"Jesus, Shep." Way rubbed at the pink skin. "So I binge-watched the last season. Maggie, you gonna arrest me for that?"

"Last time I checked, questionable taste isn't against the law."

"Hey, sometimes the challenges—or what they call opportunities—are interesting," Way said.

"So *that's* what interests you." Maggie's smirk meant she was baiting their brother.

"Fine, so there are usually hot women on the show. And sometimes by the end, they're..." He cast a quick look at Maggie.

To prepare for guiding the group, Shep had watched every *Do or Die* episode last night, so for once, he knew exactly where Way's mind was. "What Way is trying to say is that even though the women are sometimes dirty and probably smelly, they tend to lose articles of clothing. In the Maui show, some actress was down to a thong and a lacy bra by the end of the competition."

"She won, too," Way said.

Maggie snorted. "I wonder why."

"Hey. She was the last woman standing. She deserved to win."

"Actually," Shep said, "the comedian guy in that episode would have won if the thong girl hadn't bent over while they were crossing that rope bridge. She shifted her center of gravity, and it threw him off-balance."

"No, Shep," his brother said. "I think her perfect ass cheeks were what affected his balance. And speaking of perfect, I heard a rumor that one of the contestants in this episode is Joss Wynter."

"Who told you that?" Maggie asked.

"Ran into Dan the Man at Triple B last night." Way pointed toward where Dan was, if his wild arm movements were any indication, regaling a group of women with a tall tale. "Couple of tequila shots and his lips got loose."

Shep grunted. He'd known these celebrities would probably be challenging, but Joss Wynter? From what Riley—his sister and a big Scarlet Glitterati fan—said, the musician made Jennifer Lopez look low maintenance. "Riley told me that Joss Wynter owns over three hundred wigs. But if there are only three natural hair colors, why would someone need that much fake hair?"

"Two words for you. Hot and Sex." Way grinned at him. "Can you imagine going to bed with a pink-tipped blond on Monday and then having a pixie redhead go down on you the next morning?"

"If you took two women to bed at the same time, you could easily have that," Shep said. It was just logical.

"My God, you two are pigs," Maggie scolded. "Dad would be ashamed to hear you talking that way."

"Oh!" Understanding dawned in Shep's brain. "I get it. It's like that time Mom dyed her hair really blond and Dad chased her around the dining room table. I think her hair increased his sexual appetite."

Way laughed and clapped Shep hard on the back. "And now, my man, you know the value of three hundred wigs."

Murmurs rippled through the crowd, and Maggie turned on full cop mode again. Eyes scanning, missing nothing. "I'll see you two Neanderthals later. Maybe when you've made it to the Stone Age."

She stalked away but had only made it about twenty feet when the *schwoop-schwoop-schwoop* of rotors rumbled overhead. Shep spotted a helicopter off to the west over the treetops.

The crowd went quiet.

"That's gotta be them," Way said. "They rappel down ropes sometimes."

"That is flying too low for a skydive."

"Oh, hell. That's not a... Do they have a..." Way sputtered, and Way never did something as wishy-washy as sputtering.

But when Shep spotted what was dangling below the

helicopter, he totally understood, and it was all the proof he needed that these TV people were idiots. And that they didn't give a damn about safety. He wanted to grab Puck's leash, get in the truck, and drive directly home.

"Do you think the contestants have any kind of harnesses on?" Way asked.

Not that Shep could see. Sure, the bulky PFDs— personal flotation devices—they were wearing would help keep the three people inside the raft from drowning when they hit the water. But what was going to keep them from breaking their necks if they fell out of the raft from that height?

From the chop of the rotor blades and the breeze coming from the south, the inflatable raft was swinging round and round like a yoyo at the end of its string. A cameraman—who *was* in a harness—was leaning out of the helicopter to catch the action from above.

Shep scanned, looking for more people up there, but that was it. A cameraman and three idiot contestants. Buffalo Moody and the rest of his crew must already be somewhere on the ground.

What kind of decent guide would let his group dangle in the air while he had his feet safely on the earth? "That guy's a douche, letting them swing up there alone."

"They won't be swinging long," Way said. And as he said it, the ropes tethering the raft to the helicopter began to extend. Fucking fast.

And someone from up there screamed. Shep was already in motion, running toward the water, with Puck keeping pace. "Don't do what I think you are going to do, you fuckers," he yelled up at the helicopter.

Faces peered over the side of the raft. At least they'd had the good sense God gave a turnip and had settled their asses on the bottom of that inflatable boat. The helicopter bucked, sending the raft into an even wider, wilder circle.

Noise swelled from people on the ground—gasps, shouts, and a few encouraging hoots. When the raft was about twenty feet above the water, the ropes harnessing it to the helicopter completely disengaged.

The helicopter banked right and swooped over the crowd.

The raft plummeted down, down—

Whomp!

The sound of rubber hitting water and screams rolled over Shep and echoed off the mountains. He shoved his way through a cluster of young pine trees and made for the creek bank. This area of Deadman's—more river than creek —was known for being a fast run when the water was high, and Steele Ridge and the surrounding area had received a decent amount of rain at the end of the summer.

Those stupid TV fuckers had dropped the raft less than thirty feet behind a class IV rapid. Good thing the contestants in the raft—two in front and one in the guide position —were at least wearing helmets and the PFDs.

As Shep watched the boat hurtle toward the churning water, the person on the front right gingerly dipped a paddle into the water. Big mistake. It was ripped away by the current and went whirling downstream.

"Shit! Someone do something!" a man yelled from the front left spot. "Or we're all going to die."

Shep cupped his hands around his mouth and hollered, "Paddle right!" If they could get closer to the left bank, they'd miss the killer drop between two massive rocks well known for pinning rafts and spitting out rafters.

He had to give the person in the back credit. He or she tried like hell to steer them to the left, but the guy in front was also digging deep on the left, sending them to the right. Unexperienced rafters didn't always understand directional commands, and paddle right meant to paddle only on the right side of the raft.

They were headed directly for the boulders.

"You in the front, stop paddling and slide to the right side of the boat!" Shep yelled at the dude screwing up their direction. "You in the back, keep paddling!"

The rafter in the back followed his commands, but in combination with the flow of water, the movement almost pulled the person out of the boat. Whoever was in the back position was short.

"Hook your feet under the thwart—the inflated cross tube—in front of you!" he yelled. "Stay in the damn raft! Don't fall out."

To do as instructed, the competitor had to pull the paddle partially out of the water, and the movement just wasn't enough to change the raft's course. It slammed nose-first into the leftmost rock and went into a wild spin.

Hell, they were about to go over the rapid sideways. Hopefully, Moody had explained what to do if they fell out of the boat. To never, ever put your feet down and try to stand up. Look for an oar. Grab on and let someone drag your ass back in the boat.

But if no one was left in the boat...

Sure enough, the raft hit the hump of the rapid and the entire left side dipped sharply. The person who'd initially lost a paddle went sliding across with the force of gravity and body checked the other rafter in front. That was all it took for both of them to go over the side and disappear under the swirling water.

The only rafter remaining in the boat used the oar to push off the rocks and navigate clumsily through the passage. Once the raft was over the rapid, two heads popped out of the water. Limbs flailed and it was obvious they were both trying to fight the current. One head went back down. Damn.

Downstream, Dan was wading into the water, angling toward the spot where the rafters had been dumped into the water. His progress was slow, though, because he was also fighting the force of the rapids.

"Puck, stay," Shep told his dog.

Then he ran upstream and executed a shallow dive. Slick as a seal, he turned on his back and let the water navigate him toward the rocks. He'd probably only get one chance at this, so he had to make it count. A few feet from the rocks, he flipped over and kicked his way underwater.

Sure enough, one of the rafters had a foot caught between two rocks on the creek bed. And the current was keeping the person's head under water. Dan had actually beat Shep to the rafter and was yanking the person by the underarms but making no progress freeing them.

So Shep grabbed an ankle and worked what felt like a female foot out of a Keen sandal. Freed, the woman kicked out, catching him in the solar plexus.

They both came out of the water gulping for breath, with Dan right behind them.

Shep called out to the woman, "Don't put your feet down. Float on your back until the water is calmer."

"But—"

"Do it!"

The other person who'd been dumped out of the raft was already a good fifty feet downstream, apparently having had the good sense to work with the current instead of against it. The raft was bobbing its way toward a bridge spanning the creek.

Shep grabbed his floater's arm and towed her toward the bank.

"Don't! Stop! I can't get out here. I have to make it to the markers."

"What?"

She ripped out of his hold and pointed downstream. "If I don't make it down there, I don't get any points."

For. Fuck's. Sake.

"If you don't get out of this water, you could drown."

Rather than answering, she took off swimming. Away from him.

This was even worse than Shep had imagined. Maggie *should* call him Mr. Optimism because he'd obviously painted too rosy of a picture about this whole clusterfuck.

Dan said to him, "Let her go! It's not your job to interfere with the game."

Then what the hell had Dan been doing?

"And for your information," Dan continued, "I would've saved her. You actually slowed me down."

With Dan dogging him and yapping about how he'd had everything under control with the drowning chick, Shep swam toward shore and called out to Puck, "Release!"

Tongue lolling and tail wagging, Puck came loping up from where Shep had left him on the bank. His dog was a lot happier than he was right now. Happy was no longer in Shep's vocabulary. The word should be ripped from the dictionary.

Still, Shep grabbed Puck's leash and squished his way back toward the waiting crowd. Miraculously, all three rafters had made it to the green markers, two on their feet and one in the boat.

From this vantage point, Shep spotted turquoise hair spilling out from under the lone rafter's helmet. Based on what Riley had told him, that rafter had to be Joss Wynter. She was smaller than he'd imagined—probably five feet if she was an inch.

But she'd fought and stayed in that raft. That would've been a feat for someone twice her size.

Even though the smartest course of action would be for Shep to walk away, leave these nut jobs to their own devices, he couldn't. And only partially because of Dan's threats about his job.

He had to get a better look at the itty-bitty woman who'd conquered that Class IV. Because right now, if he had to put money down on one of these contenders, he'd lay a solid hundred on her.

3

JOSS WAS A FREEZING FRENZY OF MOLECULES. EVERYTHING inside her was pinging around and knocking together. The chaos would probably never stop.

Yes, the water on her skin and soaking her sneakers was cool, but they didn't account for the gut-deep shudders radiating from the very center of her body.

They had put her, Lauren Estes, and Bradley Woodard into a flimsy rubber boat and dropped them. From the sky.

When Joss had set eyes on that helicopter, she'd turned around and walked away. Unfortunately, one of the production assistants apparently had Jerry's phone number because Joss had found herself on the phone with her manager.

He'd promised her anything—any gig, any arena—if she would just get on that helicopter. It would be fine, he said. She'd asked for this, he said. It was time, he said.

No, it hadn't been time. It would *never* be time for the insanity she'd just been a part of.

After outfitting the contestants with a helmet, a life

jacket, and a paddle, the guys in the helicopter had simply cut the ropes. *Adios. See ya later. Bu-bye.*

And what Joss had thought would be a fluffy play at a survival game for a few days had become real damn real as that raft hurtled downward. How she'd stayed inside it without passing out, she still had no idea.

She couldn't do this. She'd been an idiot to think she was ready. As soon as she could get off this water, she was calling Jerry and backing out. Who cared if she had to return to being a hermit inside her house?

She looked around wildly for a way to escape, to get to shore. She blinked down at the paddle in her hand. Should she be doing something with it?

Probably, but her arms were frozen.

Slowly, the buzzing in her brain began to change frequency and morphed into the shrill sound of people on the water bank yelling and clapping. They reminded her of arena crowds, fans just waiting to get their hands on her, gleefully anticipating snatching a piece of her.

Her already rapid breath shallowed even more, and little spots played ring-around-the-rosie at the periphery of her vision. The water would take her downstream. Away from these people.

Go, go, go.

If she could make it past the bridge ahead of her, she'd somehow navigate her way to shore. And run screaming all the way back to California. But before she and the raft could rush under the bridge, two shirtless muscular guys waded waist deep and caught the boat. Then Bradley and Lauren came dog-paddling down the river past her. Some other guys kneeling on the bridge snagged them under the arms and lifted them up.

Woozily, Joss looked up at the bridge to see that Buffalo

Moody was standing there, smiling and waving at the throng of people. He was saying something, but the words seemed to disintegrate before her ears could catch them. Buffalo's teeth were big and white. Made her think of the wolf in Little Red Riding Hood.

Joss rubbed her hands over her face and tried to get herself under control.

Focus on what's in front of you.

As people continued to hoot and holler, two camera operators were panning the spectacle. The Western North Carolina mini-season of *Do or Die* was obviously underway.

Was this what she got for failing to stream a single episode of the show? For popping a sleeping pill before stepping a foot on the airplane from LA. She thought luck was with her when she conked out and slept the entire way to Charlotte. Especially since she hadn't suffered through the dark demon dreams that had become her constant companions lately.

Or maybe *this* was the true nightmare.

She opened her mouth to ask if all this was real, but the only sound that came out was a moan.

"Ma'am, are you okay?" A man with short blond hair peered down at her. A frown marred his apple-cheeked, All-American good looks. The kind of looks that could get him cast in a reboot of *The Waltons*. No, *The Waltons* on steroids.

"Uuuuhhhh."

The other man shot an alarmed look at John Boy. "Gage, I don't think she's okay." This guy was tall, probably almost a foot and a half over Joss's minuscule five feet. He too had short hair, but his was dark and looked as though it would curl if left to its own devices. Yep, coloring aside, he could play John Boy's brother in *Waltons: The Buff Years*.

"Ma'am, we're gonna get you to the first aid station. Deke, let's tow her in," the blond said.

But they were intercepted by another big man wading into the water straight toward them. This guy's hair was longer. Wet, it clung to his head and neck, making it hard for Joss to tell if it was dark blond or light brown. He cut through the water with determined strides, water dripping down his golden torso. He wore a pair of low-hanging cargo shorts, giving her a glimpse of strong hip bones and perfectly formed abdominal muscles that seemed to have the singular purpose of drawing a woman's attention to what lay behind a man's zipper.

"Am...Am I dreaming?" she forced out.

"No, ma'am," the blond man said. "This is as real as it gets, and Shep doesn't look too happy about it."

As the other man drew closer, the guitar intro to Imelda May's "Big Bad Handsome Man" began to pound in Joss's mind. Then she heard the lyrics join the guitar. This man was definitely tall, mad, mean, and good-lookin'.

He was Devil Divine.

Divine's nipples were drawn tight and so was his mouth. And with the way he was bearing down on her, he was looking to take something out on her.

"Wh...Why is he mad?" All she'd done was try to make it down the river alive and with a sliver of her sanity.

With a rough jerk, Devil Divine grabbed the cord ringing the raft and said to the other men, "I have her. I don't know how the hell they roped the two of you into this idiocy. But she is my responsibility."

"God help you." The blond man laughed. "And I thought my job wrangling Reid Steele was tough sometimes."

Without saying a word, Devil Divine started to drag her raft toward shore.

No, this was not okay. She lunged toward him and grabbed his wrist.

With a quick shake, he threw off her hold. Alarm ricocheted through her, and she forced out a hoarse "Stop!"

That, at least, earned a glance from him. "Why?"

"Because I don't know who you are or where you're taking me."

"I'm Harris Sheppard Kingston. Adventure guide at Prime Climb Tours. And we are getting out of the water." As the water shallowed, the man's saturated shorts drooped further, revealing the top curve of his ass cheeks. Joss's chilled skin began to warm.

She couldn't help but give his backside a quick peek, and holy guacamole. Something told her this gluteus beauteous was most likely homegrown, as were his bulging triceps and Atlas shoulders.

For the first time in a long time, Joss experienced a jolt of something besides self-loathing. It felt a lot like lust.

And if she was capable of that spark, was it possible she might be capable of competing on *Do or Die?*

Maybe.

That *maybe* grounded her, helped her shake off a little of the terror still trickling through her.

"Why are you pulling my raft in?"

"Because I am the local guide," he said, striding toward land and dragging her and the raft onto the bank with a *scritch.* "And they were stupid to drop you the way they did. Unsafe and stupid."

Amen and hallelujah. Joss held out a hand, expecting Devil Divine to take it and help her out of the raft. But his attention was focused back on the water.

"That one." He pointed toward Lauren, standing on the bridge beside the show's host. Lauren had stripped out of her life jacket, giving the public a good view of her leanly muscled body, showcased in a thong bikini. Strangely, she was only wearing one sandal. Still, with chin up and chest out, she looked like the warrior princess that she played on the Netflix exclusive, *Amazon Rises*. "She almost drowned."

That statement shocked a little more sanity back into Joss's brain. "Lauren Estes?" When Joss arrived in Steele Ridge and realized she'd be competing against the actress, her competitive instincts had been sparked. Because winning—both the game and the hearts of the public— would be tough against her. Bradley Woodard, the third competitor, wasn't as physically fit as Lauren, but people liked him because he was the son of George Woodard and Beverly Blaise—Hollywood royalty—and he gave a great deal of his family's money to different environmental chari- ties across the world.

"And the guy—"

"Bradley Woodard."

"—didn't have any idea how to steer that raft. They should have put him in the back because he's the biggest." He looked Joss over with a dispassionate study and clearly found her wanting. "You should have never been placed there."

She never should've let the show's producers push her onto that helicopter. But they'd reminded her that she'd signed both a whopper of a hold-harmless release and a contract of completion. If she didn't compete in *Do or Die,* there would be a lawsuit, and she couldn't withstand any more bad press at the moment.

Tell that to her stomach, still twisting itself into impos- sible shapes.

"You would have been a liability in front, too, because you are so little," the man continued on about the raft. "One major rapid and you'd go flying like a projectile out of a catapult."

A spark replaced all the gastro-gymnastics inside her. She clambered out of the raft and said, "Should I remind you that I was the only one who *didn't* fall out of the raft?"

"Pure luck."

That made her want to punch him in the kidney. But his lower back looked just as impenetrable as the rest of his body. Asshat. At least he wasn't part of the show. And realistically, anger and annoyance on her part was infinitely better than total terror.

"Puck, release," the man called out. A gorgeous golden-red dog trotted to his left side and gazed up at the man with adoration in his brown eyes. Maybe Devil Divine had better rapport with animals than he did with people.

"He's beautiful," she said. "Is he a retriever?"

"Yes. A golden."

She ran her fingers lightly over the dog's back, but he didn't spare her a glance. That hurt more than the man's scorn. "Then I'm surprised he didn't jump in the water."

"Puck is well trained. If I tell him to sit, he stays in place until I release him."

"Wow, I wish I had a dog like that."

"A lot of people do. But they do not understand what it really takes to train one. They take one look at Puck and want him. They can't have him."

What a strange thing to say. "Of course they can't. He's *your* dog."

"He's my best friend."

Her heart cracked a little at that. Yes, dogs were known as man's best friend, but from the way Devil Divine behaved and talked, she got the impression that he might not have many friends. And it made her realize that she was following him up the bank from the water just as loyally as his dog was. She glanced back toward the bridge. Now that her pulse was slowly returning to normal, it was clear to Joss that she had no choice but to buck up and play this game. Fear or no fear. "Um... I probably need to get back to the crew."

"They are meeting over here." He nodded toward an open-sided canvas tent. With *Do or Die* banners hanging from all the metal supports, it had obviously been set up for the show.

She, Devil Divine, and Puck were almost inside the tent when someone yelled from behind them, "Joss Wynter, can I have your autograph?"

That was all it took for a crush of people to break away from the main crowd and rush toward Joss. The rumbling and noise level rose, decibel by decibel, until it seemed as if it was invading her chest and pressing against her ribs.

"You don't want her to sign a damn thing," a man shouted. "She's a selfish bitch!"

"Joss, Joss, look this way!" someone else hollered.

A little girl called out, "Can I get a selfie with you?"

Joss's ability to breathe was restricted by the panic building inside her. She should've demanded the show allow her to bring bodyguards. But both she and Jerry thought the mini-series would be filmed in the boonies, away from both fans and haters alike. That she would be safe.

"I...I can't face those people," she gasped out to the man—Harris, he'd said his name was Harris—striding half a pace in front of her, but he didn't even spare her a glance.

Unable to shake the feeling of being threatened, she broke into a run and darted around him and the dog. Maybe if she could just make it under the tent awning, people would back down.

Why wasn't this guy helping her? It was as if he didn't recognize that she was in danger.

Joss lunged for the tent, tripping over a support rope. Oh, God. She was falling. Falling. Losing control. She would plunge into the crowd from high above them, and they would surround her, jump on top of her, smother her.

Joss took a headfirst slider into the dirt and tried to flip over to ward them off, but she couldn't seem to make her muscles work.

That was when she heard the man say, "All of you, stay behind the red line. You cannot step past it. This area is only for people associated with *Do or Die*."

Now? *Now* he decided to come to her aid? After she'd almost blacked out with panic?

Finally, Joss managed to flop to her back and saw that he was standing like a human shield, arms out and legs wide. The dog was on alert too—ears up and tail lifted like a furry sword.

A man with a dark beard and mean eyes stepped over the red spray-painted line that Joss hadn't seen when she hurtled across it.

"You do not have an ID badge," her now-protector said. "Step back."

"I just want to tell her—"

"Now." He flattened a palm on the other guy's chest and easily pushed him away. No anger, no violence, no rush. Just put him back in his place.

That did more to calm Joss than all the Valium in her medicine cabinet back home.

While Devil Divine was holding back a mass of people who wanted to get close to her, Buffalo Moody strode through them without acknowledging anyone. The host of *Do or Die* had tanned skin and a face that could be described as craggy. Joss guessed his hair was supposed to look sun-bleached. But she had colored her own hair enough to recognize drugstore dye when she spotted it.

Although he looked like a big fake to Joss, female fans apparently loved him. And the Hollywood rags made it clear he'd *loved* plenty of them, too.

The crowd parted for him and the entourage trailing him. Lauren looked a little worse for the wear with one shoe missing, but the confident expression on her face didn't waver, and she stopped to pen a few quick autographs. Some on paper, some on body parts.

Bradley wasn't a sign-my-tit kind of celebrity, so he just smiled and shook a few hands. Two camera operators flanked them from behind and herded them toward the tent.

And here Joss was, lying on the ground. She was already shorter than both of her opponents by at least half a foot. She didn't need them towering over her.

Get your ass up, sister.

She scrambled to her feet.

Red dust clung to her palms and tiny rocks were embedded in her already abused knee. She brushed at it, setting off a sting. A trickle of blood oozed down the outside of her calf.

She could handle a few scrapes and a little blood. She could handle more. She *would* handle more.

She hadn't built a successful music career by letting fear get in her way.

As kids in the suburbs of Omaha, she and her sister Kellie had been allowed a long leash. They—well, mainly Joss—had roamed free, climbing trees and exploring the neighborhood. That was where she'd first learned to be tough. Then when she struck out on her own to play her music, she'd learned another type of toughness.

Mental toughness.

"There she is," Buffalo boomed, swaggering toward her. "Joss Wynter! No one on the crew imagined you would win the first opportunity."

Opportunity? Is that what he called being dropped from a helicopter? She called it a reason to be admitted to the psych ward.

He swung an arm around her and grinned for the camera. His fingers brushed the side of her breast—an accident or on purpose? Joss tried to ease away, but Buffalo was a strong guy and gripped her shoulder.

Another boob brush.

Yeah, that was not an accident.

Joss smiled up at him, but she put a little teeth behind it and not the friendly kind. The spectrum of wild emotions she'd run through since she left LA were coalescing into something heated. Something that could easily boil over and burn the hell out of everyone here. "So you're telling me that I'm the *Do or Die* underdog?"

Buffalo laughed. *Hehuhhe. Hehuhhe.* "Well, you have to admit that between you, Lauren, and Bradley, you're the most physically underwhelming."

"And though she be but little, she is fierce," she gritted out.

"Hey now," Buffalo said, "no need to get your feathers rustled."

"They're ruffled," Devil Divine told him as he pulled a dry T-shirt over his head, covering up that amazing body. "And she was quoting Shakespeare. *A Midsummer Night's Dream.*"

Interesting. Her big-bad-handsome-man knew something about literature. Hidden depths.

With a blink, Buffalo turned back to the crowd and flashed a toothy grin. "If you'll excuse us now, it's time for our competitors to get ready for the first leg of the show." He nodded toward the corner of the tent and the person stationed there lowered the canvas tent flaps, casting the space into temporary darkness.

Buffalo took that opportunity to do more than skim Joss's breast. He gave it a good cantaloupe-ripeness squeeze. No. No one was allowed to grope her like that. After that horrible night on stage, she didn't stand for that shit anymore.

So Joss also took advantage of everyone's blindness and grabbed the show host between the legs.

She twisted and said in a low voice, "Touch me like that again and I will take these as a souvenir." And then bright lights flipped on suddenly, clearly illuminating her hold on Buffalo Moody's junk.

Fabulous. The cameras were trained right on them, and this would be definitely be a clip that made it through the editing process. As if she didn't care that she'd been caught holding Buffalo's balls, Joss casually released him and crossed her arms.

The groping host had the audacity to wink at the camera.

"Well, well," Lauren sneered as she saw Joss's hand leave their host's crotch. "If we're going to play this game that way, then I'd better pick a partner." She turned to Devil Divine with a predatory look. "Yum, cutie. I choose you."

He didn't even acknowledge that Lauren had said anything, just turned to Buffalo and said, "We're behind schedule. If we don't leave here within ten minutes, we won't make it to the spot I picked to overnight."

"Son," Buffalo said, holding out his hand, "we haven't been properly introduced. I'm Buffalo Moody and this is my show. So you just put out the fire in your pants. I say when we leave."

"I am Ross Kingston's son. Not yours." Devil Divine's gaze seemed to land somewhere around Buffalo's left ear.

A man at least fifteen years older than Devil Divine insinuated his way into the group and flashed a smile at Moody. "Hey, there. I'm Dan Cargill, owner of Prime Climb Tours. This guy is Shep Kingston, and he's the local guide I helped your producer handpick—"

"No," Shep cut in. "The producer asked for me. You didn't have anything to do with it."

Dan ignored Shep and kept his attention on Moody. "Sometimes Shep's a little abrupt, but you'll find he's pretty good at what he does. Second to me, of course, but I wasn't available so—"

"Son, if he's second to you, then why was he the one to pull Lauren out of the drink?" Moody cut the man down with a scathing stare. "If it had been up to you, she'd have drowned."

"I... I'm sure it was hard to see from where you were standing on the bridge, but Shep and I worked together to free Ms. Estes from a very dangerous situation. One she wouldn't have been in if—"

Moody snapped his fingers at the guys keeping people from entering the tent. "Escort Mr. Carr outside."

"The name is Cargill, and I—"

Two men took Cargill firmly by the upper arms and frog-marched him out of the tent. Moody swiped his hands against one another as if dusting away an annoyance. "Now, where were we?"

Devil—no, his name was Shep Kingston—said, "We were about to get moving."

"Well, Shep. We don't move until I give the word. And we've got a little business to take care of before we hit the trail." With a careless hand, Buffalo gestured toward a group of grips, who toted forward three full-size suitcases, two Bottega Veneta satchels, a leather trunk, and Joss's carry-on and guitar case.

"Thank God," Lauren sighed, waving the grips toward her as she said to Buffalo, "I assume we'll have a support van for our things."

Buffalo's chuckle held a cruel edge. "Not exactly."

One of the grips passed out small knapsacks to each of the competitors.

"You can pack whatever you can fit into the backpack," Moody said, his tone smug. "And one personal item if it doesn't fit inside. But you and you alone will carry anything you bring along. We're using a skeleton crew for this show. Just two cameramen, the local guide, me, and the three of you. You've got five minutes to choose your items."

4
———

WHILE THE ASSHOLE MOODY WAS GRINNING LIKE HE'D JUST unwrapped the best Christmas present of all time, the three contestants stood with open mouths, bags dangling from their fingers. Shep's dad and Way would probably describe them as shell-shocked.

Shep felt a little like that himself. He didn't mind going into the backcountry packing light. In fact, he preferred it. But there was light and then there was dangerous. "Moody," he said. "So the show crew will be packing in food, water, and other essentials, right?"

"Why would you think that?"

"Because these three people are not accustomed to the wilderness."

"Kingston, the people who watch this show want to see the contestants struggle. Even suffer. And since they won't be climbing a massive mountain or scaling a glacier like in some seasons, we needed to up the ante a little. Dan Cargill assured me that you were an experienced survivalist. And that's what you'll be teaching these three on camera. How to survive."

Shep pointed to the far corner of the tent and said to Moody, "Let's step over here."

Moody's megawatt smile didn't dim as he accompanied Shep and Puck across the tent, but he walked stiffly, as if his butt muscles were contracted. That usually meant someone was unhappy about something.

"I did not agree to be filmed." Without looking down, Shep reached out to skim Puck's head, trying to keep himself centered. Calm. "Dan Cargill was supposed to make that clear to you. I do not want to be on camera."

"Son," Moody said. "This is my show. Do you understand what I'm saying?"

"Technically, it's the network's show. But what I think you are trying to say is that you like to make all the decisions, whether or not they are good ones."

"You're getting paid to carry out my decisions."

"Prime Climb Tours is getting paid." But the man wasn't completely wrong. Shep's compensation would come in the form of keeping his job, allowing him to pay his minimal bills. Staying on top of normal things like that on his own meant he didn't need another person to help or remind him. Puck was the only companion Shep needed these days.

"Whatever." With a wave that said he didn't give a shit what Shep wanted, Moody said, "Cargill assured me you would be more than happy to accommodate any requirements of the show."

Damn Dan. And damn Buffalo Moody. "I will teach these people survival skills, not because Dan agreed for me to, but because they will not be safe if I don't."

Moody slapped Shep on the arm, and Puck nosed between them. He knew Shep's equilibrium was being threatened. Hell, his equilibrium had been shot ever since

Dan told him about this show. Moody glanced down at Puck. "Who's the pooch, and what's he doing here?"

"This is Puck, and he is my dog."

"Lose him. He can't make the trip with us. He shows up on camera and he'll upstage the celebrities. Besides, he doesn't seem too friendly."

"He is very friendly to my friends. You are not my friend. I won't leave him here because Puck goes everywhere I go."

"Not this time, son."

Moody took a step, but Shep—knowing this was the kind of man who couldn't be swayed by words alone—grabbed his arm and gripped it hard. "Mr. Moody, do not call me son again. Now, Puck *will* be making the trip with us. He is a service animal and if you violate my right to have him with me at all times, I will consult my attorney and have him file a discrimination suit against you."

"Service animal. Sure he is." Moody snorted and stepped away, breaking Shep's hold on him. "And I thought the celebs were divas. You sure as hell don't look disabled. I bet if I asked you for legal paperwork that you couldn't produce it."

"On the contrary, Puck's papers are in the glove compartment of my truck if you would like me to present them to you."

"What the fuck ever," Moody grumbled. "Just keep him off camera."

"And what about me? Dan promised I would never be filmed."

"But I never promised any such thing." Moody rounded on Shep and puffed out his chest so that it brushed against him. Disgust, as thick as a nasty green smoothie, oozed through Shep, and he shifted away. Still, bits of Moody's spittle landed on him when he said, "Sure, our priority is camera time for the contestants, but you will be filmed, too. So get over it."

Shep could take Puck and walk away this minute. Just slide into his truck and return to the sanctity of his cabin. No, that wasn't true. No job meant no cabin. No cabin meant no independence.

And Shep very much liked his independence.

There was no choice here, so Shep said, "Puck, let's go." He turned away from Moody and strode across the tent to the contestants. The Amazon woman and the soft-looking man were sitting on the ground pawing through a bunch of shit they didn't need to take with them. He said to the woman, "You don't need that much underwear. In fact, you don't need any."

"Excuse me?"

"And that lace will chafe."

"Not if I don't wear it for long." She was trying to say something to him with her smile and quivering eyelashes, but Shep didn't bother to try to figure out the message.

"If you are wearing a pair of underwear now, that's all you need. You can turn them inside out tomorrow."

"Ugh," she said. "And the day after that?"

"If you have to, then you can wash them out and put them on wet."

"That sounds... disgusting."

Shep pointed to the half dozen T-shirts covered with charity logos that the male competitor was stuffing into his bag along with a glass bottle of cologne. "Leave that behind."

"I don't think so." The man chuckled and shook his head. "If I can't change underwear, then this is a necessity."

"Maybe if you want to get it on with a bear," Joss Wynter said to the man. Shep *thought* she was teasing, but he wasn't certain. "I read they like anything that smells remotely like food," she continued. "So if you're looking for a little ursine love, you pack that right up."

The bottle slipped from the man's grasp and hit the packed dirt serving as the tent's floor. The glass cracked and sickly sweet-smelling scent rolled through the tent.

Shep ground his teeth at the overpowering odor. This was exactly the reason he didn't work inside a building with other people. Overwhelming smells, too much conversation, complete lack of logic. He covered his nose with his palm and stepped away.

"Are you okay?" Joss put a light hand on his arm, a touch that would normally be uncomfortable if not downright painful to him. But with her, for some reason, it was... bearable.

"I don't tolerate strong scent well." Puck sneezed and shook his whole body as if confirming Shep's intolerance to stuff that smelled chemically fake. Shep ducked out of one of the tent flaps, with Puck and Joss Wynter right behind him.

Thank goodness, it looked as if most of the crowd had become bored and left. Shep took a few gulps of fresh air. The scent of pine and the hint of cool the mountains were promising soothed him. Once his head was clear again, he glanced down at the tiny woman beside him. Blood streaked one of her legs.

She was a mess, but she didn't smell like a perfume factory. If he had to describe her scent, he would call it clean and warm. She had her knapsack slung over one shoulder and the strap for a soft guitar case on the other.

"You shouldn't take a musical instrument, either."

Her mouth twisted. "I traded my extra underwear for it.

Besides, it's not that heavy, and I'm sure not leaving it with someone else."

"We will be hiking up to fifteen miles a day. It will be slapping against your back the entire time. It is an awkward shape, and not necessary."

"Not for you, maybe," she said as she gazed toward the mountains humping up from the ground to the west. Although she may have been teasing the other contestant a few short minutes ago, now Shep thought she might be sad. "But this is *my* best friend."

"A musical instrument can't be a friend."

"So says the man who's BFFs with a dog." She glanced up at him, but her eyelashes didn't twitch like the other woman's. Suddenly, he realized that Joss Wynter was pretty. With her turquoise-dyed dark hair, pink lips, and tiny stature, she looked a bit like a fairy. Maybe like Tinkerbell's older sister. The one who probably snuck out at night and back-talked their fairy parents.

"What?" she asked. "Why are you staring at me like that?"

Shep tried to regain the thread of their conversation and flailed around inside his head for a few seconds. Guitar. Best friend. Puck. "That's different," he finally said. "Puck is alive."

"Doesn't make it any less sad."

"Puck makes me happy." More than that, he made Shep whole.

She lifted a hand, let it drop back to her side. "So you understand why I need my guitar."

"I have heard your music."

"Oh really?"

"I do not like it."

Her laugh was a single puff of air. "Hey, why don't you tell me what you really think?"

"I just did. It's too loud. The guitar makes my ears hurt and your voice is screechy." Just thinking about it, the strident sound of her screaming lyrics on stage or over his radio, prompted Shep to take two steps away from her.

"Good thing you're an adventure guide and not a music critic." Her voice had turned hard, harsh.

"I am sorry, though."

"Nothing to be sorry about." She turned her back on him and started for the tent. "Different musical tastes for different people."

"No, I'm not sorry about that."

"Then what?"

"I'm sorry you killed your bandmates."

Joss locked her knees to keep them from kissing the dirt again. There was a sucker punch, and then there was an emotional knockout. One word reverberated through her head: *killed, killed, killed.*

Puck trotted over to her, leaned his head against her thigh, and whined up at her.

"I said something wrong, didn't I?" his owner said.

"You... you think?" Sudden low-level nausea rocking her stomach, she shot a glare his way that should've twisted up his balls worse than her claw hold on Buffalo earlier.

"I am actually not sure. But when Puck makes that sound, it usually means someone is hurting. I didn't mean to hurt you."

She'd had some terrible things said to her and about her over the past months, but few people had the sheer nerve to outright accuse her of killing her band. "Then why did you say what you did?"

"Because it was a tragedy." He dug into his pocket and pulled out a long, slim length of paracord. "I might not enjoy Scarlet Glitterati's music, but my little sister is a huge fan. I know many more people are, too."

Joss stroked Puck's ears, but the feel of the silky fur did little to ease the pain inside her. "You think I'm some kind of monster."

"I didn't say that." With one hand, he manipulated the cord, giving it all his attention. Dammit, a person should look you in the eye when they called you a monster. "I think I stepped over some line, but I'm not sure."

What huffed out of her wasn't a laugh. It hurt too damn much to be that. "I get that guys can be clueless. In fact, I'm pretty sure I've dated every clueless one on the west coast. But I thought Southern men were different. You know— polite and all that. *Yes, ma'am. No, ma'am. Let me hold the door for you, ma'am.*"

He looked up from whatever he was doing with the cord, but he still didn't meet her gaze. His darted to somewhere around her chin and back down again. "My parents did raise their children to be kind and courteous."

"You just happened to fail charm school."

"I didn't go to school." He rubbed a hand over his drying hair—now a sun-bleached light brown—making it stand up in electrified whirls. "That's not true. I went to school until I was ten."

"And then you just ran wild like Mowgli?"

"Mowgli did not run wild. He had two families—one wolf, one human. I only had a human family."

"My God, you are the most literal human being I've ever met."

He bent over the cord and turned his back on her. "I am not making the soup right."

That was it. After he stood up for her, she'd thought they had some type of connection, but obviously not. He was rude, insensitive, and distracted.

Devil, yes. Divine, no.

He might look like over six feet of sexiness, but Joss could not suffer this man another minute. He was either playing the most elaborate mind-fuck she'd ever encountered, or he was psycho. And she had plenty of madness inside her own mind these days, thank you very much.

"Look," she said. "It might be better if you and I keep our distance during the next few days. It's obvious you don't like me, and I don't know how soup figures into all this, but—"

"Soup is conversation."

Intrigued in spite of herself, she approached him again and Puck followed. "What?"

"That is the way my dad taught me to talk to people. It is like making soup. They put in one ingredient. You look at the ingredient and then add something else." The cord dangling from his fingers, he pantomimed dropping food into a pot. "But not like radishes to their sweet potatoes."

And there was her answer. Definitely psycho. "Oookay."

Attractive on the outside, but awful on the inside.

The man growled. Actually made a low rumbling sound that shot through Joss's body and made her hair rise with awareness. Apparently, she was psycho, too, because something about that sound cranked up her hormones. But even a psycho knew when to edge away from danger.

"You say one thing and then I say something back that makes sense with what you said," he said, pacing a tight circle around her, preventing her from escaping. "Which means I have to listen. Hearing and listening are not the same thing."

"Well, that's self-aware. Good for you." *Keep things light and friendly.* She didn't like how intense this had suddenly become.

"I wish Puck could talk," he said so miserably that Joss's heart jolted. Puck fixed a concerned gaze on his owner and whined again.

"You would be a very rich man," Joss said as she sidled away a half-step. "I have a feeling Puck is a highly intelligent dog. I bet he could teach physics if he put his mind to it."

For the first time, she witnessed a true grin spread across the man's face. "Or neuroscience."

Okay, good. They'd apparently backed away from some weird precipice, so Joss nodded. "Why not? The sky is the limit for a dog like Puck." As if he understood every word they were saying, Puck looked back and forth between them. *Zip.* Right eyebrow up. *Zap.* Left eyebrow up.

"Can we start over?" Shep asked her.

"Do I have to get back in the raft?" she joked, even though the thought of the raft and the drop made her want to vomit.

"That would not be very efficient since we are about to start our hike."

"Of course it wouldn't."

He turned to her, squaring his shoulders with purpose and meeting her gaze. And oh, wow. Just wow. His eyes were green. Why hadn't she noticed that until now?

Because...because this was the first time he'd looked at her eye to eye.

He held out his hand, and with the feeling that she was embarking on something life-changing, she put hers in his.

The feel of his callused skin on her softer palm buzzed up her arm and settled in her chest.

"Hello," he said. "My name is Harris Sheppard Kingston. People call me Shep. I work as an adventure guide for Prime Climb Tours. Steele Ridge is my hometown. My parents and most of my brothers and sisters live here. I love the mountains, my family, Puck, my cabin, and homemade ketchup."

And damn, that little autobiography charmed her. "That would make quite a Tinder profile."

"My dad taught me to make conversation because I could never understand how to do it on my own. He told me I don't always have to look people in the eyes, but sometimes, when something is really important, that it's a good thing to do. Because regular people see it as a sign of truthfulness and sincerity. My family knows I don't lie, so I don't always have to look them in the eye."

"You're looking me in the eye." And neither of them seemed inclined to drop hands.

"Because I somehow hurt your feelings, and that was not my intention. I want you to see my apology is sincere."

Charmed? This man had gone from running a blade of burning steel through her heart to melting her into a puddle of disbelieving attraction. "Thank you. I accept your apology."

"However, it's likely I will do it again. Because even Puck can't stop me from saying the wrong things."

"You hurt people's feelings a lot?" Made sense if he hit everyone with this type of verbal whiplash.

Shep finally dropped her hand, glanced away and swallowed. Took a bracing breath and met her stare again. "I don't always understand things like body language, intonation, sarcasm, and subtext. I try, I really try, but sometimes I just... can't."

She couldn't imagine there was anything this man couldn't do if he put his mind to it. He was obviously smart, conscientious, well-read, and he loved his dog. "I've never changed a tire, I don't understand geometry, and I don't know how to ride a bike."

"Really?" he said, his eyes going wide. "For the tire, the first step is to jack up the car and... Oh, soup. You don't want me to tell you how to change a tire, do you?"

"Shep Kingston, I don't think I've ever met a man like you." And it made her wonder if she'd been missing out.

"You probably have, but you just didn't know it. Because we're estimated at one out of every two hundred fifty to five hundred people. About two to four times as many men as women. They don't really know why."

"You lost me again."

"Backstory. Yeah, people need that sometimes," he said. "When I was eight, I was diagnosed with Asperger's Syndrome. It's no longer listed in the *Diagnostic and Statistical Manual of Mental Disorders,* but once you have a diagnosis, they don't take it away. Now, it's called being high on the autism spectrum. Autism Spectrum Disorder."

What? This...this incredible man was *autistic*? "I... uh...wow..."

"Don't worry," he said quickly. "It's not contagious or anything. It just means that my brain tends to work a little differently than most people's."

Yes, she was beginning to understand that. And for some reason, it made her feel not so grief-stricken and guilty. "Shep Kingston, I wasn't sure at first, but you're growing on me. Who knows, we might even become friends."

Friends. Joss Wynter wanted to be Shep's friend. And she no

longer looked as if she was going to cry, which released something knotted deep inside his gut.

Had he ever experienced that feeling—Worry? Guilt? Compassion?—before?

He didn't think so. Amber had made it clear he didn't have feelings like a regular guy.

He thought she'd understood he was different when she agreed to marry him. But for some reason, she'd believed he would change.

And when he hadn't, she'd left him, her only explanation jotted down on a crumpled napkin. *I can't handle you anymore, Shep. I need to be with a normal man, and you will never be normal.*

"Friends?" he asked Joss like a moron. "That would be—"

"Let's saddle up, you two!" Buffalo Moody stuck his smug face through the tent flap and told them, "It's time to get this show on the road." *Hehuhhe. Hehuhhe.*

Joss turned to Shep and asked, "Does his laugh sound like a constipated jackass to you?"

"I do not think I've ever heard a constipated jackass laugh," he said, nodding slowly. "But I am going to assume you know more about the digestive issues of hybrid equines and agree."

"Let's go kick this mountain's ass, Shep Kingston." Joss looped her arm in his and squeezed hard. Her firm touch electrified him, zipped up his biceps, and flooded his brain with confusion. With attraction.

How did she know the kind of touch he could tolerate? Could enjoy. Could come to crave.

Don't read anything into it. She wants to be your friend. That is all.

Together, they returned to the tent, where the two other

competitors had their bags strapped to their backs and wore expressions even Shep could tell were pissy. Having two sisters helped with recognizing those types of mood indicators.

Joss withdrew her arm from his, and Shep remained on the fringe of the group until Moody waved him up to stand next to him. "Son, why don't you tell these folks what we have planned for them today?"

"I don't know what *you* have planned," he said instead of reminding the man—again—that they were not related. "But like I told the producers last night when we discussed the route, I intend to lead the group up Bertram trail about five miles and then make camp for the evening."

"What about food?" the woman named Lauren asked. "We weren't allowed to put anything edible in our bags."

"A human can go approximately twenty-one days without eating," Shep told her. "Hydration is much more important. So we'll start with that." He looked at Moody. "The trailhead is about half a mile on the other side of Deadman's Creek. Do you want to transport—"

"From now on, no more rides. Foot propulsion only."

Lauren—Shep was already starting to think of her according to her attitude and behavior so in his mind, she was The Bitcher—still only wore one sandal. "Then someone needs to get her another shoe. I won't take her on the trail like that."

"Yay!" she said. "I do get something else from my suit-case." She rushed over to dig into her bag and pulled out a pair of Chuck Taylors. Not the best for hiking, but they were definitely a step up from taking to the trail barefoot.

Shep shouldered his own pack—a large Osprey with an internal frame—and Bradley said, "Whoa—I thought we only got small bags."

"I'm not competing," Shep told him. "So the rules don't apply to me."

And they'd be damn glad the rules didn't apply to him when they needed first aid. "Puck, let's go!"

Puck trotted to his side, and with a combination of dread and strange joy flowing through him, Shep pushed his way out of the tent and away from the oppressive scent of men's cologne.

5

THEY LEFT THE TENT, ONE AFTER THE OTHER, MAKING JOSS think they looked like a line of ducklings following Mama Shep. Lauren was on Shep's heels with Joss behind her and then Bradley. Buffalo Moody brought up the rear.

Shep's long legs ate up the distance back to Deadman's Creek. When he angled toward the bridge where Moody stood earlier, the show host marched up from behind their duckling parade and told him, "Take them through the water."

"There's no need for that," Shep said calmly. "Not when there's a perfectly good bridge right—"

"We aren't trying to make this trek easy. Get that through your head, son. The camera operators will use the bridge." Moody held out an arm to keep the contestants in place. "The three of you wait here until Greg and the new camera guy are on the other side." He pointed at a twenty-some-thing man with a shotgun mic equipped video camera on his shoulder, "Hey, you! Baby Camera Boy, get your ass to the other side. Hustle!"

The two cameramen jogged across the expanse. Once

they were across the water and Greg gave the signal, Moody waved Joss and the others toward the water. Although they were crossing at a spot much calmer than the rapids Joss had luckily made it over earlier, the current was still running fast.

You can do this, Joss. You will do it.

After pointing Puck toward the bridge to make the crossing, Shep took off his boots and socks and clipped them onto his pack. Then he waded into the creek, and Lauren quickly splashed in after him.

Joss and Bradley followed the guide's lead in taking off their shoes.

Shep got about a quarter of the way out before pausing and looking back. He shook his head at Lauren, now tiptoeing toward him. Her approach surprised Joss. Was the woman a badass or a weenie? Shep said she almost drowned. Maybe Lauren couldn't swim.

"Keep walking," Shep told her.

A few steps before reaching Shep, Lauren slipped. Just enough that he had to lunge toward her and grab her arm to keep her upright. "So nice to know we have a strong man with us," she said in a flirty tone.

Joss swallowed to keep her gag reflex under control. So this *was* the way Lauren planned to play the game. By using her assets to seduce the men into helping her. Taking care of her.

The Amazons would be so ashamed.

Shep released Lauren as quickly as he'd caught her. "Stand right here while the others catch up."

Bradley went in the water next, using his arms and legs to propel him. Joss hefted her guitar over her head, hoping she could keep her balance. As she neared Lauren and Shep, he reached for Joss's guitar. "Give that to me."

"No," she said out of instinct. She didn't trust anyone with Fiona, but she covered her actions by saying, "Buffalo said we all have to carry our own gear."

While she, Lauren, and Bradley waded forward, he side-stepped his way through the water, keeping a keen eye on everyone. When they approached the far side, he helped them all trudge out of the water and up the bank.

But when Buffalo came splashing up, Shep didn't offer him a bit of help. Maybe he took for granted that the show's host should know how to get his own ass out of the water. But Joss happened to see Buffalo take a step, lurch sideways, and slap the water to keep his balance.

Shep seemed to ignore the whole incident, but Buffalo aimed a glare in the other man's direction.

When Buffalo made it out of the water, everyone but Lauren sat to put on their shoes. She frowned down at her tennis shoes. "Mine got wet. What am I supposed to do?"

"Wear them or go barefoot," Moody said cheerfully.

Shep said, "You might want to put some moleskin on your heels first."

"Believe it or not, that wasn't something that made it into my minuscule bag." Lauren glared up at him. Good grief, the woman needed to make up her mind about her game-playing method.

Without hesitating, Shep unzipped a pocket on his pack and pulled out two flesh-colored pieces. "Pull off the backing and apply the sticky side to where your shoes rub your feet."

Pouting, Lauren did as he said, but she didn't complain, which was an improvement as far as Joss was concerned.

"How far did you say we were going today?" Bradley asked. "Because it's already after four o'clock."

"Originally, I'd planned for eight miles." Although Joss

was in decent shape from trail running, that seemed ambitious in the few hours until sunset. "Now we'll be lucky to make it five."

"I don't guess you have half a dozen tents packed in that backpack of yours, do you?" Bradley eyed Shep's pack on the ground. Joss wouldn't be surprised if that bag was like Hermione Granger's purse, with the ability to bring forth palatial tents and other camping gear.

Shep said, "Only one tent."

"Too bad," Bradley said, but his smile was good-natured.

Shep shrugged into his pack and secured the straps across his chest and waist, accentuating the breadth of the first and the trimness of the second. Although Joss had been struck by the man's physical appeal immediately, this flare of attraction she was feeling was throwing her off-balance. "The trailhead is this way," he said. "Please stay within sight of the person in front of you and behind you. No wandering off trail. If you need to stop for some reason, send the message up the line to me."

They queued up in single file and somehow Joss ended up fourth this time, which meant Buffalo's *sight* would include a view of her ass. Fabulous. She shrugged into the straps of her backpack-style guitar case, and then secured her small pack over her arms so it rested against her torso.

And although her guitar should cover the majority of her posterior real estate, she turned to Buffalo and ramped up the evil eye. "Don't even think about trying to feel me up while we're hiking. Not today, not tomorrow, not at all. I don't know if you do this to all the female contestants, but I am not playing your game. Do I make myself clear?"

"Aw, sweetheart, you're too sensitive. Back there in the tent, that was just my way of welcoming you to the show."

Joss put a layer of frost into her voice when she said,

"Then I guess you won't mind if my way of saying thanks for the warm welcome is by plastering your name and the MeToo hashtag all over Twitter."

His for-he's-a-jolly-good-fellow expression immediately soured into a scowl that highlighted the grooves around his mouth and the interstate system of lines at the corners of his eyes. "Bunch of diva bullshit," he grumbled.

MeToo was anything but a diva movement, and Buffalo's dismissal of it made Joss want to give him a black eye and a definitive case of testicular torsion. "Don't push me," she warned him.

"Come on, you two," Bradley called back to them. "Or we'll be hiking in the dark."

If they couldn't hike five miles before sunset, the group was already doomed. But Joss didn't want to antagonize her competition so early in the game, so she bared her teeth at Buffalo, then jogged to catch up with the group.

The trail was easy to see but narrow, so they hiked into the forest single file. Once they were inside the tree cover, the temperature dropped by a good ten degrees, probably putting it somewhere in the mid-sixties. Under the weight of her load, Joss rolled her shoulders back and just breathed.

Her lungs seemed to expand more than they had in months. As if the North Carolina mountain air might be able to fill up the emptiness inside her.

All she had to do right now was put one foot in front of the other. It was that simple.

As the day's overwhelming tension slowly seeped from her muscles, for the first time Joss considered that this trek might be about more than the redemption of her public image and career.

Maybe this change of scenery could bring her some kind of peace. Maybe she was supposed to come here to heal.

The heady scent of the dirt beneath her hiking shoes made her think it had rained recently. Nothing but freshly wetted earth smelled like that. Musty yet clean.

How long had it been since she smelled it? Not even when she'd been running in the rain yesterday. It was as if her senses, her ability to take in and absorb stimuli, had been stunted since the accident.

But today, everything seemed sharper, clearer. In the trees, birds called out to one another—hoots, squawks, and sweet whistles. The sound of the water receded as they hiked up the trail and it dog-legged to the right. Although fall had yet to descend here, the leaves were beginning to hint at the rich yellow, orange, and red colors they would take on.

If she didn't have to think about the lech behind her and the competition in front of her, the hike might be completely peaceful. Then again, Shep Kingston had done more than a little to add to her chaos today. He'd confused her, pissed her off, charmed her, and ultimately impressed her.

And his dog?

Well, Puck was like a shining light. A furry beacon of hope.

As if she'd called him, the retriever trotted down the trail in her direction. Bradley put a hand out, trying to waylay him with a "good boy" and a scratch, but Puck just flashed him a doggie smile and zeroed in on Joss. He made a U-turn and stuck to her right side. "Hey, buddy. Do you love this?"

He glanced up at her, his warm brown eyes so dark and wise. It was as if he understood what she was asking him. His luxurious fur was dotted with a few leaves and some pine straw, so as they hiked, Joss picked the detritus off him and tossed it back into the forest. With sure feet,

Puck padded along beside her as if they'd been friends for years.

Maybe he'd decided he liked her because his owner had warmed to her a little.

The feel of Puck's fur under her fingers eased the remaining tension in Joss's shoulders. She could imagine—for just a little while—that she was out here on her own. That Puck was her dog, and they were free to go anywhere, do anything.

No guilt. No fear. No confusion about her future.

Unfortunately, the snap of twigs off to her left reminded her that the camera operators were out there filming. Every step. Every expression.

It took so much energy to wear her game face these days. For years, she'd done it out of habit. After all, it was required when she was performing.

When she was hustling for the sound of an audience's applause.

But Puck wasn't her normal audience and she didn't have to impress or entertain him, so she just talked to him in a low voice. Asking him questions that he couldn't answer. Like where he lived, if he was a North Carolina native, if he enjoyed being brushed. She stopped herself from asking the dog about Shep. She did not need that to be picked up on a camera mic.

When they'd been hiking for about two hours, Moody tapped her on the shoulder. A very perfunctory, impersonal tap.

Good, he'd paid attention.

"Send it up the line for Shep to stop."

Joss gave the message to Bradley, and to her disappointment, Puck seemed to understand that he needed to head back to Shep because he loped uphill. Once Shep came to a standstill and everyone else in the group caught up, Moody clapped his hands and said, "It's time for the second opportunity!"

Joss glanced around. Whatever the *opportunity* was, the show hadn't set up anything. They were still surrounded by forest and nothing else. However, three of the trees did sport yellow ribbons fluttering with the sway of branches.

Moody held out his hands, palms up. "These are sweet gum trees. Each of you will climb and gather ten sweet gum balls and then carry them from the tree with you. You can't throw them down to the ground. The first person to gather ten gum balls, get to the ground, and return to me wins the opportunity."

"And what do we get for winning?" Lauren asked.

Buffalo told Lauren, "You'll get a premade shelter to sleep under tonight."

"I like that," Lauren said. "So I plan to win."

Joss barely registered the woman's flirty tone because she was too busy staring up at the tall trees with rough bark. As a kid, she would've been all for climbing one of these.

But one night on stage had changed the way Joss would look at heights forever. As usual, secured electrical cords snaked across the floor, but navigating them in five-inch heels was second nature to Joss. This time, as she strutted close to the stage's edge, she became tangled in the power cord from her electric guitar to the amp. With her hands full of her favorite Fender Stratocaster, she couldn't catch herself and toppled headfirst into the crowd.

When they caught her, she thought it would be okay. But mob mentality set in, and the fans all wanted a piece of Joss Wynter. Hands grabbing, fabric ripping, everyone— including her—screaming. A guy wearing a baby blue trucker's hat grabbed the guitar from her hold. Two drunk girls ripped apart the sequined shirt Joss was wearing, leaving her in a cami bra that exposed her left breast.

Joss was on the floor, fighting off the grabbing hands. An earring here, a shoe there. By the time security reached her, the only thing she was still wearing were her jeans and they were unzipped.

Her Fender was swept off into the crowd and apparently ripped apart for souvenirs. But Joss had gone back to wardrobe and come out fifteen minutes later with another guitar as if nothing had happened. As if her heart hadn't been ripped apart along with the Strat.

Because they only applauded if you finished the show.

And now she had to scale a damn tree.

Buffalo held out three popsicle sticks. "Draw a stick to figure out which tree you'll be climbing."

Joss drew the number three and went to stand by her tree. Above her, it looked about a billion feet tall, branches stretching up and out. And the lowest branch was a good three feet above her reach even if she stood on tiptoe. Her already scraped-up hands were sweating and her stomach was pitching. "What...what happens if one of us falls? Shouldn't there be some kind of safety net or something?"

"Sweetheart, this show is called *Do or Die* for a reason." Buffalo said. "You don't have to climb that tree, but you'll immediately go on the dead list."

That wasn't an option. Not only did her pride demand that she beat Lauren, she didn't want to look like a scared little girl in Shep's eyes. She whispered the mantra she'd begun using on stage after the fall. "They only applaud if you finish the show."

Falling—and failing—wasn't on today's agenda, no matter how shaky she felt after the helicopter from hell.

Buffalo waved his arm like a flag and yelled, "Go!"

Joss quickly found that her tree's trunk was thicker than she'd realized. Her arms and legs barely went halfway around. The bark bit into her inner thighs and upper arms. It took every ounce of her strength and concentration to hold on, much less clumsily shimmy her way skyward until she could grab the lowest branch and pull herself up. Her arm muscles burned, and although she tried not to look, she couldn't help but notice both Bradley and Lauren were above her by at least ten feet.

Better trees or longer arms and legs. Didn't really matter which. She was behind.

She shifted her concentration back to her own tree and made more progress.

Yes! A cluster of spiky balls hung two branches above her. Looked like at least half a dozen individual gum balls. By stretching, Joss was able to grab an overhanging branch and sort of walk her way up the tree trunk. Pretty it wasn't.

But effective it was.

She did the same for the next branch and somehow flipped herself over it so she could inch her way out to the sweet gum fruit. She grabbed them and yanked. Not as easy as it had looked. The struggle was real, and by the time she worked them off the branches, she was breathing like she'd run a sprint. And she hadn't given much thought to where she planned to store these things. With quick hands, she stuffed the balls down her shirt and into her sports bra. And damn, it was like inviting a porcupine into her underwear.

She backtracked and groped her way up to another limb on the other side of the tree. More balls. Excellent. These came off with less of a fight, but when she shoved them down her shirt, three that she'd already gathered made their escape, tumbling out of her sports bra, bouncing off the limb beneath her, and dropping to the undergrowth-covered ground.

During it all, she tried like hell to filter out Moody's voice, but she couldn't help but catch a few of his comments. When he called out, "Nice, Lauren," Joss knew the other woman was in the lead.

That gave her the impetus to reach for a few sweet gum balls overhead. She skimmed them with her fingertips. Just a little farther.

From below, Shep called, "Don't overreach. If you lose your grip, you'll fall and probably break something."

The only word Joss heard was *fall.* She was going to fall.

Her heart seemed to pulse in her throat, and the tree bark in front of her wavered in and out of focus. Dizziness threatening to make her black out, Joss inched her way back to the safety of the trunk and clung to it, her breaths coming fast and shallow.

"Joss? Are you okay?" Shep's voice filtered through the staticky fear in her head. "You have to keep going."

They only applaud if you finish the show.

She needed to pretend that Shep was her audience, and the only way he would approve of her was if she finished this damn opportunity. Blocking everything else out, Joss climbed again.

By the time she knew she had more than ten sweet gum balls stuffed in her bra, with at least one of them stabbing her in the right nipple, Joss slowly backtracked her way out of the tree. Slid the last few feet and tore the crap out of her inner thighs. Joss did a noodle flop onto a nearby log, not caring that Lauren and Bradley—standing there watching without so much as a labored breath—had both beaten her by a wide margin.

Moody boomed, "Lauren wins the second opportunity. Congratulations! You'll be sleeping in comfort tonight."

"Comfort is relative," Bradley drawled. "Since I doubt we'll find a five-star hotel out here."

Puck dashed over to Joss and rested his chin on her thigh—thankfully an area that wasn't afflicted with tree rash.

The sun suddenly disappeared, and Joss looked up to see Shep standing in front of her. Water bottle in one hand and blue cloth in the other, he hunkered down and pushed her knees apart. He grunted what she assumed was unhappiness.

Without a word, he wet the cloth and proceeded to clean the abrasions that ran from her knees to a couple of inches below her vagina. At least her shorts had protected *that*.

Shep was thorough, so thorough that Joss's terror receded, being replaced with something just as instinctual. He pressed the wet cloth against every inch of her damaged skin, sometimes angling his face so close to her thighs that she could feel his breath. Which only created a tingly pain that had nothing to do with her reddened scratches.

Did he have any idea how erotic their current position was? Or that her body was responding to his closeness? When he blew on her skin, presumably to dry it, Joss almost skyrocketed off the log.

"Damn," Moody chuckled. "Now that's a bang hole shot."

Joss looked up to find both camera operators recording the scene from different angles. One over Shep's shoulder, getting what had to be a straight-on view of her crotch. Moody was grinning lecherously, as if Joss had stripped off her shorts and panties and given *him* a bang hole shot.

6

For the span of breath, Shep went still. Not a threatened-animal still, but a poised-predator still. Then, without a word, he dropped the cloth and Joss caught it. With his hands in tight fists, he stood and stalked toward Moody.

Puck gave Joss a quick you're-gonna-be-fine lick and trotted to catch up with his owner.

"You are an asshole. You may host this show, but that doesn't give you license to be a dick. Apologize to her." Shep didn't seem to realize the cameras were still rolling as he just grabbed a handful of Moody's shirt and jerked the shorter man to his toes.

Oh, my. This...this was Devil Divine.

Joss's already humming hormones turned into a frenzied flash mob.

And why were women still programmed to get a sexual thrill from a blatant show of male domination? If Joss's thighs hadn't stung so badly, she would've crossed them to soothe the sudden ache between them.

She was hot for an untamed wilderness guide. A man

who had nothing in common with her world, with her. Hell, he'd admitted he didn't even like her music.

But as Chris, one of her bandmates, had always said, "The twat wants what the twat wants."

Undoubtedly crude. Also inexorably correct.

"He's delicious, isn't he?"

In her trance of unexplainable attraction, Joss hadn't realized Lauren had sidled up next to her. "A little rough around the edges, for sure," Lauren continued. "But that's excellent in bed. In public, not so much." Lauren tilted her head to one side and studied the arguing men. "He's different. I can't put my finger on it, but he's just a little...off."

Joss wasn't about to divulge what Shep had explained to her earlier. "You just think he's off because he hasn't tried to lure you behind a tree and nail you against it."

Lauren's laugh was genuine. "Thanks for the idea. I'll definitely put that on my list. My original thought was some juicy action in Deadman's Creek. But I'm flexible."

"Don't mess with him, Lauren." Joss had no idea if Shep found Lauren attractive or not, but she knew enough to realize the woman would treat him like a dildo and then walk away. A man from a small town might not understand a Venus flytrap like her.

"Oh, my. Does someone else have her sights set on him?"

"No, and that's not what we're out here for." She avoided Lauren's knowing gaze by tending to the scrapes on her arms. "Surely even you can go without getting all your itches scratched for a few days."

"Well, well. Thumbelina is taking this whole show seriously. You actually want to win this thing."

"Is that so hard to believe?"

"Maybe not. You're competitive, I'll give you that. Maybe I should've expected it because if rumors have any truth to them, you have a heart of stone and balls of brass. But if you think you can win..." Lauren patted Joss on the cheek. "...you're fooling yourself."

Call her delusional, but Joss had a hidden reserve of something she doubted Lauren even knew how to spell.

Determination.

After the gum ball opportunity and Moody's subsequently grudging apology to Joss, Shep had insisted she follow directly behind him as they hiked. The whole wagon train had fortunately shut their mouths and just moved their feet.

At one point, when the rest of the group had fallen back a few steps, Shep asked Joss, "Why are you doing this?"

"Because you told us we had to keep hiking."

"No, why did you come on this show?" Because Moody sure wasn't treating her like a serious competitor.

"It's a way for me to make a good impression on the American public."

"So you don't really care about winning."

"I definitely care," she said. "Because everyone loves a winner."

By the time the group stumbled into the clearing he'd chosen for them to spend the night in, the sun was just a distant glow through the trees on the ridge line above them. If he and Puck had been hiking alone, they would've been here hours ago.

Shep checked his watch for the sixth time in the past hour. It was fifty-four minutes past Puck's normal dinnertime. He'd been patient, only nudging Shep once and looking up at him with a soulfully sad where's-my-bowl expression. But being off schedule was making Shep's muscles twitch. Sure, he was used to nature's ever-changing moods, but the things he could control—like his dog's feeding schedule—he did.

He set his pack on a flat rock and located Puck's collapsible bowls and kibble. When his dog was happily munching away, Shep finally turned around to survey the flock of albatrosses around his neck.

Moody might be a misogynistic douche, but he'd made the hike fine. He was smiling and full of energy as he placed his belongings along the southern edge of the camp. He said to the young camera operator, "You, take all yours and Greg's shit over there near the tree line. I don't want your tents in any of the shots."

When he didn't move fast enough, Moody shouted, "You looking to get fired, Baby Camera Boy?"

"Name is Zach," the guy mumbled, but he hustled away. He and the other camera operator unloaded their gear from their shoulders and dropped down to sit cross-legged near a pair of pine trees.

The Bitcher had found a lush tuft of grass and was frowning at the screen of her phone. Bradley—aka The Bleeding Heart because of his connection with so many charities—was poking around at the edges of the clearing, picking up kindling-size sticks.

Joss had been a trouper on the second half of the hike after the stupid sweet gum tree opportunity, never once complaining about her shredded legs and scratched arms. Later, he'd check them for signs of infection.

And if that meant he had to get physically close—very close—to her, he didn't plan to tell anyone that he found the prospect pleasant. More pleasant than he was comfortable with.

For now, she was sitting apart from the others, carefully wiping down her face and under her arms with a Wet-Nap.

Once finished, she dropped the wipe and its wrapper into a plastic baggie and sealed it up.

At least one of these yahoos had done their research and understood the concept of leave no trace.

Moody swaggered in Shep's direction, apparently unfazed by their disagreement earlier. "Not too bad for the first day. They all made it."

"You mean some people don't?"

"It's not unusual for at least one of them to pull a chick-enshit move and quit before the second opportunity."

That gave Shep a different perspective on the contestants. All of them had already made it further than many others on *Do or Die* had. "Maybe these three will go the distance."

"Oh, I sincerely doubt it." Moody chuckled. "Having them quit is half the fun."

Shep didn't understand. To him, the point of hiking was to enjoy nature. Savor it. Respect it. Nature wasn't a game to be won. That was one reason he'd never been interested in competitive rock climbing. He felt no need to race against another human. When he climbed, it was about communing with the rock, not about conquering it.

But to enjoy nature, you had to know how to survive in it.

"First thing I plan to teach them is how to make shelter," he told Moody.

"Not happening," Moody said. "Bradley and Joss will just have to fumble their way through tonight. It'll make them hungrier to learn tomorrow. But I want you to build a shelter for Lauren and I'll give her a little water."

"Because she got down a tree with some sweet gum balls?" This man was endangering these people. As short as Joss was, she could've easily fallen from that massive tree and broken her fragile neck. Yes, it also could've happened to The Bitcher or The Bleeding Heart, but for some reason, Shep's insides knotted tighter when he thought about Joss lying broken on the forest floor.

"Hey. That's what this show is about. We're not here to treat these three like they're on some fancy trip where they get massages and drink wine at night. That show would be called *Spa and Sip,* not *Do or Die.*"

"Has anyone actually died?" A question he should've asked Dan.

"Um... well..." Moody shifted from foot to foot. "Last season, a guy suffered a heart attack while we were on the southeast coast of Sri Lanka. Unfortunately, the medical care he needed wasn't close enough and he passed. But afterward, the doctors said he was a time bomb waiting to go off."

"Did these three go through any kind of medical clearance?"

"Oh, yeah... um, sure."

Which meant hell no. Shep knew some survival medicine, but he was no Cash. Maybe that was something he needed to get more training in. Although he'd never been a caretaker when it came to other people, he found the idea of learning something new appealing.

But for now, he would teach these people how to build shelters, regardless of what Moody wanted.

"Hey, you three," Shep called out, his gaze never touching Joss. Maybe he was embarrassed by what happened earlier. Maybe he'd realized his simple medical attention had incited Joss's hormones, and he was uncomfortable with her now. "Gather up over here."

"I'm too tired," Lauren whined. "And besides, I can't get reception on my phone."

"Coverage is spotty this far out," Shep said.

"I didn't know places like this existed," Lauren said. "It's like we've hiked off the edge of the earth."

As she walked by her, Joss bumped the sitting woman on the shoulder. "A little dramatic, don't you think? Even for an actress."

"There is no edge of the earth," Shep said. "Because the planet is round."

"I just meant we're nowhere close to civilization."

"We're exactly 11.2 miles from the center of Steele Ridge," he told her.

"I wouldn't consider that civilization." Lauren's pout turned into a smirk. "How far is it to a real city?"

"It's 145 miles to Charlotte," he said. "But if that's not civilized enough for you, it is 719 to New York City and 2,278 to Los Angeles."

"Whoa, how did you know that?" Bradley asked as he patted Shep on the back.

Joss was the only one who seemed to notice the way Shep shifted from under the other man's hand. "I like maps." He strode over to Lauren and stared down at her. "Get up."

"Why? I don't have to make my own shelter."

"Maybe not tonight, but you will."

"Surely I can handle three nights sleeping out in the open. It's still warm."

"What if it rains?" Bradley said.

Lauren looked up at the dark sky as if she was able to predict the weather. "Then I'll just find someone who'll let me snuggle up with them."

The way Bradley rolled his eyes made it clear he wouldn't be Lauren's snuggle buddy. It should've relieved Joss, but that state of affairs just meant it was more likely that Lauren would try to bed down with Moody or Shep. She was welcome to Moody, but Shep? No, Joss didn't like the idea of that at all.

"There's always a risk of hypothermia," Shep said. "Even in late summer or early fall. It has everything to do with core body temperature, not the temperature outside. Shelter is critical to avoid hypothermia."

"But it's dark," Lauren said, "We can't build anything now."

"Where's your headlamp?" Shep asked her.

"You mean that hideous headband thingie? I left that back in my other bag."

"Then you'll just have to follow close behind me," Shep told her.

Lauren flashed a triumphant smile in Joss's direction.

Whatever. Joss would much rather know how to do something herself than to be reliant on a man to do it for her. She would build her own damn shelter, and it would do its job.

The four of them trooped out into the trees, with Lauren tailgating Shep, one hand on his shoulder. He rolled it, but Lauren didn't drop her hold.

Both camera operators were crashing through the woods on either side of their group.

"First," Shep said, "try to use whatever you have around you."

"Like that Christmas tree back at our camp," Lauren said. "I call dibs on that one!"

Did Lauren have any idea what she was dibs-ing on?

"That's a cedar," Shep said, "and you don't want—"

"Anyone else to get it," Joss cut in with a tiny shake of her head in Shep's direction.

"But it's—" he continued, obviously not picking up what she was putting down.

"—got the lowest hanging branches and it's very fluffy—"

"Still, she will—"

"—sleep better under it than she would on a down mattress."

When Shep turned to glare at Joss, she mouthed, *This is a game, and I'm playing it.*

Finally, he said to Lauren, "If that's the tree you want, then it's yours."

Joss repressed a self-satisfied smile, but inside, she was twerking. *Miley, I'll match my booty shake to yours any day!*

She might be a midwestern girl, but she knew enough about cedar trees to understand they were messy with sap and often harbored all kinds of creepy crawlies, including ticks. Her conscience told her she should feel bad for helping set up Lauren, but this was after all, a competition. Survival of the fittest.

Or most creative.

Shep marched them over to a fallen branch about twice as long as Joss was tall. "A debris shelter is your best bet when you don't have any tools."

Bradley snorted. "We'd have tools if we were allowed more than a carry-on."

"You want to get a few branches if possible," Shep continued as if Bradley hadn't spoken. He grabbed the branch and began scanning the area around them. He found what he wanted and grabbed two more. "One for a ridge pole and a couple for support poles. A forked one is especially helpful for the support poles." As if he'd done so a thousand times, he quickly used the shorter sticks to prop up the longer branch on one end to make a sort of triangle.

"Now you need to load up on smaller twigs and branches that will follow the angle of the two support posts."

"How much?" Joss asked him.

"Armloads."

Lauren stepped away, leaned against a tree trunk, and fluttered a hand toward Shep. "You just do that for me, cutie."

His face a scowl-a-palooza, Shep pulled out a thin silver tarp thing and began piling what looked like kindling onto it. Yeah, that would definitely make getting materials back to camp a little easier.

Once Shep was done piling, Bradley asked him, "Can I use that thing too?"

"Sure. I've got another one in my pack."

Greg the cameraman called out, "They're only allowed to use their own equipment."

"Seriously?" Bradley yelled back. "That's not equipment. It's a damn space blanket."

"Only your own supplies."

"Fuck me," Bradley sighed.

Joss hurried back to camp and pulled a pashmina from her own pack. She wouldn't be able to drag it, but it would make carrying sticks and brush much easier.

When she returned to Shep and the others, Bradley had gathered a small pile of short limbs, but was missing his ridge pole and support pole. He tossed down the branch he was holding and said, "Forget it. It's only one night. I'll be fine."

Bradley marched away with Lauren following him. She gave a lazy wave over her shoulder. "See you two back at camp. Oh, and I'd like my shelter to be a little more Four Seasons and a little less Motel Six."

Joss scouted around and found her three poles. She glanced up to find Shep watching her. "You can go on back. I'm fine."

"I'm not leaving you alone."

As she gathered branches, Shep followed her and every few minutes, he would whistle, accenting the first and third syllables. He repeated it five times in quick succession.

"Why are you doing that?"

"It's the call of a whippoorwill. When we were younger, my brother Cash and I used the sound to let each other know when we were around. Sort of a 'I'm here and everything's cool' signal."

Shep was reassuring her, communicating that he wouldn't let anything bad happen to her out here. A lump of emotion lodged in Joss's throat, but she cleared it and whistled back at Shep.

"Hey, that's pretty good."

"I've been told I have a decent musical ear," she said, smiling.

By the time she carted her last load to camp, Moody had set up a tent that would've slept everyone. He sat outside it on a stump and stirred a pot simmering over a healthy fire. Whatever was in it smelled delicious, and Joss's stomach roared.

"Well, yay," Lauren said as she sashayed over to Moody's fire. "Daddy made us all dinner."

"Oh, no." Moody laughed. "This is for me and the camera guys. You're welcome to eat if you can find any food and make a fire, but what's here is off limits to you."

Her mouth tight, Lauren kicked at the dirt near his fire, sending particles into the flames and the delicious-smelling pot of food. "I hope you enjoy being a complete prick."

"I do," he said, with a shit-eating grin. "I really do."

While Shep carried branches toward Lauren's beloved cedar, Joss picked out a spot across camp. She wanted to be able to see every move Shep made. He tried to get Lauren to stand there and listen to him explain his construction techniques, but within three minutes, she wandered away to chat with Greg and the other camera operator.

Moody was keeping a watch over the trio and reminded the guys that they weren't allowed to share any of their supplies with the contestants.

Bradley, without any shelter supplies, found a flat grassy spot and lay on his back with his head propped on his pack. Within minutes, he was letting out a soft snore with every third breath.

Joss was scurrying to arrange her leafiest branches parallel to the support poles. She didn't want holes in her roof in case it did rain.

"That's pretty good for your first time," Shep commented as he stood over her inspecting her work. "Now use some leaves to overlap all that and for a bed. You want the dry soft leaves for inside. That'll give you a little more comfort." He gestured toward her ridge pole. "You're lucky you're short."

"I think that's the first time I've ever been told that."

"Just logical. Less body length, less area to cover."

"You have a point."

He didn't offer to lend a hand, probably because Moody would've stomped over and taken away both their birthdays, but he did nod from time to time and say, "Nice" and "Good job" or "A little to the left."

When she was out of branches, Joss sat back on her heels and looked up at him, her breath catching once again at the sexy angularity of his face. Of his unsmiling mouth. A mouth she suddenly wanted to feel against hers.

Which seemed like a major long shot right now. Most men would be gaga to have a woman like Lauren draped over them. In fact, a lot of men who were now in their twenties had probably hung her famous poster on their teenage bedroom walls. The one where she was dressed in a brass bra, a red leather bikini bottom, and crotch-high leather boots. In fact, if Lauren received royalties from the sales of that perennial favorite, she could buy the known universe.

"I suggest putting on a long-sleeve shirt and pants," he told Joss. "Not only for warmth but to keep the branches from poking you so much. But before you do that, I want to check your legs. I could put on some antibiotic cream."

Oh, no. She didn't know if she could survive that twice. If he hunkered down between her legs again, she might throw herself at him more shamelessly than Lauren had. *Here, baby, kiss* this *and make it feel better.*

"That's okay," she said quickly. "I wouldn't want to be scolded by Moody. My legs are already feeling better. They'll be good as new by tomorrow."

"No, they won't."

"Good enough to hike ten miles, then."

"Remember, you need to tell me things straight out," he said. "Are you saying you want me to go away?"

No. Yes. No. "I... I'm just tired. And if I get some sleep, it'll be easier to forget how hungry I am."

"You're already skinny."

The words most women longed to hear. But Joss's appetite had been in hiding for months, and she knew she needed to gain a little. Wasn't likely to happen over the next few days.

She stood and patted her rear. "I've still got a little reserve back here. It'll see me through the next few days."

With a frown, Shep walked around behind her, and she could feel his considering gaze on her ass. It was nothing like Moody's slimy once-over. "If I had to guess, your BMI is below eighteen, which means you are underweight. And although your rear end is still somewhat curvy, you don't have any hips to speak of."

Said that like, she sounded like a total sexpot. Not.

Joss didn't know whether to laugh or lay her head down and cry.

He circled back in front of her. "It's difficult for women to get pregnant if they have either too much or too little body fat."

Yeah, she had to laugh. Because Shep's randomness was so entertaining now that she understood it. "Then lucky for me that I'm not in the market to get knocked up."

"My ex-wife was."

A blade of shock ran through her and she gaped at him. He'd been married.

And why should that be a surprise? You'd expect any other man his age to have been seriously involved with someone.

But she still didn't know quite how to respond, and she desperately wanted to understand the ex part of Shep's equation. Maybe having kids was a factor in their divorce. "Was that a problem for you?"

"I...uh...I do not want to talk about this." And with that, he walked away.

7

THE WINNER STOOD JUST INSIDE THE TREE LINE, WEARING THE shadows like a superhero cape, and watched Buffalo Moody dump a half a pot of soup onto the ground on the other side of camp. Wasteful bastard.

Still, the winner could appreciate not wanting to give anyone the unfair advantage of a full belly. Those things needed to be earned.

The show's host had also spent a good part of the evening watching Kingston and Joss Wynter. With every minute they spent together, Moody's expression had soured. Jealousy, most likely.

Even the winner could see the sparks arcing between those two. A wilderness romance wasn't totally surprising. Being out in the woods tended to get folks' juices up.

But a rock star getting hot for that weirdo? Definitely unexpected.

Moody smothered his fire. Then he carried his cook pot and swaggered out through the trees in the direction of the river west of camp.

Oh, yeah. Perfect.

The winner tailed him, each footstep calculated to hide the sound. The host took his sweet time, meandering along as if he was enjoying a sunset stroll down the beach.

They finally made it to the river, where the land fell away into a gorge. With cocky confidence, Moody took a rocky track down toward the water's edge. A few pebbles rolled under his feet, but he kept his balance like a skier coming off an Olympic jump. He might be a jerk, but the man did have a little skill.

Once at the water, he rinsed the pan and stood. Looked out over the river as if he owned every inch of it. Every inch of North Carolina.

In his dreams, maybe.

The winner hunkered belly-down on the ridge above to keep an eye on Moody.

With a smirky grin, the man stripped down and carelessly kicked his clothes and boots aside. Should the winner sneak down and take them? Watching him trudge his naked ass back to camp would be fun. Even more fun if a coyote snuck up and bit off his dick.

It would be easy enough, seeing as Moody was gazing moon-eyed at it and stroking it into a monster woody.

But a different plan was forming in the winner's mind.

Unfortunately, that plan required the winner to watch Moody yank on his dick for half an hour and spurt into the water twice. The man had no respect for the environment, that was clear. His prick finally limp, Moody climbed out of the water, shook like a dog, and pulled on his pants and boots.

Bare-chested and walking a little bow-legged, he hiked up the narrow path out of the gorge. Apparently, his masturbation marathon hadn't been enough to satisfy him because he rubbed his palms across his chest, playing with his nipples.

The winner took advantage of Moody's nip tweaking to army crawl backward and into some brush. *Snap!*

Shit, the winner's knee had landed on a brittle branch. Moody whirled toward where the winner hid and frowned into the darkness.

Okay. This was okay. A complete stealth approach would've been boring anyway.

An owl screeched from another direction, distracting Moody for long enough for the winner to belly crawl to the right, back toward the gorge's edge. The winner tossed a big pinecone, and it made a soft crunching sound as it bounced its way down to the water.

As expected, Moody approached the ledge, leaned over a little. "Anybody out there?"

The winner didn't answer.

"If you're down there, don't be a douchebox," Moody called, a telling quiver in his voice. "Say something."

Move now or let this play out a little longer?

It was already late, and the winner needed to rest. So in one fluid motion, the winner pushed off the ground and nailed Moody in the lower back.

That screwed up the man's balance, and he stumbled forward. Trying to stay on his feet, he took a big step like a gymnast coming off the uneven bars. And that was Moody's last mistake.

A millisecond too late, he seemed to realize there was nothing under his foot. He attempted to shift his weight and fling himself backward.

But the winner was ready, shoving the man over and into nothingness. The sound of Moody's groans and curses filtered up as he tumbled down. The winner didn't wait for the final splash before hightailing it down the trail.

Nothing could be left to chance.

When Moody surfaced in the river, the winner was there and dunked the man's head underwater. Between the impact of Moody's fall and the element of surprise, it wasn't hard to hold him down.

And when the final air bubble surfaced, the winner smiled with satisfaction. "Adios, jackass."

Joss was drifting toward oblivion when the pad of four feet sounded outside. Her multi-tool was at the ready, tiny knife out, when an animal crawled into her half-ass shelter. Brandishing the knife, Joss tried to scramble back, but there was only so much room and her feet knocked against the ridge pole where it met the ground.

When she flicked on her headlamp and realized her visitor wasn't a bear or mountain lion, she dropped the weapon.

Puck pulled himself forward with his front paws, ooching his head and shoulders in with her, and grinned as if he'd just executed the best dog trick ever. And when she saw that he was wearing a light pack that held a small bladder of water and an energy bar, her heart stuttered and her stomach cramped. Should she trust this gift?

What if Lauren was using the dog to disqualify her? Or poison her?

Okay, let's rope in the wild imagination a little, okay?

She patted the pack and whispered to Puck, "Are these for me?"

His head on her shoulder and the swish of his tail were

all the answer she needed. This wasn't Lauren playing some trick. The food and water were from Shep.

His kindness took her off guard, made her feel shakier than hunger ever could. She wrapped her arms around Puck's neck and pressed her face into his fur. He finally wiggled, and she reluctantly released him, consciously ignoring the wet patches left where her eyes had been.

"I get it," she told him. "You don't have all night." She popped open the bladder and took a tentative sip. The water that trickled down her throat was cool and sweet.

The protein bar, she broke in half. And although she knew it was risky, she wrapped up the remaining piece and stashed it inside a freezer baggie in her pack. She pulled off a corner of the other half and held it out to Puck.

Gently, so gently it tickled, he nibbled it out of her palm.

"You're a sweet boy. The sweetest boy I know," she said close to his ear.

Then she savored her piece bacon-maple flavored protein bar bite by tiny bite. Normally, she would choose something that tasted more like chocolate and nuts, but if this was what Shep carried, it had to be good for an energy boost.

In between bites, she sipped the water. Slowly, drawing the experience out as if it were a seven-course meal. When she finished the half portion of energy bar and licked her fingers, she tried to tuck the bladder into Puck's pack, but he scooted back and avoided her.

"Are you sure I'm supposed to keep this?"

His answer was to stand and lightly touch the tip of his nose to her cheek. Then he turned and trotted away.

In the morning, Joss woke with sunlight striping across her

face through the overhanging branches. She blinked and stretched. It had taken her too long to finally fall into sleep last night.

So this morning, with the sun warming her face and body, she reached into her pack and retrieved the rest of the energy bar. Again, she ate slowly, appreciating each sweet-salty nibble and hoping that by drawing out the experience, her energy would last longer today. She made sure the bladder was tightly capped and shoved it deep into her bag. She didn't want to risk someone—anyone—seeing it.

In camp, people were beginning to stir, the murmur of voices making it seem as if this were a pleasant vacation among friends. But that was the last thing *Do or Die* was. And Joss couldn't afford to lie around while her competition was awake.

She pushed through the branches that had sagged overnight and out into the clearing. Sure enough, the camera operators were sitting outside their one-man tents shooting the shit and checking over their equipment. Bradley was peering into his knapsack as if he might find a delicious breakfast in there. And Shep, with Puck by his side, was carefully folding up his own small tent and stowing it away.

Lauren and Moody weren't around. They were either still asleep, or maybe they'd gotten up early and were somewhere together. And if they were together, that likely meant Lauren was trying to screw her way in to the winner's seat.

After all, she'd made it clear she planned to win, no matter what it took.

The thought of Lauren's sex strategy made Joss feel less guilty about taking gifts from Shep last night. Trying for casual, she adjusted her own bag and propped it and her guitar case against a rock before meandering toward Shep.

"Good morning," she said.

He glanced up at her, and she was once again pulled in by his green eyes. As quickly as he'd met her gaze, he dropped it again.

"I wanted to say thank you," she pitched her voice low to make sure no one else heard.

"How are your legs?"

She'd barely thought of them after her surprise visitor last night. Giving Puck a good ear scratch, she told Shep, "Better with long pants. I think I'll keep these on today."

"Good."

Was he angry at her for some reason? Maybe the offer of water and food had actually been some kind of test. One she'd failed.

"I... um... I thought I was supposed to eat it."

He blinked up at her in confusion.

"You know," she whispered. "The protein bar and water. If you want the water back then—"

"Why else would I have told Puck to take it to you? Of course, you were supposed to."

"Oh... okay." This man had a way of keeping her off-balance. "So what's the plan today?"

"Hell if I know," he said, glaring over at Moody's zipped-up tent. "He hasn't issued orders to his minions."

Joss cupped a hand around her mouth, but couldn't hold back the laugh that popped out. "Sorry."

"Why?"

"What?"

"Why are you sorry? If you're apologizing to me for something, I don't understand what it is."

Excellent question. "I guess I was apologizing for laughing at your comment. Maybe because I think it's pretty accurate."

"Then the appropriate response would be to say, 'I agree that Buffalo Moody is a condescending dickhead.'"

"I agree that Buffalo Moody is a condescending dickhead."

Shep's smile, when it came, did something to transform his lean face. It made him look younger, carefree and relaxed.

"You're very handsome," she said before she thought better of it.

"And you're very pretty," he said, his gaze skimming over her face and across her body. Not in a creeper kind of way, but in an objective-yet-interested way. "I think you'd be prettier if you gained a little weight. But last night I remembered that my sisters told me it's not polite to talk about a woman's weight."

He'd mentioned his family yesterday, and Joss was suddenly ravenous to know more about the people who'd helped form this fascinating man. "How many sisters?"

"Two. One is the oldest and one is the youngest."

"So there are three of you?"

"No," he said. "Five. I have two brothers as well."

"Wow." She was one of two, but she and Kellie had never shared much in common. While Joss was into dressing and behaving in any way that was the antithesis of normal Midwesterners, her sister was all about fitting in. Their parents had praised Kellie's conformity and criticized Joss's lack of it. "I'd love to hear more about them."

"Why?" His forehead crinkled. "You don't know them."

"I'm just interested. I think they have to be pretty special."

"I don't understand why you would think so. They are special people, but you have no basis for thinking so."

Although she had the overwhelming urge to run her

hand over his hair and try to soothe his confusion, she rubbed Puck's head instead. Shep watched the movement with keen eyes. "You're a pretty special guy, so my logic says they're probably really cool, too."

"They are the best. I love them..." He trailed off and stared down at his hands. "At least I think I do."

At his uncertain tone, a piece of Joss's heart broke off and tumbled to the ground. A sharp instinct told her that how he felt about his family was a subject best discussed when they had plenty of time. Because she had a feeling that she'd only get one shot to really make an inroad with Shep Kingston.

And for some inexplicable reason, she wanted to know him.

"Maybe you'll tell me about your family at some point during this trip."

"Maybe I will."

Joss scanned the clearing, but still neither Lauren nor Moody had made an appearance. "Have you seen Buffalo or the Amazon Queen?"

"Amazon Queen?"

"Sorry. Lauren."

"Oh, you mean The Bitcher."

This time, Joss didn't bother to cover her mouth. She just let the laughter roll out, and it felt as if her body and soul had undergone an emotional spring cleaning. "That..." She couldn't stop her chuckles. "That is perfect."

"The women in my family don't always like it when I do that either. Label people by their function or personality trait. But to me, that makes more sense than names."

Fascinating. Shep had an entire system of logic and thinking that made him unique. Special. It was a gift, but Joss realized probably not everyone would agree. "Have you given anyone else on the show one of these handy-dandy labels?"

Shep grunted, but a tiny smirk lifted one side of his mouth. She wanted to bite it. So naturally, she took a step to the side and tried to breathe through the surprising spear of lust.

"Moody is The Bombastic Bullshitter. Bradley is The Bleeding Heart. I don't have anything for the camera guys. They don't say much."

"And me?" she asked quietly, even though she was fairly certain she didn't want the answer.

Shep ducked his head and tied the loose ends of his pack straps into knots. Untied. Tied again. Cleared his throat. Fiddled with the straps.

"Whatever it is, I won't get mad."

"It's...um... The Pretty Prima Donna."

She plastered on a smile even though she hated everything about his name tag for her. She *had* been a prima donna and that was why her band was dead. How could a man who'd known her for less than a day see that so clearly?

"You were right," she blurted out. "I did kill them. My band. I put them on that helicopter."

"I should not have said that. Just because some magazines blamed you doesn't mean it is true. I know that."

Joss swallowed and took a shaky breath. "Instead of getting in that helicopter with them, I took a limo that day. I told myself it was because of my fear of falling. But the truth was I rented that helicopter because I wanted privacy to discuss my solo career with a new record label. And although the helicopter company itself was reputable, it came out later that this particular pilot was inexperienced. The Santa Anas were pretty strong that day and..."

"And you put all the blame on yourself."

"Maybe I should have checked references. I shouldn't have tried to shut my band out."

Shep lifted his arms, let them hover midair for a few seconds, and then dropped them. "We... ah, should probably wake up The Bitch... uh... Lauren." Shep stood, which only reminded Joss how wide his chest was. At first glance, it was the kind of chest a woman could rest her head on and allow to absorb some of her pain. But not her. Because he obviously had nothing to say to her confession of guilt.

What did you expect?

"Yes," Joss forced herself to say, "she does seem the type that might sleep the day away."

"What about you?"

"When we're... I'm... touring"—just thinking the word and what it meant now made her want to coil into a ball of self-protection—"it's normal for me to sleep until noon. My body rhythm changes in order for me to get enough rest. But when I'm home, I'm usually up by seven." She gestured to Lauren's shelter, which still looked in good shape, unlike Joss's shotgun shack. "Why don't I try to wake her?"

Relief was so apparent on Shep's face that Joss reached to pat him on the arm, but she remembered that he didn't care to be touched and dropped her hand.

So she strolled over to Lauren's shelter, and just for kicks, shook the cedar branches above it. "Rise and shine, sunshine!" she sang out with totally false cheer. "The day just isn't the same without you. Get up, sleeping beauty!"

Lauren's answer was a cross between a groan and a curse, so Joss rustled the tree again and knocked the toe of her hiking shoe against the support branches. "Oh my goodness, Moody is out here cooking bacon and eggs!"

Lauren moved so fast, diving out of the brushy shelter

and scanning the camp wildly, that Joss rolled her lips in to keep from laughing.

Really? Laughing after what she'd just told Shep? How was that even a possibility?

The truth stunned Joss.

This... this was actually good for her. She'd only thought of *Do or Die* as a way to improve her public image, but instead, it was changing her image of herself. She wanted to win, yes. But playing and laughing and enjoying it along the way were just as important.

"Where? Where is he?" Lauren's words tumbled one over the other as she pushed her wild hair from her face, revealing a cheek creased with leaf marks. Her eyes slitted, she sniffed the air. "Where's the food? Have you already eaten?"

Okay, maybe this *wasn't* funny. They were all hungry, which could easily turn into hangry. "Lauren, listen. I'm sor—"

"Because we better all get what we deserve."

Was that the way the world worked, that people ultimately got what they deserved? If so, Joss deserved nothing.

8

When The Bitcher lunged out of her cedar shelter like a lion leaping on a gazelle, Shep went on alert. At his side, Puck did the same. The woman was obviously not a morning person, so something must've happened to motivate her to abandon her bed so quickly.

Shep shifted his attention to Joss's face. Her lips were pinched tight. Was she about to cry?

"Where is he?" The Bitcher called out. "Where is Moody and the damn bacon?" She lifted her face, reminding Shep once again of a starving predator, and took a deep sniff. "I don't smell frying pork!"

"What's this about bacon?" The Bleeding Heart asked.

The Bitcher pointed at Joss. "She said Moody was cooking us a big breakfast."

"Unless he snuck off into the woods and is whipping up pancakes somewhere else, I don't know how," The Bleeding Heart told her. "I woke up at five, and Moody hasn't been around."

"Five in the morning? That's uncivilized."

"No," he said mildly to The Bitcher, "that's sleeping on the hard ground."

"You think I didn't suffer?" She turned an I-smell-a-nearby-latrine sneer at her own well-constructed—if Shep did say so himself—shelter. "I slept like a homeless person." She climbed to her feet and brushed off her clothes, now dotted with cedar sap and wrinkled like towels left too long in the dryer.

Shep hated when that happened. The few times he forgot about his laundry and it came out a mess, he had to start all over again. Rewash them, promptly put them in the dryer, and then watch them tumble until the buzzer went off.

The Bitcher rounded on Joss and loomed over her, making the difference in their heights very apparent. "Were you lying to me?"

"I wasn't lying exactly," Joss said. "I was *motivating* you."

"You deceitful bitch." The taller woman lunged, getting herself a nice handful of Joss's turquoise hair. As hard as she pulled, Shep was surprised she didn't yank Joss off her feet. "I'm going to teach you a lesson you won't forg—"

To Shep's everlasting surprise, Puck dashed toward the two women and bared his teeth at The Bitcher. The pitch of his growl was something Shep had never heard and it lifted the hair on his arms. It meant he needed to put an end to all of this. Now.

He strode toward the women and gave Puck a "Don't!" command. His dog let his lips drop, but he didn't back down, just continued to give The Bitcher the canine equivalent of the stink-eye. "Puck, heel!"

Rather than turn a circle against Shep's left side as he usually did, Puck walked backward two steps and kept his attention centered on The Bitcher.

She put both hands to her throat in a gesture even Shep could tell was the work of a drama queen. "Did that mangy mutt just threaten me?"

"He was afraid you were hurting Joss." And by the number of loose blue strands clutched between the woman's fingers, she'd succeeded.

"It would've been justified," The Bitcher huffed. "That... that was mean."

The Bleeding Heart laughed, a snicker that quickly turned into a hearty guffaw. "What is this—middle school? Lauren, you diva, you would've played the same trick if you'd thought of it."

Letting go of her drama queen persona, she dropped her hands from her throat and wiggled her fingers, letting Joss's dislocated hair float to the ground.

"Are you hurt?" Shep asked Joss. First, she fell before they even started the trip, then she ripped off skin coming down that tree, and now she'd been snatched bald. If they stayed out here much longer, he'd have to drag this woman back on a litter.

"Stings a little," she said with a grin. "But it was kinda worth it."

The Bitcher swung their way and bared *her* teeth. But when the fur on Puck's ruff rose, she shut down her aggressive expression and turned to Shep. "Please tell me there *is* some breakfast."

"I'm sorry, ma'am. But I'm not in charge of food around here. That's up to Moody."

Her expression soured again. "Then that bastard needs to get his ass up." She stomped toward Moody's tent and when it dawned on her that Greg and his counterpart had filmed the entire catfight, The Bitcher shot the two men a double-barreled bird.

"A charmer, she is not," The Bleeding Heart commented.

"But a communicator, she is," Joss lobbed back.

The Bitcher unzipped Moody's tent and stormed inside. "You little fucker, I'm hungry and you..." The tent shook and dipped like two wild boars were mating inside it. Shep squinted his eyes, trying to blur the mental image of Moody and the woman as humping javelinas.

The Bitcher shoved her way outside and put her hands on her hips. "He's not here. And by the looks of it, he didn't sleep here. His sleeping bag hasn't even been unrolled."

"Damn," The Bleeding Heart said. "To think I could've had a little cushion."

"Where is he?" Shep asked the camera operators.

"No idea," Greg answered. "He doesn't really tell us much other than when he knows there's some good footage coming up. We're supposed to be ready for anything at any time."

It was possible Moody had meandered off to answer the call of nature, but Shep had been up for over an hour himself. That would mean the man was taking the dump of a lifetime.

"Do you think he got lost?" Joss asked him.

"Or maybe a bear ate him," The Bleeding Heart said hopefully.

Shep contemplated for a few seconds. "Moody is a jackass, but he does know a little about the backcountry. I doubt he's lost. Besides, he had a compass. As for the bear, there would probably be some evidence, and since there's no blood—"

Joss grabbed his arm, and the firm pressure felt good. Felt so good, it made Shep want more. Did she want more?

"Bradley was kidding," she said.

"Oh. Yeah. Right." Her touch wasn't about him. She was

concerned for Moody. He pulled away and said to the group, "All of you stay here. I'll go look for him." Then he lowered his voice for Joss's ears only. "I have more energy bars in my pack. You're the only one I trust to get them and portion them out fairly. One per person."

"If it would shut Lauren up, I'd stuff them all in her mouth."

"As my dad says, that would be cutting off your nose to spite your face."

"He sounds like a wise person."

"He made me the man I am today."

"Then he's a helluva guy." She smiled up at him. "Now go find Moody so we can get this show back on the road."

"We won't be on a road. We will—"

"I know. Be hiking the trail."

Shep took to the woods with Puck trotting along beside him. As they spiraled out from the campsite, he thought about Joss Wynter. With the way she sang on stage and her band's music, he'd expected her to be shrill. Sharp. Maybe even savage.

But she wasn't. Tough, yes. Especially for a person her size. Then again, maybe when you were that small, you had to develop a certain toughness. Kind of like him when it came to interacting with people who had the capacity for emotion that he seemed to lack. In order to make it in the world, he had to use what he had—his intelligence—to navigate social situations.

It didn't always work for him, but he'd gotten better at it over the years. As a kid, he'd felt like a turtle being constantly ripped out of its shell and left naked in the middle of a highway.

Joss was being tough now because she wanted to win *Do or Die*. She was playing the game, but he didn't know if her heart was really in it. That could be because she believed she didn't deserve to, or because he wasn't reading her right. Her revelation about the accident that had killed her band had shaken him. Made his brain pinball inside his head.

Sure, he'd read one article about the event, but he should have known better than to believe it.

The problem was that Joss *did* believe it.

The other thing consuming his mind was how Joss had touched him several times, and he hadn't felt like moving away. He shunned touch from most people except his parents and siblings. And yet, he *liked* the feel of Joss's hand on him.

But was it possible he was reading things—sexual things —into her touch?

After he'd gone through puberty, a girl touching him had done one of two things—hurt him or made him horny. Either had felt uncontrollably painful. So he shied away from casual skin-to-skin contact. A hug from a family member, he could handle, but they knew him. Knew his thresholds and when to back off.

His dad and brothers had spent a lot of time trying to teach him the difference. But human flirtation and mating rituals held a complexity that Shep could never completely crack. It was one of the reasons he'd been so happy to marry Amber when he was twenty.

In the beginning, things had been good between them. When Shep was interested in something, he often took that interest to the edge of obsession. Amber had enjoyed being his obsession.

But once they were married, she hadn't understood why his intense focus on her shifted to something else. At that time, it had been rock formations. Another, it had been native plants.

He'd believed he'd secured companionship that would reassure his family and allow him a relatively independent life. Companionship, Amber had explained to him, was not the same as love.

Their marriage had failed. He had failed.

Something he would never do again because he now understood that he did not understand women. Accepted that he wasn't capable of loving a woman the way she wanted to be loved.

He needed to stop thinking about this. About Joss and what she wanted from him, if anything. Right now, the most important thing was to find Moody and get this group farther up the mountain.

To his everlasting frustration, he made six circles of camp, increasing the radius each time, but Moody didn't seem to be within shouting distance. Shep patted Puck on the side. "I think he's screwing with us, Puck."

Puck looked up, and his eyebrows seesawed, making his long eyebrow whiskers wave.

"And if we don't get back to camp soon, there might be some kind of war. For all we know, we'll discover that the three contestants have tied up the camera guys and are fighting to the death over a handful of energy bars."

But when he and Puck cleared the tree line back into camp, the camera operators were busy filming the progress of a snake as it wound its way toward the woods. The younger guy said, "I saw one of these last night when I was in the woods taking a leak. I bet it's a pit viper. Probably the most poisonous snake in all of North America."

"It's a rat snake," Shep told him. "There are only three venomous snakes native to North Carolina. Well, five if you count the types of rattlesnakes separat—"

"There are snakes out here?" The Bitcher screeched.

"Jesus, Lauren, didn't you buy a guide book or anything?" The Bleeding Heart drawled, doing a pretty damn good job of sounding like a Carolina good ol' boy. *Jay-sus.*

"I guess Moody didn't show up while I was out looking for him?" Shep asked the group at large.

"No sign of him," Joss confirmed.

Well, hell.

Shep squatted down to unzip his pack and withdraw the sat—satellite—phone he'd insisted Dan provide him for this trip.

The Bitcher was at his side faster than Barry Allen could race around Central City. "You have a phone! Does it work? I need to make some calls and—"

"No."

"Yes. I can see quite clearly that you have a phone. Now hand it over, cutie, and I'll pay you for it later." She winked, which meant she either had something in her eye or there was some subtext he wasn't getting.

"No, I mean this phone is for emergency contact only." And although Moody's disappearance wasn't officially an emergency, it felt like one to Shep. He didn't want to be out here with all these people by himself. Moody was a jackass, but he was the one ultimately calling the shots.

Shep walked away from The Bitcher and dialed in the number for Prime Climb. It rang half a dozen times before someone picked up. "Prime Climb Tours, Celia speaking."

"I need to talk with Dan Cargill."

"Can I ask who's calling?"

"Harris Sheppard Kingston."

"Oh, Shep, you should've just said so," Celia said. "But Dan's not here right now. You'll have to call him on his mobile."

"Thanks." Shep hung up and dialed Dan's number.

"'lo?"

"We can't find Moody."

"What? Who is this?"

Who else was hiking through the backcountry with a guy named Moody? "Shep Kingston."

"Oh, yeah. Moody. Now what's up?"

"Moody disappeared sometime between last night and this morning. Everyone else is accounted for," Shep said. "But when we checked his tent this morning, it looked like Moody hadn't slept in it."

"Did you search for him?"

Shep was slow on the uptake sometimes, but he was not dumb. "Yes. But he wasn't within shitting distance. I think I should bring these people back to Steele Ridge and—"

"Not even when the devil buys a fur coat."

What? What did fur coats have to do with anything? "That doesn't make any sense. What do devils, fur coats, and Moody have to do with one another?"

"Kingston, sometimes you wear me smooth out." Dan sighed on the other end. "Now let me tell you what's goin' on here. Ol' Moody is pulling your leg. He's probably hiding somewhere. This is a show stunt, you see? He wants to watch how the contestants react to this. He knows where you plan to make camp tonight, right?"

"Yeah," Shep said.

"Then he'll either show up on the trail somewhere or he'll be waiting for you at camp."

Why the hell couldn't people do things that made sense? Shep didn't know what Moody would be trying to accomplish by playing hide-and-seek today. Even if he wanted to screw with the contestants, he should've clued in Shep or the camera guys. "And if he doesn't meet back up with the group?"

"Kingston, don't worry so damn much."

When Shep returned to camp, Joss looked for some sign of success in his face. Instead, it held complete misery and more than a little consternation.

This was the face of a man who wasn't expecting Buffalo Moody to pull a disappearing stunt. The face of a man who was afraid he was stuck with people he didn't particularly care for.

"Who were you talking to?" Lauren demanded of Shep as she held out her hand, clearly expecting him to surrender the phone. "My turn next."

"No," Shep said, a definitive edge to his voice. "You are not using my phone, so stop asking."

"You work for us," she shot back. "You have to do what we tell you—"

"I do not now nor would I ever work for someone like you. It's time for you to shut up."

"Well, I—"

Joss grabbed Lauren by the arm. "Leave him alone. He wasn't expecting this either. Give him a break."

"I hate this whole damn show," Lauren grumbled.

Joss wasn't a big fan right now either, but sometimes life gave you shit you didn't like. You could either whine about it or get up and do something about it.

It was clear to Joss now that she'd spent entirely too long whining and hiding the past few months. How could she expect to process and move past the deaths of her band by behaving that way? How could she reestablish her career? She couldn't.

So the first step back was to play this game to the best of her ability.

Which meant it was time to take action. "Shep, what do you recommend that we do?"

"Dan said Moody probably planned this and that we should continue the hike. That Moody will show up somewhere on the trail or at camp tonight."

"Only problem with that," Bradley said, "is that Moody sets up the opportunities and basically decides who wins the game. How's he gonna do that if he's not around?"

Joss wouldn't put it past the slimeball to be observing them this very second and judging their actions and reactions. In fact, the hair on the back of her neck had been doing a crowd wave ever since they discovered Moody was missing, as if someone was out there in the trees watching this whole scenario like a living diorama.

She shivered and crossed her arms to ward off the chill sweeping over her. She nodded toward the camera operators. "Greg and Zach will be filming us. If Moody misses anything, he can review the film. It's honestly not that big a deal."

"You call starving to death not a big deal?" Lauren said.

"You gobbled up a damn protein bar like a bear just coming out of hibernation," Bradley said. "You won't be starving anytime soon."

Lauren stomped over and pushed her face close to Shep's. Shep took a mother-may-I step back, but Lauren simply followed. "I know you have more food in that pack." She thrust out her hand. "I want you to hand it over."

"No."

Her face contorted, and she lunged at him and shoved him in the chest.

But Shep didn't budge, and Puck trotted over to lean

against his leg. "Don't do that again," Shep said in what Joss could tell was forced calm. "I don't like to be touched. Especially by you."

"What man doesn't like to be touched?" Lauren sidled close to Shep again and stroked his arm. "Maybe one who isn't a real man?"

Okay, that was more than enough. Joss marched over and yanked Lauren out of Shep's touch zone. Capitalizing on the bigger woman's surprise, Joss dragged her to the edge of camp and lowered her voice. "Stop it," she said.

"Why should I?"

"First, because you're making an ass of yourself on camera. The guys film everything. And second, because you're taking your frustration out on a man who's just trying to help us through the next few days."

"If he was really trying to help me, he would give me food and that damn phone of his." Lauren shot a glare in his direction. "What is wrong with him?"

"He didn't sign on to run the show, and I'm sure the last thing he wanted was to be saddled with all of us."

"He's being compensated for it."

"He's not being paid for you to abuse him." If Joss was a betting woman, she'd wager that Moody didn't pay his local guides all that well. And if Shep's employer was taking a cut, that meant he wasn't getting rich by babysitting a trio of spoiled pseudo-celebrities in the wild. "And if you're nicer to him, I have a feeling you might benefit from it."

"So you *do* think he can be screwed into submission."

The impulse to slap Lauren made the muscles in Joss's arm quiver. "Screwing has nothing to do with it. Shep Kingston is obviously a professional. Allow him to do his job—his way—and he'll help us get through this."

Lauren huffed and glanced away.

"I mean it, Lauren." Joss shifted around, where Lauren would be forced to look at her again. "Besides, you do not want the fallout if I go to the entertainment rags after filming is over and give them the inside scoop about how Lauren Estes behaved out here."

"You already said the film crew is getting everything. How could you add to that?"

"Oh, I have an unlimited imagination."

Lauren's mouth was frowning, but her forehead didn't so much as wrinkle. Using Botox in LA was like popping a breath mint. Almost everyone did it, but it still stunk of desperation. "So you're saying you'd lie."

"I would figure out a way to make you look so bad that you'd be lucky to be cast in a toilet bowl cleaner commercial."

"What makes you think I wouldn't retaliate?"

"Maybe you would"— Joss lifted her hands, palms up —"but quite honestly, I don't have any further to fall in the public eye."

"Fine," Lauren finally said. "But you better watch your back once Moody shows up."

"Just try to behave until then, and you can give me your best shot."

9

"LET'S PACK UP CAMP," SHEP TOLD EVERYONE WHEN THE women returned from their little convo at the edge of the trees. Even he could tell neither Joss nor The Bitcher were totally happy, but apparently they'd come to some kind of truce.

"What about Moody's stuff?" Bradley asked.

Shep lifted a shoulder. "Far as I'm concerned, whoever packs it up and carries it can have it for now."

Bradley and The Bitcher were off in a sprint to lay claim on Moody's tent and supplies, and it looked as if The Bleeding Heart was winning. He already had the stakes pulled out of the tent and was dragging it away from the woman like a coyote with a poodle carcass.

"Bradley!" she called to him. "Bradley, wait! Let's talk about this tent thing."

Shep glanced over at Joss. "Aren't you going to try for it?"

"And listen to more of Lauren's bitching and moaning? No thank you. They can fight to the death over it."

"Less competition for you, huh?"

She smiled, and it knocked Shep directly in the chest,

making him want and ache at the same time. "That wouldn't break my heart," she said. "But they're both tough, so I'm not counting on any miracles."

Once the other two competitors had negotiated over Moody's possessions and the camera guys had packed up their gear, Shep waved everyone back toward the trail. "Today, we're hiking twelve miles."

"You're kidding," The Bitcher said.

"Lauren..." Joss's voice was low and carried a message Shep wasn't privy to.

"Can't wait!" Lauren said cheerfully, so cheerfully that it gave Shep whiplash.

"And we'll gain about four thousand feet in elevation," he said. "But a lot of that will happen during switchbacks."

"Why can't we just climb straight up the damn mountain?" The Bitcher asked.

"Because," Bradley said, "doing that would kick all our asses."

On the trail, Shep took the lead and said to Greg, "Do you mind bringing up the rear since Moody's not here?"

"As long as I can still film, it's no problem," he said. He turned to his colleague. "Why don't you get in the middle of the stack, say between Bradley and Lauren."

To make the pattern even, it really should've been guy, girl, guy, guy, girl, guy. But it ended up guy, girl, guy, girl, guy, guy. The lack of symmetry made Shep twitchy, but no twitchier than the fact that he was now in charge of this group.

For the first couple of hours, they made decent progress since everyone had some protein bar in them, but midmorning, the whole group started dragging. Shep wanted to push, hoping to stumble across Moody around the next turn. Not that he liked the guy, but he'd be damn happy to hand back the reins of this ridiculous rodeo.

When The Bitcher flopped down on a fallen tree and sighed, Shep realized nothing he did or said would prod her farther until she was good and ready. She waved Bradley over and said, "Hon, give me a sip from Moody's water bottle, why don't you?"

"Only if you share his food."

"You might want to pace yourself," Shep warned. "Be sure not to gorge now or you won't have anything left later."

"When Moody shows up again, he'll take it all away. Better to gorge now and repent later," The Bitcher said. "Actually, all the better if he shows back up and doesn't have a bite or sip left."

Shep wasn't going to argue with her. After all, it wasn't as if the mountain was barren. He could come out here with nothing and survive for months, if not years. "Then while all of you take a break, I'm going to scout up ahead. Stay here until I get back."

"You wouldn't want to leave us here unprotected, would you?" The Bitcher asked. "Maybe you should leave us your phone just in case."

He was torn because she had a valid point. Then Greg piped up and said, "Don't worry about it, man. Zach and I both have sat phones."

"Really?" The Bitcher said. "You've been holding out on me all this time? Give it to me so I can call civilization."

"Nope," Greg said with a grin. "Moody would have my job, my head, and my balls. You might be worth a couple of those, but I value my testicles."

Dear Jesus, Shep was never doing something like this again. He didn't care what Dan threatened him with. People were the worst.

Twenty to thirty minutes where he and Puck were on their own sounded like heaven to Shep. If they found Moody, great. But what he really needed right now was time alone, away from these people and the static they created in his head.

But before he could take a step, Joss cornered him and said, "Would you mind if I came with you to look for Moody?"

Yes. No. Honestly, he didn't know.

"How about if I promise not to talk to you?"

Shep blinked. Could she possibly understand his need for silence? For a little serenity?

"I won't even talk to Puck so you don't have to hear a human voice at all."

She *did* get it.

"Promise?"

Her smile lit her gray eyes, and she drew an X over her chest. A chest that Shep was now having a hard time looking away from. What would it feel like to slip his hands under her shirt and...

"Joss is going with me," Shep abruptly said to the group. He trained his gaze on Joss's guitar case. "You should leave that."

"I..." She took a step back as though reconsidering. "Are you sure it'll be safe here?"

"Those four are not going anywhere," he said. "And as long as you haven't hidden food in there, I think it'll be fine."

"If you're sure." She carried it over to Bradley and asked him to look after it.

She, Shep, and Puck returned to the trail. It was wide in this area, with room for them to walk three abreast. *Stop thinking about breasts.* Shep was careful to put Puck between Joss and himself.

Still, as they strolled away from the others, their three-some almost seemed like a little family.

Although he was one of five kids, Shep had never really considered having children of his own. When Amber had hit him with her desire to get pregnant, he hadn't known how to respond. Later, after they split, he'd heard she'd told her friends that she'd wanted a couple of *snotty-nosed brats* because she didn't want to work at a job.

Needless to say, Shep's mom had never been in Amber's fan club. Oh, she'd tried to get along with her for his sake. But the two women couldn't have had less in common if they came from two different planets.

His mom had recently retired from her job as an environmental engineer, and Amber was still a cashier at Hoffman's Grocery. Shep didn't like to shop at Hoffman's, but when he couldn't avoid it, he tried to check out through another clerk's line. Because even now, more than five years after their divorce, Amber still liked to yap his ear off.

Joss shrugged out of her pack and dug through it as they continued to walk. Without a word, she offered him half of a half of a protein bar. The one he'd sent via Puck last night.

Most of time, his emotions were what most people might consider muted, especially compared to the way NTs seemed to feel everything so keenly. But Joss had a way of touching something inside him with her small gestures. His instinct was to hand the bit of protein bar back to her, but he remembered something his dad had told him. That people who care for one another offer little gifts to each other. Half of the giving was to accept the gift gracefully and gratefully.

Shep broke off a piece for Puck and gave him a sit

command. His retriever's focus never wavered from Shep's face. No sly side-eye glance at the food. Just pure eye-to-eye from human to canine. It was one of the few types of eye contact that never made Shep feel uncomfortable.

"Okay."

Puck politely took the bit of food from Shep's hand.

Clearly enjoying the ritual, Joss smiled. But she didn't speak. Even Shep's sisters would've had a hard time doing that. "You can say something," Shep said to Joss, realizing he meant it. He liked the sound of her voice.

"Oh, thank goodness." Her words came out in a rush of breath. "He's amazing, just an incredible dog."

"He was well trained."

"By you?"

"Some, but mostly by the puppy raisers and the organization that matches them with people like me free of charge. When a puppy is ten to twelve weeks old, volunteers take him into their home. Until the dog is about two years old, the puppy raisers socialize him and teach him basic commands."

"And then what happens?"

"They return the puppy to the organization for advanced training."

Mouth open, she blinked up at him. "You mean they just give him up? But... but isn't that horribly hard?"

"Yeah, it is tough even though they go in to puppy raising knowing the dogs aren't theirs to keep. Some people do it again and again, raising multiple puppies in hopes of them being placed."

"God, that takes a lot of commitment, and a lot of love," she said, smiling down at Puck. "Do you have any idea you are just a big offering of love wrapped in fur?"

Puck grinned up at her, his lolling tongue belying her effusive praise and his innate intelligence.

"We should probably go off trail," Shep said, even though he was pretty convinced that Moody wouldn't show himself until he was ready to. "Not too far, but I figure the group needs a few more minutes of rest."

"Sure won't hurt."

Although Puck remained close to Shep's side, he weaved right and left, sniffing the fallen leaves and pine needles.

"You think he could track Moody?" Joss asked.

"Maybe. But he's not really trained as a hunting dog." But in direct contradiction of Shep's words, Puck suddenly set his legs and buried his nose in leaf debris, his snuffling becoming audible and labored. "Sit, Puck."

He did as directed, but his entire body vibrated. Shep hunkered down and brushed away a few leaves. When he spotted something blondish-brown, his whole body stilled. He took a breath and held Puck's leash out to Joss. "Will you take him for a minute and walk him about ten feet that way? His command is let's go."

"Sure." She took the leash, gave Puck his command, and led him to a cluster of maples that were starting to show the promise of fall's vivid colors. "Do you think he found something?"

"Probably just a sack of trash someone tossed off the trail." But Shep had a bad feeling about this. Something wasn't right here, and he didn't want what was buried here to tempt Puck. He usually had a gut of steel and had been known to eat just about anything, including a few of Shep's mom's not-so-delicious baked goods.

It only took Shep a few seconds of digging through the debris to realize Puck hadn't stumbled across some carelessly disposed of garbage. Under the decomposing leaves was the body of a dead fawn. By the looks of it, a June or July baby.

"What is it?" Joss called out.

He didn't want to tell her. But he also didn't lie well. "It's... uh... it's..." He tried to scoop pine needles across the fur he'd uncovered. "Why don't you take Puck back to the trail? Straight through the trees. It's not far."

"Shep, what is it?"

"Nothing."

"You're lying to me."

Yeah, and it crawled over him uncomfortably. "Please do what I asked."

"What did you find?"

Resigned, he said, "You're not going anywhere, are you?"

"No."

Goddammit. "It's a baby deer."

"Oh. Oh, no."

Shep looked over his shoulder to see Joss looping Puck's leash to secure him to a tree. She set aside her pack, rushed to Shep's side, and knelt beside him. "What should we do?"

Nature was normally something to be left alone. Most of the time, humans interrupted life cycles that shouldn't be tampered with. But this was different. This was a baby. Babies should not die. And he couldn't stand the idea of something coming along and eating this one. "I'm going to bury it."

"I can help."

"I really don't think you want to—"

"I *need* to help."

He nodded. "There's a small spade tied to the side of my pack. Take that off and you can start on a hole. Doesn't have to be very deep. We'll lay him in it and cover it with rocks and heavy branches."

Joss retrieved the spade secured with bungee straps and found a spot between two of the maples. Without asking, she went to work, scooping away leaves and attacking the soil beneath.

Shep dug through his pack for a pair of gloves. Although wrapping the deer in a survival blanket might help keep predators away, it wasn't environmentally sound. Burying him and letting the earth take him back would have to be enough.

Expecting to uncover the body and find some evidence of illness, Shep rocked back on his heels when he saw what had killed the deer.

The poor little guy's throat had met the business end of a knife, and recently.

Why the *fuck* would someone do this? Hunting for food was one thing, but hunting for sport was cruel, inhumane, and useless. It was shameful.

Shep set his teeth. He'd seen death and decay, but carelessness and cruelty, he could not accept. "Joss, go back to Puck, please."

Unfortunately, she took his words as a direct invitation to return to him and look over his shoulder. "Oh my God. Who would do something like this?"

Exactly his question. "Someone shitty."

"It looks like it happened recently."

Shep touched the fawn's flank, and the warmth of the body confirmed Joss's guess. He didn't like the idea that someone had stood in this exact spot, probably less than half an hour ago, and killed. He hurriedly picked up the small body, careful to take a wide step around Joss, and placed it in the shallow hole. He covered it with the leaves Joss had dislocated. "We need rocks and branches. Anything sharp or with thorns is good."

"Will... will he be okay there?"

Probably not for too long, but Shep wasn't about to tell Joss that. And the instincts he'd honed out in the backcountry for years were insisting that it wasn't safe here for them, either. "We need to hurry. I don't want to be here longer than we have to."

Within a few minutes, they'd gathered enough stones and brush to visually obscure the little grave, but Shep doubted it would mask the fawn's scent for long.

Regardless, it would have to do, because his nerve endings were jangling with the warning that he and Joss needed to get back to the group.

Although Shep's face was completely blank of expression, Joss knew he was disturbed by what they'd found. It was if the energy field around his body was vibrating with a different frequency, even steeper waves than it had when they left the others. He unclipped Puck from the tree where she had secured him and strode away from the burial spot.

Although Puck was sticking to Shep's side, by the time they intersected with the trail, the muscle in Shep's jaw looked as if it could deadlift a hundred pounds. He dug into the pocket of his cargos and withdrew the piece of cord she'd come to understand was, like Puck, a source of comfort to him. Without looking at it, he tied intricate knots, one after the other, as they hiked.

Something told Joss he needed space, so she marched along beside him, focus forward on the trail. Step after step, they continued in silence. But from her peripheral vision, she saw that Shep's tying movements eventually became slower and less jerky. Finally, he loosened the last knot, slipped the cord back into his pocket, and stroked a gentle hand over Puck's head.

"I am sorry you had to see that," he said gruffly.

She nodded, but felt as if she needed to say something back. "I'm sorry you had to see it, too."

That stopped him. Head down, he stood still in the middle of the trail, and his hands clenched and unclenched. "Someone killed it."

"Yes."

"I've seen dead deer before."

"I'm sure you have." Although Joss desperately wanted him to look at her, she knew by now that his avoidance didn't mean he was avoiding *her.*

"Then why did you say that, about being sorry that I saw it?" he asked.

"Because it affected you."

He looked up and pinned her with his green gaze. *Whoosh.* Joss's breath flew the coop. "Why do you touch me?" he asked.

What? Joss blinked to try to follow the hard left he'd turned. She had to stay present around this man and learn how to play an endless game of Chutes and Ladders. Joss thought for a few moments because she understood she couldn't answer his question with an off-the-cuff comment. This was important to him. Maybe more important than she could grasp.

"I don't actually touch a lot of people," she said finally. "My family isn't filled with huggers. And having fans grasp at me..." She tried to get her breath back, but it was avoiding her lungs for a different reason now. "...it used to be flattering in a way, but now I find it terrifying."

"You didn't answer my question."

"I'm working on it." She tilted her head and looked up

into the leafy canopy over them, trying to grab on to some equilibrium. "Touch has been totally missing in my life since..." She couldn't get the words out of her mouth even though she'd already laid herself bare to Shep.

"Is it true that you and Chris Lively were lovers?"

Joss blinked. Chris had been one of her bandmates from the very beginning, from the time she was discovered in a little dive bar on the outskirts of Omaha and ultimately signed a recording deal.

Most people would be thrown off-balance being asked such a personal question, but it was so much better than talking about the crash again, so she jumped on it. "At one time, yes. When we were in our early twenties. But it hadn't been that way between us in a long time." In fact, Chris had been most recently involved with a woman Joss had believed he would marry.

She'd been so happy for him.

Then she'd been selfish, and he was dead.

A topic she didn't want to delve into again. Talking with Shep about touch was so much better. "I touched you because... well... I guess because I felt—feel—some type of kinship with you."

"Oh," he said, and went broodingly silent.

"Just 'oh'?"

"I don't do this well."

"If you'll explain what it is we're doing, I'll try to help."

Shep simply reached for his security cord and began walking again. It was maddening, but she tried to stay calm. Tried to truly understand. But even Puck kept looking up at Shep as if he expected him to respond to Joss's offer of help.

"I'm not trying to be difficult," she said finally when it became apparent Shep wasn't going to answer her. "I'm just unsure."

"That is nice," he said. Finally, he released a long breath. "I'm not making sense to you, am I?"

"Not completely." Although she knew Shep wasn't trying to be funny. Or difficult.

"I am usually the one who has to apologize for not understanding and being unsure." His quick glance in her direction made it clear he was earnestly trying to explain himself. "I said it is nice because it makes me feel good that someone else is unsure."

"It makes you not feel so alone when that happens, huh? When someone knows exactly what you're going through."

"It's a pretty rare occurrence for me." He worked his cord into a particularly complex configuration and handed it to her.

Joss ran her fingers over the smooth bumps and humps of the knot.

"It's a monkey's fist."

"It's beautiful."

His eyebrows rose, and he frowned down at the knot. "Really?"

She held up the knot, studied it closer. "Seems like an art form in a way."

"Do you want to have sex with me?"

Well, okay then. Shep had obviously decided that their conversation soup needed a habanero thrown into it. "This is where you were going by asking me why I touched you." She passed him back the length of cord, instinctively understanding he would want it while they delved into this topic.

"I know I'm supposed to say things that go with the things you say. I just..."

"Can't always do it?"

"It wears me out."

"I can imagine."

"Can you really?"

"It's like anything that doesn't come naturally to someone. For example, riding a bike for me. I have to concentrate really hard when I try to do it. And I end up falling a lot."

"Yes," he said, his shoulders relaxing. "You do understand."

"I'm not sure if I want to have sex with you."

"Hey, you did it, too."

"I'm learning from the best." She smiled up at him.

"Do you know when you might be sure?"

Joss paused in the middle of the trail and turned to face him. "Can you look at me or will that make you uncomfortable?"

"My brothers say it's important to look at a woman you like."

He liked her. She was a twenty-nine-year-old woman, and that made her as giddy as a preteen at her first Justin Bieber concert. "You don't have to look at me."

"I want to." His gaze met hers, veered off. Came back and bam! She suddenly didn't want any other woman to look into this man's eyes. They were that potent. Truly windows to a complex and beautiful soul.

"I like you," she told him. "I'm attracted to you. My body is totally on board with having sex with you, but..."

Shep rocked forward on his toes and back on his heels. Like a little boy's nerves inhabiting a man's body.

"...my brain and my heart don't know quite yet."

"Okay," he said and turned to walk away.

"Hey." She grabbed his wrist. "That's not a no. It's just an I don't know. Besides, you mentioned that you don't like to be touched." She looked down at her fingers wrapped around his golden skin. The silky hairs there mesmerized her. Seduced her. "Does this bother you?"

"Tighter," he said.

She squeezed.

"I like that."

"And lighter than that?"

"I don't really understand it, but what other people say tickles them hurts me."

Fascinating.

"And you're really small," he added.

She gripped harder. "You're worried about hurting me?"

"Maybe."

"Don't." Suddenly feeling stronger and more sure of herself than she had in months, Joss shifted close to him. "Because I am unbreakable."

10

SHE CAME AT HIM FAST. NOT ONE TO LET SOMEONE ELSE GET A jump on him, Shep was startled to find himself shoved back against a tree and Joss's hand stabbing into his hair. Puck got into the spirit and somehow wound his leash around Shep's knees, lashing him to the tree.

Before he could get his balance, Joss yanked his face down and smashed her lips to his. Although she was small, she was leaning into him with all her weight, wedging him between her body and the tree's rough bark.

Her kiss was edgy. Unrelenting lips, aggressive tongue, and sharp little teeth. Her bite did it for him, just enough pressure and pain to electrify the skin all over his body. The zing of it spiraled down and shot to his dick.

The impulse to return her aggression—to grab hold of her breasts, her ass, her anything—rolled through him. Just go from the parking lot to the Indy 500. He wanted to strip off her shirt. Stuff his hand down her pants. Then he wanted to brace her against this tree and fuck her blind.

Which meant he needed to keep himself under tight

control. As Cash and Way had made very clear to him, women did not go from zero to sixty in two-point-six seconds. They needed to be stroked and revved.

So Shep kept his hands by his sides and let Joss tongue-fuck his mouth. The grip she had on his hair, the way her other hand was curled into his T-shirt, she was stronger than he'd realized. If her inner thighs were as powerful, could grip him hard, he might be able to lose his mind in a very good way when—if—he got between them.

Suddenly, Joss took her mouth from his and she stared up at him, eyes blazing and breath heaving. "Not working for you?"

"It's working quite well."

"Audience participation is appreciated and encouraged."

"I... Women need different stuff from guys."

"Oh really? Who told you that?"

"My brothers." But realistically, it hadn't been Cash and Way who'd planted that in his brain. Amber had never wanted to have sex without being properly pleased and petted beforehand. Shep had no problem with physical foreplay. He got that. But Amber's idea of foreplay had many times eluded him. "Actually, my ex-wife."

"So what is it she told you that women need?"

Jewelry. Fancy dinners in public. "Nice words. Soft kisses. Time to... uh... get in the mood."

"I like nice words and soft kisses as much as any other girl," she agreed. "But it's not a prereq. And you've been pretty upfront about what your thing is. It's about you, too, you know."

"What?"

"Kissing. Touching. Sex. The whole thing. You get a say, too."

Somehow in Shep's mind, women always had the key, got to turn the lock any way they wanted. Since he didn't always recognize the physical cues, the tone of voice, he waited. Always. "I don't know what to say."

"If you weren't trying to filter yourself through the things other people have told you are okay, what would you say to me right now? What would you do to me?"

Uh-uh. Nope. He did not share those things. It wasn't like he was a complete perv or anything, but his imaginings weren't roses and candlelight. Sometimes, he didn't even visualize a woman's face. Just her body and what he wanted to do to it. Shep tried to unwind Joss's fingers from his hair, but she didn't loosen her grip. If anything, she tightened it, and his dick jumped.

"Am I making you uncomfortable?" she asked him.

"No, you're making me hard."

She tugged his hair, and his hips jerked against her.

This wasn't right. Women wanted to make love, and making love did not entail hair pulling and the kind of pressure Shep preferred. That was, at its nicest, fucking.

And girls did not like to be fucked.

They wanted to be pampered and coddled and loved.

How the hell was he supposed to do that when he didn't understand what other people meant by the concept of love?

"Will Puck stay here if we move a few steps away?" she asked.

"Yeah, but why..."

"Puck, stay." Joss yanked the leash out of Shep's hand, unwound it from around his legs, and dropped it to the ground. Then she grabbed his hand and dragged him behind a nearby tree. "Will you let me do something? If you don't like it, you just say the word, and I'll stop immediately.

If my touch doesn't feel good, tell me. It won't hurt my feelings."

He wanted to believe her, but Amber had said similar things a few times. And every time, she'd ended up crying and curling herself into a ball on the other side of the bed. "You don't mean that. She never did."

"I am not her," Joss stately flatly. "I am me. You have no reason to trust me, not really. But I want to show you that you can."

"I...Okay."

She shoved him against a tree. He was really becoming fond of this forest. Then she went for the button and zipper on his cargos, pulling open one and ripping down the other. His cock liked the idea of getting out of his boxer briefs and pushed against the fabric.

Joss yanked down the waistband and hooked it tight beneath his balls. And holy fuck, that was... amazing.

"You still with me?"

Shep could swear he could see his dick pulsing with every beat of his heart. He was absolutely with her. "Yeah," he croaked out.

"Tell me the second you aren't," she said. "I'm not into unwilling partners."

An emotional fist rammed into Shep's gut. That was the way he'd often felt with Amber—like he'd coaxed her into something. "Okay."

But if Joss kept her current trajectory, there was no way in hell he would stop her. His abs were tight and quaking in anticipation. But first, he had to tell her something. "If you're thinking about going down on me, don't."

For the first time since she'd pulled him in for her kiss, her eyes widened in surprise and confusion. "What? Why?"

"I don't like it."

She blinked. Just once, but it was obvious he'd stumped her. "Okay, this is a topic for another time. A man who doesn't want a blowjob. Wow. Just wow."

Another thing Amber hadn't understood. Every so often, she'd decided to blow him because she thought it would soften him up to one of her requests. She'd never understood it, never believed, that he detested the way her mouth felt on him. Once, he'd dragged her off his dick by pulling her by the hair. She'd cried for three hours that time. And not because he'd hurt her physically. He hadn't yanked out a single strand of her blond hair.

But Joss just said, "Good thing I had something else in mind."

She wedged herself against his right side, her breasts hugging his ribcage and her right leg over his. He could feel the heat of her center against his outer thigh. Then she fisted his dick. Hard. Harder than she'd gripped his wrist.

It made Shep's knees feel as if they had been replaced by Silly Putty, and he grunted out his pleasure.

"Okay?"

"Better than."

"Perfect." She didn't stroke him, didn't gently test the glide of skin over cartilage. She flat-out jerked on his dick.

Forget Silly Putty. Shep no longer had knees. He dug his heels into the ground to keep his balance.

Joss's fist was the best thing he'd ever felt. Ever. Working him over, hard and fast.

His own grip was probably a little tighter. After all, his hand was bigger. But she was fisting him with an intensity and speed and pressure that made his brain go blank. He watched her stroke him, her dainty-looking fingers pulling at his dick in a definitive rhythm. One-two-three-four. Five-six-seven-eight.

"You..." he panted. "You're jerking me off in an eight count."

Joss smiled up at him, and for a second, Shep regretted what he'd told her about blowjobs. If her hand felt like this, maybe she could—

"So I am. Is that a problem?"

"No." In fact, the pattern soothed him even as her touch enflamed him.

It didn't take many more measures for Shep to feel the pressure build in his balls. He had to warn her. In his experience, women liked to back off before the mess. "I'm about to come."

"Great," she said cheerfully. And without breaking her grip, she dropped to her knees and applied her teeth to the crown of his dick. The feel of those sharp little canines against his swollen skin made napalm detonate behind Shep's eyes.

He couldn't have stopped his orgasm if someone had aimed a gun between his eyes. It was a beast, rolling and roaring and destroying everything in its path. He came for what felt like a decade, just pulsing into Joss's mouth. And when he was finally spent, she released him quickly. Touching him one second and gone the next.

No cuddling or patting or gentle kisses. Thank Jesus.

Joss wiped at the corners of her mouth with her fingertips as if she'd just dined at some fancy Los Angeles restaurant.

"Wh...why did you do that?"

Worry clouded her smoky eyes. "I'm sorry. I thought maybe that would be okay at the end."

"It..." Where was his brain? Probably somewhere in Joss's palm. Possibly in her mouth. "I... It was. I meant why you swallowed."

That chased the worry away. "Well," she drawled. "You know what they say. Leave no trace."

Shep grabbed her hand and drew her up until their faces were close. "Tell me when you've made up your mind about having sex with me. Because, Joss Wynter, I would very much like to have sex with you."

Shep's eyes were still glassy and unfocused as they retrieved Puck and hiked down the rest of the trail toward the others. He'd definitely enjoyed himself, but the firm line of his mouth was a hint that he wasn't completely happy about it. Finally, he said, "We've been gone too long."

"I'm betting Lauren and Bradley don't mind."

"They will when they realize how much farther we have to hike today."

When they rounded the last bend in the trail, they found the foursome playing cards on a fallen log. Strip poker by the looks of it. Lauren was down to underwear that showed off her legs and a lacy bra that showed off her Amazonian boobs. The younger camera guy couldn't seem to take his attention off of them. Two of his cards dropped from his hand, and he didn't even realize it.

"Good to see you kept yourselves occupied," Joss said with an infusion of forced sarcasm to mask the fact that she and Shep had *occupied* themselves as well. Still wet and achy, Joss planned to *occupy* him again at some point.

"Did you find Buffalo?" Lauren asked.

"Yeah, Lauren. They tucked him in a backpack." Bradley pantomimed handing her something. "Here's your sign."

Lauren rolled her eyes at him. "I don't understand you."

"It's a style of joke told by Bill Engvall," Shep told her.

"Whatever." Lauren toyed with the strap of her bra, probably with the hope of snagging Shep's attention. "What's the news on our illustrious host?"

"No sign of him," Joss said as she slid a glance toward Shep to find him staring at Lauren's face, his set in a grim expression. Inside, Joss smiled. The other woman might as well be wearing a nun's habit for all Shep cared.

"Everybody grab your gear," he said. "We have five more miles to hike today."

"You can't be serious," Lauren said. "That's impossible."

"She might be right," Greg said. "Because we need some kind of physical opportunity today as well. Those normally take an hour minimum to film."

"Moody isn't here," Shep said. "So no *opportunities*."

"That's not acceptable," Lauren said. "If we don't complete the daily opportunities, we'll have to extend the trip." She turned on a high-voltage smile. All in all, she *was* a decent actor. "Not that I would mind more time in this paradise, but..."

But nothing. Lauren wanted out of these trees in the worst way, but she had a point. "If we film the opportunity, then Moody can review it later," Joss said. "We have to do it, Shep."

"But Moody thinks those up." he protested.

"Why don't you do it this time?" she said softly, hoping he would understand that she needed this, too. If they didn't finish the game, the mini-series would never be aired. "It's not that big a deal."

"What kind of opportunity?" he asked her.

"No," Lauren cut in before Joss could answer. "She can't tell you that. You have to decide on your own so everyone is on a level playing field."

"Fine," Shep grunted. "Get your packs and let's go."

"So what's the opportunity?" Bradley asked him.

"I'll let you know when I've figured it out."

11

WHEN THE GROUP WALKED BY THE TREE WHERE JOSS HAD given Shep the hand job of his lifetime, he couldn't help but stare at it. It should be awarded a plaque, a medal of honor, a gold star.

"Why are you grinning at a tree?" The Bitcher asked him.

"I like that tree."

"Why that one?"

Joss coughed from somewhere behind him, but Shep just said, "Because it's a good tree."

"Better than the trillion others on this mountain?"

"Yes."

The Bitcher wagged her head back and forth. "I keep trying to understand you, but I think you might be hopeless."

"I don't care if you understand me," he said. "After we finish this trip, I won't ever see you again." It suddenly struck him that the same could be said for Joss. Once they were off the mountain. She would go home, 2,278 miles away from Steele Ridge.

"God, I hope Moody shows up soon," Lauren said.

So did he. He hadn't been alone with these people for more than seven hours, and they were already dragging at him, leaching energy out of him like vampires. Well, mainly The Bitcher. The Vampire? He tried it out in his mind. Nah —The Bitcher still suited her best.

And this crew was slow. Even Puck kept looking up at Shep, eyebrows working, as if asking could they move this wagon train along any faster. At this rate, they wouldn't make it to his designated camp spot before the sun sank or someone decided they wouldn't take another step.

"Hey, man," Greg hollered from back down the trail. "I thought we were going to stage an opportunity for these guys."

"Once we make camp," Shep called back to him. "Not much farther. Just a mile."

"Yay," The Bitcher said. "That means we've already walked four."

"No," Shep informed her. "Y'all are too slow, so we're only doing three."

"And does Buffalo have any idea that we won't be in the original location?" she asked.

"How could he?" Shep shook his head. Didn't she *think*? "No one has talked with him since I told you my plan one point three seconds ago."

She tossed her hands up in the air and huffed.

Joss came striding around the other woman and said, "Lauren, why don't you drop back for a few minutes and visit with Zach? I'm betting that if you flash him your tits again, he'll share his food with you later."

The Bitcher did an about-face and marched toward the younger camera operator.

"Is that true?" Shep asked Joss as they forged a few steps ahead of the group.

Joss lifted a shoulder. "Maybe. Probably. The way he was ogling her during their strip poker game, I don't think it would take much to push him in that direction."

"She likes men."

Joss chuckled. "No, Lauren likes Lauren. She uses men to get the things she wants."

"So she's like a prostitute."

Joss's chuckle turned into a strangled cough, and Shep slapped her on the back. Finally, she wheezed. "I don't even know how to respond to that."

"Do you like men?"

"Are you asking me if I try to manipulate people with sex?"

"You want to win this game."

"Of course, I do."

"Would you...did you...jerk me off to win?"

The smile on her face disappeared. Just *poof*.

Not good. *Not good, Shep.*

But it was too late to backtrack. And even when he was able to backtrack, he usually stumbled over his own feet. "Never mind," he mumbled.

He didn't have any problem interpreting the glare she leveled at him. She was a hundred pounds of pissed-off woman. That was a certainty when she marched on up the trail in front of him, her guitar shifting side to side just enough to reveal her butt muscles flexing with every angry step she took.

Probably not the time to check out the flex. But the shift and play of the muscles entranced him the way he enjoyed looking at complex patterns. Only three muscles in the human posterior, but if they were in good shape, they had the ability to transfix a man. One muscle in the female vagina, and it could lobotomize a man.

"I can feel you staring at my ass." Her words were clipped, like little chunks of wood flying away from a lumberjack's ax.

"I'm sorry."

"For what? Staring at my ass or calling me a game whore?"

This was bad, even he knew that. And if it was bad, that meant Joss might change her mind about having sex with him. He jogged to her side and said, "I still want to have sex with you."

"Even though I'm a whore."

Her using that word twice was an even worse sign, so Shep shut up before he screwed up more.

Thirty minutes later, they were the first ones to arrive at the turnoff for the alternate campsite he'd chosen. It was only a few steps off the trail, so he turned around and called back to everyone besides Joss, who was still stomping up the mountain. "Camp will be to your right. Turn here at the big loblolly pine and you'll see the clearing within twenty feet. Once we get there, let's unload gear and packs. Then the opportunity will start in half an hour."

"What is the opportunity?" Bradley asked.

"I'll tell you in thirty minutes," Shep said. Then he turned and jogged up the hill to catch Joss. "Hey." He snagged her elbow and pulled her off the trail to the right and backtracked to a small meadow. "We're making camp here."

"Great."

But it wasn't. He could tell that from her tone of voice. So he told Puck, "Puck, down." His dog dropped to the ground and stretched out on his side. "I'll be back in a minute to give you water."

With his grip still on Joss, he led her into trees surrounding the site he'd chosen. "I was not calling you a whore," he said.

"Sure sounded that way."

"If I thought you were a whore, I would say it."

Joss rounded on him, fists tight and chin up. Shep's heart gave a hard bump against his ribs. There was just something about this woman that threw him off-balance and made him feel totally comfortable at the same time. He had feelings for her, but he didn't know why or what they meant.

Finally, she blew out a long breath and dropped her fists. But her chin remained in the air. "I want to win this damn game, but I will not screw anyone—especially you—to win it."

"Why *not* me?"

Her laugh was breathy. She closed her eyes and gave a slow head shake that Shep had seen numerous times from his female relatives. His dad had told him it basically meant *you're a total dumbass, but I'm trying to have patience and forgive your dumbassness.* "Because I could care about you."

She had feelings for him, too.

Which meant he definitely needed to make this right. Since there was no way he was going to understand the intricacies of this conversation and whatever he'd done to piss her off, he just sucked it up and said, "I know I said something that upset you, but I'm not sure exactly what or why. I tried, but the conversation had too many threads for me to trace them all."

"You're telling me that you couldn't pick them all apart if you wanted to?"

"Well, if I had enough time, but the conversation

happened so quickly, and I knew it had gone wrong right away. I didn't think you would be happy if I waited any longer to say something else to you."

"That's very insightful of you."

"Do you want to fight about it?"

Another laugh, which he took as a good sign. A hopeful sign. "No, I really don't," she said on a sigh. "And I'm sorry that I tried to turn this into a situation you couldn't possibly be expected to navigate. Hell, a normal man couldn't..."

Her words trailed off and this time, when her eyes clamped shut, it wasn't because *he'd* made a mistake.

"It's okay," he said softly. "I'm not normal."

"That's not what I meant."

"No one in my family is, though," he told her.

"You mean you're all..."

"On the autism spectrum? No, but we are kind of loud. We like to give each other a hard time, and we all have our problems. So I guess if having problems is normal, then maybe we *are* all normal." Hell, he was even confusing himself now.

"Because there really is no normal, is there?"

He'd never really considered that before. Even though his family understood him, accepted him, he'd always believed he was on one of the far ends of the normality bell curve. But if there was no such thing as normal, there was no real standard for him to be measured by.

And that was something he wanted to let sink in. "Are we okay now or would another apology be appropriate?"

Joss laughed, and the smile he was coming to treasure made a shy appearance. "We are absolutely okay."

She shouldn't have snapped at him, Joss knew that. Even

when Shep said something outrageous or hurtful, he wasn't being a prick. Not really. He was just stating what he saw and asking questions he wanted the answers to.

And when you threw in sex, well... That topic was a minefield for anyone.

God, could she have been more insensitive—insinuating he wasn't normal? He was right. So right. There was no such thing as normal in this world. And thank God for it because Joss herself had benefitted immeasurably from not being normal. It had brought her incredible fortune. Outrageous fame.

And if she were being honest with herself, sometimes unmanageable fear.

"You're not just saying that we're okay, are you?" Shep asked her. "Because I need to go give Puck some water."

Joss did an internal check and made sure she was being absolutely level with him. "No. Everything is really okay."

He nodded and walked away. Not in the least ashamed, Joss watched his butt, the swing of his muscular arms, the width of his shoulders. He wouldn't be an easy man to have a relationship with.

Relationship. Why would she even think that word? That hadn't been in her vocabulary even before the accident. She'd been too caught up in the next move of her career.

She hadn't come to North Carolina to bond with anyone but her adoring public. So why was she so drawn to Shep Kingston?

Possibly because he was WYSIWYG—what you see is what you get. That was uncommon these days and almost unheard of in Joss's world. Everyone was out for something, had an underlying motive that they dared not share.

But this man was different. In a way that made Joss feel

clean again. Made her feel as if the oily guilt inside her might eventually recede. That she might be able to stop loathing herself.

"Goddammit!" Shep's roar came from the vicinity of camp, and Joss took off running, her pack and guitar bouncing against her spine.

"What?" she said as she skidded into the open area. "What happened?"

Shep pointed at his unzipped pack. "Someone drank the fresh water I had for Puck."

Any second now, Shep was going to...

And there it was. He shoved his hand into his pocket and pulled out the length of cord. He tied a trio of knots in rapid succession with jerky and intricate movements of his fingers.

"Someone better tell me who stole my dog's water or I'm going to strap every damn one of you to a tree and use you as bear bait." With the storm brewing in his eyes and the way he was starting to pace around the camp, Joss had no doubt that he had not only the skill but also the capacity to do exactly that.

But the other four people were just standing around, looking anywhere but at Shep.

"Tell him," she demanded. "You owe him that much."

Finally, Lauren pointed at the young camera guy. "I'm sorry, Zach. But I have to tell them you were the one."

"But it was for..." he started to protest and then suddenly pokered up.

If Joss had to guess, she'd bet he took it to give to Lauren, but that mattered less right now than getting Puck water. "Don't the two of you have any extra? Especially since we have Moody's supplies?" she addressed the camera operators.

"We... uh... we drank it this afternoon while you two were off exploring."

"All of it?" Even she knew that was a bonehead move before Shep had warned them not to gorge on Buffalo's supplies.

Four pairs of eyes avoiding her gaze was all the answer Joss needed. "If you wanted to be stupid, that's the choice the four of you made," she snapped. "But we're talking about an innocent animal here."

"Dogs drink out of toilets all the time. Just get him to the river, and he can have his fill," Lauren said with a casual wave of her hand.

"I don't let Puck drink from non-potable sources," Shep said. "Dogs can contract Leptospirosis that way."

"Don't you have something in your magic pack to purify water?" Bradley asked Shep.

"It takes at least thirty minutes until water treated with purification tablets is drinkable. Puck needs water now."

"Lighten up, dude," the younger camera operator said. "He's just a fucking dog."

That idiot. Puck was anything but just a fucking dog. Joss shrugged off her guitar and slipped out of her own pack. She rummaged through it until she found the half-full bladder. She looked up at Shep. "Do you have his bowl?"

"Where the hell did you get that?" Lauren demanded.

Joss ignored her.

At least she did until the taller woman charged over and tried to wrestle the container from Joss's hold. "Hand that over, you little cheat." Lauren tugged so hard that Joss was afraid she would damage the bladder and spill the water.

No. Ma'am. Not gonna happen.

Joss let go of the bladder with one hand, curled it into a

fist, and whacked Lauren with a hammer smack to the cheekbone.

With a satisfying squeal, Lauren released the water and fell on her ass in the dirt. "You hit me."

"Good. You *were* paying attention." Joss motioned to Shep for Puck's collapsible silicone water bowl. Carefully, she filled it just shy of the rim and passed it back to him.

"As soon as we get back to civilization," Lauren held a palm to her reddening cheek, "I'm filing a lawsuit against you for assault."

"Go for it." Joss twisted the cap back on the bladder, making sure it was tight, before stowing it in her bag. She'd sleep on the damn thing tonight if that was what it took to keep Lauren away from it. Not so long ago, Joss had believed she was mess of cracks and shattered pieces, but she was beginning to believe what she'd told Shep earlier. Maybe she was unbreakable.

If all the things she'd been through before now hadn't crushed her, that meant something. She'd been rejected, told she couldn't sing, told girls couldn't be the front man for a rock band. She'd had beer bottles thrown at her, received hate mail, endured more than her share of death threats. Especially after the accident.

He guarded Puck while he drank his fill of the water. After, Shep strode back over to the group. "It's time for the opportunity."

"Finally," Lauren sighed. "Let's get this over with so we can eat whatever food is left in Moody's bag."

Lauren was the delusional one, if she thought that was happening.

"The opportunity has two parts," Shep said. "First, you'll build a stable shelter."

"That's not fair," Lauren protested. "Joss built her own shelter last night. She already knows how to do it."

"I guess luck favors the fortunate, doesn't it?" Joss said.

"What exactly does stable mean?" Bradley asked.

Shep swiped a hand over his forehead as if trying to wipe away a massive headache. "Puck has to be able to crawl into it without the whole thing collapsing."

"And the second part of the opportunity?"

"Find and bring back to camp potable liquid." Shep glanced down at the rugged watch he wore. "You have exactly ninety minutes from... now."

"But...but..." Lauren sputtered. "Aren't you going to give us more information? More guidance?"

"The show is called *Do or Die*," he said without an ounce of inflection. "And right now, when it comes to you, I really don't care which option you choose."

And Joss couldn't stand around listening to the two of them if she planned to win this opportunity. She knew how to build her shelter, but the water might be more of a challenge. Which to do first?

"Do we have to do the tasks in order?" she asked Shep.

"My one piece of advice to all of you is to complete the task you think will take the longest first."

"Let's go, Bradley." Lauren threaded her arm through his. "We'll get water first since that won't be too hard."

They each took a water bottle and headed east, tramping into the trees with the young camera operator trailing them.

Joss took a few minutes to dissect Shep's instructions. She knew what it took to build the shelter, which encouraged her to jump in and construct hers. Maybe that meant it would take her longer to find water. She couldn't just find a creek or stagnant water source because Shep said potable. Then where?

"Can I use Puck's water bowl?" she asked him. "I want to take it into the woods with me."

With a tiny smile, Shep handed it over. "Are you sure?"

"Yes."

"If you need shade, find the type of tree you tied Puck to earlier."

Shade? It would get dark soon. Why would she need...

Water. Shep had said *potable liquid,* not water.

Greg followed her out of camp, and it didn't take Joss long to find a maple. Her attempt at tapping in to get... maple juice??...wasn't pretty, but she used her multi-tool to drive through the bark and into the tree's flesh. Not much liquid sluggishly dripped out into her bowl. It sure wouldn't keep anyone from succumbing to dehydration, but Shep hadn't mandated quantity.

When she jogged back to the meadow, Greg was still filming her. Fine by Joss because she was grinning at her success. She sought out Shep, sitting cross-legged with his eyes closed in front of his compact tent. Three deep breaths that expanded and contracted his broad chest, and he opened his eyes.

Joss held out the bowl. "You asked for potable liquid, but you didn't say how much. I hope this is enough. I got this from a maple tree."

"Quantity isn't important for the opportunity." He eyed the few drops she'd coaxed from the tree. "You do realize you could've just given me the bladder, right?"

"That would've been cheating."

"Not based on what I asked for, but thanks for playing a fair game. Good work. You're currently in first place."

Yay, her! Hopefully, Lauren and Bradley were still out there trying to find the river.

Joss had branches for her shelter gathered and the

support poles in place when Bradley and Lauren came crashing back into camp. "We have water," Lauren called out.

"You each need your own," Shep told her. "No sharing."

"Here's mine." Lauren thrust a filled water bottle toward Shep. "Bradley has one, too."

Shep brought the water close to his face and sniffed. "I said potable."

"It's from the river, which last time I checked, runs constantly."

"It's not potable as is."

She kicked a rock toward him, but it just hit the toe of his hiking boot and rolled away. "You are impossible."

"No. Those are the rules."

"If we boil it, will it be considered potable?"

"You tell me," Shep said.

"You're a real dick, you know that?" Lauren stomped over to Bradley. "I guess we'll have to boil it." That was when she must've realized that Joss was making solid progress on her shelter. "The river is quite a distance from here. You might want to get your hustle on."

"I don't need river water." Joss continued to lay branches to cover her debris shelter. "I already gave Shep something potable."

"You poured water from your stash!" Lauren accused.

"No, I found it fair and square."

"You could be lying. It was just the two of you here in camp. And with the way he looks at you, he'd probably let you turn in a cup of pee."

No reason to continue engaging in a conversation that wasn't helping Joss with her shelter, so she turned away from Lauren and began crisscrossing branches over her shelter frame.

"He probably helped you with that, too," Lauren accused.

Joss didn't bother looking away from her work. "Nope. But if you want proof, Greg has been filming the entire time."

"For all I know," Lauren's volume climbed. "You could be blowing him, too."

My God, Joss thought she'd met the sharpest clawed cats in the entertainment industry. But Lauren's were honed to a fine point and dipped in poison. Shaking her head as if to shoo off an annoying fly, Joss ignored Lauren and trekked into the woods to gather leaves for her shelter roof and mattress. When she returned, one of her support poles was at the wrong angle, compromising an entire side of her shelter.

Lauren's handiwork, no doubt. But Joss simply moved the limb back to its proper place. Then she finished off her roof, covering every hole. It might not be completely rain-proof, but she was proud of it.

She'd even made it big enough to slide her belongings in beside her. And since Lauren and Bradley were both still trying to build structures that didn't collapse like a house of cards, Joss took the time to move her pack and Fiona inside her new home.

One last look at her handiwork and she raised her hand and waved at Shep. "My shelter is finished."

He strolled over and gave it the once-over, his face not revealing a single thought. After a thorough visual study, he called for Puck to stand beside him. Then he rolled a ball into Joss's structure and said, "Puck, retrieve."

Puck, tongue lolling and tail wagging, took off like a golden-red freight train in the direction of Joss's shelter. Oh. Oh, no.

"Check it out," Bradley called out. "The dog is about to decimate Joss's shelter."

Yeah, she was having terrifying visions of the three little pigs. But it wasn't going to take a single huff or puff. Just a swish of Puck's tail.

Unbelievably, the dog raced to the entrance, then dropped to his belly. That was great, but his tail was still wagging like mad. As he army-crawled into her shelter, his tail took a swipe at both support poles.

Joss held her breath, just waiting for a full collapse. But her poles held strong.

Whew.

Then it occurred to her that once Puck retrieved the ball, he had to make his way back out. He probably weighed seventy pounds, and if he bumped anything when he turned around in there...

Please, please, please.

Incredibly, he exited the way he'd entered, but in reverse. He must've been very proud of himself because his tail was even more active. *Whap, whap, whap.* One support pole leaned a little, making the roof shimmy.

But the shelter stood its ground, and that was all that mattered.

"Here, Puck," Shep called to him.

"Well, I'll be damned," Bradley muttered.

"Joss wins the third opportunity," Shep stated.

"That's... You can't..." Lauren sputtered. "That's not fair because she had practice last night!"

"Lauren, the show is called *Do or Die* for a reason. You have to *do* something if you want to win." A wide smile spread over Bradley's face and he said, "Good job, Joss. Congratulations."

12

SINCE LAUREN WASN'T REQUIRED TO FINISH BUILDING HER shelter after the opportunity was over, she sidled up to Zach and offered to share Moody's tent with him.

"Hey, what about me?" Bradley said, but by the laughter in his voice, Joss could tell he wasn't really interested in sharing his shelter.

Lauren pointed at his lopsided—but standing nonetheless—structure. "Seriously, you want me to sleep in *that*?"

"No, Lauren," he said. "I wasn't serious, but your answer just confirms that you're a self-serving bitch."

"If I don't take what I want in this world, no one's going to just hand it over. So you're damn right I look out for myself."

The humor swept off Bradley's face. "If you think you're going to commandeer what's left of Moody's food, you've lost your mind."

"Of course, I planned to share with you, Darling Bradley." She cut a sharp look in Joss's direction. No words needed there. If Joss wanted so much as a nibble, she was shit outta luck.

"Do you think Moody will disqualify us all when he finds out Shep gave us each a protein bar and that you helped yourself to his food?"

"It's called *Do or Die,* as you so nicely reminded me. If Moody has a problem with us eating his food and using his supplies, then he shouldn't have left it all for us to take. I consider this playing the game, and playing it well." She strode off toward the younger camera guy's tent and disappeared inside.

Afterward, camp was blissfully quiet for long enough for Joss to scoot inside her shelter and close her eyes. While she was drifting in a theta state, lyrics began to come to her. Tiny phantoms darting around one another, trying to find a space to become tangible. Touchable.

Wanting someone out there to belong to me and truly understand,

What drove my heart to beat and left a mark on me, a burning brand...

A shriek cut through Joss's beautiful creative fog. *No, no, no.* The Muse hadn't gifted her with a song in much too long. This one was still a ghost and didn't sound like any kind of rock anthem. More of a folksy ballad. But she'd take anything she could get right now.

"Someone help me!" Lauren yelled. "I burned myself on this stupid soup pot. I need medical attention."

And like tiny iridescent bubbles, Joss's lovely lyrics began to disappear.

"Where is that damn guide when we need him?" Lauren demanded, but Joss could hear the tears in her voice. She had truly hurt herself.

Joss didn't have more than a couple of Band-Aids in her pack, but she unzipped it and found them.

She was making her way out of her shelter when Shep came striding into camp, Puck trotting along at his side, and answered Lauren's question. "He's out looking for the asshole responsible for all you people." He stalked over to Lauren and stared down at her with his hands bracketing his hips. "What the hell have you done to yourself?"

"I touched the pot and—"

"You grabbed the handle without protection?"

"How was I supposed to know it was hot?"

"Because that's what happens to metal over an open flame."

"Like I often boil up some shitty canned soup over a bonfire in my backyard."

"Why would you..." He cut a look at Joss as if asking for her help, and she shook her head, telling him Lauren was being sarcastic. "Never mind. Let me get the first aid kit and see what I can do."

But when he crawled back out of his tent, his hands were empty, and he sat back on his heels and surveyed everyone in camp with disgust. "Taking Moody's crap is one thing, people. But I didn't think you would actually steal from me."

"What do you mean?" Lauren asked, true tears forming in her eyes as she held one hand with the other.

"The first aid kit is missing," Shep said flatly, "and one of you stole it."

After The Bitcher's meltdown, Shep had taken a much-needed break from the group and hiked out to the river to get water he could purify for Puck to drink, and he'd kept an eye out for any sign of Buffalo Moody. He damn well should've known he couldn't leave anything behind with that pack of hyenas. The camera operators wouldn't have stopped the thief, but they might've gotten it on film.

"Do you know how to boil water?" he snapped at Bradley.

"Fire, pot, water. Pretty simple."

"Then do it, so we have something to clean The Bi... Lauren's hand with." He passed the other man the water bottle he'd carried to the river. "Less than half a cup should be plenty to clean her burn. The rest I'll purify for Puck."

"I'm happy to boil it all."

Shep stared him down. If he did something stupid and Shep had to hike back to the river tonight, he'd take Bradley with him and hold his head under the water.

"Hey, man." Bradley lifted his hands and leaned back. "Whatever's putting that look of murder on your face, you need to stop thinking it. I'm just offering to deal with the water. No double-cross involved."

It would be fucking handy if Shep could tell if the guy's expression was sincere or not. So he turned to Joss. "Does he mean what he's saying?"

She strolled over and studied her competitor. "I think so."

"That the best you've got?" he demanded.

"It's not a science, you know."

"If it was, I could do it myself." He sighed and told Bradley, "Don't make me regret this."

Dismissing that situation as a done deal, Shep turned to the camera guys. "Which of you was filming while I was gone?"

"Why?"

"Because I want to see the footage. If none of you are willing to squeal on the supply thief, then I'll get the answer myself." He glanced over at Joss to find her frowning at him. Like *he'd* done something wrong? She was the one who wouldn't come forward and tell him who'd done it.

Unless *she* had taken his supplies.

"No one sees the clips until Buffalo does," Greg protested.

One in each hand, Shep drew the camera guys up by their T-shirt collars. "I'll remind you one last time that Moody is not here. I am. And that makes me the boss. If you don't show me what you taped, I will not think twice about taking your fancy equipment and smashing it with a rock. Then I will make you pick up every tiny piece, every sliver so you can pack it back out with you."

Zach shot a side-eye glance at Greg. "Man, he's not right. It's like he's mad. At least I think he is. But he doesn't look or sound mad. Like his tone of voice and body language don't match his actions and his words."

"I said exactly what I mean," Shep articulated clearly so they would understand. "I want to see anything you filmed since I walked out of this camp."

The older guy quickly reached for his camera. "I'll show you what I got, but I promise you, I didn't see anyone get close to your tent."

Shep hunkered down and watched the playback on the camera. Unfortunately, Greg was telling the truth. No one had approached Shep's tent. And no one could've snuck in undetected because the tent never moved. Not a single wiggle or wobble.

The lack of a clear target to blame sent a feeling up Shep's spine that he'd never felt before, as if his body knew something that his mind did not.

. . .

Enough with all the damn drama.

Joss was half tempted to drag her shelter into the trees and away from the group. Even away from Shep. Because it had been apparent he'd expected her to narc on someone and was disappointed when she hadn't.

Look, Devil Divine, I didn't see anything.

And Joss wanting to dodge drama was kind of humorous. Normally, she was the high maintenance one, but since her life had taken a sharp dogleg, she'd become calmer.

But between Moody's disappearance, the fawn she and Shep found earlier in the day, the thefts, and Lauren whining about the small burn on her hand, Joss wanted to shove her fists in her ears and find a place where she could be alone. Maybe the lyrics that had made a fleeting appearance earlier would return. Visit her like tiny inspiration fairies.

Please come back.

Shep strolled over and hunkered down beside her. "You hungry? I've got a few MREs—ready-to-eats."

Really? He'd obviously doubted her earlier, and his face was still a frown-fest.

"Why would you want to share with me when you think I'm covering up who stole the first aid kit?"

Shep's normal eye contact avoidance became a hyperactive game of beer pong played with his eyeballs.

That was it. She was hungry, thirsty, tired, and music-deprived. She could not take any more bullshit right now, not even Shep's.

Using both palms, she hit him square in each shoulder. Gravity failed him and he landed on his ass.

"You think I took your Band-Aids and Tylenol? Well, screw you, Shep Kingston." She snatched her pack from her shelter, not giving a damn that some of the roof leaves rained down on her. With her teeth set, she whipped open the zipper and dumped everything out on the ground. "Look through it all if you don't believe me. Crawl in my shelter and make sure I didn't bury anything under the leaves. Whatever you want. Because I want you to feel like a jackass when you don't find anything."

"I really think you need to eat," he said softly. "And yes, it did cross my mind that you might have taken the kit. I am sorry. I know you didn't. Why would you when you know I'd give you anything and everything out of it? You don't have to steal to take what's mine."

Joss's thumping heart stuttered. He was admitting that she only had to ask and he would do anything for her.

She began to slowly pick up her belongings and place them back in her bag. When she came across the Band-Aids, she said in a quiet voice, "I had my own."

"Let me apologize to you with food. It's nothing fancy, but it will be hot."

Did she have an appetite? She didn't even know. Before coming out here, food had been repulsive to her. Knowing that Chris, Winston, and Miguel would never eat again, she'd barely been able to force a few bites down her throat.

"They don't taste that great," Shep said. "But they're full of protein."

His simple, no-strings offer extinguished the last of Joss's anger and hurt feelings. "Maybe we could share one?"

"If we do, is this like a first date?" His smile was seriously like the sun rising from behind the lush green forest. A blessing. A benediction. A bounty of male beauty. "Or are you one of those women who wants a fancy dinner and dancing and all that?"

"I don't mind a nice restaurant." She held her hand up toward the sky, where the stars were winking like fireflies in a velvet-shrouded sky. "But it would be hard to beat this candlelight."

"Then come on over to my place." He took her hand and pulled her to her feet.

"Wait!" After the first aid kit incident, she didn't want to leave her things unattended, especially not her guitar. She grabbed Fiona and her pack.

Shep's beautiful smile turned into a grumpy-old-man scowl. "You're not planning to play that, are you?"

"I don't know. Maybe," she said, even though she knew it wasn't true. Even touching her guitar case caused her pain. But lyrics had come to her earlier. Maybe...maybe this time, she could actually unzip the case. Possibly touch Fiona's smooth Sitka spruce. Run her fingers over the strings. The thought made the breath stall out in her lungs.

Shep stared at her case much like he had eyed the camera guys earlier. A touch of loathing and a whole lot of suspicion. "Do whatever suits you."

Something in his tone continued that sentence with *because you will anyway.*

She started to place the case back in her lopsided little shelter, but her spine straightened, and she tightened her grip on the handle. Shep was silent as he led her to his tent where Puck was resting in front of—guarding—the entrance. Shep's scowl stayed firmly in place as he dumped the contents of a small silver package into a pot and lit the gas below it.

"What are we having?" she asked.

"Chicken and rice. Most of these ready-to-eats are soaked in some kind of disgusting sauce. Not the chicken and rice."

Joss flipped through the handful of packs peeking out of Shep's backpack. Chicken and rice, all of them. She'd noticed all his protein bars were the same flavor, too—uncured bacon and maple.

While he stirred the contents of the pot, she ran her fingers lightly over her guitar case. She'd felt the slick, cool fabric under her fingertips a million times, but now it seemed as foreign as a stranger's skin. She skimmed the zipper pull, found it cold and unforgiving, as if the metal could slice her to pieces.

She pulled back her hand and tucked it carefully into her lap.

Without talking, Shep scooped the food out into two collapsible bowls. But Joss desperately needed the distraction of a discussion right now, so she said, "You mentioned that your sister is a Scarlet Glitterati fan."

He grunted.

"Is that the older sister or the younger?" Joss didn't really want to talk about the band, but she did want to learn more about Shep's family.

"Riley is the baby," he said, handing her a bowl of steaming chicken and rice that smelled strangely tempting.

"So she's the youngest and then..."

"Can you ask the actual question you want the answer to? I rarely understand implied ones."

"Sorry. Will you tell me your siblings' names, the order they were born, and what they do for a living?"

"Mandrell Margaret Kingston is the oldest. She's the sheriff of Haywood county. She's very bossy, but my dad says it's because she cares so much about people. She is involved with Jayson Tucker."

The Jayson Tucker? "You mean Jayson Tucker, the quarterback who plays for the North Carolina pro team?"

"Yeah."

"Wow." Joss had met the huge handsome man when

Scarlett Glitterati played the halftime show at the championship game earlier this year. Before...

Don't think about the crash. Distract yourself with Jayson Tucker.

He was...well...wow. A North Carolina sheriff and one of the best quarterbacks of all time. Now that was an interesting combo.

"Then came Kristofferson Cash Kingston. He's a firefighter and paramedic. He also works with the local SWAT team. His high-school girlfriend, Dr. Emerson McKay, recently came back to Steele Ridge. They apparently have sex regularly."

Joss choked back a laugh. "Good for them?"

"It's not a booty call. He loves her." Shep blinked, as if he was thinking over that concept and not entirely understanding it. "She's a good doctor. She's part of the SWAT team, too. She and Cash are on what's called the TMT, or tactical medical team."

Well, so far, his family sounded like a crew of movers and shakers. "And who's next in line?"

"West Waylon Kingston. He's—"

"Wait a second." Something about his brothers' and sisters' names tickled at Joss's brain. Harris Sheppard. Mandrell Margaret. Kristofferson Cash. West Waylon. "What's Riley's middle name?"

"Riley."

"Then what's her first name?"

"Wynette."

Holy crap. He and his siblings were an homage to country music. "And your parents?"

"Ross and Sandy."

Okay, so maybe not the mom and dad.

"Do you want to know their dog's name, too?"

"Why not?"

"Nicksie."

Hm, that didn't seem to fit. Maybe his parents had run out of beloved country artists. "Who's the big country music fan?"

"My mom." His smile returned, and Joss realized she wanted to hug it close and tuck it into her pocket like a personal prize. "My dad finally put his foot down when it came to the dog."

"Nicksie..." Joss mentally rolled her eyes at herself. How could she have missed it? "Stevie Nicks?"

"Yep."

"I think I'm in love with your family already."

He tilted his head to one side and studied her. "That doesn't make any sense."

Yeah, not to her either. But for some reason, she was forming fond feelings for a family she'd never laid eyes on. "Tell me about Waylon."

"He goes by Way." Shep scooped up a bite of rice. Chewed and swallowed before continuing. "He used to be a Marine. Now, he makes custom bullets."

"That's a thing—like a real job?"

"Just as real as a rock star."

Touché. "And then there's Riley."

"She's been in Africa recently and is home on a visit. She has a boyfriend named Coen, and as a little girl everyone called her the Kingston Menace."

Joss chuckled. "I definitely want to meet her."

"Because she's your fan."

Normally, that would be the case. Joss loved nothing better than to be approached by a superfan. Her need for that admiration had been the driving force when she shuffled her band members off to a practice session without her.

She'd been looking to gather up all that adulation for herself. Looking for a way that she wouldn't have to share the stage, divvy up the limelight.

Afterward, she'd hidden from the world, and it had left a void of uncertainty inside of her. Because if she wasn't Joss Wynter, most lauded living female guitar player and rock star, who was she? If she couldn't hear the sound of screams for more, the light from thousands of cell phones, and hands clapping, what was the point of listening?

"Did you know that I was on the cover of *Rolling Stone* when I was twenty-one?"

"No."

"And that Scarlet Glitterati has had seven singles hit number one on the *Billboard* charts?"

"I told you I don't like the music," he said, tone matter-of-fact. "Why *would* I know that?"

The chicken and rice had become infinitely less appetizing and Joss held it out in front of her. "Can I give this to Puck?"

"No, he's already eaten." Shep's hand grazed hers as he took the bowl, and the connection zinged through Joss. "I'll finish it."

"I'm one of the most famous musicians in the world."

"Uh-huh," he mumbled around a bite of chicken and rice.

"But I haven't touched an instrument, sung a note, or written a lyric since my band…"

"Died."

"Yes."

"Do you want to talk about it?" The hesitation and reluctance in his voice told Joss it was a stretch for Shep to say such a thing. How could he offer true compassion when the public had been so unwilling?

"Not tonight." Because for the first time in so long, her palms itched with the need to hold her guitar. What if she took Fiona from the case and she burned Joss? Scorched her as punishment because she'd been indifferent to her music for so long.

But what she felt, what was ripping her up, wasn't indifference at all, was it? Shame and blame and bone-deep fear. Those were the monsters keeping her from her music.

Fear that she might be nothing without the others. Without the rest of Scarlet Glitterati. Blame because she'd put them on that helicopter. And shame because she'd been secretly angling for the opportunity to go solo. To leave them behind.

And now, being alone in the spotlight was the last thing in the world she craved.

13

JOSS WAS GAZING AT HER GUITAR CASE WITH SUCH AN expression of misery and hope that even Shep could see and recognize it. He had zero desire to hear her play, but it was as if she believed that instrument could save her life.

And what would he do if she were drowning in the river?

He'd throw her a PFD and jump in to save her.

His job, yes. But more than that, his moral duty. A good wilderness guide did not abandon his group when they were needy and hurting. "Open it," he said.

"What?" Her head came around, her eyes wide as she stared at him.

"If I can recognize how much you want to play what's in that case, then you want it bad."

"Wanting and being able to are two different things."

He reached out, took both her hands and turned them over in his. "Is there something wrong with your hands? Your fingers?"

She closed her eyes, but he thought he might've seen a lightning strike of pain in them before she did. "I've tried a hundred times."

"Have you really?" he asked. "Or have you sat there looking at it, all down in the mouth?"

That opened her eyes. "Down in the mouth?"

"My Granny Kingston used to say it. You know, moping, pouting, brooding. She always claimed that a swift kick in the ass was the best way to cure it." Although he hated it when other people touched his things without an invitation, he picked up Joss's case and balanced it across his thighs.

Joss's fingers clenched—maybe with the need to defend her belonging or maybe to smack him for handling it without permission.

Slowly, one tooth at a time, he began unzipping the case.

"Shep, don't."

"If I don't open it, will you?"

She simply stared at the place where his fingers were touching the zipper pull.

So Shep finished the job, unzipping it and folding back the top. He'd expected a pristine, glossy guitar. Fancy and fussy. But the instrument Joss was afraid to touch looked as if it had been through hell and back. The wood was scratched, and at some point, someone had taken a Sharpie marker to it, doodling designs that were no better than a toddler's. One of the tuning knobs was broken in half and another was held together by a slim strip of silver duct tape.

Dings and scratches marred the whole thing, but Joss was gazing at it as if it was her lover's body. A body she had been painfully denied and simply wanted to touch one more time.

Her face was filled with heartbreak and desire.

Good God, if this was what other people saw, how did they deal with it? If they could recognize all the emotions on others' faces, how did they have time to do anything *but* study faces? Especially those of the people they loved.

Because recognizing the sheer want in Joss's face was overwhelming to Shep, making his heart feel as if it was pounding everywhere in his body. Whipping him from worry to panic to lust. Beneath the guitar case, his dick hardened and throbbed. He wanted her to look at him the way she was staring at her instrument.

"She's not pretty, is she?" Joss finally said.

Pretty, no. But beautiful all the same. The guitar made him think of an old stuffed pig Riley had carried around until she was nine or ten. And of the story of the Velveteen Rabbit his dad used to read to them as kids.

The only things this shabby were those that were well loved.

"It's special to you."

Joss blinked at him.

"Because sometimes we mistreat the things we love the most," he said, understanding with a clarity that stunned him. "They take our casual abuse and stay for more."

"My grandfather gave it me." She reached out as if to touch the guitar, but her fingertips hovered an inch away from the wood. "He was a dreamer. He saw things, heard things others didn't. My mom tried to take it away from me because she resented her dad. Her family didn't get him, didn't understand why he couldn't be persuaded to go to an office from nine to five and bring home the same paycheck week after week. Instead, he played in the bars until two in the morning and painted when he woke up in the early afternoon. This was his guitar. His pride and joy."

Family members were supposed to love one another, Shep knew that. But in Joss's case, some of them had given and some had taken away. Which was real love?

Her smile, when it came, was deep and dreamy. "He gave it to me on my eleventh birthday, and I was never the same.

It was if he'd handed me a piece of my body that had been missing my entire life, only I'd never realized."

And now, she'd purposefully lopped off that piece.

"Less than a year later, he died." Her smile wavered and melted away. "Sometimes I've wondered if it's because he gave me Fiona."

"Who is Fiona?"

"My guitar."

She'd named an instrument? Then again, if she felt about Fiona the way he felt about Puck, that made total sense. "Your grandfather saw something in you."

"That's exactly what he used to say. 'Jojo, I see something in you. Something special—a sparkle, a sharpness. It's gonna take you further than your biggest dreams.'"

Jojo. Shep liked that. Made her seem more like a real-life woman and less like a big-name performer who stood on stage and sang for thousands. "Is he the only person who called you that instead of Joss?"

"I'm Jojo to the few people who really understand what music means to me. Joss Wynter is my stage name. My birth certificate says Jocelyn Mae Winterburn."

"Pretty." Almost as pretty as she was sitting there in her grungy pants and shirt, looking at her beat-up guitar as if it was the answer to all the world's problems. So Shep slid the case from his lap to hers.

Joss tried to scoot back, but he caught her wrist and looked into her eyes. That simple contact amazed him because sharing this intimacy with her didn't make his stomach hurt as it normally did. "You need to do this. It's always hardest the first time."

"I... I have the craziest feeling she hates me now."

Shep tried to think like his dad would in a situation like this. Ross Kingston had a lot of thoughts on relationships.

He always said people were puzzles, that they said things that misdirected, that weren't exactly what they meant. And in a relationship, it was the other person's job to figure out the puzzle, determine where the map really led.

Joss thought her guitar hated her. Which was clearly impossible since a musical instrument was inanimate. No soul, no ability to experience emotions.

She believed her guitar harbored bad feelings toward her, but she was actually projecting her own negative emotions onto her guitar. "Then do something to help her love you again. Show her how you feel about her."

Joss wiped her hands down the sides of her pants, and they were visibly shaking when she reached into the case. She probably had no idea that she let out a little sigh when her fingers closed around the guitar's neck.

It was a sound of relief. Of satisfaction. Of completion.

He shouldn't be having the kind of thought that sound drove through him, if Joss would sigh like that after an orgasm slid through her.

She lifted out the guitar and ran her hands over it lovingly. Sensuously.

Even if Shep could control his thoughts—and he was having a hell of a time wrangling them—he couldn't will away his erection. As long as Joss kept stroking her guitar like a lover, he would be aroused. He shifted around for comfort, but thankfully, Joss wasn't paying him a bit of attention.

Her fingertips brushed over the strings, barely creating a sound, but the vibration shimmered through the night and skimmed over Shep's skin. The pressure behind his zipper intensified until his cock was the only part of his body he could feel.

With a long exhale, Joss pushed the case aside and

settled the guitar fully in her lap and cradled it. She merely toyed with the strings for several minutes. From fear or pleasurable anticipation? But when the first note sang into the air, it was pure and clear.

Completely absorbed and within herself, Joss quickly tuned the guitar and began to pick out a melody. Something soft and secret. Haunting. Healing.

It was nothing like the sounds from the strident electric guitars she played on stage. It was almost as if Joss was talking to herself, reassuring herself. Becoming herself.

Joss Wynter wasn't at all the woman he'd thought she would be. And she was somehow making him want to understand how to love.

Joss was jerked painfully from sleep by a scream. Not an owie-I-burned-myself scream, but one of bone-deep fear and terror. Heart booming, she thrashed her arms and legs, trying to throw off whatever was wrapped around her, holding her down, suffocating her in the predawn haze. "Oh, God. I need out. I need out."

"Jojo, you are okay." Then she heard the three quick notes of a whippoorwill call. They continued in a musical circle until she stopped struggling.

Shep. She'd been with Shep last night outside his tent. Eating, talking, playing Fiona. She'd *played*. Not much, just plucked a few strings, but still.

Joss took a breath and tried to get her bearings. She was in a sleeping bag, and fighting against ripstop fabric and duck feathers wasn't doing anything for her. She shoved the whole thing down her legs and realized Shep was lying beside her. "Who screamed?" she asked him.

"Probably Lauren," he said without much concern, even

though Puck was standing and peering into the trees, his ears and the fur around his neck raised.

"That wasn't like her scream last night," Joss said and hurried to put on the shoes Shep must've slipped off her feet last night before tucking her into his sleeping bag.

"She's an actress."

But when Lauren stumbled into camp, Joss knew she wasn't acting. Her skin was paler than watered-down skim milk and tears were streaking her wild face. That she could've fabricated, but her nose was running as well, and Lauren wouldn't fake that. "He's—oh, God—he's just there. He's hanging. He's dead."

That brought everyone in camp to their feet, and Shep demanded, "Who? What are you talking about?"

"Buffalo Moody," Lauren sobbed out and wiped her nose on her shirtsleeve. "He's...he's dead. Someone hung him."

"Maybe you made a mistake. Could you have seen an animal strung up? Hunters do that to ward off predators."

"I know what I saw."

Shep coaxed sketchy directions from Lauren, then told everyone to stay in camp. Yeah, that didn't happen. They followed him into the woods.

Still unnerved by the authenticity of Lauren's screams, Joss stayed close by Shep's side. The trees seemed to lean together, conspiring with one another and sharing dark secrets. "Maybe...Do you think she saw something else and just imagined it was Moody?"

He grunted. "Don't know what to think since I haven't seen it yet."

They smelled death before they found it, a putrid sweetness Joss had never inhaled before. But she didn't have to have experience with the scent to know what it was. Her eyes watered, and she covered her mouth and nose with her palm.

"Everyone should stay here," Shep said. "Let me go on and see what's what."

While the others seemed grateful to hang back, Joss forged on behind Shep and Puck. They weaved through the trees and slipped into a tiny clearing.

It was still and quiet. It was horrible.

She'd thought she was prepared from the scent, but the sight of Buffalo Moody sent Joss to her knees. Try as she might to fight it off, her gag reflex engaged, her stomach convulsed, and she heaved.

"I told you not to come." Shep's tone was impatient and unsympathetic.

"Just give me a minute, and I'll be okay." Untruth. She would never be okay again. From the corner of her eye, she watched Shep stride up to the body, hanging about two feet off the ground. Moody's right foot—bare and bloated— swung back and forth like a gruesome pendulum. He was wearing only pants, and his torso and arms were also swollen.

Now that she was looking, Joss couldn't tear her gaze away. His face was so puffy and distended that it looked as if someone had blown him up like a helium balloon.

"He wasn't hung," Shep said.

Joss staggered to her feet and Puck leaned against her thighs, steadying her. "But he *is* hanging."

"That's not how he was killed." Shep stepped back as if to take in the entire grisly scene at once. "He hasn't been here long. If he had, there wouldn't be this much of him left. The animals—"

"Got it," she wheezed out, holding one hand out to ward off his words and pressing the other hard into her stomach. "Wh...what do we do now? Should we take him down or—"

"No, we need to call the authorities and let them handle this." Shep patted his pockets. "Damn. I left camp without the sat phone."

"Maybe I can run back and get it." Because the alternative was for her to sit here guarding Moody's body from predators, and she wasn't sure she could manage that without losing her mind.

"Go back to the others and have one of them bring it me. I'll stay here in the meantime."

"You said he wasn't hung. What do you think...How did he...What happened?"

"By the looks of it, Moody drowned. The river we camped not far from last night runs near here." He stepped even closer to the body, making Joss want to yank him away. Making her want to run and run and run. Shep pointed toward Moody's head. "If he'd been hung, we'd see broken capillaries in his face."

"I...I'll take your word for it."

"So how the hell he found himself strung up in this tree, I don't know." Shep studied the ground under the body then followed a shallow twin-grooved trail to the edge of the trees. He used a stick to drag out a bright orange PFD similar to the ones Joss and the others had worn in the raft. "Looks like someone used this to float the body down the river. It was dragged for a few feet here, but any other tracks that might've been made have been covered. Joss, once you get back to the group, stay there with two people, and send the other two back with the phone."

Everything inside Joss compelled her to do as he asked, to flee, but she didn't want to leave him here alone. "Why don't you come with me? After all, it's not like he's going to

—" Something erupted from her throat—a disturbing combination of laughter and a gasp—cutting off her words.

"I'll be fine," Shep said. "Take Puck and go now."

Relieved to turn her back on the horrific sight and smell, Joss grabbed Puck's leash, and they jogged back the way they'd hiked.

But the rest of their group was no longer waiting.

14

Something crashed through the trees toward Shep, and he braced to defend himself from threat—animal or man. But it was Joss, her brightly colored hair falling out of its ponytail and whipping around her face. Puck trotted along behind her, shooting worried looks up at her and then toward Shep.

"What's wrong?"

"They're gone," she puffed out. "The others."

"Are you sure you went back to the right place?"

"By the pine tree that looks like a broken finger."

"Did you call out for them?" he asked, although he wasn't sure which he preferred—that she had or hadn't.

"Yes, but nothing. No answer." She cut a quick glance at Moody's body, still hanging from the branch smelling like ten days of ass-ripe roadkill. "Do you think someone...He obviously didn't do this to himself. Do you think whoever did this hurt the rest of the group?"

It would take some real doing to snatch up four adults—three of them men who weighed over 170. "Any sign of a fight or struggle near the tree?"

"I... I don't think so."

Damn it all to hell and back. He'd known from the get-go that this *Do or Die* show was a circle jerk waiting to happen. But had Dan listened to him? No. No, he had not. And now the man would shit a llama when Shep called and told him this situation had become a full-on clusterfuckin' orgy.

No way would Shep send Joss back to camp alone to get the sat phone, which meant he either had to cut Moody down and drag him back with them or leave him here. Shep didn't like either option. But when it came down to the safety of the dead or the safety of the living, there was no question.

Moody would just have to wait.

Shep turned back to the man's body and spent several minutes studying everything about it.

"What are you doing?" Joss asked him.

"Trying to remember everything I can."

"Because..."

"Because we have to leave him here and get back to camp for the phone. He won't look like this the next time we see him." He turned to see Joss shudder and wrap her arms around her torso.

Oh, hell. She was probably scared and freaked out. This was way more than she'd signed on for. And he was standing around subjecting her to a dead body.

He hurried away from Moody and touched Joss lightly on the arm. "I'm sorry. You shouldn't have had to see this." God, between the fawn and Moody, she'd seen more death in the past twenty-four hours than...

No, she'd seen death before. And if the news reports had been accurate, she'd seen it up close and personal. Her band went down less than a mile from where they took off, and the tabloids had run pictures of Joss's car racing to the scene. Of her kneeling amid the burning wreckage, her face buried in her hands.

In response to his touch, she turned into him and burrowed against him, so close that it felt as if she wanted to open a door into his chest and walk inside him. "I'm scared."

Shep carefully enfolded her in his arms, tested it out to see how the tender hold felt to him. Not bad. In fact, verging on good.

And the closer she pressed, the better it felt.

"I'm here," he said. "Puck's here. And we would never leave you. As of this second, I'm not letting you out of my sight. Not until we get down off this mountain."

She looked up at him, her eyes watery. "You promise?"

"Cross my heart and—"

"Don't say that."

"Jojo, I'm a trained survivalist. So when I tell you that I will make sure you survive, you can believe it." He kept his arm around her shoulders as he led her away from the scene. He hadn't liked Moody worth a damn, but he wouldn't have wished this—whatever *this* actually was—on anyone.

But what concerned him more was *who* would've killed the man. There wasn't a lot of love lost between the show's host and several others in their group. Moody had seemed to get along with Greg okay. But he'd jumped the younger camera guy's shit several times. Bradley seemed disdainful of Moody. And the host and The Bitcher had been playing at some sort of love-hate relationship.

Everyone had left camp at some point over the past couple of days, giving them opportunity.

The only one Shep didn't suspect was Joss. Whoever had

strung up Moody had done it this morning, and Joss had been sleeping next to Shep all night.

But The Bitcher had been out and about this morning. Shep hadn't smelled death on her. But she was smart. What his brother Way would call cunning. Could she have devised some type of pulley to hoist Moody up in that tree?

"We need to start back," he said to Joss.

She straightened her shoulders and took a deep breath, but she stayed beneath his arm as they hiked back toward camp. "I thought he left the group to screw with us."

"So did I."

"He wasn't a very nice man."

"He was a dick."

Joss's laughter was combined with a snuffling sob as she gestured vaguely in the direction behind them. "But no one deserves that."

"As soon as I get a call in to my sister Maggie, she'll have people up here. She's the best at what she does. She'll figure this out."

"This means the show is over."

"I know you wanted to win."

Joss stumbled, and he tightened his grip around her shoulders. "It sounds horrible and shallow now," she whispered.

"Moving forward is never horrible and shallow. You were doing this for a reason."

"Then is it horrible and shallow that I hate that our time together is almost over?"

Fuck. He hadn't given that a single thought.

He'd call Maggie, help would come, and he and Joss would return to Steele Ridge. Then she would leave. Because the show was the only reason she was anywhere near North Carolina. Anywhere near him.

He tightened his hold on her shoulders until she squeaked. Immediately, he dropped his arm.

"What's wrong?" she asked, stepping in front of him. It was either stop, go around, or plow her down. Shep stopped.

"We need to get back to camp," he said, his voice gruff because his throat was tight. "And we'll take it from there."

"What does *take it from there* mean?" She moved in and rested her head on his chest, making Shep's heart pump double-time. "Once we get back to Steele Ridge, the police are going to have a lot of questions, right?"

"Yeah."

"Then it will be impossible for me to get back on a plane to LA right away. I'll need to stay in town."

The tightness in Shep's gut eased a little. "For how long?" Hopefully for long enough for that sex they both wanted to have. "You could stay..." He didn't want to freak her out. "...with my parents."

No, no. That sucked. If she was in his parents' house, it might be hard to have sex.

"Or at the B and B in town," he hurried to say, trying like hell to keep from reaching for his paracord to bolster his courage. "Or with me."

She smiled up at him. "Then taking it from there means I'll stay with you for a few days."

"How many days?" He needed to know. Exactly.

"Is three too many?"

No, he wanted to tell her as he wrapped her in his arms, three was far too few.

To Joss, the walk back to their campsite seemed to take years. The forest and animal calls that had once sounded friendly now surrounded her, pressed in on her. This wasn't some sweet nature show. It really had turned into Do or Die.

She reached for Shep's hand and held it tightly. He didn't pull away, so the pressure must've been okay.

Every couple of minutes, Puck let out a low whine, as if he intuitively understood that things were not right in the world. Shep laid a hand on his dog's head and the retriever calmed.

Silently, so silently a whisper would've sounded like a shout, a man stepped onto the trail in front of them. His clothes were made from multiple raccoon tails strung together that hung from around his neck and waist. When he spoke, his voice was rusty and low. "You are not welcome here."

Shep dragged Joss behind him, but she peeked around. The other man stood, feet spread, arms wide, and chin up.

Shep said, "We're just heading back to our campsite. We don't want any trouble."

"You are on the land of Juney Whank. You are trespassing on the graves of my ancestors and her children."

"No," Shep said calmly. "This is the Nantahala National Forest. Public land, public access."

"Your government may have laid claim to this ground, but in the eyes of the Sacred Mother, it is mine."

Wow. Was this guy for real? He honestly believed that he and his mother had some type of ownership of this land.

"Well," Shep said, "you can tell the Sacred Mother that we're just passing through and will be on our way."

"The Sacred Mother demands payment."

Joss coughed to cover her nervous chuckle. She'd never once been mugged in LA, and now they were being shaken down in the boonies of North Carolina. The universe officially made no sense.

"If you're looking for money," Shep told him, "you're hitting up the wrong guy. I don't bring my wallet when I'm leading a group."

"Your paper money means nothing to me."

Him or the Sacred Mother?

"The Sacred Mother requires a sacrifice."

Alarm skittered through Joss. After seeing Moody's body, the word *sacrifice* wasn't something she wanted to get up close and personal with. It made her think of hooded robes, stone tables, and ritual knives.

"Not from us, she doesn't," Shep pulled Joss and Puck around to circumnavigate the man, but he was quick and cut them off.

His eyes shining like bright black marbles, the raccoon guy said, "I will take your animal as payment."

"Not in a million years." Although Shep's words were delivered in a casually matter-of-fact way, his body was one long line of tension.

"Then I will take your woman." He reached for Joss's arm, and his nails and knuckles were crusted with dirt.

Shep knocked the raccoon man's hand out of the way and angled his body so that he would have to go through over six feet of muscle before getting to Joss. "Mister, I don't know what mushrooms you've been making tea out of, but I am not handing over my dog or my...woman. The answer is no. Now get the hell out of my way or—"

"But the Sacred Mother—"

"I get it. You care about your mother," Shep cut in. "I feel strongly about mine as well. But you'll just have to find something else to—"

The man leaned forward, sniffed Shep from abdomen to throat, as high as the shorter man's nose could reach. "You smell of death. Have you come from the underworld?"

Sacrifice. It reverberated through her again.

Could he *actually* mean the sacrifice of a life? If so, maybe he'd come across Buffalo and decided he had to be killed for tromping around on sacred ground.

Shep placed his palm against the man's sternum and pushed him back several paces. "You need to get out of our way. If you don't, the Sacred Mother will be very displeased."

"How could you know of the Sacred Mother's wishes and pleasures?"

"She and I are on speaking terms." Shep drew his shoulders back, making him look twice the size of the other man. "Now, move aside or I will knock you down and walk over your body. Your decision. I am okay with either."

Raccoon Man took a grudging step aside, and Shep strode past him, dragging Joss and Puck with him. They were half a dozen paces beyond the man when he called out, "The trespassers who would foul the Sacred Mother's earth will pay with their lives."

Joss plastered herself against Shep's side. For most of her life, she'd been confident and self-assured. She'd had to be to make it as a musician.

But being out here made her realize that her self-concept was purely situational. She wasn't anything against nature. And apparently nothing against a man who might want to hurt them.

"Do you think he's truly dangerous?" she asked Shep.

"You're wondering if he's the one who killed Moody."

"It crossed my mind."

"He's part of a group who think they're the offspring of the Juney Whank Falls."

"So this Juney Whank is the Sacred Mother?"

"That's the even nuttier thing. Juney Whank wasn't a

mother at all. He was a guy named Junalaska Whank. But this group of people are convinced the falls gave birth to them. They live out here, claiming they've taken back their land from the US government. I've come across them from time to time."

"You've met this guy before?"

"Not him specifically, but others like him. They're big on talk, but I've never had any real trouble from them." That might be the case, but Joss didn't miss the fact that they were hiking so fast that she might have to break into a jog any second.

When it came to trouble from Mama/Papa Juney Whank and her/his acolytes, there was always a first time for everything. "So you're saying you don't think he had anything to do with Moody's…"

"Murder," Shep said flatly. "Moody didn't hang himself," Shep said. "Which means someone else put him in that tree. My bet is on the person who drowned him."

"Is it weak of me to say I'm scared?"

"No," Shep's voice gentled. "It means you are smart enough to respect danger. That is never weak. But don't worry. Once we get back to camp, I will contact my sister Maggie and let her know what's going on."

"And she'll come get us? How quickly could she be here?"

"Most areas can only be accessed on foot. That's one reason it's smart to respect the forest, the mountains. But there are a couple of places to land a helicopter—"

"No." Joss's feet stopped moving. "No helicopter."

"It's the fastest way out."

"I don't care," she said. "'I'll walk a million miles if I have to. If you want to fly out on one, that's fine. Just tell me how to get back to Steele Ridge and—"

He grabbed her arm, gave her a little shake. "Stop. I would never leave you alone out here, so stop being stupid."

Her breath began to hitch, and before Joss could control it, she was hiccupping through a tsunami of tears.

"Jojo. Shit. Don't... I'm sorry. I'm sorry I called you stupid. You're not stupid. You're very smart. Let's just get back to camp, and everything will be okay. I promise."

Dumbass.

Shep felt about like he had when he was still enrolled in elementary school and kids had called him names because he was different. *Window licker. Brain dead. Fucktard.*

He'd heard them all. And back then, they'd made him feel small, isolated, unloved.

But this time, he'd done it to Joss. Of course she didn't want to fly out of here in the helicopter. And he'd called her stupid.

His stomach was sick with the knowledge that he'd hurt her. Reduced her fear to a single word that wasn't true. And now—on a day when everything had already been an award-winning shit show—he'd made it worse. Made everything feel off-balance and fragmented.

He needed to fix the jumbled, jagged pattern of events happening around here.

Moody disappearing.

The first aid kit disappearing.

The fawn carcass.

The Moody carcass.

Something was at play here. Something Shep couldn't put his finger on. He hadn't lied when he told Joss he didn't think the kook back there on the trail had anything to do with Moody's death. But something definitely wasn't right.

Details kept zooming on a speed track in Shep's head, but rather than staying in their own lanes, they were crashing into each other like bumper cars.

It's okay. You don't have to fix this by yourself.

Maggie would help figure what was going on and bring order back to the trees and mountains Shep loved.

But when he, Joss, and Puck made it back to camp, Shep came to a complete standstill. He looked around, slowly taking in the entire scene.

Almost everything was gone. The camera guys' tents, Moody's tent and supplies. Lauren's and Bradley's packs. The flattened areas of grass were the only hint that the camp had ever held more than two people.

Shep's small tent was still standing, but by the way the front flap was fluttering in the breeze, it was obvious someone had been inside.

"Where *are* they?" Joss asked him.

Well, since no kidnapper would take the time to snatch four people and all their shit, he was fairly certain the others had hightailed it back here and fled.

Fuckers.

"They packed up and left."

"What do you mean left?"

They hadn't taken Joss's guitar case. Probably didn't figure a musical instrument would help them in any way. "They either started hiking down or they—"

A sick realization hit Shep. He dropped Puck's leash and Joss's hand and lunged for his tent. He dived inside, and sure enough, his pack looked like a band of drunk raccoons had thrown a party in it.

The Bitcher, The Bleeding Heart, and the camera guys—now collectively known as The Shitheads—had been nice enough to leave his water container, but it was empty. The water purification tablets, his remaining protein bars, and the burner and MREs were missing.

But shittiest of all, the sat phone was gone. He and Joss now had no food, no water, and no way to contact the outside world.

15

"Shep?" Joss called from outside the tent. "What's wrong?"

Pretty much everything. Which was the dead last thing he wanted to tell her.

But lying wasn't in his lexicon, and besides, he didn't have the extensive amount of energy that it always took for him to manufacture and deliver social lies. He stuck his head out the flap to find her sitting on the ground with Puck on one side of her and her guitar case on the other as if they were protecting her.

"They were inside your tent, weren't they?" she asked, but looked away from him as if avoiding a straight answer.

"Yeah."

"So no one snatched them after all. Those assholes left us up here with a dead Moody. At least we can still call and..."

Shep squatted down beside her and let his eyes close. For once, he didn't relish the idea of telling the truth, either.

"What?" she asked. "What aren't you saying?"

The feel of her palms pressing on either side of his face

produced a painful pleasure. Shep opened his eyes to find her nose to nose with him. Her eyes were a kaleidoscope of pewter and smoke with a thread of slate blue. If he looked into them long enough, he might be sucked in, whirled around, and kicked back out.

"Shep! You're scaring me."

Scared females were not something he liked. He'd learned that when Riley was eight, and he left a southern devil scorpion on her pillow. He'd thought she would appreciate the natural beauty of the *Vaejovis carolinianus*. Instead, she'd screamed her head off when she woke to find it staring directly at her with its stinger raised.

"They took what was left of my water and food."

"Okay," she murmured, backing off and releasing her grip on his face.

He wanted to ask her to squeeze him again, but knew that would seem weird.

"You showed me how to find water. And we can do without food for a little while, right? Wait!" Her mouth screwed up into the cruelest expression Shep had ever seen on her. "Did they take Puck's food, too? If they did, I swear I will hunt every last one of them down and make them eat dog food for the rest of their lives. And not that good tender cuts stuff, but the cheapest dry bag food with all sorts of crappy fillers in it."

"They left the dog food." He quickly reassured her.

"Thank God. But they're still shitholes."

"Heads," he said. "I'm now thinking of them as a whole —The Shitheads." Unfortunately, she didn't yet know how shitty they were. "That's not the worst of it," he said. "They stole the satellite phone."

She jumped to her feet and paced a circle around Puck. He watched her, turning his head right, then left, then bending it back, trying to track her progress. "Okay," she said, half to herself. "Maybe they called for help, right? They can't be too far away. If we just pack up and head back down the trail, surely we can catch them."

It was possible, but Shep didn't know that he wanted to travel with that pack of hyenas anymore. Moody's killer was still in question and they'd obviously thought so little of Joss's, Shep's, and Puck's lives that they'd stolen from them and left them behind.

"I don't think that's a good idea."

"Why not..." She whipped around to look at him and froze. "Are you saying that you think one of them did that to Buffalo Moody?"

"They ripped off our supplies and our only communication device."

"That's a long way from murder."

To Shep's mind, there was no scale on lying, cheating, and stealing. You were either a liar, a cheater, and a thief, or you weren't. "Do you really want to sleep beside people who are capable of swiping the items most critical to staying alive?"

She crouched down and cradled his face, this time more gently. But Shep found himself wanting to lean into it. "No," she said softly. "If they'd wanted to really take what's most likely to keep me alive, they would've taken you."

A feeling that was hard for Shep to identify seemed to fill his chest, inflating it to the point he thought it would burst. The sensation made it difficult for him to catch a breath, form a thought.

Joss touched her lips to his, but didn't give him time to do more than blink before she drew back.

"Because you, Shep Kingston," she continued, "are the most capable, most reliable man I've ever met in my life." A little smile started at the right corner of her mouth. "In fact, you would be the number one draft pick on my Zombie Apocalypse team."

"You don't really believe in zombies, do you?"

"It never hurts to be prepared." Her smile disappeared and she rocked back onto her butt, plopping onto the ground. "So what do we do now?" Before he could answer, she held out a hand. "No. Wait a minute. It's not fair for me to ask you to think for me. Give me a few minutes here."

Intrigued by her request, Shep ducked back inside his tent and set his pack to rights. Multi-tool and flashlight in the front pocket so they were accessible. Spare clothes stuffed into the bottom of the main compartment. He rolled up his thin mat and secured it to the pack with compression straps. Once he was done in here, he'd drop the tent and do the same with it. His remaining supplies back in their proper places, he crawled outside and leaned his pack against a rock.

Joss was staring across the small clearing to where the camera guys' tents had flattened the grass. She tapped her lips before speaking. "Okay, so an immediate evacuation is out for now since we have no way to get in touch with anyone in Steele Ridge. Which means we need to be prepared to handle a couple more days out here. You taught us that shelter and water were most important." She blinked. "Did they take your gas burner, too?"

"Yeah," he said. "They grabbed almost everything but my clothes and tent. And honestly, I'm surprised they didn't steal it."

Joss shook her head. "They didn't need it. Why carry more weight than you have to?"

She was really starting to understand. Gazing up at the sky, she said, "I'm figuring it's about one o'clock, right?"

Shep consulted his watch. "One-twenty-two."

With a satisfied nod, she said, "That gives us between five and six hours to hike."

"Don't forget that it's easiest to deal with water and shelter while it's still light out."

"True. So more like four hours. How far do you think we can make it in that time?"

"Well, we won't be taking the trail in the direction we hiked up, since that's the way The Shitheads probably went." Although the camera guys knew this trail made a circle, which meant they may have urged the group to continue on around. He and Joss needed a different option.

"There's another trail about five miles from here. We'll have to hike southeast to pick it up and then it winds back and forth across the mountain some." If it were just him, Shep would consider ditching the trail altogether and walking straight down the mountain. Not with Joss. She might be getting the hang of all this, but she was still a soft city girl in many ways. An extra day on the mountain wouldn't make or break them. Besides, if the other group showed up in Steele Ridge without Shep and Joss, Maggie would come looking for them pronto.

After she chewed on some asses.

The thought of their ragged asses made him happy.

"Will you be okay to walk a little before we get water?" he asked. "I figure Puck can probably go another hour."

Joss's smile was fierce as she hopped to her feet, picked up her guitar, and held out a hand to Shep. "Whatever Puck can do, I can do."

They made it to the other trail in under two hours, even

though they were trudging through what seemed to Joss like a haunted forest.

Shep approached a big maple and used his multi-tool to tap it. The sap definitely didn't flow like water from a spigot, as Joss well knew. But Shep stood patiently, filling Puck's water container.

"How did you learn all this nature and survival stuff?" she asked him.

He lifted a shoulder as he watched the liquid drip out. "Some from my dad. Some from reading. A lot from actually doing."

"What's the longest you've ever been out here by yourself?"

"About six weeks."

"Six? As in forty-two days and nights?" She couldn't imagine. "But you had plenty of supplies, right?"

"Actually, that was before I got Puck," he said. "So the trip was what you might call minimalist. Enough basic supplies to allow me to live off the land."

"As in gathering all your own food and water?"

"And making shelter."

"Why would you willingly do that when you probably had a perfectly usable tent?"

At that, he twisted to look at her. "Why did you really come on *Do or Die*?"

"Because my manager set it up to repair my reputation. To get back into the public's good graces. Because everyone loves a winner, right?"

Shep simply sat there as if waiting for the real reason.

"Because I don't know who I am anymore." Her words came out in a whisper. "I've been playing some weird popularity contest for the past decade, and I have no idea if that's what I want anymore."

"People like your music."

But did she? Did she like what she'd built? What she'd become?

She wasn't sure she had anything inside her that was truly worth other people's regard and respect. Because she wasn't sure she had anything inside her that *she* could respect.

She'd gone from playing music she loved in dive bars to superstardom and all it encompassed. She'd believed her own press, believed she *was* Scarlet Glitterati. What the hell did she need the guys for when she was the one everyone idolized?

She was no idol. Most days, she barely felt alive.

Until she'd come to North Carolina.

"I... I think I needed to figure out something."

"And have you?" Shep exchanged Puck's container for the bladder he'd given to Joss.

"I'm still working on it," she said, walking over and taking the container collecting liquid from the tree. "Let me hold this while you take care of Puck."

Puck poured maple sap water into Puck's collapsible bowl, and the dog lapped at the stuff that had come from the tree and looked up at Shep as if asking what he'd been served.

"It's all we've got right now," Shep told his dog. "So drink up."

Puck put his head back down and emptied his bowl. For some reason, that loosened the tight sickness that had been Joss's constant companion from the second she'd seen Moody hanging from that branch. "Puck will be okay, right?"

"Bradley wasn't wrong. Dogs do drink from toilets. They're pretty hardy. But it's still best if they have a clean water supply. As long as he'll drink this, he'll be fine." Shep capped the water container and eyeballed the one she was holding against the tree. "That'll do for now. Enough for us to get down the trail some and make camp. Let's get going."

Shep hadn't been kidding when he said this hike would be more challenging. Up to now, they'd either been gaining elevation or cutting across the mountain, so Joss hadn't realized just how hard hiking downhill was on the knees. The switchbacks they were forced to take helped, but this trek was still more challenging than the ones up the mountain.

But she wasn't about to complain. She was alive to feel pain, unlike Buffalo Moody. *Don't think about his feet, his face, the fear he must've felt.*

"We need to find you a little food before we make camp." Shep waved her off the trail into a small meadow. "There's usually some Queen Anne's lace—wild carrot—in this area."

Although she wanted to sit right there in the middle of the trail and let him hunt and gather, Joss just smiled. "I'm not even that hungry."

"You will be," he said. "And you need the fuel for a full day tomorrow."

And there was Puck. "Will he eat wild carrot?"

Shep smiled at her. "This dog is pretty much a canine garbage can. About the only thing we've found he won't eat is my mom's eggplant bread."

"Eggplant bread? I don't blame him. What about kale?"

"Yep."

"Avocado?"

"Loves it."

As horribly as it had started out, her day was taking a good turn. Shep and Puck simply made Joss happy. "How about lime?" she teased.

"Not his favorite, but he's been known to give it a taste."

"He's like an everything-a-vore."

"Means he's easy to please. Unlike some people."

Hopefully, he meant The Shitheads, because Joss would not be one of those people. Not tonight. Not ever again. "What are we looking for?"

"A plant with small white flowers in an umbrella shape with three-pronged bracts under the flowers. The leaves look like a fern or flat-leaf parsley and when you crush them, they smell a bit like carrots."

Determined to be the one who found dinner, Joss scanned the forest floor as they walked through the trees. There were plenty of leaves and what looked like briars with the summer berries long gone. "Parsley, parsley, parsley," she whispered under her breath.

Wait! Was that...

Little white flowers in the shape of bursting fireworks. Yes!

She rushed over and knelt down to yank it out of the ground. "I found it! I found dinner!"

Shep glanced her way. "Don't pull that."

"Excuse me?"

"It's poison hemlock. If we eat that, we'll both overproduce saliva, have convulsions, and possibly go into respiratory and renal failure."

Well, that was picturesque. This was harder than she'd imagined. Joss sighed and got back to her feet. "So when you came out here by yourself, you lived off the land?"

"Plants, nuts, and small game."

"Oh."

"You're against hunting, aren't you?"

"I...never really had to think about it. Hunting your own meat in LA means stopping by the butcher counter and asking for a special cut of steak." But she was curious about how Shep had hunted. "So you brought a gun with you?"

"No." He gave her such an offended look that Joss laughed.

"You're telling me you caught animals with your bare hands?"

"It's possible, of course," he said. "But no. I constructed a small trap. And I made a bow and arrow."

"Made. You just whipped up a bow and arrow out of thin air?"

"No." He snorted. "I made it from a hickory sapling and some string. I did bring a knife with me. I don't go anywhere without a knife."

"Even to the airport? I can't see you getting through security with something like that."

"I don't fly."

"What?" Was he scared, too? She stared at him, mouth open wide enough that some forest bug zoomed in and down her throat. She coughed until her eyes watered. When Shep gave her two hard pats to the back, she waved him off. Finally, she wheezed out, "I think I just got my protein for the day."

He grinned. "Bugs are definitely another food source."

Joss swallowed a dozen times, imagining she could still feel the insect lodged in her throat, little wings vibrating in hopes of a desperate escape. She popped herself in the chest with her fist. Gah—what had it been? A moth, a mosquito, a fly?

Fly. That was what had started this whole debacle. "You said you don't fly," she wheezed at Shep.

"Yep."

"Fear of flying?"

"Not really. I don't like crowded places. And airplanes

are crowded and stuffy and noisy. They're packed with people."

"So how do you travel?"

"Drive mostly," he said, turning to a plant that looked almost identical to the one she'd pointed out. "But I don't do it all that much, either."

"I can't even imagine." Extensive travel was a given in her profession. Planes, trains, tour buses, limos. She'd done it all except for space travel. What would it be like to live in a nice little town instead of constantly being rushed from one concert to another?

"We're pretty different." Shep's voice was low and Joss felt as if he was pulling away from her even though his body remained in the same place. "I like where I live. Plenty of space to be outside. My sister Riley goes all over the world for her research. Loves it. That's just not for me." With his fingertips, he rolled a couple of the plant leaves and held them out to her nose.

Hm. It did smell like carrot.

Joss looked closely at the plant Shep was gathering from, then spotted another a few feet away. She pointed it out to him and he nodded, so she began gathering the Queen Anne's lace. "You shouldn't apologize for living a life that you like. Do you have any idea how many people hate their lives? They have no idea until they wake up one morning and realize they're trapped in something they never really meant to get into in the first place."

"Has that ever happened to you?"

Yes, but she'd tried to go the opposite direction. Push away the doubts and double down. Become even more of what she was beginning to question. "I don't think I want to talk about this."

His brows lowered and mouth flat, he looked over at her.

"I'm sorry. I tend to push when I want to know something. I don't always understand boundaries. It's none of my business."

Now she'd hurt his feelings and made him feel uncertain. That was the last thing Joss wanted. She couldn't remember the last time she'd had an open and honest relationship with someone else. After all, she'd been lying to her band for months before she betrayed them.

Jerry was probably the one person she'd always been upfront with, but that was sad, considering she'd paid his salary.

Joss joined Shep and handed him the plants she'd gathered. "I didn't mean it that way," she said softly. "I...It's just that you're making me look at myself in ways that make me uncomfortable. You're asking me to say things aloud that I've never been able to."

"Forget I asked."

She placed a hand on his upper arm, remembered to grip instead of caress. "You didn't do anything wrong. Me, on the other hand, I've done plenty." She glanced up. The sun was starting to dip, which meant they needed to get going. "Do we have enough food for tonight?"

"Yeah." Shep brushed the dirt off the plants and carefully put them in his pack.

When they were back on the trail, they didn't restart the conversation, which gave Joss a little breathing room. Allowed her to enjoy once again the sound of bird calls and the breeze through the tree branches. Made the trees seem friendlier, less menacing than earlier in the day.

Shep did that, made her feel safe and centered.

He led her and Puck into a clearing covered in lush grass and ringed with flowers that ranged from the palest of yellows to majestic gold. It was stunning, the kind of place hiking tour companies might feature on their websites. The air was cool and untainted. Something about the way the trees ringed the area made it feel magical and protected, as if a spell had been cast to lure in travelers.

"This is gorgeous," she said. "Did you know this was here?"

Shep ducked his head and turned away, but not before Joss spotted a patch of pink high on his cheeks. "It's just a place to sleep, like any other."

No, it wasn't. It could've been a bridal bower. A place to celebrate, laugh, and love. Whether Shep would admit it or not, he'd stopped here for her. "Could I hug you?" she asked. "I could really use a hug right now."

"I guess."

The poor guy stood in the center of the clearing as if he was facing a firing squad, arms held awkwardly at his sides. Joss went to him and threaded her arms under his. Then she wrapped him in the tightest bear hug she could manage. When she couldn't hold it anymore, she quickly dropped her arms and backed away.

"That wasn't terrible," he said.

The only way to respond was with humor, so Joss grinned up at him. "I'm taking that as a compliment."

"My turn now," he said, and wrapped his arms around Joss. Not in a wrestling hold, but a sweet, gentle embrace that softened her heart. How had he understood exactly what she needed? "Relax. It's okay."

"You're sure?"

"Yeah."

It felt so good, so right, so natural to loop her arms around his waist and rest her head lightly against his chest. They were like a couple, like two people who cared for one another and wanted to comfort each other. Even Puck got in on the act by sitting next to them and leaning heavily against their legs.

"This is really, really nice," Joss whispered.

"Maybe The Shitheads did us a favor by taking off."

Maybe they had. And maybe she and Shep would find a way to make the most of it tonight.

16

SINCE THE SECOND JOSS PRESSED HER BODY AGAINST HIS, SHEP
had been aroused. But they had important things to do and
based on the way he'd asked intrusive questions earlier, he
doubted Joss was interested in his interest in her.

So he pitched the tent while she fed and watered Puck.
With a satisfied sigh, his dog circled three times, curled up,
and propped his chin on Joss's guitar case. Maybe he was
hoping she'd play again.

If Shep were being completely honest, which he was
99.6 percent of the time, he wanted her to play. And from
the expression on her face last night while she was intent on
her guitar, Joss needed to.

"Would you like a fire?" he asked her.

"It's not like we really have anything to cook." She
looked up and smiled. The day had been hard on her. Her
face was smudged, her skin was pale, and her eyes were
tired. She needed more than a hug. She needed someone to
take care of her, and not just by providing her with shelter,
water, and food.

"There's a waterfall not far from here," he blurted out. "With a small pool at the base. We could swim. It'll be a little cold, but we can make camp near there afterward. Have a fire."

"That would be wonderful." Her smile didn't look quite so tired now. Shep's chest felt unreasonably warm all the sudden, and he rubbed at it.

He scrounged up two small microfiber cloths The Shitheads hadn't taken to use as towels. Although he knew the way to the falls, he was careful to notice landmarks. The old sweet birch had lost a couple more limbs since the last time he was here, but it was still crooked at the top. He pointed it out to Joss. "One of the reasons you have to be careful when you hike away from the trail is because people actually tend to walk in circles when they get lost. Some people have a natural sense of direction, but most don't. Only those people who are very observant and know their landmarks will stay calm when they find themselves farther from the trail than they planned."

"Do you do that? Catalog landmarks?"

"Always," he said. "Less because I need them. I've always had a good sense of direction, but more because it forms a pattern."

"You like patterns. Like the patterns of the knots you tie? It seems to soothe you."

"Most people don't understand that about me."

"I think we already determined that I'm not most people."

Shep reached out for her, took her hand. He held it in a firm grip, but didn't feel the need to apply more pressure. This was just right. Joss was just right.

"Tell me about where we're going," she said.

"It's a small waterfall that most people never hike out to see. It's not one of the big ones like Linville Falls. It's also not near a more popular trail, so they don't bother with it. But it's pretty and quiet."

"Sounds perfect."

The sound of the waterfall hit Shep's ears before it was within view. A rhythmic rushing roar that canceled out other sounds around them. When they cleared the trees surrounding it, Joss said, "Wow."

The air was cool and moist. It blew with a clean freshness that could revive the most exhausted hiker.

"Set the supplies and Fiona over there." He pointed to a flat rock out of the direct trajectory of the water spray. "And please secure Puck's leash to that tulip tree. He would stay on his own, but I don't want to chance him getting too close to the edge and falling in."

While Joss clipped Puck to the tree and arranged their meager supplies, Shep scaled the rocks down to a spot where he could reach out and wet the cloths. He climbed back up to Joss. "You... uh... should wipe down before getting into the water. The less stuff we put into it, the better. No soap, but plain water should do the trick."

She took the rag and immediately scrubbed her face. "Oh God, that feels good."

"All over," he said. "If you want, I can go back down and you can toss the rag to me when you're finished."

"Are you asking me if I need my privacy?"

"That is the socially polite thing, isn't it?"

"In case you haven't noticed, we're not exactly in the middle of civilization. But if you'll feel more comfortable, feel free to turn your back."

"I would feel comfortable watching."

Joss swept out her hand in an expansive motion, indicating he could make himself comfortable. Shep sat and
adjusted his cargos because his dick was already getting
hard just from him thinking about Joss taking off her
clothes.

He held his breath as she unbuttoned her overshirt and
tossed it onto a rock, leaving her in a skimpy tank top. She wasn't
wearing a bra, didn't really need one. When she washed the
back of her neck and under her arms, the fabric pulled tight
across her breasts, clearly showing the erect state of her nipples.

He'd never really liked Amber's breasts. They'd made
him feel claustrophobic when she pressed them against his
face. Cash said that was probably because Amber was
stacked with boobs the size of the Rocky Mountains. "You
have small breasts."

Joss paused and looked down at him. "Yep. Want to
know the exact minuscule cup size?"

"That wasn't the right thing to say, was it?"

"It's the truth."

"But it's not flattering or romantic."

"I'm finding that I don't need flattery and romance from
you." Off came her hiking shoes. She unbuttoned and
unzipped her pants, then shimmied them down her legs
and kicked them off. She stood there, within touching
distance, in bright pink panties and that tank top.

She really was small all over—narrow hips, slim legs,
ankles he could easily circle with his fingers.

One by one, each muscle in Shep's body was tensing at
the visual stimulus in front of him. But maybe that was as
far as she planned to go. Although her remaining clothes
were probably sweaty, she could certainly choose to swim in
those.

Her choice, not his.

But then she reached for the hem of her shirt and stripped it over her head.

Shep went light-headed. *Breathe, dumbass, or you are going to pass out. That's definitely not romantic or sexy.*

If he tried, he could probably cover both her breasts with one hand. One pink-brown nipple would touch his palm and the other would rub against his middle finger. Even if he put his face against them, they wouldn't smother him. They were nice. Joss washed her torso, and her nipples pointed out even farther.

Shep's dick liked that. A lot.

If he'd thought his head was woozy when she took off her shirt, it was nothing compared to the vertigo he experienced when she pushed down her panties and stepped out of them. A tiny patch of dark hair triangled between her legs. "Your real hair color is brown," he said.

She laughed and flipped turquoise-tinted strands behind her left shoulder. "Did you expect the rug to match the curtains?"

"What?"

Joss patted her head. "Curtains." Then her pubic area. "Rug."

"Oh."

"I've done it in the past," she said as she continued washing, bending this way and that, making Shep so short of breath that he was forced to lie back on the ground. His heart was freight-training in his chest and little spots—turquoise ones—were bursting in his peripheral vision. "I dyed it pink once."

"Like cotton candy," he murmured. He wasn't a big fan of sweets, but something about spun sugar had always appealed to him. As a kid, he'd described it as sugar fur. Soft and sweet.

Would Joss taste like cotton candy?

Just as he'd never been much for having oral sex performed on him, he had never particularly enjoyed putting his mouth near that part of a woman's body. It reminded him of a rain forest—sort of hot and humid. An entire tropical ecosystem.

"You're thinking something funny," she said as she swiped at *her* ecosystem.

"A woman's vagina is… sort of a foreign environment."

"Like say the moon?"

"I was thinking more along the lines of the Monteverde Cloud Forest."

She snorted a laugh. "Who knew I had an entire jungle between my legs?" She finished with her washing and stood there with one hand on her hip, her other leg cocked just enough to give him a glimpse of what was behind her cotton candy. "You have the same dislikes when it comes to going down on girls?"

His face burned. Just lit up and flamed. Now he knew how other people felt when he said things that he thought were completely reasonable, but they thought were outrageous. "I think maybe I could learn to like it." At least with Joss.

"What flavors do you like?"

"Isn't there only one?"

"Oh, baby," Joss's tone was teasing. "I have worlds to open up to you."

"What kind of worlds?"

"The kind where licking a woman's pussy is like eating birthday cake."

"I like birthday cake, especially with buttercream frosting."

"It's a deal." Leaning toward him she held out her hand for... She grabbed his and gave it a hearty shake. "I'll serve it up and you try it once. If you don't like it, you never have to eat birthday cake again."

Joss standing there naked, his hand in hers, and the talk of her tasting like birthday cake had given Shep the stiffest hard-on he'd ever sported. "You might have to hold my hand when we climb down to the falls," he said.

"Why?"

"Because all the blood from my head has been rerouted to my penis."

She smiled. It was wide and possibly a little shrewd. "Your turn." She fanned out her shirt like a blanket and sat down, knees up and crossed. It was probably meant to be a modest pose, but Shep could still see her—

With a head shake, she said, "None of that until you show me yours."

Taking off his clothes wasn't that big of a deal to him. His body looked pretty much like all the other human bodies. Couple of legs, couple of arms, etc. He took off his boots and was careful to lay his socks over them to air out. Then he pulled his shirt over his head and smoothed it out on a rock. He followed Joss's lead, washing the areas that felt stickiest.

"Do you have any idea what you look like?" she asked him.

"Like a guy without his shoes and shirt on?"

"No, like over six feet of a delectable buffet, but just the appetizers. I'm waiting to see the main course and dessert."

Now, he *was* self-conscious. Once he took off his pants and underwear, there would be nothing between them. Full exposure. *Just do it.*

He hurriedly stood, unfastened his cargos, and shoved them off. He didn't look at Joss, just concentrated on finishing his wipe down.

"You are seriously the most delicious man I think I've ever seen," she said in a hushed tone Shep had heard in church a few times. One of awe and reverence, his dad had said. Although he wasn't quite sure how to take Joss's praise, his body was lapping it right up. "If I were a sculptor, I'd make a statue of your cock and call it The Perfect Penis."

That made him laugh. "You're teasing me."

"If I were a painter, I'd be like Picasso and paint a man with three of your penises." She tapped herself on the chin and looked up at the early evening sky. "I'd be rich because there would be a bidding war on that painting."

"You're already rich."

She batted her eyelashes at him. "It really would be a waste not to suck on it. Think you might reconsider?"

His dick jerked against his stomach. It had none of Shep's inhibitions. It might even lean more toward kinks than quirks.

"Not today," she said, "but when we get back to civilization."

"Maybe... I guess... Okay."

"Excellent," she said cheerfully and hopped to her feet. She grabbed his hand and dragged him toward the rock's edge. "Then let's get wet."

Joss made the comment with a smart-ass grin, but truth was, she was already plenty wet. The man was seriously beautiful, and she'd seen her share of rock stars and Hollywood celebrity bodies. But Shep's shoulders, chest, and killer abs were in another class. No glossy gym time for him. Those muscles had been sculpted through being outside and doing cool shit. And holy God, she'd never seen more beautiful inguinal creases than those carved to show off Shep's gloriously stiff cock.

Somehow, she and Shep helped each other climb down to the gorgeous little pool below the waterfall without falling on their heads or bruising anything that she planned to make use of.

Joss slipped into the water—the Arctic cold water—and yipped. Like a Pomeranian. A spoiled one accustomed to wearing a cashmere sweater.

Goose bumps domino-ed up from her toes to her scalp and she immediately crossed every appendage that hadn't frozen into immobility.

"Move around and it will help some," Shep said as he slid in without so much as a hiss.

Before she could commit to any movement, Joss needed to satisfy her curiosity about what the water had done to Shep's stupendous erection. Underwater, she skimmed her hand across him and found him still hard and pointing due north.

Now that was impressive.

And now she had to get warmed up. She started out treading water, but that didn't do enough to fight off the chill seeping into her bones, so she struck out and swam a few laps back and forth across the pool.

Six million more and her temperature might be back to a normal 98.6. She was on lap number twenty when she plowed into a rock. She surfaced to find the "rock" was actually Shep's ass. "Hey, you're in my way."

He swirled around in the water to face her and his grin took her breath more fiercely than the cold water had. When he did that, smiled like he really meant it, the world was simply a different place. A brighter, more bountiful place. "I know. I meant to. Do you want to see behind the waterfall?"

She looked at him from the corner of her eye. "How do I know you're not just trying to lure me back there to do something nefarious to me?"

"Is fucking nefarious?"

"Only if you do it right."

He grabbed her around the waist and strode—strode! Who could do that in water?—toward the waterfall. Out of self-preservation, she gripped his shoulders and wrapped her legs around his waist. It was either that or be dragged through the water.

With each of Shep's steps, his penis nudged her butt. Not entirely uncomfortable, but if the man was iffy about oral sex, he definitely wouldn't be into backdoor action. Joss did a little monkey shimmy and pulled herself up his torso.

She was considering kissing him—or maybe biting that amazing muscle on his shoulder—when water rained down on her. Sluicing into her mouth, surging up her nose, and almost slicing through her hold on Shep. When she was free from the deluge, she sputtered and sneezed. Very sexy.

No doubt she looked like a rat clinging to a piece of drift-wood. Granted, a very big, very solid piece of driftwood, but still.

Shep shook his head and his hair slicked back like he was a Calvin Klein model. She hated him—just a bit—right this second. "That wasn't very nice."

"What?"

"Almost drowning me."

"I told you I was going to show you behind the waterfall."

"Isn't there a side entry?"

"Yeah, but the shortest—"

"—distance between two points is a straight line."

"Exactly."

Oh, fuck hating him. She could love a man like this.

Love? No. She didn't deserve to feel that. Not with what she'd done to other men she cared for.

Joss put a chokehold around Shep's neck and dug her knees into his sides like he was a prize racehorse. And then she kissed him.

It was a savage mashing of lips and teeth. Wide open mouths and hot breath. Violent, just a few notches down from vicious.

But she knew Shep could take it. Would like it. Suddenly overcome by the stress of the day, the uncertainty of her career, and the loss of her music, Joss wanted to claw at him.

Let physicality and ferocity bruise away all her fear. Because if she was steeped in her body's pain, there was no room for hurt inside her heart.

Shep bracketed her hips and pushed her back, scooting her ass across a smooth shelf of rock. Still she clung and clawed.

But he was stronger and broke her hold on him. They stared at one another, their breaths coming in fast, mean gasps. "Jojo?"

She dropped her face into her hands, felt the hot leak of tears coat her palms and slip through her fingers.

"Jojo, are you okay?" Shep's tone held confusion. She didn't want to confuse him or tease him. "I didn't mean to scare you or hurt you."

She shuddered out a watery laugh. "You didn't. I... I'm the one who jumped you. I don't know what got into me. I've never kissed someone like that." She peeked out of her hands and spotted a trickle of blood at the corner of Shep's lips.

My God, what had she done?

In her desperate attempt to shove away her own pain, she had physically assaulted and wounded him.

Who *was* she?

No one she or anyone else wanted to idolize.

17

SHE WAS CRYING. SHEP DID NOT LIKE TEARS. THEY ALWAYS meant something, but he never knew what. Once, when he was seven, he'd given his mom a necklace he'd made from wild purslane, and she bawled. He'd immediately snatched up the gift and hidden it deep in his closet. He'd also hidden himself behind a collection of old coats.

The homemade present had made her unhappy and that had left an empty pit of anxiety where his stomach normally was.

It didn't take her long to find him even though he'd hunkered down like a frightened hermit crab. His mom took his hand and gently withdrew him from the tight dark space.

"Honey," she said, "it's okay."

"But you are crying!" She still wore tear tracks on her face, and that made him want to rock back and forth, bashing his head into the wall. "I hate Dad!"

"What?"

"He told me you would like it. The necklace. He was wrong."

Even though he was almost as tall as her, she'd drawn him into her lap. "No, Shep. He was exactly right."

"Then why are you crying?"

"Because I liked it so much that my happiness and love for you welled up inside me and spilled out. It was so much that I couldn't hold it all." She smoothed her hands over his head with a firm touch and he'd rocked in her embrace.

"I do not like tears. They make me feel..."

"Unsure?"

"Like Godzilla ripped my stomach out and ate it for breakfast."

She laughed, a sweet sound that never failed to soothe him, and he rested his head on her shoulder. "Baby boy, I love you so much. I don't think I can even tell you how much. You are special and smart and sensitive. Not everyone will understand that. And because of that, sometimes you will feel unsure. Scared even. But try not to run away. Running away makes you feel like you're someone else's prey. And Harris Sheppard Kingston, you will never be anyone's victim." That was when she'd given him a slim length of cord and suggested he see how many knots he could learn to tie within a week.

He'd been fashioning fifty different ones within two days.

But now, standing here watching Joss's shoulders shake and tears streak down her face, Shep didn't have his paracord. It was up on the rock inside his shorts. So beneath the cover of the water he was standing in, he manipulated his fingers and said to Joss, "You are not crying happy tears like my mom, are you?"

Hesitantly, she raised her hand and brushed her fingers across the corner of his mouth. When she drew back her hand, it was smeared with blood. "I hurt you."

He automatically licked his lips and tasted the coppery flavor of blood. It wasn't the first time in his life that he'd had a busted lip. "I am okay. I am not in pain. Please stop crying."

His request only made her cry harder.

Shep released his grip on her upper arms and waded back and forth in front of her. "I don't like this. It's not fun. I wanted to have fun."

He'd thought if he could show her that he was fun, that he could kiss her, and make her feel good, that she would like him. Really like him.

And he wanted that desperately.

"I thought I knew how to be with you," she said. "But when I kissed you, I attacked you. I was using you to work off my fear."

"I did not mind."

"I do."

"Then I guess we will not have sex."

Her laugh was a watery snuffle. "You are such a guy."

"Because I have a penis."

"No, because you have a one-track mind."

"Maybe we should climb back up and—"

She pressed her fingers to his mouth. "I'm sorry I messed this up. I love the pool and the waterfall. It's very pretty. Very romantic."

Okay, this was good. She actually liked something he'd suggested. Maybe she did like him even though he wasn't fun.

"Maybe we could try this again?" she asked quietly.

Oh yeah, he was all for that. But if a wild kiss made her cry, she might not like sex with him. And if they got started and he couldn't handle her touch, because it was too light or gentle, he would have to get away from her. She definitely wouldn't understand that. His brothers always told him it was better to be up front and discuss issues before having sex with a woman. Saved your ass in the long run, they said.

He stared at the rock facing behind her. "I like to have sex a certain way."

"Not gentle. No soft touches."

"You won't like this, but sometimes I don't like women to touch me at all, while we are..."

"That's kinda tough since by the very definition of sex, two people are touching. Unless, of course, we're talking about phone sex. But we don't have a phone."

"Do you have phone sex?" he asked, rolling that around in his mind. He liked the sound of it. Why hadn't he ever tried that before? All the mental stimulation and none of the touching.

"Not regularly." She laughed. "But I'd do it with you."

"But not now because we don't have a phone. And I really want to have regular sex with you."

"Tell me what you need to make this a good experience for you."

"Could you... uh... keep your hands to yourself?"

She immediately braced her palms on either side of her hips, placing them flat on the rock.

"And no kissing," he said quickly before she decided he was too weird. Too much trouble.

"At all?"

"Not until I see how this goes."

"Okay," she agreed with a nod. "You can touch me, but I can't touch you. Got it."

"And you have to tell me if I'm too rough. I don't always know."

"Our safe word can be Zimbabwe."

"Safe word?"

"If one of us says it, the other has to stop what he or she is doing immediately."

Yeah, he liked that idea. "A safe word is good."

In Joss's opinion, a good hard screwing would be even better right now, but she had to let Shep approach this his own way. She might not be able to touch, but she could tease. He'd enjoyed that before they climbed down to the waterfall. Joss shifted her hands and arched her back.

And from the way his gaze tracked her movement, she knew she had him hooked. Might as well go for broke, so she spread her legs, let him get a good long look. "Anything look appealing?"

"Yes."

"Then do whatever you want."

When he surrounded her breast with his rough palm, took her nipple between two fingers, heat and need spiraled down and she squirmed against the rock. She had a feeling she'd be squirming a lot more before this was over. Shep didn't seem to be a man who rushed.

He pinched, and her hips bucked. "Oh, God."

He immediately released her and started to back away, but she growled at him.

"Don't. That was a good 'Oh, God.' More." Although she wanted to grab his hands and put them on her breasts, she restrained herself. Luckily for her, he seemed to understand. With both his big hands on her, her skin warmed and she felt surrounded and sheltered.

It scorched her and softened her.

He pinched and plucked her nipples with such focus, pushing Joss toward the brink of orgasm. One touch between her legs and she would go boom. "Ah... could you...

would you... I need..." She shifted restlessly on the rock trying to give him the hint.

But hints didn't work well with Shep.

"Could you move one hand between my legs and do the same thing there?"

His delicious torture on her breasts stopped. "I don't like the way that feels on my fingers."

"You're not a fan of the clitoris?"

"No. Inside."

"Why not?"

"It... ah... feels like... um..."

"Just say it."

"Pudding. It feels like pudding."

Pudding? She pinned her lip with her teeth because now was not the time to laugh. Still, she would never, ever look at those little snack packs again without thinking about this conversation. "And you don't care for pudding."

"I like chocolate."

Yeah, she could work with that. Later. "Fine. Then I'll take care of the rain forest. You can go back to the mountains." Although she'd much prefer his rough hand between her legs, a girl had to do what a girl had to do. So Joss reached between her legs and played.

Shep, however, did not return to the regularly scheduled program. Instead, he was staring like a man in a trance at where she was touching herself.

"Never seen a girl masturbate?"

"Amber didn't do that."

"Poor Amber."

"Does it feel good?"

"Does it feel good when you touch yourself?"

"Yes."

"Then there's your answer," she said. "But it would feel even better if you returned to what you were doing."

"I like that." He pointed between her legs.

She couldn't laugh. She could not. Or he would back away. But the man needed to make up his damn mind.

Sounded like his ex-wife had done quite a number on him.

"Would you like to trade? I'll take the mountains."

"You mean your breasts, right?"

"Yep."

"Okay."

Joss cupped her breasts and tried to replicate Shep's movements. It felt good, but wasn't quite the same. He, on the other hand, was staring between her legs like her vagina might be sporting teeth.

"It won't bite."

His wide-eyed gaze flew to hers. "Some of them do?"

Joss bit her bottom lip until she had herself under control. "I was teasing you."

"Oh. Good." Now, rather than reaching down with his hand, Shep lowered himself into the water until he was eye level with her. Then he pushed against her knees, opening her wide. Exposing her. He studied, tilting his head left and right, as if memorizing every fold.

Only the tightest control kept Joss from grabbing his hair and pulling his mouth toward her.

Finally, he touched her clit and she jolted. "It's okay," she gasped. "That was a good touch."

"I like this," he said, half to himself. "It's like a vagina nipple."

Dear God, please help me get through this without cracking up because I really need to come.

"It really likes you, too."

Shep manipulated her clitoris with a single-mindedness she'd never experienced from another man. Usually, they thought it was some kind of starter button and that once they'd gotten the motor cranked, they never needed to touch it again. Shep, on the other hand, was getting a PhD in female anatomy down there.

Eyes closed, she rocked against his touch and fingered her nipples. This would get her there, and then she'd get him off any way he wanted. Just a little more. Another circle and—

"Ohmygod!" Her eyes flew open at the feel of Shep's long fingers pushing inside her. "I thought you didn't like that."

"I thought you might feel different." His face was a study in concentration, making it clear he was seriously considering the texture of her vagina. He worked his fingers in and out, steadily and ruthlessly, until Joss couldn't seem to catch her breath. Her heart was pumping out of control and her muscles were tightening.

"I'm... Shep... I'm about to come."

"Okay."

"Do you want to take your fingers out?"

"No."

That was the single first time the word *no* had ever sent a monstrous orgasm hurtling through Joss's body. She clamped down on Shep's fingers and lost her mind.

That was interesting. Joss's vagina hadn't made him think of pudding. It reminded Shep of something strong and powerful. A fist. A silky vise. He thought he liked it.

And with the way her body was sagging against him, Joss herself reminded him of a floppy doll.

Her eyes still closed, she said, "Do you have any idea what you just did?"

Shep stiffened as he withdrew his fingers from her body. Questions like that normally meant he was about to hear something unkind. Possibly even cruel. He braced himself.

"You just brought me to the most surprising orgasm of my life."

Sometimes surprises were good. Sometimes they weren't.

Joss's mouth curved into a loopy-looking smile. Maybe this surprise was good. Her lids opened slowly to reveal glassy eyes. She'd either done drugs or she was happy.

Since he hadn't seen her take any pills in the past few minutes, he was going to go with happy.

And that made him happy.

"I had a good time," he said.

She laughed and lightly slapped him on the upper arm. Her eyes opened wide and she dropped her hand. "Oh. I'm sorry. In my post-orgasm haze, I forgot."

"It's okay. I think I like it when you touch me."

"How about you stand up?" She scooted toward the edge of the rock she was sitting on. "This is the perfect height for... oh, shit."

"What?"

"We're in the water."

He glanced around. Had she just realized that? "Yes."

"Without a condom."

Oh. "Oh shit."

"Yeah," she sighed. "And I didn't exactly pack for a holiday fling."

"I have condoms in my backpack."

"Are you serious?"

"My brothers told me to never leave home without them."

"I love your brothers."

Shep frowned. He didn't like that. He didn't want Joss to love Cash and Way.

Why?

Because... because he wanted her to love *him*?

"You'll have to give me a few minutes before my legs are steady enough to make that climb," Joss said.

No. If he gave her a few minutes, she might decide his brothers were better than him. "Stay here and I'll be back."

Shep was an experienced climber, but today was the first time he'd ever scaled rocks naked with a hard dick. Wait. Had he double-checked for the condoms after The Shitheads stole from him and took off?

He couldn't remember, and that disoriented him as much as having no blood flow in his brain.

Back at his and Joss's small camp, Shep snatched up his pack. And in his frenzy to find protection, he tossed everything else out onto the ground.

He'd packed three. The rule of three. He ripped open a side pocket and there they were. Three condoms.

The Shitheads were partially forgiven.

As he rushed back toward the rocks, Puck gave him a dude-you-are-crazy look. Shep said, "You would be crazy too if there was a pretty little retriever waiting on you."

When he ducked under the waterfall, Joss had leaned back against a rock wall and appeared to sleeping. "Jojo!"

"Hmm?"

"Are you asleep?"

"Sort of."

"I have condoms. Three of them."

Her lips curved. "That's not very many. But we'll have to make it work."

She opened her eyes, and his heart bumped hard against his ribs. She looked soft and sweet and satisfied. Had he done that? Yeah, he had. "Can we make the first one work right now?"

"Any time you're ready, big boy."

Now, Shep felt awkward. Since they'd experienced a pause, should he make her come again or should he...

"You're overanalyzing something. And it's okay to ask questions. This isn't a test where you aren't allowed to share answers. Can't fail here."

He didn't know whether to just dive back in or if they needed to start all over. "I'm just not sure what to do now."

She held her arms wide and wiggled her fingers. "How about you return to where you left off a few minutes ago?"

"Are you still..."

"Wet? Yep. Why don't you put one of those on?" She nodded toward the packages he was fisting.

Shep tossed two on the rock beside her and tore open the other. When he rolled it on, it was like a glove three sizes too small. But that suited him perfectly. If every part of sex could feel like that—pleasure laced with pain—he would never want to do anything else.

"Right here." Joss waved him in between her legs as if she was directing air traffic. "I think this is what you're looking for."

Good to her word, Joss didn't try to wrap her arms around him or touch him in any way. She just shifted forward and spread her legs wider, allowing him to line up with only the insides of her thighs touching his hips.

"Are you sure...Is this okay?"

Her breath warm on his collarbone, she said, "Don't worry about hurting me. I'm fine. I promise."

He palmed her ass for leverage and drove inside her.

His brain did a cartwheel inside his head. She was hot and tight all around him. Slick heat. Supple strength.

He tried to catch his breath, but it was nowhere to be found.

"This is great," she whispered. "But it's even better if you move."

And it was. Shep pushed into her with jerky movements of his hips. Harder, faster, closer. But he wanted more. He didn't want to just plunge in her. He wanted her to surround him. "Put your arms and legs around me."

"Are you sure?"

"Yes."

When she wrapped around him, something happened inside Shep's chest. A slow roll and surrender. He worked his hands under her ass to lift and tilt her.

In. In. In.

His hips pistoned against her. He could do this forever.

Then her muscles began to ripple the way they had earlier, and he almost lost his rhythm. It felt like the most mind-bending massage ever, and by the way his balls drew up in response, Shep knew immediately that he would lose it long before forever. "Kiss me," he told her roughly.

"But—"

"Now, Joss."

She bracketed his face between her hands, held him firmly, and pressed her lips against his. Not fiercely, like before. This was like the best bottle of maple syrup being poured over waffles crunchy on the outside and fluffy in the middle.

Joss made urgent noises in the back of her throat and

writhed against him. She went rigid and moaned against his mouth. The contraction of her muscles around him was incredible.

Shep pushed in—as far as he could—and allowed himself to let go. His dick jerked inside Joss's body, and he orgasmed with a power he hadn't known was humanly possible.

His heart jerked inside his chest, and he wondered if it was possible for him to love just as powerfully.

18

AFTER SHE AND SHEP DRIED OFF WITH A PIECE OF MICROFIBER the size of a tissue, they climbed clumsily back up the rocks. Joss felt like a giddy teenager after her first all-night drinking party. She was also freezing. Not to mention starving. "I could eat a bear."

"We don't have bear," Shep said as he handed over her clothes. "We have wild carrot."

"That's my favorite." She shimmied into her clothes, then ducked into the trees for a quick pit stop. When she returned, Shep had already gathered some kindling and branches.

Puck glanced back and forth between her and Shep with a look that said *I know what you did down there.* Joss rubbed his head and gave him a big hug. "Don't worry, buddy, we both still love you."

"Do you?" Shep asked, wiping off a handful of Queen Anne's lace root with one of the cloths and passing them to her. "Do you love Puck?"

"Of course." Joss studied the wild plant, smaller and skinnier than normal carrots. She sniffed it and took a cautious bite. Not bad. Not great, but her stomach wasn't particularly picky right now.

"But you haven't known him very long."

"It didn't take long. He's very lovable."

"Do you love a lot of people? Earlier you said you loved my brothers, but you don't even know them."

"It was an expression."

"So you don't love them?"

Her brain wasn't tracking with what Shep was really asking. "You know how you've told me to ask you direct questions? I need you to do that right now."

"Have you ever left someone you said you loved?"

Suddenly, Joss felt as if she'd stepped into a minefield. This was about something more than a casual expression or her affection for his dog. "Even though my family and I don't really understand one another, I still love them. But I had to leave Omaha to have the career I wanted."

"Would you leave again to have the career you want?"

Joss honestly didn't know anymore. She wasn't sure she had a career or a life she wanted. "Maybe."

Shep turned fully away from her to clear a space for a fire. With efficient movements, he used a stick and some sort of small bow he'd fashioned from another piece of wood and his beloved paracord to coax a flame to life. Incredibly, sparks started to lick through the kindling. He blew on it to nurture it to a flame and fed it twigs and dried grass. "It's cold and your hair is wet. We probably shouldn't have had sex."

Suddenly, her chest hurt and she took a step back even though he couldn't see her. "Regrets already?"

"Having sex is not a survival skill."

"According to evolutionary theory, it is."

"Evolution can hold its own for the few days we're out

here," he said. "But the water reduced our body temperatures, and the sex used up energy that we can't properly refuel."

"I would argue the sex raised our body temperatures." She couldn't refute the expenditure of energy, but she would do it again, no question. After all, they'd be off this mountain soon. She would buy herself the biggest cheeseburger ever cooked. Then she and Shep would have a talk about the energy needed for sex.

He removed his cord from the fire bow thingie and tied it one-handed. If he could do something similar with his tongue...

Cool it, Joss. The man is upset about something.

"I don't want to argue with you," she said, "If you think having sex wasn't smart, then I believe you."

"Come over to the fire so your hair will dry." He added some bigger branches to the fire.

"Okay." She plopped down beside it, but she wasn't sure it would thaw the sudden coldness inside her. Was Shep—a man she'd thought was the most honest she'd ever met—playing games with her? "How many more miles to Steele Ridge?"

"About fifteen. We had to hike farther from town to pick up this trail. Why?"

"Do you think we could hike them all tomorrow?"

"I could," he said. "But I don't think you can."

"Have you heard me complain about how physically tough this trek has been?"

"No. But you are five feet tall. The average stride for a person your height is 24.78 inches. I'm six foot two and men have slightly longer strides than women. If you do the math, then—"

"I get it," she said with a little sulk in her voice. "Then I better get some sleep so I can do my best tomorrow."

"Your hair is still damp."

"So?"

"Being wet affects your body temperature. Your body will produce shivers to warm you, even in your sleep. And when you shiver, you are—"

"Burning energy."

"Exactly."

If Joss had a pair of scissors right now, she'd chop off her hair and toss it in the fire. And whoa, that sounded very much like the old Joss.

She turned so her back was toward the growing fire and held up her hair to dry the stands underneath.

Shep settled beside her. "Let me help."

That surprised her since she assumed he wouldn't enjoy the texture of her hair against his skin. But he gently took the mass from her and slowly pulled down pieces as they dried.

"I like your curtains."

Dammit. She did *not* want to be charmed by him right now. Not in any way. But she couldn't help herself. He'd already gotten to her, made her think about her life. Made her wonder if he could ever be a true part of it.

"I also like the rug."

"You hurt my feelings when you said we shouldn't have had sex."

"I am sorry. I didn't really mean it. I just..."

"Just what?"

"I didn't like talking about you leaving people you love."

Were they falling in love with one another? The idea left her feeling shaky and unsure and... strangely hopeful.

Swish. He let more strands fall against her neck, and she shivered. "Are you cold?"

"No." But if he kept doing that, she might get hot. And that was not what needed to happen tonight, not when they were both feeling uncertain and off-balance. "Is it dry enough for me to go to sleep?"

He released the rest of her hair and smoothed a hand down it. Sweetly, gently. "Not completely dry, but enough. You crawl in. I will make sure Puck takes a rest stop and put out the fire. I... um... thought we could both sleep in the tent, but—"

"Yes." She didn't have a firm grasp on what was happening between them, but she wanted to be close to him.

"Okay." He rose and patted his leg for Puck. They strolled toward the tree line, and Joss admired them both.

Sleek, smart, and so, so sweet. How could anyone meet the pair of them and not fall a little bit in love?

She sure wasn't that strong. But it wasn't fair to Shep for her to make her feelings too clear. He obviously wouldn't understand that she could care about him and still care about her music more. Not that she was seriously considering a long-term relationship after knowing a man for less than three days. But North Carolina was hardly a music mecca. And he'd made it clear this was his forever home.

It suited him. Suited him and his dog.

Joss crawled into the tent. Shep's sleeping bag was arranged just so on his thin air pad. He would need all that space, so she moved to the far side of the tent and used her pack as a pillow.

The day caught up with her, and she let sleep take her under.

It was full dark when Joss blinked out of sleep at the feel

of an arm wrapping around her torso and a hand covering her breast. She opened her mouth to scream when she realized where she was. Safe. With Shep.

Maybe he'd just rolled over in his sleep and done what tended to come naturally when two people slept together. But then warm lips brushed the back of her neck.

He was kissing her neck. Kissing her with the softness of eyelashes sweeping a cheek. The sensation made Joss's heart swell and stilled her breath. "Shep?" she wheezed out.

He froze. "This wasn't okay, was it? You were asleep. That means no consent. Consent is important. Consent is required."

She caught his hand before he could pull away, pressed it firmly to her chest. "It's perfectly normal for lovers to touch one another, sometimes even when they're sleeping. Of course, you really want to make sure he or she is awake for the main event. But a kiss or caress is fine."

"But you did not say yes."

"I'm saying yes now." Her words propelled them both to action, and it was a crazy tangle of arms to shed their clothes inside the small space. Joss flung her shirt, and it landed on Puck. He gave a disgusted grunt and curled up tight in the corner, his back to them.

Joss giggled. Seriously giggled. "My bathtub back in LA is bigger than this tent."

"Next time, you can say yes in your bathtub," Shep said, putting his hands all over her recently bared breasts.

But would he be there for her to say yes to? Joss didn't want the truthful answer to her own question, so she asked, "How do you want to do this?"

"I'm not sure."

"You're telling me you don't have a plan? That you didn't

have the whole thing mapped out in your head when you were kissing me?"

"Maybe."

"Then lead on, General Kingston."

"I like that." And she liked hearing the smile in his voice. "You may call me the General."

"Great," she teased. "Now I find out that you're into dominance."

"No," he said as he handled protection. "I am going to be into you."

He was good to his word, flipping Joss onto her back and somehow settling himself between her legs as if he'd choreographed the whole thing as the most efficient ballet ever danced. Sleep was still fogging Joss's brain, and she instinctively ran her hands up his arms to rest lightly on his shoulders.

Then she remembered and tried to pull them away.

"Don't," he said. "I like it when you touch me."

"Even like this?" She purposefully skimmed her fingers up and down his biceps.

His big body shuddered, one all-over earthquake. "Again. Just a little more pressure."

This time, she pressed with her nails, outlining his triceps muscles, bulging from holding his weight off of her. He shuddered again, and a guttural groan rolled from his throat.

That sounded promising. Joss used her short nails to trace the same path. Shep's hips jerked, and his erection rubbed against her lower belly. Even more promising.

She lifted and opened her knees, offering herself. "Come inside me."

She wasn't prepared for what he did next. Shep didn't shove his way inside.

He slid. Slowly. Sinuously. Sensuously.

Joss's eyelids drooped with the pure pleasure of it. "Oh. Oh, yes."

When he was fully seated, he lowered himself to his elbows and pressed his cheek to hers. And if his gentle entrance into her body hadn't twisted something inside her, this would have.

"Okay?" he asked.

"So okay."

He rocked into her. Slow, lazy strokes that wiped her mind, stoked her body, and stripped her heart. It was deep and dreamy and so intimate that Joss wasn't sure if she wanted to wallow in it or run away from it. The power of it engulfed her because she knew that Shep was touching her in a way he'd never touched anyone in the past.

With a long stroke down his strong back, she shifted her touch from his shoulders to his butt. Work of art. Each cheek was an overflowing handful of perfection.

As he slid in and out of her, his muscles flexed and relaxed. With her fingertips, she pressed into the hills and hollows. Shep's rhythm picked up tempo. Not too fast, just enough to let her know he was affected by her touch.

"I like the way you feel, Shep Kingston," she breathed, turning her face into his neck. He smelled so good—like cool water and woodsmoke. "I like the way you feel against me, inside me."

Gently, she set her teeth against the cords in his neck and nipped.

That quickened his rhythm as if she'd spurred him in the sides and hollered Giddy-up! Three powerful pumps, driving her head up against the wall of the tent.

"Slow, easy, slow," Shep chanted to himself like some sort of sexual mantra. His hips slowed again, rolling into hers with the movement of ocean waves. Inexorable, incessant, unstoppable.

The coiling tension in Joss's belly twisted and spread—up, down, all around. He was taking her to a different place, a location that didn't exist on this plane, in this world. Her heart thrummed against his, whispering a prayer and sending out a plea.

Be with me.

Care for me.

Accept the real me.

"Shep, I... oh..." The sensations, the feelings swept up, over, and simply swamped her. Overloaded her until her body and brain were blindly tossed into a primitive mode of seek and connect.

It curled through her, sensation breaking over sensation. Her orgasm was nothing less than indulgently luscious. Like the finest chocolate melting on her tongue. She didn't want it to end—didn't want the flavor and texture to fade. She wanted to taste it forever even as she swallowed it all.

Still, he moved against her, rocking his hips in an ongoing pattern of pleasure. Her fingers digging into his glutes, he surged against her like those ocean waves whipped up by high winds. Crashing against her until she surrendered fully, and he did the same.

Puck barked—a raw, sharp sound—and Shep shot out of the most satisfying sleep of his life like a marble fired from a giant slingshot. Joss was draped across him with a boneless pressure that was more comforting than the thickest blanket in his home. Her little body was putting off heat, making Shep sweat.

Making it feel as though a dragon was licking at his skin.

Murky shadows danced and flickered outside the tent. *Just a full moon.*

He shut his eyes against the light. Puck nudged his shoulder and whined, a sound of fear and concern. Shep's eyes popped open again. He shouldn't be able to see anything outside the tent because the moon was a waxing crescent.

The illumination wasn't anything so benign.

He grabbed Joss by the shoulders and shoved her to the side. "Wake up. Right now!"

"Wha..." She thrashed against him in her sleepy confusion, catching him just under his left eye with her fist. "Don't—"

Another shake and a light tap on her cheek. "Now, Jojo. Our camp is on fire."

By this time, Puck was on his feet, pacing back and forth in front of the zipped tent flap and whining. The flames outside were higher than the dog was tall.

Joss was flailing, trying to find her clothes and put them on.

"We don't have time for you to get dressed," Shep said. "You and Puck have to get out of here." He flicked open his multi-tool and cut an inverted T shape into the opposite side of the tent. He wriggled halfway out the hole to determine if the fire had surrounded them.

Almost, and the flames were climbing higher with every second that passed. They didn't have time to waste. They needed to be on the opposite side of that fire wall. He crawled out of the tent and immediately reached back in and dragged Joss out into a naked, confused heap. "Puck, outside!" he said.

His dog lunged out, but tried to back up when he saw the fire.

"Sit."

Puck's haunches hit the dirt, but he didn't look away from the circle of flames around them.

Shep swept an arm inside the tent to hook his pack, Joss's guitar, and anything else handy. How was he going to get Joss and Puck out of this fire without hurting them?

The pieces of microfiber he and Joss had used to wash and dry with earlier were still damp. Shep dumped what was left of their maple water over Joss's head and over Puck's head and back.

"What the hell?" Joss asked.

He thrust one of the microfiber cloths at Joss. "Put this over your head and face."

"But—"

"Do it."

He tied the other around his dog's head like a do-rag. When he turned to look at Joss's progress, she was fumbling, and the cloth kept falling to the ground.

"Come here," he demanded. He used his length of cord to tie it over her head.

"Now, take Puck and run."

"Through the fire?"

"There's a narrow gap." He pushed her forward. "That's the only way out."

"What are you going—"

"Shut up and do it," he yelled. "Drop to the ground and roll when you get to the other side. Do it now."

Joss's eyes were huge in her pale face, and Shep wrapped her fingers around Puck's collar. Then he snapped his fingers and said, "Release, Puck."

Following Puck, Joss ran toward the ring of fire. Shep's stomach tried to claw its way out of his body as he watched them plunge into the tiny gap in the orange and white wall and disappear.

If anything happened to either of them, he... He didn't know how he would survive.

Shep glanced around for anything he could use to fight the fire, but he just didn't have enough supplies to kill it from inside. He needed a water source.

He gathered up the clothes and shoes scattered on the ground and shouldered his pack and the guitar. Then he ran like hell.

19

His hair is burning. It was the only thought Joss's brain would produce as Shep lunged through the flames surrounding the tent they'd been sleeping inside less than three minutes earlier. He released his grip on his pack and Fiona, and then, as he'd demanded she do, he dropped to the ground and rolled, but his movements didn't extinguish the licks of fire on his head.

Joss stumbled toward him and did the only thing she could think of—she whacked him with a small cedar branch, slapping him in the head with the green needles.

Smack, smack, smack.

Smack, smack, smack.

Smack, smack, sma—

The branch was wrenched from her hands. "Jojo, it's okay."

No. No, it wasn't. He'd forced her and Puck to leave him behind. What if he hadn't been able to escape? He could've fallen. Broken a leg. Been burned to death.

Her legs gave out, and she crumpled to the ground. Her

face found a safe resting spot in her palms, and she blocked out everything. The night, the fire, Shep.

"We need to move back," he said and grabbed her by the arm to drag her up. "Closer to the waterfall. I have to put out this fire. If the fire spreads this way, you and Puck can climb down and get in the water."

They made it to the ledge, but Joss was fairly certain she hadn't carried her own bodyweight. She dropped down to sit, and Shep was right there, squatting in front of her and running his hands all over her body. "Are you okay? Are you burned anywhere?"

"No. I don't know. I don't think so. Check Puck."

Shep did the same with his dog. "Roll, Puck."

Puck lay down and rotated to his back so Shep could inspect his paws.

"Is he okay?"

After inspecting each paw, Shep gave Puck's release command and the dog rolled to his stomach. "His paws might be a little sore for a while."

"I'm so sorry. I could've carried him."

"How much do you weigh?"

"What?"

He eyed her. "A hundred pounds or so? Well, Puck is seventy-five. If you had tried to carry him, you would have been unsteady and possibly fallen into the fire. You're both better off because you didn't carry him."

Shep grabbed the bladder and climbed down the ledge. He returned with water, but when she would've stood to help him put out the fire, he said, "Stay here with Puck. I don't want him to accidentally stumble into the fire."

To hell with that. Joss hurried into a pair of shorts, one of Shep's T-shirts, and her shoes. Then she tethered Puck to a sturdy bush and gave him a down command. She grabbed all the clothes she wasn't wearing and climbed down to dunk them. When she made it back to the campsite, Shep had doused some of the fire.

With the wet clothes, she slapped at the remaining flames, knocking them down. Shep glanced at her, and his face hardened. "I told you—"

"Save it," she snapped. "And let's make sure this thing is out."

It took them several more trips down to the water and back again to refill the bladder and rewet the blackened clothing. Silently, they worked side by side, with Shep kicking up the last smoldering areas and Joss smothering them with her clothes.

From the scorched circle around Shep's half-burned tent, Joss realized the fire hadn't been as huge as it had looked. Dangerous, yes. But the whole thing was no bigger than her living room rug.

Finally, Shep grunted his satisfaction with their fire-fighting efforts and said, "We need to check on Puck."

Back at the ledge, Puck was still lying near the shrub, so Joss turned to Shep and demanded, "Come here. I want to look at your head."

"I'm fine."

"Now, Harris Sheppard Kingston, or I am going to lose my shit this very second."

He blinked and sat with his back to her so she could paw through his hair like a flea-seeking orangutan. In the pale early morning light, she muttered to herself as she checked him for scalp burn. Except for the spot around his crown, his gorgeous hair was unscathed. And even that scorched area was just burned down to a crewcut. It stunk. Hell, they all stunk. But that was it.

Joss pushed Shep away and huddled into herself, wrapping her arms around her legs and shoving her face into her knees. She didn't want to see Shep's head or his face.

She didn't want to see anything, especially not the memory of the fire's menacing glow.

"We need to assess what to do next."

"No."

"What?"

"I don't want to reassess. I want to sit right here until a search and rescue group comes and—"

"We can't do that because—"

"Dammit, Shep! I need a minute here!" She immediately felt like crap for yelling at him, but she couldn't manage both of them right now. Holding herself together was stretching it.

"Okay. Then I'm going to go look and see if I can figure out how the fire started." A strong hand passed gently over Joss's bowed head. "Puck, stay with Joss."

She heard him stride away, and a sudden chill swooped over her skin. How was that possible when they'd almost burned up a few minutes ago? Joss abandoned her armadillo impersonation and stretched out on the ground to curl around Puck, absorbing his warmth and his steadiness. "Puck is a good boy. The best dog in the world. So strong and brave."

He raised his head at the praise, his ears lifting as well. Joss stroked the silky fur to comfort them both. "Nothing fazes you, does it? Not dead bodies, raccoon men, or raging fires."

Puck dropped his head, resting it in the crook of her neck. It didn't escape Joss that the position gave him a perfect view of their destroyed campsite. He would see the second Shep walked back this way. He would see if anyone else snuck up.

Joss stayed snuggled up with Puck until he lifted his head and his mouth stretched into a doggie smile. Because she knew it was Shep approaching, her stomach relaxed a little.

"Your shirt—well, my shirt—is on backward," he pointed out.

For whatever reason, that made her smile. "And the clothes you grabbed didn't seem to include a pair of under-wear." Hell, she'd just run through fire naked; she could handle going commando for now.

"You used everything else to help put out the fire. I was mad when you did that."

"I'm sorry, but there wasn't any way I was going to let you put it out alone."

Shep sank down beside her and sighed. "I never imag-ined you would have to be this brave. Jojo, I'm sorry about the fire."

"Why would you say that?"

"I thought I made sure the campfire was out last night."

"Of course you did."

"Then why did our camp burn?"

Joss squinted, recalling the arc of the fire, how it looked as Shep jumped through it, as she beat him with a branch. "Doesn't it seem strange that it would've burned in a circle around us instead of in a line? That wouldn't have happened if it sparked from the campfire, would it?"

"Why didn't I think of that? Are you saying you think someone set it?"

"Yes, and I'm wondering if whoever did this is the same person who... who..."

"Killed Buffalo Moody."

She hadn't wanted to say it aloud. Because once the words were in the air, they couldn't be pulled back and covered up. So she just nodded.

"All I know is that I don't like this. We need to get back to Steele Ridge as soon as we can."

Joss forced herself to her feet and put Fiona on her back. "Then I say we get going."

Disappointment ate through the winner at the fact that Kingston, the woman, and the dog were all still alive. Barely even hurt. A bad burn or a busted leg would've been nice.

This contest didn't have a lot of time left on the clock, but the winner was secretly happy it wasn't over yet.

There were more tricks in the bag.

And just because they weren't physically hurt, that didn't mean the winner hadn't scored some major points. The rock star was curled in fetal position, and she'd yelled at Kingston.

Maybe she was finally figuring out how half-baked the guy was. She probably only planned to string Kingston along until they made it back to Steele Ridge. She was smart enough to know a man didn't leave his fuck buddy behind.

From a vantage point up in the trees, the winner had gotten an eyeful of their tonsil hockey in the water. Shep was a well-hung son of a bitch, that was for sure. But then they'd gone under the waterfall and the winner hadn't been able to see or hear anything.

Too damn bad.

But when they'd done the monster mash in the tent, the winner had seen that. Had been close enough to hear every gasped word and moan. Had heard the grunt and groan of two long orgasms.

The winner couldn't imagine Kingston getting hot and heavy enough to satisfy someone like the rock star. Then again, maybe she'd been faking it. Women did it all the time.

Whatever. They could have all the fake fucks they wanted until the winner decided it was time to finally take Kingston out of the game.

But not yet.

Because the whole match was more fun than the winner could've ever imagined. If there was a way to both kill Kingston and keep him alive to continue playing, that would be cool.

But there wasn't. So Kingston would have to bite the big one. And if the chick and the dog went down, too...

Well, that was just simple collateral damage.

Shep didn't like it. Did not like it. Did *not* like it.

As he, Joss, and Puck hit the trail again, his tendency to obsess was about to slip past his self-control and blow up like a string of firecrackers.

This whole trip into the mountains had been a mistake.

But if it was a mistake, did that mean what was happening between Joss and him was a mistake, too? Shep didn't want to believe that.

He was, however, self-aware enough to know that he dealt best in blacks and whites. Joss had introduced a gray he wasn't completely comfortable with. And now he'd led her into danger.

With thoughts and questions doing a whirling dervish in his head, Shep instinctively reached for his cord and tied half a dozen knots inside the limited space of his pocket.

And shit, by the way he was working his fingers, it probably looked like he was playing with himself.

"I'm not masturbating," he said finally.

Joss jerked her head around to look at him. "What?"

"In my pocket." He nodded toward his right side. "I'm not touching my penis."

"Should I say congratulations or I'm sorry?"

"I'm tying my cord."

"I know, Shep. I was just joking. It was a bad one. Believe me, if I had a security cord right now, I'd be fondling it, too."

"Really?" he asked. "Would you like mine?" He surprised himself with the offer.

"That's really sweet," she said. "But do you... do you think it might help you if you used your other hand to hold mine?"

Huh. That had never been soothing to him before, but a lot of things had changed since Joss white-water rafted into his life. "We could try it."

She gave a sort of smile, more of a lip twist, actually. "That wasn't fair of me. It would help *me* if you would hold my hand."

Instead of recoiling, Shep found he wanted to hold Joss's hand. He *wanted* to help her. To make her feel better. Instead of just enfolding her smaller hand in his, he intertwined their fingers.

She looked down at their joined hands and a real smile bloomed on her face. "Let me know if this starts bothering you."

"It won't."

Because Puck's leash had been one of the things left behind to burn with the tent, he was keeping pace with them, trotting along on Joss's other side. He'd become as protective of her as he was of Shep. A few days ago, that would've made Shep feel unsettled, maybe even jealous.

Now, he was glad his dog cared for Joss as much as he did.

They were all hiking quickly down the trail, with Shep keeping a vigilant eye out for any potential threats, when Puck's nose shot up into the air. One quick side-eye glance at Shep, and he shot off at an angle and into the woods.

"Oh, my God. Where is he going?" Joss asked.

"Puck, here!" Shep yelled.

But his damn dog never looked back, just crashed his way through the underbrush until he was out of sight.

"Shep," Joss gasped. "Shep, my fingers!"

He glanced down and realized he was strangling her tiny fingers. He dropped her hand. "I'm sorry. I have to find Puck."

"Do you want me to stay here on the trail?"

"No. I told you I wouldn't leave you alone and that goes double after what happened last night."

Joss headed toward the spot where Puck had disappeared off the trail. "Surely he won't go far."

Shep didn't think so. Then again, Puck had never, in his whole life, taken off like this. He was trained not to react as a normal dog would, no matter the temptation.

Temptation. What could possibly have tempted his dog to act against his training, to revert to his instincts? Shep's family often referred to Puck as the canine garbage can because he was very, very food motivated. Puck had been lured off the trail by the scent of some delicious food, Shep would bet on it.

Not just any food, but one of his all-time favorite people foods. And what was the likelihood of someone having an innocent picnic way out here when he and Joss hadn't seen a single person since they'd run into the Juney Whank guy?

"We need to catch Puck now," he barked at Joss. "Run."

"Shep?"

"I don't have time to explain. Hurry and stay close behind me."

For a dog that was so happy to laze around in the shade or on a couch cushion, Puck was a fast motherfucker when he had a mind to be.

With Joss's fingers hooked into the back of his shorts, Shep crashed through branches and underbrush, barely feeling the scratches on his face and arms. He just hoped he was protecting Joss with his bigger body.

They'd probably sprinted a quarter mile when Shep spotted Puck hunkered down over what looked like a pile of hot dogs. He was going at them like he was competing in one of those eating contests.

"Puck, don't!"

Puck shot him a guilty look and gulped down the wiener that was already in his mouth.

There was no sign of a recent campsite or picnic. And hot dogs didn't grow on trees so someone had dropped these on purpose. Shep needed to get his hands on what was left of that pile of meat. "Puck, I mean it. Don't!"

Reluctantly, Puck backed away from the food and sat. His huff of disgust came through loud and clear.

"Can you hold him while I check out what he was eating?" Shep asked Joss.

"Sure."

She grabbed for his collar, and Shep squatted next to the few hot dogs left. He had no way of knowing how many Puck had already gobbled down. Shep broke one in half and sniffed the inside. Smelled like pork byproducts to him, but plenty of shitty people knew dogs would eat tainted meat. How many guard dogs had been sidetracked and drugged that way to make it easier for a crook to rob a house?

But why Puck? And why now?

What the hell was going on out here?

Whatever it was, Shep could no longer afford to just meander his ass back to Steele Ridge. He needed to go on the offensive.

20

HER BREATH STILL HITCHING FROM THEIR DASH THROUGH THE woods, Joss ran a trembling hand over Puck's head and down his back. Hot dogs in the middle of a national forest didn't make sense. And with the way Shep was sniffing and studying them, he didn't think so either.

"Are they rotten?" she asked him.

"No. These things have so many preservatives in them that they'd probably survive a nuclear holocaust."

Realization flooded her. "Oh, crap. You're smelling for poison." She scanned the area wildly, spotted a small tuft of what she was looking for. "Here, Puck." She half dragged him to the grass. Doubtful he would graze like a cow, she ripped out a handful and shoved it into his mouth. "Swallow, dammit."

"That's a good idea." Shep joined her and took Puck's face in his hands. "Eat it, Puck."

Joss yanked out more grass, and Shep performed a dog whisperer miracle and sweet-talked Puck into eating half of what she'd picked.

"We need to get away from here," Shep said in a low voice. "Whoever left these could still be around."

"You think someone was trying to lure Puck to this area?"

"Yeah."

God, all she wanted was a safe place where she could hunker down. A basement, a closet, a vault. Because these unending acres of towering trees, fallen logs, and leaf piles felt threatening. Like the forest was stalking them. But that was silly. None of what had happened out here was the work of nature.

It was the work of man. And Joss remembered enough from high school English that Man versus Man was the most unpredictable kind of conflict.

Shep scanned the forest and finally said, "This way."

"But the trail is the other direction."

"Which is exactly the reason we are not going that way. Hold on to Puck." He pulled his cord from his pocket and fashioned a short leash. "I don't think he will bolt again, but I don't want to take any chances."

The grass, a natural emetic, didn't take long to work its magic. Within five minutes, Puck was hunched over and heaving. It sounded painful, but if the hot dogs were poisoned, they needed to come up.

And there were at least a dozen of them altogether.

Once Puck's yak-fest seemed to be at an end, the dog looked away from his porcine downfall in shame. Shep squatted down to rub Puck's head in comfort. "It's okay, bud. I know you couldn't help yourself."

Shep turned and looked up at Joss. "We need to get out of here. Who knows what else—"

Something whizzed through the air and flew past Shep's shoulder. Puck let out a high-pitched yelp that made both goose bumps and sweat break out over Joss's body.

What in the world?

Before she could register what had just happened, Shep scooped up his dog and yelled, "Run!"

With Puck in his arms, Shep could do nothing to help Joss but shout at her to get the hell out of here. Eyes wide, she ran, and he took off in a zigzag pattern behind her. "Go right! Now left!"

If they were where he thought they were, a group of caves wasn't far ahead.

Joss turned her head to look at them. "What happened?"

"Shut up and keep running!"

She did. He had to give her major credit for that. For a short girl, she was hauling ass. Arms and legs pumping. Breath heaving. Fiona bouncing against her back.

"Angle to the left up that hill."

To the left she went, no hitch in her stride. And although Puck was heavy in his arms, Shep didn't let up either. From the way his dog was panting in pathetic little whines, Shep couldn't afford to fumble or fail. He had to get them all to shelter.

"Up a little more," he panted out. "Look for a rocky ledge that opens into a cave."

Joss attacked the scrum like a billy goat, powering up, up, up. The rocks rolled under her, and she pitched forward onto her palms. She didn't make a sound, just regained her balance and climbed.

"It's here. I found it," she said, pulling herself onto a jagged pile of rocks and making as if to crawl into the cave.

"Wait. I need to check it out."

She scooted to the side, found a perch on a flat rock, and held out her arms for Puck. Shep gently laid the dog across her lap, eclipsing most of Joss's body. "Oh my God. Someone shot him with an arrow. It's... I think it's deep."

Shep couldn't think about that right now. *Check out the cave first.*

Inside, it smelled of bat shit, but he tossed a few small rocks into the corners. Nothing furry or poisonous scurried out. It would have to do.

He crawled back out and gently lifted Puck from Joss's lap. His dog was panting in distress, yet he still licked Shep's hand, trying to reassure *him.* "It's okay, buddy. I will make it okay." To Joss, he said, "I don't think anything is inside the cave."

"I'd bunk down with any animal right now. I'm just glad to be in an enclosed space." After the fire, they didn't have many clothes left, but Joss pulled a T-shirt from Shep's pack and spread it on the ground. "You can lay him here."

Once Shep had Puck on the ground, he could see the arrow had definitely breached fur, the underlying skin, and was lodged firmly. But it was impossible to tell if it had pierced anything inside. Should he try to take it out or leave it in?

"Do we take out the arrow?" Joss asked, mirroring his question to himself.

"I don't know what is best."

"He's hurting pretty bad."

"I know that!"

"I'm sorry. I know you do. I... I just feel helpless."

Yeah, so did he, and it was a feeling he never enjoyed. "I'm going to cut down the arrow some, enough that it's not sticking out as far, but not so much that I can't get leverage to pull it out if needed." He used his multi-tool to clip the fiberglass shaft. Puck yelped, a high-pitched expression of pain that bolted its way through Shep's body.

Overload. It was coming on, and he couldn't afford to lose his shit right now. But he had to lose something. He tossed the butt of the arrow aside and said, "I need to throw up."

Fortunately, he made it to the mouth of the cave in time and leaned over the rocky ledge to vomit. He didn't have much to heave up—not like Puck and the dozen hot dogs—but the bile scorched his throat and stung his eyes.

As gross as it felt, it cleared his head. Allowed him to think.

For some reason, he, Joss, and Puck were under attack. Shep couldn't ignore everything that had happened in the past twenty-four hours. It didn't matter who the attacker was. All that mattered was that Shep stopped them.

When his stomach finally let up its assault, he swiped his mouth with the back of his hand.

Joss poked her head out of the cave and held out the empty maple water container. "Here. There's a mouthful left."

"We need that."

"Just a little sip. A swish and spit. You'll feel better."

He took it from her and rinsed the taste of fear and confusion from his mouth. "Thanks."

"Come back inside."

In the cave, they both sat close to Puck, with Shep's hand on his head and Joss's on his rump. The retriever's eyes were closed, but his breathing was still labored.

"When that arrow flew," Joss said, "you had just turned toward me. Do you think it might've been meant to hit you?"

Shep thought back, remembered their relative positions. He'd been crouched over Puck just a fraction of a second before the arrow whizzed past. If he hadn't moved, it would've punctured him in the upper left quadrant from the back. "I think the shooter was aiming for my heart."

"My God, Shep." She grabbed his arm hard. "Are you sure?"

"Based on the trajectory, yes. Either that, or the person is a shitty shot. They're out there right now. And they've made it clear they're going to keep coming at us. We can't return to the trail. We'd be too exposed."

"What about the others from *Do or Die*? If they've made it back to town, won't your sister be concerned that you're not with them?"

"We can't be sure The Bitcher and the others were able to make it off the mountain, either."

"You're saying whoever started the fire and hurt Puck could've gotten to them, too? Why? Why is this happening?"

"I don't know, but I decided it doesn't matter. If we are going to get back to Steele Ridge alive, I have to find this person and stop them."

"You mean we, don't you?"

"No," he stated flatly. "I mean me."

"I am not going to sit in this cave like a scaredy-cat while you go out and possibly get yourself killed."

"Someone needs to stay with Puck."

"Okay. Point to you. But I can help. Let's talk this through together."

"I'm already working on it in my head."

"That's not good enough for me. I haven't made it to this place in my career by letting someone else make a plan for me. Not even my manager or agent. I always know what's going on," Joss said. "The facts. That's where we need to start. What's gone wrong since we left Steele Ridge?"

"Everything," Shep grumbled. Well, maybe not everything. He'd never imagined he would meet someone like Joss.

"Not helpful," she shot back. "First, Moody disappeared."

"We found the fawn, and the first aid kit went missing."

"Moody was... found." Joss swallowed as if trying to keep her stomach from reeling. "Lauren and the others took off and took more of our stuff. And we met that weird guy on the trail."

"Someone set a fire at our campsite."

"The hot dogs."

"The arrow."

"God, so many things." Joss rubbed at her forehead. "What's the point of it all? If it was just about Moody, every-thing would've stopped after he was killed."

"Maybe someone wanted to stop the filming."

"That's good. A definite thought. A publicity stunt set up by Lauren or Bradley?"

"Seems like you would want to stick around if you were hoping for publicity."

"True. A stalker fan?"

That was an angle Shep hadn't considered. "Have you ever had one of those?"

"Several. At least one a year."

"Maybe this person is after you."

"And how do we know it's only one person? What if someone followed the other group and someone else is behind us?"

Shep tried to keep all the complicated strings separate in his mind, but they were like delicate gold chains that had all been stored together and knotted around one another. Usually, he liked nothing better than to untie them and untangle them. But this time, he needed to be able to see each one individually. "We only have to worry about our chain."

"What?"

"Even if there are multiple people trying to mess with the show, we only need to worry about the one following us."

Yeah, now they were getting somewhere. If they could pick this apart just a little more, Shep would know his next move. He liked being able to talk this through with Joss. She had a cool, logical side.

"When Moody disappeared from camp," she said, "it changed the tenor of the show. But with Greg and Zach still there, the filming did go on. However, your role changed. You had to transition from local guide to the grand poohbah of the whole operation. No one else could get the group out of the mountains and back to Steele Ridge."

Puck groaned, and Shep stroked his head gently, trying to comfort him.

"I never thought the fawn might be related to what was happening in our camp. Not until we found Moody's body." Sure, it had been gruesome, but Shep didn't think it had been a big personal blow to anyone, least of all him. He hadn't liked Moody. He would've never wished him dead, but his death hadn't changed much in Shep's world.

"Then The Shitheads took most of your stuff and the sat phone. That was a big blow."

"But they left, and that was a good thing."

"You were still stuck with me. More than stuck. Then you felt responsible for someone you weren't all that keen to take out into the wilderness in the first place."

That was true, but by that time, he'd begun to feel differently about her. "Maybe whoever followed us saw it that way."

"You didn't?"

"No. I think I made it clear that I liked you." More than liked. Was there a level between like and love? Why did emotions have to be so damn confusing?

She waved away his words with a casual motion that made Shep feel as if he were the one who had taken an arrow to the chest. What did that mean? That she was waving away his admission? That she didn't believe someone like him could have feelings for someone like her?

"Then we're back to the fire, the hot dogs, and the arrow." She ran a hand down Puck's tail with an easy affection that Shep wanted for himself. This was why he shouldn't try to figure out love. What he wanted, what he was able to give, would never be enough for a woman.

And right now, Puck was the most important thing. "The hot dogs were for Puck."

"Yes," she said, her hands going to her hair and pulling, "but don't you see that's about you, too? Puck is your best friend. How better to get to someone than to harm someone they love?"

How would he feel if someone hurt Joss? Would he crawl to a ledge and throw up? Just the thought made Shep's stomach pitch. Yeah, he'd definitely heave if something happened to her.

"There were four famous people with our group and you want me to believe that all this bullshit was about me?"

"Dammit, Shep!" More hair pulling. "You're supposed to be the logical one. Look at it clearly, closely. And you'll see it's *all* about you."

21

JOSS KNEW WHEN SHE'D FINALLY GOTTEN THROUGH TO SHEP. He dropped his head. "Puck, I am sorry. I'm the reason you are hurt."

"No," Joss said forcefully. "Some shitty person is the reason he's hurt."

"I should not have brought Puck with me."

"Would you have made it four days without him?"

"That doesn't matter." Shep was avoiding her gaze, actively turning his head away when she tried to catch his eye.

"How do you think he would've felt if you'd left him back in Steele Ridge? He wouldn't have understood."

"I would've left him with Maggie and Jay," he insisted. "He loves both of them."

"I'm sure he does, but you're his person." She took his hand, made sure her hold was tight. "You, Shep. No one else."

"I have to figure out a way to get him out of here as fast as possible."

"Can we drag him like you would someone with a broken leg?"

"Yes. It would be painful, and we shouldn't get back on the trail if someone is after us."

"That just means we'll have to leave the son of a bitch up here on the mountain, doesn't it?"

"And the best way to do that is to set a trap he or she can't get out of."

Even though her heart was raw and bleeding at Puck's situation, she knew Shep needed her encouragement and support. "Now we're talking. Let's nail this heartless SOB."

Kingston and the rock star were holed up like scared mice in a cave about a quarter mile away. The winner had especially enjoyed seeing Kingston lean over the ledge up there and puke like a teenager who'd guzzled a six-pack of warm beer.

The guy was usually so stoic. So superior. So fucking strange.

Now, it was pretty funny to see he did have some kind of heart.

Kinda too bad about the dog, though. The winner would've taken him as a prize. A few months without Kingston, and the dog would forget he ever existed. Dogs were dumb that way.

But that dog was the smartest stupid animal the winner had ever met.

When the arrow hit his dog, Kingston had run like a bat outta hell, so the injury was serious. Now, if they hid out in that cave for too long, the dog would definitely bite it. They didn't have much in the way of supplies.

After all, the winner had made sure to slowly swipe anything that would make survival too easy.

The dog's bad luck.

That was okay. The winner could get another dog. No hand-me-downs from Kingston needed. The winner's dog would be better. Smarter and more loyal. Loyal *only* to the winner.

But how to end the contest with Kingston now? Having him and the rock star die of dehydration, starvation, or hypothermia in that cave wouldn't be a lick of fun. A total chickenshit way to kick the guy's ass.

It was time to make a new plan.

Although Shep didn't have many of his original supplies to work with, he had a whole damn mountain of options beyond the mouth of the cave. But if he were the one tracking prey, he would be keeping an eye on wherever the prey had settled. Which meant their hiding place in the cave wasn't a secret.

Caves were tough places to wage an attack against because there was little chance of approaching unseen. However, they also had a fatal weakness. Only one point of escape.

Sometimes.

"I need to explore this cave."

"If you're making a plan, I don't want to be left out," Joss said.

"No plan yet," he assured her. "But a little time alone in the dark will help my mind start to work one out. I won't be gone long." He handed Joss a rock. "It's not the best weapon in the world, but it's better than nothing." Then he stood and turned toward the darkened inner recesses of the cave, but Joss caught him by the hand.

"Shep?"

"Yeah?"

"This would be a good time to kiss me."

"We cannot have sex right now."

"I'm not talking about sex. I'm talking about the kind of kiss that reassures your lover that you care about her and that you are coming back, no matter what."

That made a sort of logical sense. Shep leaned down and put his lips on hers. Joss met him with a fierceness that he hadn't expected. Warm lips and shallow breath that carried affection, yes. But something more. A sort of uncertainty colored lightly with desperation.

Was this the kind of kiss soldiers received before they left for war?

He grabbed a lock of her hair and pulled her face closer to his. With his mouth, he tried to answer the questions she seemed to be asking.

Will you come back?

Yes.

Will you figure out a way out of this?

Yes.

Will you keep us safe?

Yes.

Do you love me?

His mind stuttered. Maybe he was reading things into Joss's kiss that weren't really there.

She'd never said she loved him, and he was wrestling with imaginary questions.

Reluctantly, he broke the kiss that his brain had probably made entirely too much of. "Thank you for caring about Puck."

"He's part of you. How can I not care about him and for him?"

Her question trailed Shep as he set off to explore the cave. Did what she'd said mean she cared about *him*?

She and Puck were counting on him to save them, and if he could find another way to get them all out of this damn cave, he would feel a lot better about their situation.

His footsteps echoed around him, and the *scritch* of little feet told him they weren't completely alone in this cave. As long as the other cave dwellers weren't interested in being overly neighborly, that was fine.

The farther he explored, the darker the passage became. He desperately wanted to save the battery power on their one remaining flashlight. But when he rammed his head into a low-hanging rock, he had to surrender. The flashlight clicked on, but the beam was a ghost of what it had been. They'd be without artificial light soon, probably before he made it back to Joss and Puck.

Shep dropped to all fours to ease his way through a tight stretch. The rocks above jutted downward, making him feel claustrophobic. Making him feel desperate and uncertain.

Making him reach for his pocket.

Dammit, he didn't have the time or the space to fuck around with his piece of paracord right now.

Keep going.

Before he could navigate his way out of the coffin tunnel, his flashlight gave up. Just blip. One second, a thread of hazy light. The next, nothing.

Although he was crawling blind, Shep realized when the tunnel opened up. The quality of the air changed, seemed more expansive. He reached above him to feel for the ceiling. Sharp rocks bit at his hand, but there was definitely more space.

And it seemed as if a shaft of light was filtering toward him from up ahead. Could be his imagination, so Shep blinked again and again to clear his sight. The path *was* brighter. Still shadowy, but light was seeping in from somewhere.

He crawled faster.

His heart was beating like crazy inside his chest. Beating with hope.

Shep shimmied through an arch of rock and into a chamber high enough for him to stand. And there... there to the right was the lucky break he'd been searching for.

22

IT SEEMED AS IF SHEP HAD DISAPPEARED INTO THE DARKNESS behind her decades ago. Every sound, every scurry made Joss jump. She had to calm down. Her anxiety couldn't be good for Puck.

His breathing was becoming more irregular. More worrisome.

"It's okay, Puck. He's coming back. And we're all going to be fine and live happily ever after." Well, probably not all together, but they could each be happy in their own spots on opposite coasts. Joss would return to her music, and Shep would return to leading adventures for noncelebrities.

Unfortunately, now Puck wasn't even bothering to open his eyes when she spoke to him.

"You have to hang on. You have to." She couldn't imagine a world without this amazing animal in it. Joss scooted around so she could keep a close eye on Puck and see both the cave mouth and the dark recesses behind them. Surely if Shep had been gone this long, he'd found something. Something good.

Or gotten lost.

Or been bashed on the head with a loose rock.

Or been speared through the chest with a stalactite.

That's not helpful.

A shuffling sound echoed from the darkness, and Joss scrambled to her feet, squatting near Puck to protect him from whatever bloodthirsty animal might be coming for them both. "I will mess you up," she whispered. "Just try me, and you'll see what a crazy-ass, blue-haired rock star can do."

More shuffling, and huffing, and what sounded like the clatter of bones. Bones. Oh, God, it had already eaten Shep!

That was it, she had to do something.

Joss jumped to a standing position and raised her arms like she was the biggest, baddest animal ever to terrorize a forest. Then she charged into the gloom, screaming like the world was ending.

The animal's shape started to take form. It was big, much bigger than her.

OhmyGod, OhmyGod, OhmyGod.

It was standing on its back legs. Had to be a bear. A Kodiak. But Joss couldn't back down now. It would feast on her and then have Puck for dessert.

"Get the fuck out of my cave, you motherfucker. I will fuck your bear ass up so bad that you'll be ashamed to show your face in the woods. Aaaaaaah—get out!" She tried to dance around it to the right, herd it far left. But it dropped something and lunged for—

"Jojo!"

She fought it like a wild thing. Nails, hands, teeth, feet. She thrashed against the bear in a frenzy.

"Jojo, it's me. Shep."

Brutal relief shot through her system like she'd suddenly mainlined all the heroin in Los Angeles County. Her head went woozy and her knees went gooey. She stumbled back and cracked her head against the rock wall.

"I think you need to sit down." Shep held her arms, bearing most of her weight as he tried to lower her to the ground.

"No, I have to get back to Puck."

"How is he?"

"Not great." She stumbled back to him and dropped cross-legged beside his head. "Please tell me you figured something out."

Shep stroked a gentle hand over his dog's flank and the expression of concern on his face twisted Joss's heart. "I did, but it's going to take some work, and we don't have a lot of time."

"Just tell me what I need to do."

Joss didn't look as if she was in much better shape than Puck, but her promise to pitch in however he needed was delivered with a straightened spine and a tight mouth. And truth was, it didn't matter if she was wearing thin. He couldn't execute this plan without her.

"I am going to construct a couple of traps outside the cave. If this person knows we are in here, which I think they do, then they'll come for us eventually. Fortunately, there are really only two ways to approach this cave. So when the person takes one of those paths, a trap will spring, and the son-of-a-bitch should end up with a spear in him."

"Okay. I like it." Joss nodded. "But if this person is watching the cave, how are we supposed to leave the cave to set the traps?"

"Gimme a sec." Shep went back into the darkness and

returned with an armful of sticks and limbs. "I found a small exit point way back in the cave tunnels."

"Which is how you were able to gather all this."

"We'll prep the materials for the traps here, then head for the exit point I found. While you and Puck stay just inside the cave, I'll circle around and construct the actual traps. After that, I'll come back to get you. We'll hike north and farther east for a while before heading south again."

"If we can just sneak north, why the traps?"

Because Shep wanted to hurt the person who'd shot his dog. Who'd killed Moody. Who'd set fire to their camp. Who'd terrorized Joss. "I want to slow him down, but more than that, I hope one of these traps spears him right through the balls."

"Wow. You've got a mean streak that I hadn't noticed."

"I don't love a lot of things. I don't know how to love a lot of things. But the things I think I love, no one is going to hurt or take away from me."

Joss placed her palm on his cheek. "You are an amazing man, Shep. Puck is a lucky dog."

Warmth flowed over him. Did she realize that he was talking about her, too? She was one of the things he was beginning to believe he loved.

"What do you need me to do?"

Shep sorted the sticks and branches into piles. "Leaves need to be stripped from any branches. Then we'll need to sharpen all the ends."

"What kind of trap is this exactly?"

"It's called a spring spear trap. Normally used to hunt along game trails."

"But animals are smaller than a full-grown person."

"This thing will take down a boar if it's set up properly."

"Shep, how many ways to kill someone do you think you know?"

"Enough." He pushed a pile of branches toward her. "Strip these as well as you can while I start whittling down ground spikes."

The stripping and notching took them longer than Shep would've liked. He couldn't chance placing the spear in a tree or bush and having the person see and disable the trap, so he'd have to set it up lower, which meant they needed more ground stakes to stabilize the whole thing.

When he'd sharpened the spears and stakes for so long that his hand was bleeding, Joss took the multi-tool from him and finished off the ground stakes. They didn't have to be as precise or sharp. What mattered most was that one of those spears made it into this bastard's body.

"The trip to the exit point isn't going to be easy," he told Joss. "We'll have to drag Puck through part of it because it's not high enough for either of us to stand. I'll carry him for as long as I can."

"We can use these extra branches to make a frame. And your pack will be the litter. And if the route is tight"—Joss swallowed—"there won't be room for Fiona. Do...do you think she'll be okay here?"

Although he really wanted to make her that promise, he couldn't lie. "Probably, but there are no guarantees."

"Puck's life is the most important thing."

She was stranded in the wilderness and being pursued by a psycho, yet she was calm and thinking logically. "You are a caring woman."

"Damn right I am, so don't sound so surprised."

He took her face in his hands, looked directly into her eyes and thought he caught a flash of shock in them. "I'm not. Maybe I was at first. But you are not a spoiled rock star.

You've shown me the real Joss Wynter. The real Jocelyn Winterburn. The real Jojo. You are strong and smart and fearless."

"I'm scared all the time," she said softly.

"Courageous is a better word. You aren't playing a game out here. I think you are rediscovering who you really are."

She blinked, but it didn't clear the sheen in her eyes. "And I think you may be exactly right about that."

God, Shep hadn't been exaggerating when he said getting through the cave tunnels would be a challenge. And why Joss thought he might've been was a mystery. He was the original tell-it-like-it-is man.

When they approached the area where they would be forced to crawl, they lowered Puck's litter to the ground. Joss's insides and hope sank when he didn't even whimper at the jostling.

They made slow progress, Shep crawling backward and her forward. Joss tried to stabilize the litter, making sure Puck never hit the cave's rock walls. By the time the tunnel opened up again, Joss's knees felt as if they'd been shredded on a cheese grater. She was huff-puffing air, and sweat was a slick layer all over her body.

"Does your cabin have a bathtub?" she asked Shep as she lifted the back end of the litter. They could share Puck's weight from here on out.

"Yes."

"What kind?" She was dreaming of a deep one near a window where she could gaze out from the safety of water and shelter.

"The bathing kind."

"Good enough."

"It has feet."

"A clawfoot."

"Yes."

"If we weren't carrying an injured dog between us, I would jump you and kiss you. Maybe jump you and do more than that."

"Because my house has a bathtub?"

"Yep."

"I've been thinking of adding on. Building another bathroom with an even bigger tub."

She and Shep were damn well going to make it out of this cave, get Puck medical help, and share that clawfoot tub.

"We're at the cave exit," Shep said suddenly. And only then did Joss realize the cave had brightened a little.

They both squatted and placed Puck's litter on the ground. She was terrified that Puck was fading away.

Joss grabbed a handful of Shep's hair and pulled him in for a quick hard kiss. "Set those traps and get back here as soon as possible."

He nodded once. Then he worked his way out the crack leading to the wilderness beyond.

23

SHEP'S HANDS HAD NEVER FELT THIS CLUMSY BEFORE. ANXIETY and self-doubt rose up in him, clawing their way up his throat and threatening to explode out of him. He reached into his pocket for his length of cord only to find it missing.

More nasty adrenaline spurted into his body.

Where is it? I need it. I need Puck.

I need Jojo.

Shep set his teeth and moderated his breathing. Slow in-breath, slow out-breath. His dad and Cash had taught him to meditate many years ago. He was in control. He was okay.

He remembered where the cord was. He'd used it, cut it into smaller lengths, to secure the ground stakes together. The rest of it was sitting in a pile beside him. He'd set it aside to use for the spears themselves.

His hands steadied and he quickly tied the spear into the free end of the swing arm. After securing the trigger post, he cut a notch in it. He looped the trip cord around the trigger pin and placed one end of the pin into the notch, careful to keep his legs and feet out of the line of fire just in case something went wrong and the spring released.

His notches in the trap pieces were perfect. He knew that, so he pulled back the swing arm to create tension, gently situated the trigger pin over the spear, and nodded. It would hold.

It *would* work.

He snake-crawled his way through the underbrush and positioned the spear in the second trap. It wouldn't kill whoever was stalking them. That was too much to hope for. To be high enough to kill, the mechanism would've had to be in plain sight. So a surprise injury would have to be enough.

Enough to give them the head start they needed.

He didn't want to set off the stalker's curiosity too soon, so Shep quickly constructed a very rudimentary Goldberg machine. A small pile of rocks that would simulate someone scrambling down the hill from the cave and something to set them rolling. He scooped dirt into a piece of ripstop he'd cut from his backpack and tied it off. Then he secured it to a low branch over the rock pile and punched a small hole into it. The dirt trickled out, a sluggish flow that would give Shep and Joss time to get away with Puck.

As quickly as he could, he ducked and weaved through the trees and around to the backside of the cave. A faint sound came from inside. So faint he wasn't sure he was hearing anything. But when he worked his way inside the small opening, Joss was stroking Puck's head and humming to him.

A lullaby, maybe?

God, why couldn't she sound like that when she sang on stage? It was sweet and soft, and tugged at a part of Shep he didn't know he had inside him.

Shep's return interrupted her song, and she scrambled to her feet. "All set?"

"Yeah. We need to move out." He pulled himself back through the opening, and they carefully maneuvered Puck's litter outside.

Joss wiggled through like she'd been scaling boulders her whole life. She picked up her end of the litter and said, "I'm ready."

Shep led the way through some rough, rocky terrain that morphed into a steep uphill climb filled with prickly bushes and dying wild blackberry vines. But it would cover their tracks and no one would expect they'd taken the north route out of the caves.

When he felt they'd traveled far enough north and knew they could pick up another trail due east of their current position, he said, "Half a mile and we should hit the trail. Are you okay?"

"Never better."

One glance behind him proved her words a lie. Her face was streaked with dirt and her eyes were red-rimmed, but she had a grip on Puck's litter as if it was her last possession in the world.

"Let me know if you need to rest."

They picked their way through the forest and met up with the trail.

"Any idea how far to Steele Ridge?" she asked him.

"About eight miles."

Her mouth firmed into a line, and she rolled back her shoulders. "Then we're going to run it."

"What?"

"I know you think I'm some pampered LA princess, but I live in the Santa Monica Mountains. Definitely different from these, but I trail run when I have time."

He didn't want her to wear herself out, because then

he'd have to figure out a way to carry both Puck and her. "I don't think that's a good idea."

"How about I promise to let you know if I get tired?"

"You're already tired."

"I'm motivated." Her chin lifted, reminding him that she was no softie. She'd proved that time and time again over the past few days. "And my motivation beats my exhaustion any day."

"Why don't we switch?" he said. "You take the front and set the pace."

She nodded. They gently lowered the litter, switched places, and picked up Puck again.

And damn, Joss was a machine. Tough with a capital T. Even though she was—as his dad would say—no bigger than a minute. Her arm muscles were defined from the effort of carrying the litter, but she never relented. Just ran —shoulders squared and feet flying.

"Do you think it worked?" she asked.

"The trap?"

"Yeah."

"There is no way for me to know," he said, casting a quick look at Puck and then returning his focus to the trail. It would not be good if he stumbled and fell. "But I rigged a Rube Goldberg that I think will lure this person toward the spear traps."

"You will never stop impressing me."

Unfortunately, that probably wasn't true. Shep ended up disappointing people—especially women—because he couldn't be what they wanted. Amber had often been disappointed in his performance in one way or another. She'd complained that he was never home on time. That he preferred to camp in the wilderness than to sleep in her bed. That he wasn't reliable or considerate.

Eventually, Joss would feel the same.

Get off this mountain before you worry about all that.

So he emulated Joss and just ran. But when there was no sign of trouble, he started to worry again. They'd either gotten very lucky or had been lured into some kind of trap of their own. "I can't think like that," he blurted out.

She seemed to take his outburst in stride and asked, "Like what?"

"Like we might fail." He could not let either Puck or Joss down.

"We won't," she huffed. "I can run like this all night."

That was a lie. She started slowing down at least a mile back. But if there were prizes for perseverance, she would get a first-place trophy. Because he would give it to her. "If I tell you we have three more miles, do you think you can make it?"

She stumbled. He felt it from the way the litter dropped abruptly and then righted. "Absolutely."

"Good," he said. "Then you can definitely handle the single mile until this trail crosses Talleyville Road."

"You're sneaky." She looked back at him and flashed a droopy smile that wound its way through the fog of his fear and made him hope for the future. "But I like it."

Joss's legs didn't feel like Jell-O.

They felt like a soupy platter of flan. Like flan stirred together with a pitcher full of cream. No, of skim milk.

She was pretty sure she'd formed a whopper of a blister on one heel about three miles back. She hadn't been lying when she told Shep she ran the trails. But she'd never run this fast or this far. Or for something this important.

Blisters would heal. Legs would recover.

Puck might not.

She didn't bother to ask Shep how he thought his dog was doing. She was seeing the deterioration firsthand. Because she needed a rhythm that would keep her feet moving for the last mile, she chanted to herself: *Puck is alive. Puck will stay alive.*

But that only lasted so long and she started flagging again.

"Sing," Shep said to her.

"What?"

"Doesn't have to be loud." He adjusted his hold on his side of the litter, taking a little more of the weight. "But it will provide a backbeat."

"I... I haven't... I can't..."

"Do it for Puck. It will help him."

Of all the songs—hundreds of them—that Joss knew by heart, none of them seemed to surface. *This isn't about you. Puck doesn't care what you sing, only that you do it.*

Or maybe it was Shep who needed soothing most of all.

They all needed something. Something to keep them going.

So Joss sang. She made up verse after verse of "She'll Be Coming Round the Mountain," substituting she'll with they'll. Because *they* would get off this mountain all together or not at all.

They'll be jogging down the mountain when they come.

They'll be eating raw wild carrots...

They'll be drinking maple water...

They'll be carting Puck the dog...

They'll be counting on each other...

She sang and sang, improvising the lyrics. When she couldn't think of any more, she started them all over again and would've sung them a million times more if that was what it took to get them where they were going.

But Shep abruptly said, "We're at the road."

Only then did Joss blink the sweat out of her eyes and realize they'd come to a beautiful strip of blacktop. Completely deserted blacktop. "Which way into town?"

"West," he said, gesturing to their right. "But all we need is for one person to drive by."

"They'll pick up hitchhikers?"

"This isn't the big city," he said. "And people around here know me."

If he said so, but Joss mentally prepared herself to break into a run again. She was just about to suggest they speed up when a Black Tahoe slowed behind them and came to a screeching stop. A lean man with dark hair jumped out and ran toward them. "Jesus, Shep! What's going on?"

"We need to get Puck to the vet. Now."

"Let's load him in the backseat." The man grabbed Joss's side of the litter and eased it away from her. Her hands remained in a cramped, curled position while the men slid Puck into the rear seat of the Tahoe.

Joss blinked, for some reason registering that the cargo area of the SUV was filled with stacks of tissue boxes and antibacterial wipes.

"You need to get in the car!" the other man called out to Joss, yanking her away from thoughts of whether or not he had a whopper of a cold. "Move it. Now."

Because Shep had taken the seat beside Puck, Joss stumbled toward the passenger door. The intense stranger jerked it open for her and took her arm to help her inside. He quickly shut the door and rounded the hood to jump in the driver's seat.

They went from zero to rocket ship in a blink.

The man beside her glared into the rearview mirror at Shep. Joss wanted to climb over the console and beat him with her fists. If he had any idea what—

"What the hell happened?" he demanded, his harsh words directed at Shep.

"It's a long story." Shep's head fell back and he closed his eyes. "Just get Puck to the vet and I'll explain everything."

24

His brother drove like a man possessed. Although Puck was loyal first and foremost to him, Shep's whole family loved his dog fiercely. He was family. Period.

Way might've taken the turn into the veterinarian's gravel parking lot slightly too fast, but he stopped the Tahoe with the smooth ease of a hot spoon slipping through ice cream. Shep pushed himself out of the car and turned back to scoop up Puck. His chest was barely rising and falling.

Although Shep's stomach tried to rebel the way it had back at the cave, he swallowed the bile. Puking wouldn't help right now.

Joss dashed for the front door, rattling the chimes hanging on it, and yelled inside, "We have an emergency coming in. We need a doctor now. Now!"

"Fucking hell," Way muttered as he jogged toward the entrance beside Shep and pointed to Joss's back. "That's Joss Wynter."

"Her name is Jocelyn, but I get to call her Jojo." He turned sideways to carry Puck through the door and one of the vet techs was already waving them into the back.

"In here."

Dr. Orozco quickly looked over Puck, but Shep couldn't get a read on her expression. Was the lack of facial muscle movement an indication that the situation was hopeless? Or hopeful?

Damn, he hated not knowing.

"He needs surgery immediately," she said as she palpated Puck's side. "It looks like the arrow kept him from bleeding out, but I won't know the extent of the damage until we get inside and see what's what."

Shep didn't want to let Puck go back through that door. Into the treatment area. To be put under and cut open. He had the sinking feeling that if he let him go, he'd never hold him in his arms again. Dr. Orozco must've understood because she put a tender hand on Puck's head and the other over her heart. "I will help him to the very best of my ability. And I'm very good at what I do."

Joss tugged on Shep's arm, pulling away his grip on Puck. "Let the vet have him, Shep. You've done everything you can."

The yawning space inside Shep was emptier and darker than anything he'd ever felt before. And he'd felt plenty of empty darkness in his days. "He's all I have."

Way clamped an arm around Shep's shoulders and squeezed hard, leading him out of the exam room and toward a waiting area filled with bright colors and a mini dog park. In the far corner, a sign asked people to leave donations of toys and towels for the local animal shelter. "No, he's not. You know that. Where's your paracord?"

"Wrapped around a couple homemade spears up near some caves."

"What? Why were you making spears?"

"It's a bit of a long story," Joss told him.

"I'm calling Cash and Emmy, having them meet us at your cabin," Way said to Shep. "Once they've given both of you a good look, you're going to tell me what the hell happened up there."

"But Puck—"

"Is in good hands," Way reassured him. "Dr. Orozco will keep you in the loop."

Shep shot a final look at the door leading to the rear of the vet clinic. Way was right, but Shep hated leaving Puck.

Within half an hour, Shep's cabin was under assault from his family. Way's call to Cash and Emmy turned into some kind of damn phone tree, and every Kingston was hovering around somewhere. Shep was pretty sure there were a few Steeles on his front porch, too.

He'd never had so many people in and around his home.

Cash had hunted up a thin piece of rope and pushed it into Shep's hands. "Hang on to this." But what Shep found he really wanted to hang on to was Joss's hand. They sat on the couch side by side while Cash looked Shep over and Emmy did the same with Joss.

"I can't breathe," Shep wheezed out.

"Shit," Cash barked. "He's having some kind of allergic reaction. What the hell did you get into—"

Emmy glanced over and put a hand on Cash's shoulder. "No, he's having a panic attack. Don't go down that rabbit hole with him. He needs you to be calm."

"You're right," Cash said and turned to say to the room, "Everyone but Emmy and me out of here. Give them some space." He centered his attention back to Shep. "You, close your eyes, and let's breathe together."

His brother counted him through some round breathing, and Shep's galloping heart slowed to a trot. But his fingers were still working the rope. A fisherman's knot. Then a sheepshank. And finally a trucker's hitch.

Joss's hand in his, and a rope in the other. Shep's world was beginning to right itself just a little, even though he imagined he could feel Puck's furry weight against the side of his leg.

"I can't live without him, Cash."

"Not that it'll come to that, but yes you can. You had a life before him and you'll have a life after him."

"It's better with him."

"Of course it is. Which is why Dr. Orozco is working her ass off right now."

Shep finally opened his eyes again to see Emmy and Joss both watching him closely.

Emmy said, "You're both a little dehydrated and definitely exhausted. I'd like to start a saline drip on each of you. You also need food and a whole lot of rest."

"We'll feed and water them," Cash said grimly and hitched a thumb toward the front door. "But there's not a damn person here that's gonna let them rest until they hear what happened up on that mountain."

Although Joss had been eager to meet Shep's family, they'd descended like a plague of locusts, and that had been slightly unsettling. But there was not a doubt in her mind that these people cared for Shep deeply. Loved him unconditionally. How could he believe he didn't know what love was? It was all around him.

So thick she could breathe it in. She wanted that, what he had. People who didn't expect him to sparkle before they smothered him with adoration.

Shep's paramedic brother Cash looked a bit like him.

The hair wasn't as shaggy, but there was something about his eyes and mouth. He had a lightheartedness about him that she'd seen in Shep a few times.

Emmy McKay, as she'd been introduced, checked Joss's blood pressure and glanced at the cabin's front door. "The troops are assembling."

That was good. Joss said, "Could they stay outside? Shep might need some space to tell the full story, but…"

"But what?" Cash's sharp gaze met Joss's.

"But you might want to have a few people stand guard."

"Are we guarding against your fans or something else?"

"Something else. Definitely something else."

Cash shot to his feet and was out the door. Joss heard him bark out, "Reid, we've got problems. No, I don't know what the hell they are right now. But I need you and your brothers to surround this cabin. Take weapons."

Shep smiled—a weary, trying-for-patience smile. "We are kind of a bossy bunch."

"I hadn't noticed."

"I'm surprised Maggie isn't up my ass right now."

"Oh, she was out on a call," Emmy said cheerfully. "But apparently she's on her way. So expect her to breach your posterior any minute now."

A younger woman—probably midtwenties, with brown hair in a chin-length cut and blue-framed glasses—poked her head in from the porch. "Can I do anything in here?"

"Think you can rustle up a snack?" Cash asked her.

A brown paper bag crinkled when the woman held it up and grimaced. "Mom brought what she called the-cure-for-everything muffins."

"I don't even want to know, do I?" Cash groaned.

"Crystallized ginger for nausea, red ginseng for hangover, whisky and honey for cough."

"That actually sounds like her best baked good yet," Cash said.

"Oh, and turmeric and salmon for inflammation."

"No, thank you," Shep said firmly. "I have some Epic bars in the kitchen."

"I'll get them." The woman dropped that bag, and that was when she seemed to realize Shep had company on the couch. Her gaze stopped and Superglued onto Joss. "Oh. My. God. You're... you're... Why didn't anyone tell me..."

"Snack now, Riley," Emmy drawled. "Fangirl later."

Ah, so this was Shep's younger sister. The Scarlet Glitterati fan.

"I'm on it," she said. She leaned back outside and said, "Dad, did you bring OJ? We could use that inside." She beckoned a tall, lean, older man who carried what looked like a carafe of fresh-squeezed juice into the cabin and they hurried into the small kitchen. They returned with glasses of juice and Shep's favored protein bars.

"Thanks, Dad," Shep said as he reached for a glass. "And look at you, Riley, being all domestic. Coen is a good influence."

Riley stuck out her tongue at her brother, but immediately sucked it back in. "Shit, I'm sorry. This is horrible. Shep, I'm..." She walked toward the front door. "I need a minute."

"Why is she upset?" Shep asked his dad. "She didn't like being called domestic?"

His dad clapped him soundly on the shoulder as he passed the other glass of juice to Joss. "No, I think she's worried about her big brother."

After what amounted to a post blood drive snack, Joss and Shep settled into two wooden chairs on the front porch. A woman, wearing a sheriff's department uniform with a utility belt packing a serious looking handgun, strode up the stairs and stood directly in front of Shep. "Talk to me."

The rest of the group gathered around them as if awaiting story time at the library.

It *was* a bit of a tall tale.

When things went completely quiet, and Shep didn't say a word, Joss reached over and gripped his hand. "Do you want me to explain everything?"

"You will do a better job."

She took a bracing breath and said, "We're pretty sure we evaded a murderer."

25

"Excuse me?" Maggie—glaring at Shep as only Maggie could—braced her hands on her hips. Yeah, even he knew that was unhappy body language.

"Mags," he said. "Give us a minute here before you start grilling us down to the bone. Because I have a few questions for you."

"Harris Shep—"

"Did the other *Do or Die* people make it back to town?" he asked.

"I haven't seen them. Anyone else?" she asked, looking around at the family members gathered.

"No," Emmy said, "but they were staying at the B and B before they left, right? I can call Mrs. Tasky and find out." She pulled out her phone and walked to the edge of the porch, but Shep figured they were still out there in the woods somewhere. Or one of them had turned on the rest of them.

Hell, he didn't know, and his head was one massive ache of confusion.

Joss gripped his arm and addressed his sister. "Sheriff, law enforcement needs to get out into that national forest."

"What the hell are we looking at here?" Maggie asked, hands still firmly planted on her uniform-covered hips. "A rescue mission, a manhunt, what?"

"Probably all of the above," Shep told her. "And definitely body recovery."

"What?" Shep's mom jumped off the front steps, her eyes more than wild. "Whose body?"

"Buffalo Moody's," Joss said. "We found him. Well, Lauren Estes actually found him out in the woods, but..."

"Someone had him strung up in a tree," Shep said. "But I don't think that's the way he was killed."

"Why the holy hell didn't you call me immediately?" Maggie demanded. "I don't give a flying flip that you were on federal land."

The national forests were officially in the US Forest Service's jurisdiction, but they had cooperative agreements with most county law enforcement in Western Carolina, including Haywood county. "I planned to," Shep said. "But when Joss and I made it back to the group's campsite, the others were gone, along with a lot of my stuff, including the sat phone."

"Where were you?"

"Almost three quarters around the trail loop on the east rim. But the body was in the woods off to the north. As for Moody, I'm not sure how much will be left of him by the time you get people up there."

"If you were at the east rim, you should've been back sooner. Where have you been?"

"When the rest of the group wasn't in camp, and it was obvious they'd stolen supplies, I got suspicious. What if one of *them* killed Moody?"

"Shep thought it was best for us to hit another trail," Joss added.

"And a few other things happened along the way that made us realize someone was tracking us," Shep told Maggie.

"What kind of things?"

"Maggie, it doesn't matter right now." Shep jumped to his feet and glanced around for Puck. When he remembered Puck was—*no, no, no! Don't think about Puck right now.* Shep tried to calm his jumping pulse by sheer will. "What matters is that I hopefully put a spear through someone's leg up near Stonehill caves. If I was lucky, he might still be there. If he's not—"

"—then we definitely have a manhunt on our hands."

"I'm going up with you." That was not negotiable.

"No," she shot back immediately. "This is a job for law enforcement. Maybe search and rescue."

"I have more experience in the backcountry than all those people combined. Besides, I know the exact locations of Moody's body and where I hopefully speared whoever killed him."

"You just came down off that mountain and you're not in any shape—"

"You can leave me here," he said, spinning around to loom over his sister, "and I'll hit the trail on my own."

"No, you certainly will not," his mother protested and looked toward his dad for support. "Ross, tell him that he can't—"

"Honey, he's an adult," his dad cut in. "I'd rather Maggie let him go in with her group, but I will not tell a grown man what he can and can't do. Shep knows what he can handle and what he can't."

As much as Shep admired and respected his mother, his

dad had always been his person. His rock. He was the one who convinced Shep he was worthy of being accepted by other people, just as he was.

Joss reached for his arm again and her grip tightened to the point of pain. Something was wrong.

He turned to her and ducked his head to try to gain a little privacy. "You are upset. Why?"

"I don't want you to go back up there."

"I have to." It occurred to him that she might be scared. *Good going, Shep. Get her to safety and then let her think you're going to dump her.* "If you're scared, you can go home with my parents or better yet, someone can take you to my Aunt Joan's house. My cousin Reid has security—"

"I'm not scared for me," she said. "I'm scared for you. Whoever is out there made it clear that he or she was after *you.*"

"You were in the tent, too, when that fire was set."

"But I wasn't the main target."

"I'll be hiking in with Maggie and other law enforcement. You might have noticed that my sister wears a gun on her hip. Believe me, she and everyone who works for her knows exactly what they are doing."

"Then I want to go back up, too."

Oh. No. Hell, no. Shep wanted to jump away from her—pace and pull at his hair. Instead, he took both of Joss's hands in his. "You would slow us down." She started to say something, and he squeezed her fingers. "And I need you to stay here and keep an eye on Puck."

"But your family. They can—"

"He's gotten very attached to you over the past few days. If he wakes up and I'm not there, he might be scared. But if you're there, you can help him. He won't be scared if you're there."

Her head dropped and when she spoke, she sounded a little like a frog. "How long do you think you'll be gone?"

"I don't really know."

"I want to stay here," she said. "In your house."

Shep glanced away from Joss to find every person in his family staring at them—wide-eyed and loose-jawed. What? Had they never seen two people have a conversation before? "We're just making soup," he told them.

"Sure you are, buddy." Way shook his head, but appeared to be suppressing a smile. "Sure you are."

"Dad, Joss will be staying here. I am going to give her my keys—to the cabin and my truck."

"Okay, what do you need me to do?"

"Do you think you could help track down her belongings? All the *Do or Die* celebrities had to give up most of what they'd packed before we left. I bet Moody had his support people store it somewhere."

"Absolutely."

"Honey," his mom gripped his shoulder. "What can I do? Joss will probably be hungry later. I could—"

"Take her to the Triple B. That would be a great idea. If she doesn't feel up to it tonight, maybe tomorrow sometime."

"I could do that."

He touched his mom's hand. She was trying hard to smile, but it didn't look like the proper muscles were all engaged. "You're wearing a fake smile."

"I'm trying for it to be real."

"Maggie and I will be okay."

"I know you will, honey. But I don't care how grown up and capable you both are, you're still my babies."

"Mom," Maggie said, pulling their mom in for a hard,

quick hug, "your babies need to gear up and move out while we still have some daylight."

After Shep and his sister left in her cruiser to finish prepping for the trip back up the mountain, Joss was still surrounded by his family. There were quite a lot of them. And none of them appeared to be leaving.

She'd never felt threatened in a crowd until she'd taken a header off the stage that night. Now, her fear of falling had little to do with losing control and being physically vulnerable. It was all about the emotional threat.

She swallowed to try to make her thumping heart return to its proper location in her chest. *You aren't being hunted here. These people won't drop you and stomp you underfoot.* "Um... Was there... Can I tell you anything that Shep didn't get a chance to explain?"

Riley—who'd been giddy to initially meet Joss—wore a tight-mouthed expression and body armor made of crossed arms. "I'd like to know why you're cozying up to my brother."

Another swallow, but no words made their way out of Joss's mouth. Shep's family all looked like a phalanx of shit-locked soldiers right now, even Shep's firefighter brother Cash, who had initially seemed like a totally laid-back, easygoing guy.

"He got you off the mountain," Riley continued, her tone combative. "What else do you want?"

"I... I don't know what you mean."

"I'm asking why he was holding your hand and acting as moon-eyed as I've ever seen him."

"Shep doesn't normally do moon-eyed." Shep's brother, Way, wasn't a huge guy. But with his unsmiling mouth and slitted eyes, he looked as though he might know thousands of ways to maim. Then again, he'd had a cargo hold full of what she'd realized were back-to-school supplies. So who was this guy? "So we're all a little taken off guard."

"What happened out there?" Riley demanded. "What did you do to him?"

"Riley-girl," her dad said softly. "Your mother bear streak is showing."

"I don't care." She shook her head, making her hair swing angrily. "She's a big rock star, and he's…"

"Amazing," Joss said softly as she looked around at all the unfriendly faces. Only Shep's dad's body language was relaxed. "Riley, I get why you're protective. Shep told me a little about all of you while we were out there, and it's obvious you all love him very much. So I don't have a problem telling you that I care for him deeply as well."

"*Care for.* What does that mean exactly? And how can you care for a man you've known for less than a week?"

Joss stood and looked Riley in the eyes. Maybe not directly, because Shep's sister had a more than a few inches on her. But she'd be damned if she planned to defend herself, defend Shep, while sitting. "It means exactly what I said. I have feelings for him. He's smart and funny and capable and honest. A woman would have to be a fool not to be drawn to that."

Riley's shoulders lost a smidge of their tension. "There have been a few fools through the years."

Cash snorted. "With the biggest one being Amber."

Shep's mom took Joss by the arm and pulled her in. "Shep hasn't had the most successful romantic past. Are you saying… We're asking if you're involved with him."

If having his body inside hers and having feelings she couldn't quite define was considered *involved,* then absolutely. "Oh my God! You want to know what my intentions are. Like his dad said a few minutes ago, Shep is a grown man. You all know that, right?"

"I'm not sure if you realized this," his mom said. Her volume was soft, but the thread of steel in her words was clear, "but he is... a little different."

"Of course, I noticed," Joss said. "I got my first clue when he said something that knocked my legs out from under me."

Cash groaned and shook his head. "That's Shep, alright."

Joss stood her ground. "But what I also noticed is that he's refreshingly honest."

"Some would say painfully."

"He told me about his Asperger's." She looked around, meeting each person's gaze, one by one. "That explained a lot."

"Having something explained and truly understanding it are two different things," his mother said. "You've only known Shep a few days. He's a wonderful, generous, authentic person, but close daily contact with him can be challenging. A challenge many people aren't up to meeting."

"You all seem like a nice family," Joss said. "And I can appreciate where you're coming from. He's your son, your brother. But he knows who he is and what he wants. I would never take anything from him that he wasn't willing to give. I'm not interested in turning Shep Kingston into anyone else. But I also don't know what else I can tell you about our involvement right now."

A large, dark-haired man with a military-style haircut stepped forward and wrapped a comforting arm around Riley's middle, but her expression didn't soften. She said, "There is no gray area with Shep. You need to decide if you're in—all in—or out. Or you'll hurt him, and then I'll have to hurt you. There won't be an Amber sequel if he's thinks he's fallen in love with you."

Had he? Had Shep fallen for Joss? Fallen *in love* with her? She found that to be more realistic, more appealing than she ever would have a few days ago. Who could she be with him? Who could he be with her? Who could they be together?

Joss wanted to find out.

"I don't have all the answers," she told his family. "Are things complicated? Yes. Have the past few days been intense? Absolutely. But I'm not leaving Steele Ridge immediately, definitely not until the sheriff finds out who was stalking us through that forest. But I have a favor to ask of you. If you love him, and I know you do, please give us a little time to figure out if we love one another."

Fucking Kingston. He'd set not one, but two, traps. The winner had avoided the first, but not the second. And a homemade spear to the thigh hurt like a bitch.

Every step taken back to his four-wheeler and every jolt down the trail toward Steele Ridge had been a misery.

But Kingston had also turned tail and run back to town like a little girl. What he didn't realize was that their competition wasn't over.

Not yet.

Not until the winner came out on top.

26

BEFORE JOSS LEFT SHEP'S CABIN, ONE OF HIS COUSINS HAD showed up with a bag printed with La Belle Style on the side and filled with clothes. She'd gratefully pulled on a pair of socks, protecting the blister Emmy had bandaged for her, but the other clothes would have to wait until she had a chance to shower.

Shep's dad insisted on driving Joss to find the belongings she'd brought from California. He whistled "Camp Town Races" and several other folksy songs as they bumped their way over the blacktop roads from Shep's cabin into Steele Ridge.

He rolled down the driver's side window and the breeze ruffled his hair—more salt than pepper. Joss could see where the Kingston children had come by their good looks. Both Mr. Kingston and his wife were very attractive.

Although his whistling was totally in tune, Joss couldn't stand another second of it. "'Days Are Short' by Arlo Guthrie."

"Hmm."

"From *Hobo's Lullaby,* 1972."

"Interesting." He glanced over at her, and kindness shined in his eyes. "I wouldn't have thought American folk was your genre."

"I'm not a woman you want to play Name That Tune against."

His smile—wide and genuine—reminded her of Shep's when he was truly happy. "I like you, Joss Wynter."

"You sound surprised."

"Oh, I enjoy your music," he said easily. "Overall, I'm a classic rock man myself, although you wouldn't know it by my kids' names. Sandy is a big country music fan."

"She picked great names."

He laughed. "Not sure the kids would always agree with you. Those names caused them more than a little trouble back when they were all in school. Maggie punched a boy in the nose once because he ran around calling her Mandrell the Mandrake."

What, she wondered, had kids called Shep? How had they treated the boy who didn't just march to the beat of his own drummer but drummed a whole new tune? "Emmy Lou Harris and T. G. Sheppard, right?"

"My wife says country music is the best music."

"Any of your kids have musical talent?"

"Not really. Probably for the best since they're all so damn good at their chosen professions."

"Especially Shep. He got me off that mountain alive." But Joss felt as if she and Shep's dad were dancing around the real issue here. His family, although mostly hospitable, weren't exactly platinum members of the Joss Wynter fan club right now. "If you're planning to grill me, you might want to start now," she said. "I doubt the drive to town is that long."

"Should I grill you?" he asked mildly.

He couldn't be this casual about her relationship with his son when Shep's sister wanted to dissect her with a pitchfork. "Are you really this laid-back?"

"I'm a simple guy." He swept a hand over the chest of his plaid shirt. "Just a former stay-at-home father."

That made her laugh. Ross Kingston was no doddering dad. And he might claim to be chill, but it was no mistake that he'd offered to accompany her into town. He wanted to know things. "My real name is Jocelyn Winterburn."

"Pretty."

"That's what your son said." She took a quick breath and braced her hand against the truck door, trying to steady herself. "He told me about his ex-wife. I'm not her."

"Also interesting," Ross said. "Shep doesn't usually talk about her."

"Just because you don't talk about something doesn't mean you're not thinking about it 24/7."

"Is that the way it is with your band?"

Gut punch. She should've expected it, but he was so damn affable. It was obviously his super-stealth secret weapon. The sad smile on his face told her that he hadn't meant his words to do damage. "Yes," she finally said softly. "Sometimes things that happen in life are so painful that talking about them tears a new hole each time the words come out. You learn to shut up and stop ripping yourself open."

"Because other people never understand?"

"No, because *you* still don't understand. Not what happened. Not truly. Not what you did to cause it. Not how to heal. You know nothing. Understand nothing."

"Shep wasn't responsible for Amber's choice to leave, and you didn't kill your bandmates. We get caught up in circumstances and assume causation rather than correlation. And that's a very important difference."

"Association, as opposed to direct responsibility," she mused.

"But it's easier to understand causality. Correlation is messier. So many variables. It's impossible to control for them all."

"Are you a scientist?"

"No, a farmer."

"A very smart farmer." He drove down Main Street, a charming thoroughfare that she hadn't had a chance to see since she'd been literally dropped into town. A small sandwich sign sat outside a place called the Mad Batter. Chalked on it was the message, "The most important stages of life aren't the ones you stand on."

Shep's dad made a turn, then studied her. "Do you hold yourself responsible for what happened, Jocelyn Winterburn?"

"I did."

"And now?"

What did she feel now? The past few days had been so intense—in both negative and positive ways—that she didn't know what all the feelings flying around inside her meant. As Shep would say, she needed to try to separate the strands. "Now I'm starting to see that although we can influence other people's behavior, it's pretty hard to force anyone to do something they're absolutely unwilling to do. At least not under normal circumstances."

"And your band willingly put themselves on that helicopter."

"I feel like you're trying to tell me something here. Something about Shep."

"I'd say one of the reasons Amber left and your band

boarded that helicopter was because all the parties involved weren't being honest. Not about what they wanted or how they felt. And when you're unclear with the people closest to you, it's infinitely unkind. I don't know how you feel about my son, and truthfully, it's not my business right now. But I do ask that you're honest. With him and with yourself. You both deserve that."

They pulled up in front of a huge white farmhouse painted with green shutters, and he parked the truck. She was trying to process all the lessons Ross Kingston had packed into a fifteen-minute drive. "Shep is the most honest person I've ever met in my life. He doesn't play games, and I won't play games with him."

"That's all I can ask." He pointed to the B&B with its peaceful-looking porch, complete with quaint rocking chairs. "Would you like me to go in with you? Or I can just stay here and ride back—"

"Thank you," she said quickly. "But I've been with people nonstop for the past few days. I'll just pop in and see if my phone and things are inside. Then I'm going back to the vet clinic."

Shep's dad opened the glove compartment, which looked like a cross between Whole Foods, REI, and Staples. Very neat. Very Shep.

Ross took pen to napkin and jotted down two phone numbers. "First one is my cell. Second one is Sandy's. I don't expect trouble of any sort, but if anything happens, even if you get spooked, dial 911. Maggie will have briefed her officers on what's what."

"How will you get home?"

He chuckled. "Believe it or not, we have a rocking little Uber business going on here in Steele Ridge."

Unable to let him get out without some show of appreciation, Joss put her hand on his forearm. But the thank-you she planned to say turned into something else entirely and she blurted out, "I think I'm in love with your son."

And *whoosh*. There went her stomach and her heart on the amusement park ride. The one that dropped two hundred feet. She slapped her hand over her chest and wheezed out, "Is that crazy?"

"I'm not really one to talk about crazy and love," he said. "I knew during the first date with Sandy that she was the one for me. She's been the one for me for over thirty-five years, and God willing, she will be for at least another thirty-five."

"How long had you known her when you went on that first date?"

"Twenty-seven hours and fourteen minutes."

"Wow, you work fast."

"We Kingston men tend to know what we want," he said, resting a steady, fatherly hand on her shoulder. "But for Shep's sake, don't say any words you can't take back unless that thinking of yours turns into knowing."

Shep had to hand it to Maggie, her deputies, the forest service LEOs, and the rest of the multi-jurisdictional team that had been put together. They made excellent time, hiking into the national forest with a speed and intensity that left no doubt they were taking this situation seriously. Very seriously.

And they were all looking to him for guidance and advice, making Shep wonder what it would be like to work on a team like this. One where people communicated so fluidly, where people understood and accepted each other's strengths.

"You doing okay?" Maggie drew even with him on the trail. "You've got to be exhausted after the past few days."

"This is what I do."

"I get that," she said. "But you don't normally guide a group that runs into this kind of trouble."

"Even with everything that happened, Joss and I were doing okay until Puck was shot."

"God, Shep, I'm so sorry about that." She looked up at him, but thankfully her pace didn't slow. "I forgot to say it earlier."

"Why are you sorry? You didn't shoot him."

"I'm sorry it happened. But we will find this person."

Shep scanned the trail in front of them, but it was impossible to tell if someone had traveled this way—the more direct route back into Steele Ridge. If someone had, he hadn't left any blood trace. "Maybe he or she is still up there."

"Let's go through the possible suspects again," she said, pulling out her phone and engaging the voice recorder.

They'd already done this, but Shep understood Maggie's need to be thorough. They were very much alike that way. "All the people associated with *Do or Die.*"

"Give them to me one by one."

"The Bitcher."

"Lauren Estes."

"The Bleeding Heart."

"Bradley Woodard."

"And the camera guys."

"Greg and Zach." Maggie nodded. "I've got people contacting the network to get their last names. Who else?"

"Like I said, we came across one of those guys who believes he's a descendant of Juney Whank Falls. But this seemed personal, especially when Puck was targeted."

"And you don't think those people could get personal? They claim they own the mountains and forests."

"Maybe," he admitted. "But I would have expected more direct action to get us out of the area."

"I'd say putting an arrow into your dog is pretty damn direct."

Shep's insides tensed as he thought about that arrow jabbing into his best friend. "I think it was meant for me."

"Even more personal. Shep, who did you piss off the most out there?"

He didn't take offense at Maggie's question. His family knew and accepted that he often insulted and upset people. They said they loved him anyway. "Buffalo Moody."

"Being dead tends to clear him as a suspect for stealing your gear and stalking you through the woods. Who would you say is next in the Anti-Shep-Kingston line?"

"Probably The Bitcher."

"Tell me what happened with Lauren Estes."

"She was a brat."

"And I guess you told her that."

"I didn't use the word brat," he said. "But I didn't make things easy for her like she wanted. And I sure didn't fuck her."

"Hoookay." Maggie blew out a breath. "And was that something she put on the table?"

"I know you don't think I'm good with that kind of stuff, but I'm pretty sure she was trying to manipulate me into helping her."

"And some women think that sex is the foremost manipulation technique."

"Isn't it?"

"What?"

"That's what Amber used to do. Sex if I did the things she wanted me to. No sex if I didn't."

"I'm not surprised," Maggie said.

"Maggie, do you think all women are manipulative?"

"As a woman myself, I'm trying not to take your question personally."

"You, Riley, and Mom aren't women. You don't count."

"Thanks. I think." She huffed a laugh. "But no, I don't think all women are like Amber. Look at Emmy. Or Micki and Evie. Or Tessa, Carlie Beth, Brynne, and Randi. They're all women who truly care about the men they're with."

"So you're saying Amber wasn't like them?"

"Amber thought she was marrying a man she could treat like a puppet. When she discovered that wasn't the case, she wasn't interested anymore."

"I should have listened to all of you when you tried to tell me she wasn't right for me."

"That was a lesson you had to learn on your own."

"What about now? Do I still need to learn lessons about women on my own?"

"Is this about Joss Wynter?"

"Yes."

"I don't know if she's a manipulator," Maggie said. "I don't know her at all."

"But I do," he insisted.

"Maybe, maybe not. You know the Joss Wynter who's been out in the woods relying on you a few short days. She's probably been scared, appreciative, confused."

"So you think she had sex with me because she was afraid, thankful, and out of her mind."

Maggie's mouth quirked up. "Have I told you lately how much I love you?"

"What does it feel like—love?"

"My God, you never ask the easy questions, do you?"

"Amber didn't love me," he said. His time with Joss had convinced him of that fact. "And I don't think I loved her. I don't understand love and I'm not sure I can do it."

"We all question that sometimes when it comes to relationships."

"How do I know if I even love you, my family?"

"Saying 'you just do' isn't going it cut it, huh?"

"No."

"Thought so." She released a long, low breath. "Far be it for me to try to explain something that poets and songwriters have been trying to communicate for centuries, but here goes...If I told you that Jay was being mean to me, maybe even hurting me, what would you say?"

He stopped on the trail and stared down at her. "Jay is hurting you?"

"No!" She grabbed his arm. "It was a hypothetical scenario, just to make you think. How did it make you feel when I said that? How did you react?"

"It made my gut feel like someone had set it on fire."

"Good. I mean not good, but...What else?"

"I wanted to go find Jay and break his face."

"He's bigger than you."

"So?"

"Yet you would still be willing to confront him if you believed he was hurting me." Maggie's lips lifted, just a little.

"Yes."

"That's because you care about me. You feel protective and want the best for me. That fire in the gut—that's love."

"That is stupid," he muttered. "That means love hurts."

"Oh, yeah. Sometimes it does." Maggie patted him hard on the shoulder and stepped around him to resume the hike. "But every bit of pain is worth it. Shep, you don't have to question if you love your family. You would do anything for us. You would lay down your life if it came to that. When we hurt, you hurt. When we're happy, you feel it too. Do I know exactly what love feels like inside you—your head, your body, or your heart? No. No more than I do with Cash or Way or Riley. But I think you love with a fierceness that is both beautiful and scary."

"I must love Joss, then, because she's beautiful and I'm scared. But I don't know what to do about it."

"If there's one thing I've learned recently, it's that you can't always bulldoze your way through everything and *do* something about it. Sometimes you just have to go with the flow and let things work out in their own time."

"That is the problem. I don't have a lot of time. Joss will go back to Los Angeles."

"Then, little brother," she said, "you might want to work fast."

Shep was still thinking about his sister's explanations and advice as they neared the cutoff they would take to hike up to the caves. But he quickly put it aside for the work at hand. "The cave where Joss and I were is about half a mile to the northeast. I set traps at the base so the person couldn't climb up without tripping one of them. I need to get inside the cave."

"Why? Do you think someone's inside?"

"Fiona is."

Hands on her hips, Maggie glared at him. "Fiona? Who in God's name is Fiona? And why am I just now hearing about her?"

"Fiona is Joss's guitar. And she... Well, Fiona is her family."

"Okay, let's take care of finding a killer first, and then

we'll see about rescuing the guitar." Maggie turned to the team. "Heads up, everyone. We think this person has killed before, so even if they're injured, they are probably armed and dangerous."

Everyone was silent on the covert trek through the trees. About fifty yards away from the spot where Shep had set the spear traps, Maggie held up her hand in a signal to stop. Another signal and the group silently fanned out, crouched down, and began to close in.

On the approach, they were slow. And they were stealthy. But it didn't take long for Shep to realize that one trap had yet to be sprung. The other had been tripped, but the butt-end of the spear lying in a snarl of naked brambles made it clear they were too late. The only thing Shep's trap had done was slow down the person. Maybe.

Maybe it hadn't even hit its mark.

Maggie squatted to look more closely at the broken spear and pointed toward what should've been the pointed end. "There are traces of blood here. Your spear worked, Shep."

"Not well enough."

"You didn't exactly have enough supplies on you to fashion a full-scale human trap."

"I could have if I'd had more time."

"So this guy still has part of a stick lodged in his body, lower leg most likely," Maggie said.

"I never saw blood on the trail," Shep said.

"Maybe our suspect had another way off this mountain. You were forced to hike, but I bet you anything he had an ATV."

If that was the case, it meant he could be anywhere by now. Across the state line into Tennessee. Or down into

South Carolina. Or back in Steele Ridge. Something silver caught Shep's eye, and he hunkered down to get a closer look. Recognition and sick fear hit him at the same time, and he called out to Maggie, "I know who the killer is, and I think he's probably already in Steele Ridge by now."

27

DAMN BUFFALO MOODY. JOSS DIDN'T ENJOY THINKING ILL OF the dead, but that man had been a douche face. Her personal belongings weren't at the B&B. They'd never been brought over from the tent.

Thank God she'd taken Fiona with her on the hike. Then again, Fiona might now be lost to her forever.

Although she'd wiped down with a washcloth at the cabin, she still felt dirty. She smelled, she was hungry, and she had no phone. As much as she wanted a long, hot shower and a steak, she couldn't indulge herself right now. She had to get back to Puck.

Even if the dog had no idea she was there, she would know. Shep would know. And if Shep could be brave enough to hike back into the wilderness, Joss could be brave enough to face Puck's condition.

She took a couple of wrong turns, but Steele Ridge wasn't that big, and she eventually found her way back to the vet clinic and parked Shep's truck.

Inside, the receptionist said hello. Then her eyes popped

wide. "Wait a minute. I didn't recognize you before, but you... you're..."

"Here to see Puck Kingston," she cut in.

"Of...of course. Let me just check with Dr. Orozco." She gestured toward a grouping of park benches clustered around a piece of artificial turf like a mini dog park. "Have a seat."

The receptionist disappeared through a door into the treatment area. Was Puck still back there in surgery? Or was he sleeping off the effects of anesthesia? Or was he—

No. Don't even let your brain cells move in that direction.

When the receptionist finally returned, she wasn't wearing an everything-gonna-be-all-right expression. In fact, her mouth was trembling and her eyes were red.

Joss jumped up from her seat. "Can I go back? Can I see him now?"

"Not... not yet. Dr. Orozco will come out and talk with you. But she really wants to speak with Shep. Is he coming in soon?"

Joss didn't know what she should and shouldn't divulge about the manhunt situation, so she just said, "He asked me to come for him. Anything Dr. Orozco would say to him, she can say to me."

The cute chairs didn't appeal anymore, so Joss loop-de-looped around the waiting area. Something was wrong. Something had happened to Puck. Shep would be devastated. How would she tell him—

The chimes on the door trilled, but Joss ignored them. She didn't have the energy or inclination to smile at someone else's pet right now. But she felt the air move behind her as the person neared.

"Ms. Wynter?"

No. Of all the times she didn't want to be approached.

She never wanted to sign another autograph. If this person would just walk away, Joss would give up her need for adulation for good. Forever. "I'm sorry, but I can't sign anything for you today. I—"

The beefy man who'd been snubbed by Moody in the *Do or Die* tent held up his hands. "You have it wrong. That's not why I'm here. I'm Dan Cargill, the owner of Prime Climb Tours. We didn't get a chance to officially meet. I understand from talking with Shari over at the sheriff's department that Sheriff Kingston and some others left town. I'm awfully sorry to hear about Mr. Moody and what happened on the trip."

Joss's shoulders unclenched. "Has anyone seen Lauren, Bradley, and the others?"

"From my understanding, search and rescue is out now. But the reason I swung by here is because Shep called me and asked me to check on Puck. To help you if you needed anything."

That was nice. Small-town neighborly. Or maybe this man was just worried about what kind of lawsuits might crop up against his company. *Stop being such a cynical bitch.*

She tried to smile at him, but her lips weren't particularly cooperative. "I'm just waiting on the vet now—"

"Ms. Wynter?" The vet had poked her head through the door.

"Yes?"

"You can come on back."

That had to be good news. Had to be.

Dan Cargill took Joss's arm with a familiarity that sent a shudder up her back. But he *was* Shep's boss and this was a small town. He was just trying to be helpful and supportive.

Joss wanted to bolt through the door, but the man holding her arm was walking slowly, as if he'd pulled a muscle. When they made it through the door and into the surgery area, she casually stepped away and approached Puck. He was lying on a table, an IV snaking into his leg. Bandages were wrapped around his torso and his breathing was slow. He looked so lifeless. Was it possible for a dog to look pale?

If so, he did.

"Is... is he going to be okay?"

Her dark hair still tucked under a surgical cap, Dr. Orozco gazed down at Puck. "Do you want the details or just the reassurances?"

"I want to know how bad it was and what his chances are."

"The arrow pierced the chest wall and then went through his diaphragm. Fortunately, Shep left the arrow, which helped slow the bleeding, but by the time I got in there, blood had started to seep into the chest and an abdominal hernia was forming. Basically, I had to put things back in their proper place and close up between the abdomen and the chest."

That sounded as bad as Joss had feared. "And the fact that it took us so long to get him here complicated things."

"He was pretty shocky and was in a lot of pain, but Puck is young and strong. He tolerated surgery as well as could be expected based on everything he'd been through. The next few hours are critical. It's really up to rest and time now."

"Can I stay with him?"

"Only for a few minutes. No more than ten. I promise to call when he wakes." Her smile was gentle, and when she touched Joss's arm, compassion seemed to flow from her. Puck was in good hands.

"I don't have a phone right now." Joss cleared the tears

clogging her throat. "Could you call Shep's parents? They'll let everyone know."

"Sure thing."

Dr. Orozco walked out of the room and Joss just stared at Puck. This was the dog that had tested her debris shelter, brought her food and water, and comforted her. He was Shep's best friend. "Come back, Puck," she whispered. "You have to come back. If he loses you, it will kill him."

Until something rattled, Joss had forgotten all about Dan Cargill. She looked up to see him fiddling with a small locked refrigerator. "What are you doing?"

He yanked the door hard and plastic cracked. Quickly, so quickly she couldn't process his actions, he swung open the door and grabbed a vial of milky liquid. From his other hand, he produced a syringe.

Joss's heartbeat double-timed. Needles were bad news.

Her instinct was to run, to jerk open the door and flee. But she couldn't leave Puck lying on this bed. Maybe she could pick him up and—

"Whatever you're thinking," he said easily, "shut it down. If you yell for Dr. Orozco, I will shove this needle into her neck. But if you're a good girl and come with me, everything will be all right."

No, everything would not be all right. He was filling the syringe and gazing at it like a lovesick freshman mooning over the head cheerleader. "What do you want? Money? I have a lot of it." Hell, she didn't even have an ATM card right now. It hadn't been a problem in the woods, but now it seemed like insanity. "Well, not on me, but if you'll let me call my manager, I can—"

He looked up and laughed as if she'd told a slightly amusing joke. "I don't want your money."

What then? Maybe she could maneuver him outside

somehow and get away. Run. She could work with this. "Then why don't we leave here and you tell me what you do want?" Joss tilted her head and tried for a flirty smile. "I bet the clinic has a back door. We can leave that way."

"You know, you have more brains than I thought a rock star would. You're tougher, too. The way you took to the backcountry surprised me."

What? How would he know that when they'd only met a few minutes ago... "You," she gasped. "You were the one following us through the woods."

"Yep," he said, with a proud smile bisecting his wide face.

"Why?" Maybe if she understood that, she could give him what he wanted without anyone else getting hurt.

"Because Shep Kingston needed to be taught a lesson."

"What lesson?" *Keep him talking. Distract. Disarm. Then disappear.*

"He always thought he was so much better than everyone. Than me. Bullshit. How could a guy who doesn't have all his marbles have a leg up on somebody like me? But he was never interested in actually trying to prove he was better. Just walked around like he was God's gift to the mountains or something."

"So you're saying he never took your bait."

"He isn't smart enough to realize I ever tossed it out. So when the producer from *Do or Die* called, I knew this was my chance. Kingston would never back down when people's lives were on the line."

"He's not stupid, you know," she said, edging sideways, trying to lure Cargill toward the back door. "He's one of the smartest men I've ever met."

"Not smart enough to save you and the dog," Cargill said pleasantly and jabbed the needle into Puck's haunch.

. . .

"What did you find?" Maggie asked as she jogged toward Shep.

He held up the carabiner gadget. "This is Dan Cargill's."

"Are you sure?"

"Yeah. No one would actually climb with something like this. I've always thought it was a gimmicky piece of equipment. It's his. I know because I saw him use it the day before *Do or Die* started."

"Give me a second to check in with the forest service officers, and then you're going to tell me why you think Dan Cargill was up here trying to kill people." Maggie stalked over and conferred with the rest of the group.

Shep didn't have time for all this standing around and chitchatting. He followed Maggie and shouldered his way into the group. "I'm going back to Steele Ridge," he told her. "Now." He would have to come back to get Fiona. Yes, she was Joss's family. But Joss was *his* family.

"Dammit, Shep." Frown firmly in place, Maggie braced her hands on her hips. "Give me something solid here."

He shook the carabiner in front of her face. "I don't know what else I can give you besides this."

Maggie pulled him away from the other law enforcement officers and lowered her voice. "That doesn't really prove anything. Why in the world would Dan want to create chaos during the shooting of *Do or Die*? That doesn't make good business sense."

"Is murder always about business?"

"No, but money is a hell of a motivator. And this show would have been good—very good—for Dan's bottom line. You can't buy that kind of publicity."

"He threatened to fire me if I didn't lead this group."

"That makes him a jerk, but not a murderer."

"I don't know why!" Agitation was crawling over him like a cluster of spiders. "But this carabiner is his! It's the stupid gimmicky one he carries everywhere."

"And you think he went back to Steele Ridge because he was hurt. Why don't I call the hospital—"

"No, I think he went back to Steele Ridge because that's where he knew Joss and I would go," he yelled at his sister.

"Fine." Maggie reached for her satellite phone. "I'll get someone over to her ASAP. Didn't you ask Dad to help her find her things?"

"She could be one of several places right now—my cabin, the B and B, Mom and Dad's house, the vet clinic. I don't know."

"It's okay," Maggie soothed. "We'll find her."

"I don't even know her phone number."

"This is the beauty of small-town living. Someone has seen her."

"Call Dad first."

Maggie dialed. "Dad. Hey, we think we've got problems. Is Joss with you?"

Shep paced a circle around his sister. One. Two. Three. Fou—

"When did you last see her? Do you know if she's still at the B and B? Okay, I'll call there next. But I need you and everyone else looking for her. Also, if you come across Dan Cargill, give him a wide berth." She waved a hand to punctuate her words. "I don't have time to go into all of it right now. Just look for Joss and avoid Dan." She hung up and dialed again.

"What did he—"

"Mrs. Tasky? This is Sheriff Kingston. Is Joss Wynter there? I see. When did she leave and did she say where she was headed next? Okay, thank you. You've been a big help."

Shep spun toward Maggie. "What did she—"

"Joss left a while ago, and she was going to the vet clinic to check on Puck. And before you ask, that's where I'm calling next."

Another phone call, another paced circle around Maggie.

"Stefanie, I'm looking for Joss Wynter. Is she there by chance?" Maggie's face blanked, and her hand tightened on the phone. "What? When? Please tell me you called 911."

Wait–911? Why had they called 911? He grabbed his sister by the arms. "Maggie—"

She stepped back to break his hold and kept speaking into the phone. "That's good. How is Puck?" She blinked and drew in a sharp breath. "Okay. Please keep my mom and dad informed on that."

When Maggie hung up this time and looked at Shep, her eyes held something Shep wasn't sure he'd ever seen his sister show before. It looked like fear. "What happened? You look scared."

"Dan Cargill was there at the clinic. Dr. Orozco left him alone with Puck and Joss. They heard something break and a muffled yell, but by the time they got back to the room, Joss and Cargill were gone, and the clinic's back door was swinging wide open."

"Fuck. We have to go now."

Maggie put in a call, asking for a helicopter. Before she even took her hand off her radio, Shep grabbed her wrist and started running for the location she'd specified for the landing.

"That's not all, Shep," Maggie panted as they broke into a jog. "He also injected Puck with a big vial of Propofol."

28

PLEASE, PLEASE HELP PUCK. JOSS REPEATED THE LITTLE PRAYER in her mind, but she wasn't sure if she was praying to God or Dr. Orozco.

After tying her hands in front of her, Shep's boss had shoved her into a truck and driven away from town. Now, he parked and came around to manhandle her out of the vehicle.

"Where are we?" she asked.

"It doesn't matter," he said, clearly distracted. "What matters is that once Shep gets a clue, he'll know to come here."

"I know why you're doing this," she said as he herded her toward a wood tower with multiple staircases leading up to a tiny platform.

"Yeah, because I told you."

"It's because he intimidates you." And for some reason, this guy had decided *she* was the perfect bait to draw Shep in.

"You don't know what you're talking about."

Oh, but she thought she did. It was clear that Dan

Cargill had probably once been in very good shape. But he had a softness about him, that extra layer of fat that stocky men developed when they got older and stopped pumping themselves up. Quite simply, he was past his prime while Shep was the kind of man who would always keep himself in tiptop shape. "Did you kill Buffalo Moody, too?"

"That guy thought he was such hot shit. Had a TV show and that somehow made him important. What about the people who do this all day every day? He gets all the glory for smiling at a camera while real outdoorsmen actually do what he only claims to."

It didn't look as if Cargill did the outdoorsmen thing all day long, either. He was like an aging rock star who wouldn't accept that his sex-object days were over. They still knew the music, but the shoulder shimmies and hip thrusts just didn't play to the crowd anymore.

And if Joss continued the way she'd been going with her career, compromising true artistry for applause, she'd be just as washed-up and angry as this man was.

Cargill caught her in the lower back and shoved her toward the first set of steps. "Start climbing."

"I don't think so." Already shaking from the tension in her stomach, Joss went even colder and her limbs felt like cinderblocks. But she managed to turn sideways and land a kick. Unfortunately, it caught the guy's shin, instead of his knee as she'd intended.

"Fuck!"

Joss cut left, but he grabbed her shoulder and squeezed to the point Joss was sure her arm would pop out of socket and fall to the ground. "I don't give a good crap if other people bow and scrape to you, Miss Rock Star. I think your music sucks ass and that you're a selfish little bitch. Didn't give a shit that the rest of your band ended up as splattered body parts all over some Los Angeles freeway, did you?"

Oh, God, she'd cared so much that she'd been punishing herself ever since. Maybe that was what this was—her ultimate punishment for being careless with people she loved.

He snorted. "You're not worth the energy it would take to kill you."

"Then why bother with me?"

"Because Weirdo Kingston thought enough of you to put his dick in you. That's not something he does with a lot of women. Hell, from what I hear, most women won't go on a second date with him, much less sleep with him. You must have a thing for weirdos."

Joss's fists curled against her stomach. She wanted to punch Cargill in the dick for the weirdo comment alone. "He isn't weird. He's special." So special.

Cargill snorted a laugh and dropped her arm to make air quotes. "Special. That's just another word for freak."

Yeah, this guy was definitely getting a right hook to the cock as soon as she could manage it. "I've found that people make fun of what scares them. I was wrong about how you feel about Shep. You're not intimidated. You're terrified."

He pushed her in the center of the back, sending her sprawling face-first into the wooden stairs. A splinter sliced her cheek and slipped under the skin. "You're almost more trouble than you're worth."

Joss was able to steady herself and get her feet beneath her. Her cheek throbbed and her stomach was sloshing with acid. But she would keep calm. Panic would do nothing to help this situation, and she needed all her wits about her to somehow warn Shep that he was walking into some type of trap.

The whippoorwill call. If he heard her flub the call, he would know something was wrong.

They were one flight of stairs away from the platform when a vibration rippled through the air, lifting the hair on the back of Joss's neck.

"Hurry!" Cargill grabbed her by the shirt and half carried her up the remainder of the stairs.

She hadn't noticed it as they climbed, but dark clouds were gathering, shifting over each other like a nest of restless snakes. The wind was stronger and angrier up here, pressing against Joss and forcing her to brace her legs to keep her balance.

If I fall, this son-of-a-bitch is going with me.

Cargill busied himself with some equipment—ropes and large carabiners. He gathered up a handful of stuff and turned to Joss. "Step into this."

"No." Willingly go to her death. Nuh-uh.

He grabbed her by the hair and yanked so she was forced to look into his face. "If you don't put on this harness, I'll just shove your skinny little ass off this platform. Do you know how many feet up in the air we are?"

She didn't, but it looked like a million.

Her breath was so shallow that it felt as if air was making it no farther than her throat.

Cargill rotated his fist to catch more of her hair and pulled hard, making tears gather at the corner of Joss's eyes. "Step into the damn harness," he said.

Harness sounded good. Safe. Regardless, she had a better chance of survival with ropes around some part of her body. Maybe. She maneuvered a foot inside each loop, and Cargill hitched the rig up hard, wedging it between Joss's butt cheeks like a sweaty thong.

She could do this. It was just a zip line. How hard could

it be?

She didn't know because she'd never zip-lined before. But *zip.* Sounded easy. Fast. She'd seen videos of smiling people flying through the air.

Unfortunately, Cargill didn't offer her gloves or any type of head protection. He yanked on the loop attached to her waist and clipped it into the sliding piece attached to the cable above, almost jerking Joss off her feet. "Aren't you going to untie my hands?"

"Now what fun would that be?"

If she didn't have use of her hands, she would probably zoom down that wire, across the expanse of grass, and crash into the support pole in the middle of the opposite platform. Then again, ramming into something was so much better than falling.

Cargill grabbed her by the harness, pulled her back, and let her go.

Joss had been right. With no way to slow her speed, she was whizzing through the air like an arrow.

No arrows.

However, her speed began to throttle back, degree by degree, and Joss realized her low bodyweight was working against her. The momentum she needed to get to the other tower required more bulk than she had. She thought crashing into the other platform would be bad. But this was worse, much worse. With every bit she slowed, it became clearer that she would never make it to the other side. As she feared, she finally stopped and found herself dangling halfway between the two platforms with no way to move herself.

Was he planning to just leave her out here?

No, that didn't make any sense. He said Shep would come here looking for him. Looking for her.

The vibration that she'd felt became more pronounced, shaking the air around her. Was a storm blowing in? Joss craned her neck, trying to get a three-sixty view around her. The trees waved, bowing away from her as if executing simultaneous backbends.

Whomp. Whomp. Whomp.

A helicopter.

Nooooo!

Joss didn't know what was worse—swinging here high above the ground, or the possibility that Shep might be on that helicopter.

"He's here somewhere," Shep said through the headset Maggie had shoved onto his head when they boarded the helicopter. "I know it."

"But how?"

"Because this has something to do with him threatening to fire me. He wanted me to fail out there. He wanted to get rid of me."

"Shep, I think we've already established he wanted to do more than that. And I'm pretty sure Moody was just a pawn in Cargill's game with you."

"Which means he would be willing to hurt Joss. Even kill her"—he swallowed hard around the words, to push down the guilt chewing up his gut—"if it moved his agenda forward. She's in danger."

Maggie leaned toward the helicopter's small side window and pointed. "Out there. Look at that zip line."

A person was dangling midline, almost reclining in the harness. No way in hell was Joss that relaxed about being on a zip line. Maybe her body was limp because she'd passed out from sheer terror. "I need to get to her."

"Cargill couldn't make it any more obvious that he's baiting you if he'd rigged a big-ass fishing pole and hung Joss on the hook."

"I know that. I'm not stupid."

"And I know you're not, Shep. But you're also stubborn." Still, she signaled the pilot and spoke into her mic. "Can you set us down behind some cover? I don't like what I'm seeing here, and we don't have a bead on the suspect."

The helicopter swung around, and the pilot swooped back over a clearing about a quarter mile from the zip line course. It had barely touched down when Shep bulleted out of the chopper, with Maggie on his tail.

"I'm calling for backup," she hollered. "We'll wait until—"

"Mags, it's going to get dark before too long and a storm is blowing in," he yelled over the noise of the rotors as they ducked and ran from the landing spot. "You can pull out your gun and shoot me, but I am still going out there."

"Then I'm going with you."

He swung his head around to give her a hard look. "Do *not* try to insert yourself into the middle of this. I know it's your job, but this is my turf. Dan wants *me*."

"Well, he's not going to get you."

Shep didn't plan to let Cargill get away with any of this, but first he had to get Joss off that zip line. Dan was either on tower one or two. If Shep had to guess, he'd parked in the Prime Climb parking lot, which meant he'd probably forced Joss to climb the closest tower. He cut at an angle toward it. "We're going up this one."

He took a close look at the ground around the tower and the first few steps leading up. No recent footprints. "Shit, he's on the other tower."

He'd deal with Cargill after he got his hands on Joss and

had her on the ground again. Shep had never climbed stairs as fast as he took these. With his longer stride, he ate up the stairs two and three at a time. Maggie had to run to stay abreast, but she never let up.

They were almost to the top when Shep got a clear view of Joss hanging out there on the line. Her lips were pursed, and the faint sound of a slightly altered whippoorwill call drifted toward him. She was trying to warn him away. That was never going to happen. He'd discovered he didn't like being away from her. "She doesn't have a helmet on," he told Maggie.

"And it looks like she might not have full use of her arms." She got on her radio to relay the information to her officers.

Shep had hoped to talk Joss in, explaining how to use a hand-over-hand maneuver so she could pull herself toward the tower. But that wasn't an option. He would have to go out there after her.

Now on the platform, he stepped into a harness and found a single helmet. He pulled on a pair of heavyweight gloves and then clipped in to the zip line trolley.

"He could shoot you the minute you push off this platform," Maggie warned. "I don't like anything about this."

"If he hasn't used a gun up to this point, it isn't his plan."

"He shot Puck with an arrow!"

He couldn't even think about that right now. Joss first. Then Puck. "With the wind kicking up, Cargill would have to be a better shot than I know he is to hit me." And with that, he lifted his legs and flew off the platform. His weight was a benefit, rushing him toward Joss with a speed that would have been enjoyable if Shep's stomach hadn't been one big ball of writhing muscles.

He raced toward Joss, and she lifted her head. As he

approached, he reached up and slowed his descent, braking at the last second so he didn't mow over her.

"Oh my God, Shep. What are you doing? He wants to kill you because he's jealous of your skill as a guide. And he hates himself for it, and he wanted you to come out here and —"

"Hold out your hands."

"Did you hear me?"

"Yes, I heard you." He grabbed her hands and used a pocket knife to cut through the rope binding them. "Hold on to me."

She wrapped her arms and legs around him. Hand over hand, he started the laborious task of pulling them back up the line to the tower where Maggie was waiting.

"Is he still on the other tower?" he asked Joss.

"I... I don't know." Her voice was thready, and she turned her head to look down.

"Close your eyes."

"Can't...can't unsee what I've already seen."

Shep scanned the ground below them, but there was no sign of Cargill. If he had half the brains Shep had ever given him credit for, he was hiding somewhere. Or had decided he didn't want to do something that was sure to get *him* killed.

Shep and Joss were probably twenty feet from the tower when a tremor rippled through the line, something Shep had never felt in his many years of zip-lining. Surely Cargill couldn't mess with a cable tested to hold over twenty thousand pounds.

But if he had a big cable cutter, he could—*fuck!* Shep grabbed for the line itself.

"Wha..." Joss didn't complete a single word before the sickening feeling of slack in the line hit Shep's midsection.

And gravity took over.

29

OHSHITOHSHITOHHOLYSHIT.

They were falling. Any second now, they would hit the ground just like the helicopter she'd put the band on and—

"Shep," she screamed. "We're going to die!"

With their combined weight, they were sliding toward the ground so fast that Joss saw dark spots.

"I've got you," he yelled back. She was clinging to him so tightly that she could barely draw breath. That was okay. She'd rather suffocate to death than go out by French-kissing the ground.

Or maybe they were about to spontaneously combust because she smelled animal hide burning. The line jerked taut again, whiplashing Joss's neck. The impact slid them down a few more feet.

She and Shep swung like a human pendulum. Back and forth. Back and forth.

Then *wham,* they knocked against something hard. Joss felt it to the roots of her teeth even though Shep was protecting most of her body.

They hung there—losing an inch here, six inches there

—as Shep tried to reach out and control the arc of the line. Somehow, he was able to swing them around a tower support pole. "Grab it!"

"What?"

"Reach for that pole!"

The first pass, Joss stretched out one hand and missed by inches. In a miraculous feat, Shep swung them around again, and this time Joss used her feet to catch a wooden crosspiece. She spotted Cargill, now standing between the two towers. And if she could see him, he could see them.

Still, some cover was better than none.

"Can you climb down the rest of the way?" Shep asked her.

"What?"

"Are you strong enough to unclip yourself and get away from here? Maggie saw us fall and will meet you down there. She'll help you once you're on the ground."

"No!" They were still ten feet above the ground. If she unclipped herself from this line, she would fall. She would fall and be weak and helpless.

No, they were *only* ten feet above the ground. She could do this, but she wouldn't. "I'm not going down there."

"You are stronger than you think, Joss." He stripped off his leather gloves to brush her hair away from her face and touch her chin. She turned to find him looking straight into her eyes. He gently pushed her away from him body. "Just hang on and go slowly."

"That's not what I meant. No, I'm not leaving you up here." Everything inside her compelled her to cling like a barnacle. But he'd just offloaded her weight and definitely didn't need her burdening the line again. "You're planning something."

"Hold on," he instructed and unclipped her from the cable.

She hung on to the wood like a spider monkey. "What are you going to do?"

"We don't have time for this." Shep pushed off the support beam and arced around the tower again. He released his hold on the zip line and landed on his feet. He pointed toward some trees that Joss saw Cargill disappear into.

Shep hollered, "I think he's headed for the gorge!"

From below Joss, Maggie yelled back at him, "Wait for me—"

But Shep didn't hesitate. He ran directly for the forest. Damn him.

"Joss! Can you climb down on your own?" Maggie called out to her.

"Yes. No. Yes." Joss wasn't sure if she was telling the truth or not. Her thighs protested the slightest movement and shook like two detoxing junkies. "You can do this," she whispered to herself.

Her descent took every smidge of her concentration and some muscles that—even after the *Do or Die* debacle—she hadn't been aware she had. Finally, her feet touched the lovely earth, and her knees karaoke'd a shaky version of 'NSync's "Bye Bye Bye."

They hit the ground, and she caught herself with her hands to keep from face-planting in the dirt.

"You stay here," Maggie commanded. "Backup is just minutes away."

But when Maggie took off after her brother, Joss was right behind her.

· · ·

As he'd done more than a few times in his life, Shep ignored his sister and ran into the woods. She'd already called for backup, but Shep couldn't risk that Dan might change directions and slip away from them.

As Shep had expected, Dan's tracks led toward Rasputin gorge. Formed by a fast-moving river, it dropped a good thousand feet right off the bat.

For several years, Dan had been yapping about rebuilding the old wood and rope bridge spanning the gorge. Of course, it was off-limits to any Prime Climb Tour customers. The liability was enormous. Dan had also been bitching about that for years.

But when Shep made it to the clearing at the edge of the gorge, Dan wasn't there. Wasn't on the bridge.

Had Shep been wrong to leave Joss and Maggie? Maybe that was exactly what Dan wanted. Shep turned to run back through the woods only to find that he *had* been correct.

Dan was standing fifteen feet from him with an arrow notched in his compound bow. It was aimed directly at Shep's chest. "Finally got you where I want you," he taunted.

"What is it you want, Cargill?"

He gestured by dipping the arrow slightly and then raising it again. "You out on that bridge."

"I'm not stupid."

"Yeah, not quite as dumb as I always thought," Dan said, inching closer. "You gave me a good run for my money out there on the mountain."

"Put down the bow." The setting sun made it hard to see, but Shep blinked until Dan was in focus again.

"Get on that bridge and maybe I will." Dan moved forward, forcing Shep toward the rickety structure. "If you don't, I'll shoot you in the chest and go back for your girlfriend."

Although it was likely Maggie and other law enforcement would be there to protect Joss, Shep couldn't chance it. He lunged forward, but Dan danced back and sidestepped him. "That all you got, Kingston? I smell the stink of desperation."

"And I smell the scent of a man who's scared shitless that he's past his prime."

"Fuck that, and fuck you!"

"Admit it, Dan, you've been catching the fat for a while now."

"I've had you on the run, haven't I?" Dan's smile was calm and even. He really thought this was some justifiable competition between them. Maybe if Shep let him believe he'd already won, they could end this thing now.

"Yeah, you sure did," Shep said, easing his way closer.

"Uh-uh, you aren't running this show." Dan braced his legs to stabilize himself to take a shot.

If Shep didn't do something now, Dan's arrow would find its target this time.

"Hey! Did you say something about going back for his girlfriend?" someone called out from behind Dan. "Well, you won't have to go looking for her because here she is!"

Shit! Joss was standing at the tree line. Where the hell was Maggie?

Joss ran toward the bridge. Dan turned toward her slightly, but not enough to completely take his gaze off Shep.

"Jojo, get the hell away from here!" Shep yelled at her.

"You never left me out on that mountain, and I'm not leaving you now."

Shep had to get Dan's attention back on him and him alone. He rushed the man and swept an arm up to dislodge his hold on the bow. Didn't work, but it did shift his focus directly back to Shep.

Fine, he might get an arrow to the gut, but he would take Dan into this gorge with him.

Shep grabbed Dan's shirt, pulling him too close for the bow to be effective, and tried to wrench him off-balance. Dan might've put on some lard around the middle, but he was still solid, probably outweighing Shep by twenty pounds. It was like trying to wrestle a buffalo.

Shit, don't think about Buffalo.

Something hit Dan from behind. "Ugh!" he grunted, stumbling forward, forcing Shep onto the bridge, and dropping his bow and arrow.

That *something* was Joss with a tree branch. Her hair was a wild tornado of blue around her head and her eyes blazed with a fierceness that bordered on complete frenzy.

Shep had to get Dan away from her, or they would all go into the gorge. "Jojo, you're making things worse. Get back!" he shouted at her.

In the split second of his distraction, Dan lunged forward with another arrow and a spear of pain shot blazed across Shep's left arm as the arrow grazed him. Fuck, he should've realized Dan was wearing a quiver full of arrows on his back.

Shep grabbed for the strap, trying to yank it off Cargill's shoulder.

Dan came around with the arrow again, aiming for Shep's throat. Joss whacked Dan in the arm, blocking the arrow's trajectory and sweeping his hand down. But the arrow tip sliced across Shep's chest and through the fabric of his shirt to the skin beneath. Fire chased in its path.

Dan shoved Joss, and her butt connected with the ground, but at least she was away from this damn bridge.

As he took a step back, Shep's hiking boot hit a piece of slickly rounded wood and the heavy tread couldn't steady him. His weight thrown off, Shep grabbed for the rope handhold and lost his grip on Dan's quiver.

But the feel of coarse rope strands in his palm provided Shep with steadiness and strength. Centered and calmed him.

Then Dan reached into the quiver and pulled out two additional arrows. "I think I'll use these for your eyes. When I aimed for you the first time, I was looking for a clean kill shot. But what's the fun in that? If I gouge out your eyes, you won't know when you're about to hit the bottom of this gorge. You'll piss all over yourself on the way down, just like Moody did."

"How do you know he peed himself?"

Dan lifted a shoulder. "Because he was a pussy."

"Well, if you want to toss me off this bridge, you will have to come after me." Straddling the bridge and gripping both ropes, Shep carefully began to feel his way back to the next piece of wood with one foot. One step at a time, that was all he had to do.

Dan glanced over his shoulder—either at his lost bow or Joss, Shep wasn't sure. Regardless, he had to keep Dan coming at him. "I will be across the bridge before you can notch another arrow," Shep told him. "And if you try for Joss, I'll be all over you. If you want *me,* you have to come for *me.*"

With every careful step he made, Shep's stomach wadded tighter into a ball of sick tension. The rope was disintegrating in his hands and the gaps between pieces of woods were becoming wider and wider.

That spelled death for both him and Dan Cargill. But as long as Shep took Dan with him when he went down, he didn't care. This was what Maggie had been trying to explain to him. If you were willing to sacrifice to this level to keep someone safe, you loved them.

He loved Joss. Really truly loved her like a normal man loved a woman. And that was worth dying for.

Dan charged onto the bridge and it shimmied and swayed under his weight. He stumbled and dropped one arrow in his haste to grab the rope, but he quickly righted himself. He had the advantage of seeing the steps in front of him, but Shep couldn't afford to turn his back on the man to obtain that edge.

Dan advanced faster, becoming careless with his steps in his haste. But with every slipping step, the man caught himself and kept coming. Relentless.

But Shep needed him close. *Come on, you bastard.*

When Dan was within reach, Shep shifted his weight to his arms, bracing himself on either rope, and kicked out with both feet. His heels caught Dan in the chest, but he recovered quickly and yanked Shep's foot, pulling him off-balance and compromising his grip on the ropes.

He tried to retreat and get his feet under him again, but his body felt like a bag of muscles and bones that had all decided to strike out on their own. His tenuous hold slipped and he grappled for stability. He grasped the rope on his right, and then pain exploded across the back of his hand.

Fuck! Dan had used his remaining arrow to pin Shep's hand to the rope.

Without regard for the pain, Shep grabbed the fletching and twisted his fist to break it off, but before he could free himself, Dan came up with a hard right cross to Shep's arm. Stars blinked like flickering fluorescent bulbs behind Shep's eyes. God, he hated those damn artificial lights.

He blinked them away and spotted blood seeping through Dan's pants. With his hand still pinned, Shep gripped the rope for balance and aimed a kick toward the bloodstain. Not his best effort, but it connected.

"Aaaah!" Dan grabbed for his injured leg, and Shep freed himself from the arrow piercing his hand and the rope.

The bridge shimmied under Shep's feet. More weight. Joss was on the bridge with them, but Cargill didn't seem to realize it. Shep's entire world coalesced into this pinpoint of time.

But before he could move to protect Joss, Dan screamed and reached for his neck. Joss had gotten her hands on the arrow Dan had dropped and shoved it into him. Not deeply, but it was enough.

Dan's feet slipped and he flung out a hand to grab on to the rope, grab on to Shep, grab on to anything. Caught only air.

But the man was apparently lucky as hell because instead of stumbling off the bridge, he dropped straight down with one foot on either side of a wood plank. Two hundred plus pounds of man landed with an *oomph* straight on his dick.

Possibly the first rack job that had ever saved a man's life.

"Fuck," Dan yelled as he flailed for something to hold on to.

"Shep!"

He looked up to see Maggie and her deputies with their guns drawn. "Where were you?" he demanded of his sister.

"I'll explain later," she yelled back. "After we secure Cargill."

"I don't want to chance anyone else coming out here until we get some weight off this thing." He pointed at Joss, who was breathing heavily and staring glassily down at Dan. "Go back. Now. Quickly but carefully."

Her head came up and rage was burning in her eyes. She nodded at Shep, but instead of complying, she pulled back her foot.

Gave Dan one good kick in the chin and another solid one in the nose.

Shep wanted to yell at Joss for risking her life, but he had to admire her parting shot. As he stepped over the groaning man and grabbed Joss, Shep gave his own parting shot. "You lose, Dan Cargill."

30

JOSS WOULD'VE STOOD ON THAT BRIDGE UNTIL THE END OF time kicking Shep's former boss in the face, but Shep picked her up as easily as if she were a doll and carted her back to stable ground. He plopped her feet on the grass and glared down at her. "Don't you ever do something that crazy again."

All the adrenaline that had built up over the past few days surged forward into Joss's system. Joss grabbed Shep by the shoulders and launched herself at him, wrapping her legs around his waist like a desperate anaconda. He was alive, he was safe, and he was hers.

He staggered back against a tree and just held her, his arms a reassuring weight around her body.

As the wind whipped and the rain began to pelt them, Shep's sister and lots of other people in official-looking uniforms swarmed the area and dragged Dan Cargill off the bridge in handcuffs.

Shep's big hand swept from the top of Joss's head to her ass. "I am sorry."

Joss drew back and stared into his eyes. "For what?"

"For putting you in danger."

"Your dad talked with me about the difference between correlation and causality. You didn't cause this."

"You're right." His grip on her butt tightened and then he let her go, forcing her to slide down his body and gaze up at him. "But there was definitely a correlation between Dan coming after me and your life being threatened."

She wouldn't even bother to talk him out of that one, because they would spend far too much time arguing. And she didn't want to use their time that way.

Unfortunately, Sheriff Maggie had an even worse idea. She stalked toward them and said, "You both need medical care."

"Only after we check on Puck," Shep said.

Maggie sighed, but said, "I'll have Cash or Emmy meet us at your house. Again."

She commandeered one of her deputies' squad cars to drive Shep and Joss to the clinic. On the way, Shep asked her, "Where were you while I was out on that bridge with Cargill? I expected you to keep Joss safe."

Joss hurried to say, "Don't blame her. The wind uprooted a small tree in the forest and it fell, blocking Maggie's path for long enough for me to get to the bridge."

Maggie shot her a hard look. "What you did was stupid."

Maybe so, but Joss would do it all over again.

When they arrived at the vet clinic, they were allowed straight back to see Puck. "How is he?" Shep asked Dr. Orozco. His voice was hoarse as he gazed down at his still unconscious dog.

"We gave him a stimulant that can help counteract a Propofol overdose, but there are no guarantees, Shep."

"You're saying he might not ever wake up."

"For now, he's still breathing."

Joss pressed against Shep's side and whispered, "He's strong. We have to believe in him."

Shep leaned down to his beloved companion, and Joss heard him whisper, "Puck, you are my family. And now I know how much I love my family. Don't leave me."

Her eyes sad, Maggie led them back to the car and drove them to Shep's cabin. They trudged to the front porch, where Emmy led them to chairs and began to clean and bandage wounds.

Maggie said, "I need to ask you two a lot of questions, but we can finish this tomorrow."

"No," Shep protested. "Let's do it now. I don't want Dan Cargill to take away any more time from me."

And so Maggie asked questions until Joss thought she would fall out of her chair with exhaustion.

"But he confessed, Maggie," Shep said with enough outrage to indicate he could argue for the next twenty-four hours straight. "He killed Moody."

"I know he told you that," she said on a sigh, "but we still have to have all the facts as you know them."

"So no one from *Do or Die* had anything to do with this?" Joss asked.

"We pulled them all in for questioning as well after some of my deputies found them on a completely different trail from the one they should've followed back to town," Maggie said. "It appears that the only thing any of them are guilty of is cowardice, self-centeredness, and some petty theft."

"Petty, my ass," Shep grumbled.

"Do you want to press charges?" Maggie asked him. "What they did ultimately hurt you, Joss, and Puck."

"No, I just want them gone from Steele Ridge."

Maggie stood and gave his shoulder a solid pat. "Why don't you sleep on it? You can always come by tomorrow and file a report."

"Maybe they could pay another way," Joss said quietly. Yes, they deserved consequences, but with the financial resources Lauren, Bradley, and the production company had, others could benefit. And Joss found she wanted that more than she wanted them to be crucified as she had been. "What if we demanded they pay a lump sum to the charities we choose?"

"Like the organization that gave me Puck?"

"Exactly like that."

"I don't necessarily agree, but I can understand where you're coming from," Maggie said to Joss. "Oh, and by the way, one of the cameramen knew where all the contestants' personal belongings were stashed. I'll have someone drop yours by for you."

Shep stood and drew his sister to the side, said something Joss couldn't hear. Once Maggie was in her cruiser and pulling away, Shep took Joss's hand and pulled her to her feet. "Let's go inside."

Taking her hand, Shep led her to his bedroom and urged her to sit on his bed. Then he guided her down on the mattress, and she let the lights go out.

When she woke later, her mouth was dry, her eyes were gritty, and she was still grungy. It had probably pained Shep to have her zonk out like that on the top of his comforter. She blinked and looked around. The only light came from a crack in the doorway to the bathroom.

Her body aching, she pushed herself off the bed and went to investigate. "Shep?"

"Yeah?"

"Can I come in?"

"Yes."

She eased open the door to find the room, with its roughly hewn wood walls, bathed in candlelight. The shadows flickered and danced against the golden patina of the wood.

Still wearing the same clothes from earlier, Shep was sitting on the floor near the bathtub, his long legs stretched out and his eyes closed. Beside him, Fiona was propped against the wall.

"You got her back for me." A wave of love and gratitude swept through her, almost flattening her with its intensity. Shep might not think he understood people and their complicated emotions, but he had an innate sense of what was important.

His eyes opened, and he pinned her with his green gaze. "Actually, someone from Maggie's team did."

"Because you asked them to."

"If the candles remind you too much of the fire, I can blow them out," he said.

"No, it's fine. Soothing, actually." And in addition to the candles, his clawfoot tub was filled with water and a tiny group of anemic bubbles floated near the faucet. The bathwater had obviously been cooling for a while. "Sorry I crashed like that."

"No apologies for needing something."

What she needed was this man. She was in love with him. This special, soulful man. "If I run hot water, will you bathe with me?"

"Um... that's two dirty bodies in approximately ninety gallons of water."

She chuckled. He had a good point, so she pulled the

plug and began to undress while the tub drained.

"I...uh, should go?" he asked, but by the way he was watching every move she made, he definitely wanted to stay.

"Take off your clothes."

"But—"

"I know. Dirty bodies and standing water." She pulled the curtain around and fiddled with the faucet until she figured out the shower mechanism. "Wash first and then soak. Does that work for you?"

"Does soaking just mean soaking or..."

"How do you feel about having sex in a bathtub?"

He cocked his head, and a small smile made its way across his lips. "I think I feel very good about it."

By the time she and Shep had thoroughly used the pull-out shower head to wash their unbandaged areas, Joss's skin was pink and her nipples were perky. It was like there were magnets under her skin drawing her to this man. And although he'd been all business with the bathing, his erection was plenty of proof that he wasn't unaffected.

"You sit in the back," she instructed, "and I'll handle the water." The old plumbing was stubborn, forcing her to bend over to adjust the heat and flow. When something hot and wet delved between her legs, she almost took a header out of the tub. Catching herself and gripping the edge, she glanced over her shoulder.

Oh my God. Shep was... He was...

She groaned and widened her legs. For a man who wasn't keen on kneeling at the altar, he was doing a bang-up job. Very thorough. Very dedicated.

And then—*sweet Jesus!*—he remembered the magic of the clitoris. Tongue, a sweet scrape of the teeth... and then his lips were around her and she was flying.

When Joss's brain and body decided it was finally time

to have a family reunion, her arms were shaking and the tub was perilously close to overflowing. But Shep apparently had decided he was fond of the female ecosystem because he was humming to himself and sliding his fingers along her still pulsing flesh.

"Sh... Shep. We need to... Can you stop what you're doing and pop the drain?"

"Is pop the drain a euphemism for orgasm? I haven't heard—"

"No, dammit!" She laughed. "It means you're about to have water all over your bathroom floor!"

After some maneuvering, a little overflow, and a few breathless chuckles, she and Shep were eventually situated in the tub. Him leaning back, his gauze-wrapped chest and arm above the water, bandaged hand resting on the rim, and her straddling his thighs.

"It didn't taste like birthday cake," he commented. "You said—"

"It doesn't always," she said. "You have to use a special lube and I don't happen to have any with me right now."

"That's okay. I liked it. It was hot and kind of... salty-sweet."

"Like kettle corn?"

"Exactly!"

Cracking up, she slumped forward and laid her head on his shoulder. "Shep Kingston, I love you."

His entire body—all seventy-six inches of him—tensed beneath her. Even his hard-on went completely still.

She'd scared him. Turned him into stone.

She lifted her head. Shep's face was immobile and his eyes were filled with distrust. Her hand on his cheek, she said, "Shep, I...I—"

"You need to tell me what you mean by that," he said hoarsely. "You love me like a brother or—"

"Ew! God, no. That's just wrong."

Turning his face away, he grabbed for the side of the tub, trying to push himself up and out.

But she hung on like a stubborn bull rider. "Uh-uh. No. You are not getting out of this tub. Sit your ass down and listen to me."

He settled back, but didn't look at her. Although she hadn't meant for her feelings to come out in quite this way, they were floating between them. Not softly, but with potentially razor-sharp consequences.

"Will you look at me?" she asked softly.

He swallowed and turned his head. His gaze met hers, darted away, and held for a few moments. She caressed his cheek, the stubble soft beneath her palm, and finally, he looked at her.

The spotlight was on.

"I love you," she told him. "Like a woman loves a man she wants to share things with—her body, her thoughts, her life."

"Her life," he echoed. "What does that mean exactly?"

"It means I want to be with you."

"Every day?"

"Every day I can."

"I don't love you like I thought I loved Amber."

Inside, Joss's heart began to spiderweb, like the tiny cracks on a windshield chipped by a careless pebble.

"I love you like someone I would do anything for." Her fingers tightened on his face, and he covered her hand with his. "I love you like someone I would die for."

"That's why you yelled at me when I walked onto that

bridge. You thought that to stop Dan Cargill you would have to die, too."

"It would've been okay," he said.

"No, it wouldn't have!" Tears bubbled up at the thought that Shep could've gone over or through that shitty bridge, could've fallen to the bottom of that gorge. She couldn't bear to be the reason someone else died. Call it causality or correlation, she didn't give a shit. She had to take more care, had to do whatever it took to show the people she loved that she would stand by them and keep them safe. "Because I can't live without you."

Shep woke up in his cabin with daylight just starting to seep through the windows and inch across his chest. But the fledgling sunshine was all that was in his bed. The covers where Joss had lain beside him were pulled up to the pillow and smoothed out. Last night, she'd said she loved him, couldn't live without him.

But something about the neatness of his sheets made his chest hollow out. He listened for the sound of the shower or the opening and closing of kitchen cabinets.

Nothing.

The silence surrounding him wasn't anticipatory. It was foreboding. And Fiona was no longer propped in the corner of the room.

"Jojo?" he called out, his voice cracking and swinging high. He shoved away the covers and lurched to his feet, not bothering to find any clothes.

Finding Joss was considerably more important than locating his underwear.

"Jojo?"

Maybe she was outside on the porch with her guitar, enjoying the fall morning.

But when he opened the front door, his porch was deserted. The uneasy feeling inside him ramped up another six billion notches, and he patted his hip for his paracord.

Yeah, even if he hadn't been bare-ass naked, that piece was long gone, used on the trap that hadn't stopped Cargill.

Joss. Where was Joss?

Stop and think instead of freaking the fuck out.

Maybe she'd decided to go into town. He shifted his gaze to the carport. No, his truck was still sitting where one of Maggie's deputies had parked it.

Shep ducked back inside and checked the kitchen. There on the countertop, was an Epic Bar with a folded piece of paper propped against it.

No. Notes were not good. Notes from women he cared for were horrible. Life-changing. Life-crushing.

He snatched up the paper and crumpled it in his fist.

She was gone. He knew that now.

She's Joss Wynter, you shit. Of course, she is gone. Only a dumbass would believe she would stay, would really love him.

You, my friend, are that dumbass.

He had broken his promise to himself. He had opened himself up to try to love like a normal man. But he was *not* a normal man. Joss had finally figured that out and made her decision based on it.

He couldn't blame her, no matter how much he might want to.

Where did that leave him? No Joss. Maybe no Puck. Probably no job.

No life.

Shep grabbed the protein bar and yanked open the pantry

door. With shaking hands, he dropped the bar in the trash and tossed the crumpled note in after it. Then he swept his arm across the shelf packed with protein bars and they flew everywhere. Some into the trash can, some onto the floor, some onto other shelves mixing his food in a way he normally hated.

He would never eat another one of those motherfucking bars again in his life.

31

ONCE AGAIN, JOSS DIALED THE NUMBER SHE'D PULLED FROM Shep's phone early this morning before leaving his cabin. She'd debated waking him, but he'd been breathing like a man who needed another thirty-six hours of sleep. When she'd spotted a couple of white vans parked in his driveway, she'd known she needed to lure the tabloids off Shep's scent.

She didn't mind if the whole world knew what had happened to her over the past few days. She wanted to sing it to a hundred thousand people, but Shep wouldn't want that kind of attention. With the promise of an exclusive sit-down with her back in LA, she'd convinced the tabloid reporters to trail her to California.

So she was on a plane back to LA—yes, gripping the armrests, but not drugged—to settle a few things before returning to Steele Ridge. Sans media vultures.

"Answer your phone, Shep!" She glared at the phone as she snapped it into the seat back in front of her.

A businessman in a pinstriped suit glanced back at her over his headrest. "If you stalk him like this all the time, no wonder the poor bastard isn't picking up your calls."

The old Joss would've shot back a cutting comment. Today, she simply took a breath and tried to give the man a genuine smile. "It's not what you think."

"That's what they all say right before they boil the bunny," he muttered as he turned forward again.

Okay, no more calls until she was on the ground.

Ten minutes later, Joss found herself reaching for the phone and stopped just short of popping it out again.

He was probably still asleep. She'd catch up with him once she landed.

Shep showed up at Way's front door and pounded on it. This was the first time he'd ever been to his brother's place without Puck at his side waiting eagerly for the piece of beef jerky Way inevitably slipped him.

Rocking from foot to foot, Shep was about to walk straight out of his skin if he didn't have something to do from now until the time the vet's office opened this morning.

When Way finally flung open the door, his hair was smushed on one side, his eyes were bleary, and he needed to use his razor in a bad way.

"What the hell are you doing on my doorstep at... What the hell time is it anyway? Is it Puck? Has something happened to Puck?"

"It's seven forty-two, and I haven't heard from Dr. Orozco yet today."

"Damn, I'm sorry about that. But you caught me off guard by coming around this morning. I guess I'm slacking now that I'm out of the Marines."

"You said we would test out the rifle you just modified."

"And so you decided the morning after a nut job tried to kill you and your girlfriend would be a good time?"

"Yes. It is a good time. And Joss is not my girlfriend."

"The way you and she were acting toward each other tells a different story. Why aren't you in bed wrapped around your favorite rock star?"

"Joss is not in my bed. She is not in my house." With each word, the confused agitation that had been his companion since he spotted the note in his kitchen grew in intensity until Shep felt as if it had teeth and would chew him up. "She is not in my life!"

"What?" Way passed a hand over his bedhead and stepped back to let Shep inside. "What are you talking about?"

He did not want to discuss this. Not now. Not ever. But he also knew his family. They would chip away at him until they knew the truth. "If I tell you, then you have to tell everyone else. I do not want to say this again."

"You got it." His brother arrowed toward the kitchen and went straight for the coffeepot.

Settling at the breakfast bar, Shep said, "Joss and I had sex last night."

Way paused in making coffee and looked over his shoulder. "Uh, congratulations?"

"It was very good. She had five orgasms."

"Damn." Way's eyebrows rose. "You might have to share some of your tricks with the rest of us mere mortal men."

"She is highly orgasmic."

Way snorted a laugh. "Just FYI...Those details might be TMI for most people." He turned back, dumped grounds in the coffeemaker, and punched the on button. "But you showing up at my front door makes even less sense now."

"When I woke up this morning, she was gone."

"Like gone gone? Or maybe just-ran-to-the-store-for-some-breakfast-items gone?"

"She did not go for breakfast. She set out an Epic Bar for me."

"Fuck," Way muttered, scowling at the slowly dripping coffee. "I know she's big shit and all that, but I would've sworn she was into you. I can't believe she split without a word."

"She did not say anything."

"No text? No nothing?"

"She left a note."

Way huffed and shook his head. "Why didn't you tell me that? What did it say?"

"I do not know. I threw it away. Notes are not good. If she had something good to say to me, she would've woken me up."

"I still think you should dig it out of the trash and read it. But as much as I hate to, I tend to agree with you on the note thing." He jerked the carafe out and dumped what had already brewed into a go-cup. "Gimme a few minutes to get dressed."

On his way to his bedroom, he scooped up a pile of towels and some other stuff and dumped it all in a paper sack.

"What is all that?" Shep asked him.

"Nothing. Just stuff I planned to take by the v..."

"By where?"

"The... ah... vintage resale place over in Canton."

"Those look like brand new towels," Shep said. "And aren't we headed west anyway?"

"You're right," Way said quickly. "Don't know what I was thinking."

In Shep's experience, his brother did very little without forethought. Which meant he didn't want Shep to know his plans for those towels.

Weird, but not worrisome.

"Don't go on overload while I'm putting on my pants," Way said. "We'll be out of here in five minutes, tops. Nothing like a little target practice to fix you right up."

Although Shep appreciated his brother's willingness to serve as a diversion, he had a feeling nothing would fix the hole Joss Wynter had left inside him.

32

Joss had played to stadiums that were so massive she felt like a speck on stage, but she'd never performed with nerves twanging the way they were tonight. And this venue was tiny even compared to the gigs she and the band were settling for before they recorded their first album.

But this was the most important performance of her life. It was the first time she cared only about how two people reacted—one in the audience and the one sitting on this wooden stool. She glanced down at the wicker basket on the small stage. She had so many gifts to give tonight.

Please accept them. Please accept me.

Although Joss had been full of confidence and certainty when she left Steele Ridge a week ago, now doubts were trying to slither their way inside her head. Trying to blast their way inside her heart.

Shep hadn't answered a single one of her calls, voice mails, or texts. Seven days of them.

She'd convinced herself not to take it personally because she'd learned that he liked to communicate on his own terms. Which meant face-to-face was the only way to get through to him.

And if she could outrun a killer, she could put herself on the line for the man she loved.

Randi Shepherd had been kind enough to rig a small stage curtain for Joss. She'd also been generous enough to close the Triple B to anyone outside the Kingston and Steele families. When Joss had offered to pay her generously for the sacrifice, Randi's voice had gone quiet and serious over the phone.

She'd said, "Here in Steele Ridge, we do *anything* for family. And we do it out of love."

Joss blew out a breath, but her lungs froze when she heard the sound of the door opening and people walking into the restaurant. Her ears strained for Shep's voice. For his speech patterns.

Definitely some male voices. They were ribbing one another about a paintball game. Apparently, Pretty Boy and Baby Billionaire had paired up and whipped their brothers' asses. A couple of women were protesting the whole outcome, arguing the win would've been theirs if the guys had been brave enough to let them know when the battle was going down. Verbal jabs and laughter continued until the guys agreed to a rematch, where it was predicted the women would dominate.

The door opened again and another group came in, talking over each other.

"If Cash brought another dish that includes bacon of any type, he should be permanently disqualified from the potluck competition." Joss recognized the voice as Maggie's.

"Fine by me," a man shot back. "That just means I get the benefit of eating without having to cook."

Joss smothered a laugh. Had Maggie actually *growled* at

her brother? My God, she wanted to be a part of that, a family that loved as fiercely as they fought. A family that instinctively knew how not to just accept each person for his or her quirks, but to truly treasure them. Because with them, she could be the real Jojo Winterburn, not the insecure and attention-desperate musician she'd been all her life.

And although she'd paid a visit to her own family and made amends, she knew the Kingston clan was where she belonged. But they were just a bonus that came with the man she needed.

She wanted to spend her life with Shep, the man who'd helped her see who she was, and that life was about more than applause and empty adoration from strangers. The man who was so real himself that her chest ached with how much she loved him. He was everything she'd never known she was looking for.

"I do *not* want to be here." Joss's heart seesawed at the sound of Shep's voice. His very grumpy voice. "I told Mom that. I told Dad that. But Way said he would burn all my climbing equipment if I didn't get my ass down here."

"West Waylon Kingston!" That had to be their mom.

"I am leaving," Shep said.

"No, you are not, Harris Sheppard Kingston!" his mom scolded. "Sit down right this minute, all of you."

Yow. It appeared that Joss needed to get this show on the road if she wanted to avoid a full family meltdown out there. Randi probably wouldn't appreciate it if Joss's plan turned into a Steele-Kingston bar fight.

I can do this. If Shep could put his life on the line for me again and again, I can put my heart and my pride on the line for him.

Randi slipped behind the curtain. "You about ready?"

she whispered. "The natives are getting a little restless out there."

"I was just thinking the same thing." But her stomach was so far up her throat that she was afraid she wouldn't be able to sing a note. "How does Shep look? How does he seem?"

"Honestly?" Randi said. "Disgruntled and pissed off. But I have a feeling you're going to change that with whatever you have planned."

"I hope so. It's so scary to lay yourself on the line like this."

"These two families have plenty of experience with that. Next time all the girls get together, you'll hear the stories."

"I'd like that so much."

Randi reached for Joss's hand and gave it a light squeeze. Then she slipped back out and said, "Tonight, we've got a super special treat. That's why we moved the regular Kingston potluck dinner down here to the Triple B."

"And because that meant the Steeles were invited, too," a man said, laughter clear in his voice.

"Don't get too used to it unless you plan to start contributing a dish, Reid."

"I'll have you know that I cook a mean rack of ribs."

"I won't even attempt to introduce the woman who is about to sing for you because she doesn't need any introduction." Randi swept aside the curtain and although the small stage was lit only with a warm glow, Joss felt as if she was under a fifteen-hundred-watt spotlight. She tried to smile, but her lips weren't especially cooperative. People were gathered around barn wood tables softly lit with the rustic silver pendants hanging above. An old Lance crackers sign seemed to be shouting encouragement with its *Just right... right now!* message.

"Hey, everyone," she said in a froggy voice, and then cleared the apprehension out of her throat. "Randi was nice enough to offer me her stage tonight. But this isn't a performance, not really. I'd like to think it's more of a conversation. Maybe a bit of a confession. Definitely a promise."

Shep not only wouldn't meet Joss's gaze, but he was deliberately looking away from her, staring at a side wall. His arms crossed and mouth tight. Something sharp twisted in her chest.

Had he changed his mind about her? Had he returned to his regular life and decided she didn't deserve a spot in it? Did he blame her for everything that happened, especially...

Where was Puck? Joss didn't see him in the room.

She glanced back at Shep's face. His expression was flat. Did that mean something had happened to Puck or that he was unhappy to see her?

The impulse to jump off the stool and bolt out the back door rushed through her. She could leave, catch a plane in Charlotte, and be back in LA by—

No. This isn't about getting applause or approval. It's about giving love.

"Shep," she said quietly, but he still didn't turn her way. A muscle in his cheek twitched, which could be a good sign or a bad one. "This is for you. It's called 'Lost in This World.'"

Her fingers took over, lovingly strumming the chords that had flowed from her heart, had kept her company while she was so far away from him.

> *They light me up*
> *If they all adore me*
> *They all lift up one voice*
> *Love my bitter choice*

I'm lost in this world

I own the stage
Dead eyes and leather black
I go home all alone
My life's only for show
I'm lost in this world

Wanting someone out there to belong to
    me and truly understand
What drove my heart to beat and left a
    mark on me, a burning brand
In a sea of smooth, I'm a jagged edge...
I'm lost in this world
I'm lost in this world

She played a simple break, picking out the melody, and modulated down a full step. When she sang again, her voice was darker, huskier.

I only speak
With mountains and maples
No one with me
It should make me feel free
But I'm lost in this world

A broken man
Inside I'm the biggest lie
Wanting love, then and now
Can it ever be found?
It's lost in this world

Wanting someone out there to belong to
me and truly understand
What drove my heart to beat and left a
mark on me, a burning brand
In a sea of smooth, I'm a jagged edge...
I'm lost in this world
I'm lost in this world

Eyes like a storm
Seeking and holding on to mine
Promise me a haven
When I've never had one
I'm lost in your world

Smile like the sun
With the passion to warm me
I offer everything
New songs to live and sing
We're lost in our world
We're lost in our world

When the last note faded away and hovered in the air, Shep stood. Hope bloomed inside Joss. He would walk to her and—

But no, he turned his back on her and faced his extended family. "I would like all of you to go now."

"Dude, we haven't even eaten yet," one of his cousins protested.

"Take everything and leave."

There was some grumbling, but everyone complied, piling their arms high with food. One of the men, wearing what Joss recognized as high-end jeans and a custom-made dress shirt, was holding an adorable little girl, probably a little over a year old, dressed in pink overalls. He kissed the baby's head and pointed toward the door. "Let's take this party down to the Murchison Building. It's close enough that we won't have to suffer through Reid's whining for long before he can stuff his face."

While they all filed out of the restaurant, Shep kept his back to Joss. Randi, the last one out, said, "Just let me know when you're finished here, and I'll come back and lock up."

When the door was closed behind her, Shep still didn't move except for the clench and release of his hands. He wasn't happy. Joss had put him on the spot in front of his family.

"I'm sorry," she said softly. "I thought this would be okay, but I know you aren't much for crowds and—"

"Why are you here?"

Sooty-colored anger that Joss knew was a self-defense mechanism tried to roll its way through her system. But she took a breath and mentally waved it away. "If you want the answer to that, you have to face me. I won't talk to your back. You're shutting me out."

"You shut me out first." He turned, and there was anguish in his face. Pure misery. Complete heartbreak.

Somehow, he truly believed what he was saying. How was that possible? Her first instinct was to go to him and wrap him in her arms, but she made herself stay seated. He wasn't ready for her to touch him, that was clear. "I only left for a week," she said. "I texted. Called. Left messages that you never returned. You *knew* I was coming back."

"No, I didn't."

"But I left a note and—"

"I threw it away."

Joss blinked. That he would do such a thing had never occurred to her. And it probably should have. "Why?"

"Because letters from lovers are bad."

"That isn't logical..." No, if Shep was this convinced, there had to be some logic behind his stubborn insistence. "This has something to do with Amber, doesn't it?"

His mouth was an unforgiving line. "You said you weren't like her and then you left—"

"I'm *not* like her, but how could I know you wouldn't read what I wrote?"

"When Amber left me, she wrote a note on a kitchen napkin, telling me she was filing for divorce."

Shep's lack of responsiveness made more sense now.

She said, "One of the things that you helped me see is that I don't need everyone to think the world of me. But you didn't even give me the benefit of the doubt, Shep."

"You told me you loved me and then you left without waking me. People who love each other don't do that. It's rude."

"I thought I was protecting you, but if I'm being honest, I was also protecting myself a little," she said quietly. "A couple of tabloids showed up that morning. I told myself I was leading them away from you, and I was. But I needed to go back to California to clean up loose ends. I've had too many things gaping wide open. It was painful, and the last thing I want is to start my new life full of pain."

For the first time, his rigid face relaxed. Just a little, but it was something. "What new life?"

"I want to get back to the music. Real music with a soul and essence people can connect to. I want to write and perform for real people. People I can look in the face when I play and sing for them. I want to touch them."

"That's not a good way to be a rock star."

"And that's exactly the point," she said and finally slid off the stool and to her feet. She placed Fiona in her case and stepped off the stage. "I'm done being Joss Wynter of Scarlet Glitterati. My name is Jocelyn Winterburn, and I'm just a woman who writes songs and plays them on my guitar."

"That sounds like Jojo." The painful feeling in her chest receded and her heart took up all the space. If it expanded any more, it would simply explode. *Pop!* Her feelings splattering all over the wall.

"It does, doesn't it?" She laughed and edged closer to him. His scent—all woodsmoke and pine forest—swept over her, making her tummy tight and her knees loose. "I'm sorry you thought I wasn't coming back. Obviously, just because two people care about one another, love each other, doesn't mean the communication is always going to be smooth. It's something I'm willing to work on if you are."

Ah, that seemed to do it. Shep's broad shoulders finally dropped from their resting spot close to his ears. Joss pressed against him and wrapped her arms around his waist. *Home. Real. Love.*

His heart was a steady thud under her ear. A sound she planned to listen to and cherish every day from here on out. "I love you so much it hurts, Shep Kingston."

"Before you, I did not think love was supposed to hurt. Then Maggie explained that sometimes it hurts because we care so much."

She laughed and pressed a kiss to the spot over his heart. "She's right. Love is complicated. It's not always nice and easy. Sometimes it's turbulent and troubled."

"I do not like that."

"Two people who weather bad times grow to love each other even more. Those not-so-great times make love stronger."

"Do you really believe that?"

She looked up at him, saw the uncertainty and worry in

his eyes. "I really do. There is no smooth sailing in this life. Which means the rough seas have to mean something."

"Rough seas like Puck being shot?"

Shep's words robbed Joss of breath and evoked the memory of the beautiful dog, in pain and fading away right before them. Of their desperate dash to get him help. Of Dan Cargill injecting him with Propofol. Her gaze darted around the room until it landed on something under the table where Shep had been sitting. What she saw there filled her with joy. With love.

She smoothed her hand up Shep's cheek and looked into his beautiful eyes. "If you're in the boat, I'll brave the rough seas of love for the rest of my life. But there will be plenty of joy, Shep. I promise you that. In fact, I brought you a bundle if it tonight. Will you let me give it to you?"

"What is it?"

Joss unwound her arms and retrieved the basket from the stage. Setting it on the floor, she told Shep, "Open it and see."

He squatted, his knees bracketing the basket, and flipped back the lid. Inside, was a perfect ball of black fur. The puppy was blissfully asleep on a blanket printed with bones and balls. "For me?"

"Yes," she said, "and no. I was approved to be a puppy raiser for the organization that gave you Puck."

"They gave you a puppy that quickly?"

"I promised to set up special social media accounts, and the donation I made probably didn't hurt. But when I told them I was involved with Shep Kingston, that pretty much swayed them."

"What's his name?"

"Her. She's Charley."

Inside the basket, the puppy stretched and opened her

pretty brown eyes. Her yawn was all curled tongue and high-pitched groan. And from his perch on a dog bed beneath Shep's table, Puck raised his head, ears up and alert. He stared at the basket.

But Shep's face, it was the clincher. His smile was huge. He was already in love. A goner.

"You realize we will have to give her up, right?" she said. "We have to turn her in when it's time."

Shep picked up the puppy and tucked her next to Puck. Charley snuggled against the older dog's body. Puck sniffed the pup and nudged her with his nose. Then he looked up with what Joss would swear was protective pride.

"I know," Shep said, "We have to give her back so someone else gets a companion as loyal and brave as Puck."

"Yes," she said. "Because I want those people to be as happy as you."

Shep took her by the waist and lifted her until they were eye to eye. "No one can ever be as happy as me," he said. "Because not only do I have Puck and Charley, I have Jojo, too."

She wrapped her legs around him and held on tight. When Shep pressed his lips to hers, it was all the applause Joss needed.

THE STEELE RIDGE SERIES

Steele Ridge: The Kingstons

Craving HEAT, Book 1

Tasting FIRE, Book 2

Searing NEED, Book 3

Striking EDGE, Book 4

Burning ACHE, Book 5 (Coming 2019)

Steele Ridge: The Steeles

The BEGINNING, A Novella, Book 1

Going HARD, Book 2

Living FAST, Book 3

Loving DEEP, Book 4

Breaking FREE, Book 5

Roaming WILD, Book 6

Stripping BARE, Book 7

Enduring LOVE, A Novella, Book 8

ACKNOWLEDGMENTS

It seems as if I thank many of the same people in the acknowledgments of each book. That's because I couldn't do my job without their support, encouragement, and love.

To Tech Guy and Smarty Boy (who may need a new nickname soon, seeing as he's nineteen!): In 2018, we weathered a tough year together. I'm proud of you both and proud of the family we all work so hard to keep together.

A big squishy panda hug to Adrienne Giordano and Tracey Devlyn. Steele Ridge has tried to kick our asses a few times, but we always find a path to peace. Thank you for putting up with me even though I don't always say the right things.

Sometimes, when I think of Heather Machel and Donna Duffee and what I'd do without their help and support, true tears of pain come to my eyes. Not to be too graphic, but I feel a bit like Gollum when it comes to you two.

Without our editors, the entire Steele Ridge series wouldn't be the story powerhouse it is. Thank you to Gina Bernal and Martha Trachtenberg for helping us write quality books. Also, Martha is in no way responsible for any musical faux pas I may have made in Shep's story.

A heartfelt hug of gratitude to Toby Walker and his best girl and therapy dog, Charley. Thank you for making the world a brighter place through your service to others and for allowing me to bring Charley's namesake into the Steele Ridge world.

And my lovely Sass Kicker fan group, you are simply the best. Always patiently waiting for the next book and encouraging me to write well instead of quickly. Thank you.

This book would not have been possible without some other very special folks.

To Randy Manuel of Solo Southeast in Bryson City, North Carolina, I can't even begin to repay you for your generous knowledge of the NC wilderness. I promise I still plan to come up for you to teach me important things. Just as soon as it's warm again in the southeast.

Big thanks to Reva Benefiel for being my musical sounding board when it came to Joss's character. And for helping with those damn lyrics. A girl thinks songwriting will be easy just because she can write a novel. I was delusional.

To Dr. Jennifer Peterson at Firehall 4 Animal Hospital here in Athens, thank you for not freaking out when I told you what I planned to do to Puck. Your help with some of the not-so-nice parts of this story was invaluable. (And I promise not to forward any reader hate mail to you—LOL.)

Thank you to two amazing ladies, Michelle Hawkins and Lisa Janke. You helped me believe that I could do justice to Shep's character. And once the book was written, you made sure I'd done my job. Shep and I owe you everything.

And finally, to all the Steele Ridge readers, I am so

grateful you're on this journey with us. It's a pleasure and an honor to build this world for your enjoyment.

ABOUT THE AUTHOR

 *USA Today* bestselling author Kelsey Browning writes contemporary romance, romantic suspense, and cozy mystery. Her Georgia-set, co-authored G Team mystery is described by readers as "The Golden Girls meet Dirty Harry." Her single title romances garner reviews that call her writing funny, sassy, and full of sizzling chemistry. Originally from a Texas town smaller than the ones she writes about, Kelsey has also lived in the Middle East and Los Angeles, proving she's either adventurous or downright nuts. These days, she makes her home in northeast Georgia with her tech-savvy husband, her smart-talking son, and a (fingers crossed) future therapy pup.

Kelsey can be found on:
    www.KelseyBrowning.com
    Facebook.com/KelseyBrowning
    Instagram.com/kelseybrowningauthor
    Pinterest.com/KelseyBrowning
    Goodreads.com/KelseyBrowning

Printed in Great
Britain
by Amazon